Blame it on the Mistletoe

Other Bright's Pond Tales by Joyce Magnin

The Prayers of Agnes Sparrow
Charlotte Figg Takes Over Paradise
Griselda Takes Flight

BLAME IT ON THE MISTLETOE

A Novel of Bright's Pond

Joyce Magnin

Abingdon Press fiction
a novel approach to faith

Nashville, Tennessee

Blame It on the Mistletoe: A Novel of Bright's Pond

Copyright © 2011 by Joyce Magnin

ISBN-13: 978-1-4267-1162-6

Published by Abingdon Press, P.O. Box 801, Nashville, TN 37202.
www.abingdonpress.com/fiction

All rights reserved.

The persons and events portrayed in this work of fiction
are the creations of the author, and any resemblance
to persons living or dead is purely coincidental.

Cover design by Anderson Design Group, Nashville, TN

Library of Congress Cataloging-in-Publication Data

Moccero, Joyce Magnin.
  Blame it on the mistletoe : a novel of Bright's Pond / Joyce Magnin.
    p. cm.
  ISBN 978-1-4267-1162-6 (trade pbk. : alk. paper) 1. Trailer camps—Fiction. 2. Nursing
homes—Fiction. 3. Weddings—Planning—Fiction. I. Title.
  PS3601.L447B53 2011
  813'.6—dc22

                                                                                    2011015915

Printed in the United States of America

1 2 3 4 5 6 7 8 9 10 / 16 15 14 13 12 11

For my mother, Florence Magnin
We found the dimes, Mom

ACKNOWLEDGMENTS

I can hardly believe this is the fourth Bright's Pond novel. As always, novels are not written without a village, and I once again need to say thank you to all the folks who stuck by me so faithfully through the writing: Pam Halter, the CRUE, the folks at Springton Lake Presbyterian Church who have supported and prayed me through from beginning to end, Abingdon Press for keeping Bright's Pond on the map, and my agent for taking care of business and being an encourager. And, of course, these books would never get written without the support of the readers who keep asking for more Bright's Pond. Thank you.

1

It was the tricycle parked outside of eighty-seven-year-old Haddie Grace's room at the Greenbrier Nursing Home that gave me cause for concern. I first saw it when I had brought Ivy and her dog, Mickey Mantle, to the nursing home for the pooch's weekly Visit of Convalescence. It was a candy-apple-red tricycle with colorful streamers hanging from the handlebars and a note taped to the seat: "Do Not Touch." A round, silver bike bell—the kind you operated with your thumb—was attached to the handlebars, although just barely.

Mickey Mantle loved to visit with the old folks. Ivy said he enjoyed making them smile, and she enjoyed watching their eyes light up when he let anyone scratch behind his ears. And the fact that Mickey Mantle only had three legs on account of an unfortunate bear-trap accident seemed to endear him even more to the residents, a few of whom were missing limbs themselves.

"The best part," Ivy had said, "was when Mickey Mantle was able to help that nasty, cranky Erma Crump find her nice side. Too bad she died just a week after. Only a week to be nice— imagine that."

Ivy Slocum was a good friend. Never married, she was bit on the plump side and was prone to wear oversized sweat-shirts to disguise her more than ample bosom.

I've gone on three or four of these visits with Ivy and watched how Mickey Mantle sits and lets the folks pet him and converse with him just like he's a person. I think he would sit there all day long if he could, soaking up the attention and returning the love. The pooch had become privy to many a family saga and secret. But nursing homes have their rules, and Ivy was only allowed to bring Mickey Mantle one day a week—usually on a Wednesday unless otherwise decided. And that particular Wednesday was no different—except for the tricycle and giggles coming from Haddie's room. Haddie Grace weighed all of ninety pounds it seemed to me, a tiny slip of a woman with nearly translucent skin.

"Would you look at that," I said. "Now what in tarnation is a tricycle doing at a nursing home?"

Ivy scratched her head. "Beats me, Griselda. Maybe it belongs to one of Haddie's grandkids."

"Haddie never had children. Never been married as far as she remembers."

"Then I reckon this is strange," Ivy said. "Maybe someone else's kids left it there."

I asked Nurse Sally about the little red trike when I saw her at the nurses' station. Nurse Sally was head nurse at Greenbrier, and we had become quite friendly since Agnes went to live there.

"I just don't understand it," Sally said. "Haddie Grace has been riding that thing down the hallways like she was three years old again. Scares me half to death. She can't afford no more broken bones. I think she slipped her rocker but good this time around."

"No fooling?" Ivy said. "That's odd, don't you think? Why do you let her?"

"Well, here's the thing about that," Sally said. "The residents can pretty much do whatever they want, and Doctor Silver thought that taking the tricycle away might be more harmful. You know, up here." She tapped her head.

"Maybe she should see that head jockey, Doctor Julian," I said. "I think that's his name. The doctor they made Agnes talk to."

"She has an appointment later on today. But I'm worried it might be something serious like a brain tumor making her act like a child. It can happen you know."

"Oh, I know that," Ivy said. "Brains ain't made to have growths growing inside of them. Delicate instruments they are. Why I remember when Bubba Knickerbocker got his. Made him fall down and lean to the left like one of them telephone poles out on the highway."

"That's right," I said. "Poor Ruth had a dickens of a time keeping him upright."

"He was much larger than her," Ivy said. "Kind of like a Chihuahua and a Saint Bernard going out for tea."

"I hear that," Sally said. "Funny thing is that every time I check Haddie's vitals she's sound as a Swiss watch. Can't find a thing wrong—even her blood pressure is good. It's almost like she's getting healthier."

Mickey Mantle let go a low, grumbly growl. Not a fierce, angry growl. He was only letting Ivy know that they had rounds to get on.

"Guess we better be on our way," Ivy said. "Mickey Mantle gets upset if he misses seeing his regulars. Gordon Flegal always has a Milk-Bone for him and that nice Mr. Tracy let him chew on a lollipop last week."

"That's fine, you go on without me this time," I said. "I need to stop in and see Agnes. Why don't you bring Mickey Mantle by her room when you're done?"

"Okeydokey." Ivy gave a slight tug on her dog's leash. "Come on, boy. We better get to Gordon before he conks out for the day."

I lingered by the nurse's station a minute. "How's Agnes doing these days?" I asked.

She fussed with some papers on a clipboard. "Agnes? She's doing quite well. I wish she'd get out of her room more, but she seems content."

My visit with Agnes was not what you would call "usual." I found her sitting in her wheelchair staring out the window. I loved my sister, dearly. Everyone knew that—even Agnes. Although to look at her you might wonder about us. Agnes weighed nearly seven hundred pounds when she checked herself into Greenbrier. Life had gotten too hard for her. Just getting from her bed to the bathroom was chore, and I usually had to be home to help her. But looking at her now I can see how the nursing home was helping. They estimate that she had dropped almost sixty-five pounds in the past several months and was well on her way to losing another sixty-five. I wish I could say her clothes hung on her like the skin on a hound dog after losing so much weight. But no, she still wore muumuus and housedresses—sometimes with pretty flowers and other times just white or pink.

She was wearing a beat up pair of slippers with the heels bent in, and her brown hair had been cut short for ease of handling. Her right arm rested on the arm of the wheelchair and the skin kind of dripped off the edge like expanding foam. But I noticed a sweet smell, like magnolia, wafting around the room, and it did my heart well to know that she was being cared for.

"The leaves are pretty this year," I said from the doorway. "All that rain and then that blast of sunshine and heat in August really helped."

Agnes turned. "Griselda. I'm glad you're here."

I moved closer. "Really? Why? Is something wrong?"

Agnes pushed her chair closer to me. "I'm not sure. I'm not sure at all, but something is strange."

I thought of the red tricycle. "You mean like Haddie Grace's trike?"

"You saw it then."

"Yeah, Ivy saw it too. She came with Mickey Mantle. I asked Nurse Sally about it. She says Haddie has been riding it through the halls like she's three years old."

Agnes slapped her knee. "Land o' Goshen, I know! She rides that trike and rings the bell. If it ain't a sight to see."

I sat on the visitor's chair. "Sally said they're having that psychiatrist check her out."

"I know, I know. Thing is that I don't believe that Dr. Julian will find anything more than simple elderly senility stuff going on."

"Well, Sally did mention something about a brain tumor."

"Brain tumor?" Agnes slapped her thigh. The fat under her housecoat rippled like sea waves. "I doubt that. I get the feeling what's going on around here has nothing to do with tumors or diabetes or senility. Because it isn't just Haddie. It's other folks also. There's something more going on. Something stranger than all that."

"What are you talking about? You mean there're more tricycles? More strange happenings?"

"Look out that window and tell me what you see."

"Grass, trees, a gazebo—when did they put that in? I hadn't noticed it before." It was a large octagon-shaped building with a crooked railing and a cedar-shingled roof with a crooked cupola on the top, and on top of the cupola was a rooster that seemed to be crowing to the west. "It's nice, a little cockeyed but nice."

"Never mind the crooked. Look at what, or I should say, who is in the gazebo."

I stood and moved closer to the window. "Who is that?"

"That, my dear sister, is Clive Dickens and Faith Graves. They've been out there swaying around and dancing with each other like they was sixteen years old again. I tell you, Griselda, it's like that scene in *The Sound of Music*."

"Ah, that's OK. Old people can fall in love too."

"I suppose so, but those two? I hear that old man hasn't been out of his room in three years except when they make him go to the barber or the doctor, and Faith Graves is, well, let's just say she has one foot in and one foot out. We've had more code reds on that woman in the last six weeks than anyone. But now, all of a sudden she's up and dancing like a teenager."

"Code reds?"

"Well, yeah, that's what we call it when someone walks into her room and can't tell if she's dead or alive on account of she lays there still as an ironing board and just as stiff. She is, after all, ninety-two years old."

"I guess it does seem strange, come to think about it. What do you suppose is causing this?"

Agnes shook her head and clicked her tongue. "I'm telling you. It's like a magic spell has fallen over Greenbrier. A spell of rejuvenation."

"Is it really such a problem? Maybe it's a good thing."

"But why? What happened to all these people to make them start acting like they were sixteen years old again, or in Haddie's case, three?"

I patted Agnes's hand and filled her water glass from the pitcher. "All what people. You're talking about three people."

"Then explain that." Agnes pointed to the window.

I looked in time to see Jasper York, who was Greenbrier's most recent reluctant resident, shimmy up a tree—or at least try to. He slid back down and sat on the ground.

"OK, that's weird," I said. "Jasper York would never act like that."

"What do you suppose is causing this?" Agnes asked.

I couldn't begin to imagine. "Oh, I wouldn't worry about it. It's autumn. The holidays are coming. Maybe folks are just feeling the holiday spirit. Maybe it makes them feel young again."

"I suppose that could be it, except I have this gut feeling that something ain't right around here. Not right at all."

"Try not to worry about it. You'll make your blood pressure go up or trigger an asthma attack."

"Oh, don't worry about me. I'll be fine. I just kind of wish a little of whatever virus bit them would bite me."

"Um, no, let's hope not, Agnes. That would not be fun."

But I had to laugh when I heard Haddie Grace whiz past Agnes's room singing her ABCs and ringing her bell. "Or you might be right. It could be something more than the holidays."

2

I visited with Agnes for nearly an hour. It wasn't that we had a whole lot to talk about except, of course, Cliff Cardwell. It seems that ever since that pilot fella landed in Bright's Pond, he and I have been the talk of the town. It's probably because I started taking flying lessons from him and now everyone naturally assumes we're an item or something.

"You still involved with him?" Agnes asked with a bit of a grin.

"Who? Cliff? I keep telling you and everyone else that Cliff and I are just friends and he is only teaching me to fly his airplane, nothing else."

Agnes peered out the window. "Uh-huh, I suppose there can be more than one connotation to the word *fly*."

"Agnes. That's ridiculous. Just because Zeb and me broke up again doesn't mean I'm flying—that kind of flying—with Cliff Cardwell."

Zeb Sewickey and I had been dating on and off since high school. I would have married him a long time ago—I think. But he always had one excuse or another. It usually had to do with his business. Zeb owned and managed The Full Moon Café in town. It was kind of a diner and looked a bit like a solid steel train car with windows. Zeb was also the chief cook and bottle washer, as he always said. Or he would use Agnes as an excuse to break up. But that was back when Agnes still lived with me. Except, he still finds ways to blame Agnes. I suppose everyone wants to blame things on something or someone besides themselves.

"But you do like Cliff," Agnes said. "And you did break it off with Zeb."

"I just got sick and tired of the way Zeb smothers me, and orders me around like I was one of his waitresses. I need space, room to breathe. And up there, in the clouds, is where I have felt the freest. It's like being almost weightless."

"Now that fat Agnes isn't taking up your living room," Agnes said in her best little-girl voice.

"I didn't say that, but I am not going to lie and tell you or anyone that I haven't enjoyed living by myself." I looked into her beady little round eyes. "But that isn't to say I don't miss you. I love you, Agnes. I do miss you. Many nights I wish you were still at the house, and I was making tuna sandwiches for you."

"You do make the best tuna salad in Bright's Pond."

I patted her hand. It felt warm—too warm. "Maybe I'll sneak one in the next time I come."

"Will you? That would be scrumptious."

"But I don't want to mess your diet up too much. You look like you're losing some weight. Lots of it. Seems just last week that wheelchair was a snug fit."

Agnes moved her butt in the chair. "It does feel a bit roomier. My rear end doesn't rub so much on the sides."

"Pretty soon you'll be up and running down the halls."

"Nah, not me—not unless whatever bug bit Haddie bites me too."

I was glad we had gotten off the subject of Cliff Cardwell and Zeb Sewickey.

"Well, look Agnes," I said. "If you don't need anything else I should be getting back to town. I'm taking Ruth into Shoops to shop for Thanksgiving." I saw the change in Agnes's countenance.

"Thanksgiving? You having dinner with Ruth?"

"Me and a few others. But I'll be coming by to see you. I promise to bring you a plate. I doubt even Nurse Sally would deny you Thanksgiving dinner with all the trimmings."

Agnes didn't say a word. The look in her eyes was enough to tell me that missing Thanksgiving at home would be hard. I patted her hand and then hugged her the best I could. "I know it's hard. But look, I'll come by the nursing home with Ruth and Stu and Ivy and whoever else wants to come along. We'll make it a party—just like old times."

Agnes pushed herself toward her bed. "It'll be nothing like old times. No matter how you slice the pumpkin pie, the fact remains I'm here. It's not home."

She was correct. People are supposed to go home for Thanksgiving. "We'll make the best of it. You'll see."

"You ever eat nursing home food?"

"No, well, at the cafeteria—a little. It was pretty wretched."

"Imagine Thanksgiving nursing-home style."

"It's not all about the food."

Agnes looked up at me. I watched her eyes glisten with tears. "I know that, but good food goes real well with good friends, like hand and glove, Starsky and Hutch."

"We'll find a way for you to have both."

That was when Ivy appeared at the door with Mickey Mantle. "Hey, Agnes," Ivy called with a wave. "I saved the best room for last. I always said you have the best view."

"Howdy, Ivy. Bring that pooch over here."

Ivy dropped Mickey Mantle's leash and the dog trotted in his own three-legged style to Agnes. She held his snout and looked into his big brown eyes. "What a good dog. How've you been, Mickey?"

The dog licked her cheek.

"Maybe you can bring Mickey Mantle for Thanksgiving."

Ivy looked at me.

"I was telling Agnes about our plans for the holiday. I told her we'll all come by her room on Thanksgiving and bring her a plate of food and pie and we'll have a party, right here."

"Oh, s-s-sure, Agnes. You got that right. Wild horses couldn't keep us away from Greenbrier on Thanksgiving."

Agnes smiled. "What time? What time will you all be coming?"

"Well, I can't say. Not just yet," I said. "I'm not certain what time Ruth is planning dinner. But I'll let you know. We still have a week to work it all out."

Agnes's mood deflated again. "I had no idea it would be such trouble."

"It's not trouble. It's just a matter of coordination and timing. But we'll be here with plenty of time to celebrate—good friends, good food, our many blessings."

"Blessings. Phooey," Agnes said. "I haven't been feeling very blessed lately."

"But you are," Ivy said. "You have friends. You have folks looking after you. You're getting skinnier by the day and pretty soon you'll be back in town."

My stomach wobbled. I refused to think about Agnes actually getting healthy enough to leave the nursing home and move back in with me. At least not yet. I wasn't ready. But I smiled anyway. "That's right, you'll see. Just stick with the program."

"All right. If you say so, Griselda. It gives me something to look forward to."

"Good, now like I said. I need to get back and get Ruth. Anything you need from Shoops?"

Agnes glanced around her room. "Nah. Nothing really. They give me everything I need, nothing I want but everything I need. Except maybe lemon squares. I need lemon squares, oh, and deodorant—the roll-on kind."

"OK, then I'll be back tomorrow." I kissed her cheek. "Yuck." I laughed. "Isn't that where Mickey Mantle kissed you?"

Agnes put her hand to her cheek. "Ah, there's nothing like some good dog slobber."

Mickey Mantle whined.

"Mickey Mantle doesn't slobber," Ivy said.

"No offense," Agnes said.

"Oh, I'm fine." Ivy chuckled. "But Mickey Mantle needs an apology."

Agnes scratched behind his ears. "I'm sorry, pooch. I didn't mind you kissing me."

Mickey Mantle licked her cheek again.

⁓⧟⁓

Ruth was, of course, waiting for me when I pulled up to her house. Ruth lived in an old farmhouse on the edge of town—next door to the eccentric artist Filby Pruett. She pretended she wasn't annoyed I was late, but I saw through it. Ruth didn't exactly have what you would call a poker face. She wore her heart on her sleeve and was the closest person to a best friend I had. She was a little older than me, a widow for quite some time and enjoyed staying busy as a member of SOAP—the Society for Angelic Philanthropy—which did secret charitable acts.

"Oh, Griselda, I just this minute stepped out on the porch. Perfect timing."

I smiled. But I knew she was probably standing there for the better part of half an hour. "I'm sorry I'm late. I got tied up at Greenbrier."

We walked to the truck.

"Everything OK with Agnes?"

"Oh, sure. She's fine."

I turned the ignition and off we went toward Shoops—the next town over. Bright's Pond had pretty much everything a person could need, but Shoops was a bigger town and had more shops and services. So it wasn't unusual for us to drive there for some things or just because it was nice to slip out of town on occasion.

"Glad to hear it. I think moving Agnes to Greenbrier was the best decision. I know it was hard on her. But it was best."

"I agree, Ruth. But I got to tell you. When I was over there today I saw some pretty strange things going on. Things that gave me pause."

"I'm not sure what you mean by strange? In what way?"

"It's hard to explain exactly—but it's like the old folks are getting younger or something—they have more of a spring in their step."

"Ah, it's just the holidays coming—it makes people happy."

"That's what I thought, but if you saw it, you'd know what I mean. That old woman, Haddie Grace, has been riding a tri-cycle through the halls. You should see her—ringing her bell, singing songs. It's like she's three years old."

Ruth laughed. "No, really? A tricycle? Maybe she slipped a few gears. Maybe her elevator stopped reaching the top floor finally, you know what I mean?"

"I do." I turned the truck onto the main road into Shoops. "But she's not the only one. Grown people—old people holding hands and kissing in the gazebo."

"Gazebo? When they get that? The last time I was out to visit Agnes I didn't see a gazebo. Is it white? I love a white gazebo—so Victorian."

"No, it's just that wood color and a little strange itself. Kind of crooked with a crooked rooster on top. But that's not the point. There was this old couple out there acting like teenagers."

"Ah, it's good for their hearts. And who's to say what old is? Why my Hubby Bubby and me were always what you might call frisky, even when we were fifty years old. Leastways until that nasty tumor ate his brain away but—"

"I hope you're right. I hope it's nothing. But Nurse Sally suggested that Haddie could have come down with a tumor in her brain."

"Oh, dear me, I hope that isn't the case. It's a terrible thing. Them brain tumors are like piranha, eating away. But I do remember my Hubby Bubby acting a little . . . off at times."

"I think we should pray it isn't that and instead something much simpler. Somebody once said that when you hear hoofbeats you should think horses, not zebras."

"Then we pray for horses," Ruth said. "But let's not be surprised if it's a zebra."

"Sounds like a plan. Now, where to first?" I took a breath and stepped on the gas as the road opened up. "I bet everywhere we go will be crowded. Even if it does look like rain."

"Let's see." Ruth reached into her handbag and pulled out a white envelope with what looked like a list written on it. "I need to go to the Piggly Wiggly, of course. I like their produce selection better than the one in town, even though we got all these farms around us. It's just easier to go to the Piggly Wiggly. Next I want to go to that specialty store with all the pretty linens and doodads. I was thinking to buy some new cloth napkins and—"

And Ruth was off and running. This would be the first year in I don't know how many that Thanksgiving was not celebrated at the funeral home where I had lived my whole life. Dad, the town funeral director, had been gone for many years, yet the house still looked like a funeral home. Hunter green trim, black shutters. A wraparound porch that saw many, many mourners file in and out. It was hard not to remember my mother sitting on that porch waiting to greet the loved one. She always had a compassionate smile and a plate of cookies and pot of coffee percolating in the kitchen. The Sparrow Funeral Home was my home but so much more, and now it seemed she was losing importance.

Even though everyone agreed it would be kind of sad that Agnes would not be joining us at the Thanksgiving table, it was agreed to have our celebration at Ruth's. And besides, as Studebaker pointed out, it would make a nice change.

"If the weather is nice I thought we could take our dessert and coffee outside. I was talking to that nice Charlotte Figg from Paradise—did I tell you I invited her and her friend Rose Tattoo to dinner?"

"No, you didn't. When did you see Charlotte? She's the pie lady."

"When I was up in Paradise the other day, you know doing some work for The Society. She's a very nice woman, they both are, her and that Rose Tattoo. Rose has got her arms covered with pictures, Griselda. Pictures of the whole gospel played out."

I felt my eyebrows rise. "Really?"

"Yes indeedy, seems there's some story behind them but she didn't tell me, and I figured that was fine. It's her business if she wants to have those pictures on her body."

"I hope Charlotte brings pie to Thanksgiving." I felt a smile creep across my face. "Not that yours won't be good, Ruth."

"I understand, and to tell the truth, I hope she does also. I think I might just ask her. I got my hands full with everything else."

I pulled the truck into a spot at the Piggly Wiggly. The closest one I could find to the entrance.

"I bet she'd love to bake pies for the dinner," I said. "I'm eager to taste them."

"They're delicious. I ate a slice of cherry when I was up there. It was incredible. Not too tart or sour—you know how cherries can be—or too sweet. Perfect."

"Is that right. I wonder how Zeb will take to having competition in town," I said.

"He's fine with the notion. I was at the café the other day and he said he'd welcome her pies. Maybe even put them on the menu, let them ride around in the pie carousel. He was tickled pink."

Yeah, tickled pink as in nearly fuming red. Zeb had the market on pie cornered in town. And he did serve some of Charlotte's, particularly her amazing lattice-top cherry. But I couldn't imagine him being glad to have Charlotte Figg's pies next to his in the pie carousel. Unless he had an angle I didn't see.

It was one week before Thanksgiving and the grocery store was crowded with shoppers, just as I figured. Ruth snagged a cart. She rifled through her handbag. "Now I know I put my list in here. Just this morning after adding a few last-minute items. There's always last-minute items."

"You just had it in your hand. You were looking at it in the truck."

"I know, but I shoved it back inside when we pulled into the parking lot."

"I guess you're planning a pretty traditional Thanksgiving dinner—turkey, stuffing, mashed potatoes, glazed carrots, yams with those tiny marshmallows—all the trimmings."

Ruth was up to her elbow in her bag. "Ah, there it is." She pulled a folded page from the depths of her purse. "Not exactly. I thought we'd do something more . . . exotic."

I swallowed. The page she held had disaster written all over it. "Really, Ruth. No turkey?"

"Of course, we'll have turkey. It wouldn't be Thanksgiving without one. But I saw this fancy-dancy tropical Thanksgiving dinner in a magazine while I was waiting for the doctor the other day—I had to go see the gynecologist even though I'm way past all that stuff—"

"Ruth."

"Oh, sorry. Anyhoo . . . " She reached back into her bag. "I asked the nurse permission to take the magazine home. She said I could so I ripped out the picture." She came up with a second folded sheet—this one colorful and glossy. "Look at this. Isn't it the most scrumptious table you have ever seen? It's a Hawaiian Luau Thanksgiving. Look at all the colors and the flowers and those fancy drinks with the paper umbrellas."

Oh, dear. Ruth Knickerbocker has done some crazy things in her day, but I did not think anything other than a traditional Rockwellian Thanksgiving would pass muster with the gang. "Are you sure about this? A tropical Thanksgiving?"

"Look at this. It's a turkey with a pineapple and mango glaze. And I'm going to make a macadamia nut stuffing—not that tired old chestnut stuffing people expect every year. Macadamias are the official nut of Hawaii."

I just hoped our friends wouldn't be calling Ruth the official nut of Bright's Pond. "To be honest, Ruth, I never liked chestnuts, but are you sure about macadamia nuts? Where are you going to find them?"

"I called ahead. That fancy teashop down the road has them. I don't need many."

"Tea shop?"

"Yeah, I saw it the last time I was here. It's the very last shop on Main Street. It's a little scary on account of she has a sign outside—one of them wooden tent signs touting something about having a tarot card reader psychic woman in there. And it is called Madam Zola's Teashop and Psychic Fare."

"Ew, that's weird. Not sure how I feel about all the mumbo-jumbo."

"Well, I'm sure. I hate it, too, but it's the only place to get my macadamia nuts this time of year without going all the way to Hawaii, and I can't do that. And I figured with you along it will be less scary. Hope she doesn't have skulls and voodoo stuff in there. We'll just pop in, buy the nuts, and pop out."

"OK, Ruth, let's get inside the grocery store. It looks like a storm is rolling in."

"Oh, gee, you don't think it's because I want to go into a voodoo shop, do you? Do you think maybe the Good Lord is trying to warn me?"

"Nah, I think it's because the clouds are heavy and need to rain."

"Know-it-all."

It took the better part of an hour to find all the ingredients Ruth needed for her Thanksgiving luau at the Piggly Wiggly. I was surprised we found fresh pineapple. Mangos were another issue but she found a jar of already sliced fruit that had some mango in the mix. She grabbed three jars. She bought canned pineapple also—lots of cans. I pushed the heavy cart to the checkout and we waited and waited for the line to move. It gave me an opportunity to read the sensational headlines on those extraordinary news magazines. My favorite that day read, "World's First Mutant Turkey Over Five Feet Tall."

"I ordered our turkey from Brisco's Butcher Shop," Ruth said when I showed her the headline. "But it won't be here until next Tuesday, so I'll need to come back. I ordered a twenty-pounder. Do you think that's big enough?"

I nodded. "Yep. I don't think we need a mutant turkey."

"Probably tough and dry as shoe leather," Ruth said. It was hard to know if she believed the headline or not.

"And just let me know when you're ready next week," I said. "I'll drive you back down."

We finally had all the groceries bagged and out the door. We placed them in the truck bed. I pushed some other boxes I had in there near them, like a wall, to keep the bags from toppling over when we drove over the bumps on the way home.

The Madam Zola Teashop was the last in a row of stores that included Yost's Hardware, a Rexall Drug Store, and Mrs. Deeter's Fabric and Notion Shoppe. Ruth was not kidding; there was a yellow plywood tent sign outside touting psychic readings, tarot cards, and crystals in giant red letters with an image of a crystal ball on it. It gave me the willies just to look at it.

"Are you sure you want to go in?" I asked.

"Well, it's the only place I can get my nuts, Griselda, unless you want to drive to Hawaii, and that's just not very practical now is it?"

"Whoa, fine. The place is just a little spooky. But come on, let's go inside."

"I'm sorry," Ruth said. "I think I might be a little nervous about making such a large and difficult meal. I never cooked all by myself for so many people, and I'm trying some new recipes and, well, that's always nerve-racking."

"It's OK. I understand. And don't fret, I'll be there to help, and Ivy will pitch in. And I hear Studebaker mashes a pretty mean potato—you *are* having mashed potatoes?" I had just that moment realized Ruth did not purchase any potatoes—yams, yes, but no regular russets.

"At a Hawaiian Thanksgiving luau? Nope." Ruth picked a stray hair off her wool coat.

My heart sank. Thanksgiving without mashed potatoes is like a face with no eyebrows, Snap and Crackle with no Pop.

"But Ruth. You gotta have spuds. Mashed potatoes are the most important side dish. They're like the second-in-command of the dinner."

"I bought sweet potatoes—they're more . . . tropical-looking."

"Are you gonna mash them?"

"Yes."

"OK," I said even though I knew I would not be the only guest at Ruth's table missing traditional white, creamy mashed potatoes with butter and gravy. But believe me when I tell you there will be a bunch of us meeting at the café afterward for some serious albeit sneaky turkey and gravy snacking. Zeb would most likely have some Thanksgiving specials left over.

Ruth and I took deep breaths, and I pulled open the teashop door. A buzzer buzzed as we stepped across the threshold. The store felt and looked creepy with all manner of odd items everywhere. A wide assortment of teas was arranged on a large bookcase that looked like it came out of a medieval castle. The teas were in jars and cans. A metal scale hung from the ceiling. Tables strewn with all sorts of crystals and incense burners, and other strange apparatuses made it difficult to negotiate the tight little store.

Madam Zola sat behind a counter with an old-fashioned cash register. She was heavyset, wearing a dark blue scarf with yellow stars on her head. Frizzy red hair shot like flames from underneath. She wore a long striped skirt and a gauzy white blouse. Chains hung around her neck, and long earrings with crescent moons dangled from her ears. I figured her to be in her sixties.

"Velcome, Velcome to Madam Zola's," she said not looking up from what she was doing. "I can see you've come for zome-thing . . . out of zee ordinary today."

I waved with three fingers. Ruth took a step back and whispered, "How does she know that?"

"Look around," I whispered back. "Everything in the store is out of the ordinary. It's not a tough call."

"Vhat vill be your pleasure today?" She spoke with what I decided was an affected quasi-Russian-slash-Transylvanian accent. I'll bet she was from Northeast Philly.

"Macadamia nuts, please," Ruth said as though she had just approached the Wizard of Oz.

"For tea. You like for tea? I have some nice macadamia nut tea here." She reached behind her on a shelf and pulled off a small yellow tin with orange writing. "Ve only stock zee best. And this tea is right from the island of Molokai vhere zee lepers are."

I swallowed. It didn't sound good.

"Oh," Ruth said. "I don't zink—I mean think—I want leper nuts."

Madam Zola chuckled with a boisterous chuckle. "Oh, no, no." She clicked her tongue. "Zay are harvested vis only ze best hands but grown in the most sorrowful soils—making ze best tastes for you."

"But I need whole nuts," Ruth said.

"I got those," Madam Zola said. "Zay are over dare." She pointed a gnarled finger toward the front of the store. She moved from behind the counter and took hold of a long, rickety cane with a serpent head and glaring green eyes. She tapped the cane twice on the floor. "Follow me."

We did. She limped and dragged one of her legs behind.

"Polio," she said.

Madam Zola pointed to a top shelf with jars of nuts, all manner of exotic nuts. She, of course, being chief among the nuts in my opinion. I saw walnuts, Chinese chestnuts, paw-paw nuts, and something called Allegheny chinquapin nuts.

"Zere zay are," Madam Zola said. "To ze right."

I reached up and grabbed the small jar.

"I might need two," Ruth said.

I grabbed a second jar.

"Excellent," Madam Zola said. "Vould you like me to read your palm today?"

"No, thank you," I said. "My palms are boring."

"Yeah," Ruth said nervously. "It's hard to find a palm that holds your interest these days."

We paid for the nuts and skedaddled out of there but not before Madam Zola made a second offer to gaze into her crystal ball on our behalf.

"Not today," Ruth said. "I'm in a hurry."

Once we were safely on our way back to Bright's Pond, Ruth looked at her palm. "Do you suppose it's true?"

"What?"

"That palm-reading stuff. Do you think Madam Zola can really see my future?"

I winced. "Why would you want to?"

"That's true."

"And creepy."

Ruth clung to her bag of nuts. "I hope they're not cursed or something."

"Nobody curses nuts."

"Just the same, I think Agnes should pray for—"

"Your macadamias?"

"For the whole party."

I took a moment and looked straight ahead. "Agnes is a little sad about not having Thanksgiving at the funeral home this year."

"Criminy," Ruth said. "I didn't even think about that. Maybe we can do something."

"Don't know what. She's not ready to ride in the truck yet."

"The forklift?"

"She swore she would never be driven down the road on a forklift again."

"Then we'll bring the party to her," Ruth said.

"Oh, I don't see how. I thought we'd make a plate up for her. You know, pile it up with everything—maybe make two plates and some pie and bring that to her."

"I guess that makes more sense."

"Sure. That way not everyone has to go. Maybe just you and me and Stu if he wants."

"You're a good sister," Ruth said.

I looked down the road. "No, I don't think so. Sometimes I think if I was really a good sister Agnes wouldn't be in the predicament she's in."

"Now you stop that talk," Ruth said. "You did what you had to do. Agnes let you . . . she let everybody feed her and mollycoddle her. It's not your fault."

I drove a little farther before speaking again. "Thanks, Ruth. But it's still hard to let go of those feelings. Maybe that's why Zeb and me never got married and keep breaking up."

"What do you mean?"

"Maybe I'm not my own person—like Zeb says. I spent my whole life catering to Agnes so much that I got lost along the way."

"Well, look at you now. You're flying an airplane, living alone, running the library. You'll see, God will help you make up for whatever time you lost."

3

I helped Ruth with the groceries and then headed over to the café. Even though Zeb was not speaking to me, I still wanted to see him. After what Ruth said I was hoping he'd want to talk and see if we could work out our differences. Maybe I did let Agnes get between us.

It was by now nearly four o'clock in the afternoon. The café would not be busy this time of day, but Zeb was probably busy getting ready for the dinner rush.

Dot was wiping down tables as only one customer—a truck driver from the look of him—was chomping down a fried baloney sandwich with a piece of Full Moon Pie waiting in the wings. Dot Handy was a good egg. She took over the waitress job after Cora passed away. Dot was a skinny woman, maybe not as skinny as Cora was but skinny nonetheless. Besides her work at the Café, Dot also took the minutes at all the town meetings—a job she took very seriously, carefully writing every word, rushing home to her IBM Selectric, typing it all up, and snapping it into a blue binder she kept under lock and key like she held the secret formula for Pepsi. I suppose it was her jobs that made her a natural busybody. She knew everyone's business.

"Hey, Dot." I sat at the counter so I could snag a glimpse of Zeb in the kitchen.

"Hey, Griselda," Dot said between swipes. "Zeb ain't here, if you come to see him."

"He's not? Where is he?"

"Not sure. Just said he had something to do and that he should be back in plenty of time for dinner. But he also told me to start cooking if he didn't make it. I hate cooking on the grill, so he better get back." Dot tossed her wet rag in a bucket of water under the counter. "Can I get you anything, or you just come in to make yourself feel bad?"

"No. I don't want anything. I didn't come to make myself feel bad, either. I was hoping to talk to Zeb a minute."

"He's still pretty sore at you, you know. How come you went and broke up with him anyway?"

I fiddled with a saltshaker. "Oh, I don't know. I never know. Sometimes it's me. Sometimes it's him. Guess it was my turn. I needed some space and time. It's been different since Agnes left. I kind of like having no ties, well, at least such tight ties."

"Freedom," Dot said. "Well, saying that won't make Zeb feel good. He misses you. The boy loves you, you know."

I looked past Dot out the café window. "I know he does."

"Do you love him?"

That was a question I couldn't answer. I thought I loved Zeb, but lately I had been feeling a bit mixed up.

"Well?" Dot said. "Because if you don't, then you better let Zeb know for certain, one way or the other, so he can move on with his life." She looked into my eyes. "Although to tell the God's honest truth, I can't imagine Zeb with any other woman."

I nodded.

"And you got to admit," Dot said. "The pickins are slim around here. Least you got Cliff Cardwell to turn your head."

"How many times do I have to say there's nothing going on between Cliff and me?"

"Don't tell lies, Griselda. You might not be doing anything about it, but you're attracted to more than just his air-o-plane, and it don't take a brain surgeon to see he likes you. Zeb is off in the distance somewhere."

I nodded again. "I guess I need to figure this out."

"You ain't getting any younger, Griselda. How old are you anyway, forty-one, -two?"

"Three. I'm forty-three."

"Old enough to make up your mind—and fast. Zeb or Cliff."

"Thanks, Dot. Tell Zeb I stopped by—"

"No. Not me. This is between you two."

"OK, OK. Then I'll stop by later."

I left the truck parked at the café and walked toward home. I will admit that sadness had been creeping into my spirit since Zeb stopped talking to me. The town, now in its autumn best, usually cheered me but not that day. I usually enjoyed the crisp air and the smell of wood smoke wafting through the streets. The crunch of leaves underfoot was always so playful and reminded me of my childhood. But not that day. That day the sadness I carried suddenly trumped anything that even smacked of joy. I wanted Zeb to understand that I only needed time. But he was in a hurry—a hurry that took him the better part of a quarter century to work up to.

We had been what you would call an item since our junior year of high school, but every time we even thought about marriage, something got in the way—usually it was Zeb's great big cold feet or Agnes's great big behind. This was not the first time I had called things off for some reason or other. Maybe there was some truth to what Dot said about me and Cliff Cardwell.

The dark clouds that threatened earlier had moved on leaving a brilliant cerulean sky—the kind I usually enjoyed, with wispy, wind-tussled clouds that moved like lace through the sky.

I walked on until I saw Cliff Cardwell strolling down the street. He wore his leather bomber jacket and blue jeans. He was tall, handsome and had shoulders that I would have to be dead not to admit I found . . . nice. His timing was impeccable. My knees went a little rubbery when he got closer, and I could smell his aftershave.

"Hi, Griselda," he said.

I needed to catch my breath. "Hey, Cliff. What's up?"

"I'm glad I found you. I haven't seen you in a few days. We need to talk about your pilot's test."

"I know." I looked at the ground. "I guess I'm a little nervous about taking it."

Cliff draped his arm around my shoulders and pulled me close, but not like boyfriend and girlfriend. More like chums. "Ah, you'll do great. You are my best student."

"I'm your only student, Cliff."

Cliff Cardwell had made an emergency landing on Hector's Hill several months ago. He only needed some repairs. But as it turned out, he liked Bright's Pond so much he stayed, and now he keeps his plane parked on Hector's Hill and makes deliveries for folks. I fell in love that day—instantly. Not with him, but with his plane, a cute little blue and white airplane. Cliff had been giving me flying lessons and that, I suppose, is what had started the latest problem with Zeb and me. Zeb had a jealous streak (the color of a gherkin) running down his back. I didn't know if I should have been flattered or angry.

34

"I can reserve a place for you at the Scranton airport," Cliff said. "Just let me know."

"Oh, I don't know. Maybe I should take a couple more pre-test test flights."

"I don't think you need it. But we can do that if it'll make you more comfortable. We can go up right now if you want. I was just heading down to the Full Moon for a sandwich, but I can eat later."

I looked back toward the café, and a feeling burbled up inside me. Zeb had brought this on himself. I might have been with him right now if he wasn't acting like such a jerk.

"Fine. Let's go."

The walk to Hector's Hill was not long, but it was uphill and by the time we got there, I was huffing and puffing a little. The plane looked great. It had been a week or more since I had flown and just seeing her there made all the sadness of the day drain right out of me.

"Matilda looks great," I said. Just seeing her helped me forget my trouble with Zeb. "Did you wash her or something?"

"Yep, and I even touched up the paint."

I walked toward the plane. I ran my hand over her wing. It was cold and smooth.

"You might as well take her up," Cliff said. "I wish you could just fly her yourself, but rules are rules."

"I know. That's fine. I'm just eager to get behind the stick."

After going through the preflight checklist I started Matilda down the small makeshift runway, and just before the ground ended at the edge of the cliff, I pulled back on the stick and in seconds we were off and climbing into the wispy clouds. There was no feeling in the world like it when the plane left the ground.

"Why not head over to Greenbrier?" Cliff said. "You can tip your wings to Agnes."

"Ha, sounds good. Even if she'll never see me."

"Maybe someday she'll see you fly."

I had to bank just slightly north, then east, and then straighten her out for a direct shot to the nursing home. We flew over the Paradise Trailer Park first. "Hey, look," I said. "What's that in the middle of all those trailers?"

"Looks like a fountain of some sort."

"No kidding? I think you're right." I took Matilda around for another look. "I can't believe it. They got that old fountain up and pumping again. It's been years since water has flowed through those old pipes."

"It's pretty," Cliff said. "All trailer parks should have a fountain."

I had heard that Charlotte Figg and that Rose Tattoo woman had started to make some important changes in Paradise. And now that Studebaker's cousin, Asa, was the new manager, it looks like they had started to accomplish a few things. It made my heart glad to see some more bright spots in Bright's Pond.

"Next stop, or next flyover, I should say, is Greenbrier," I said.

From the air, the nursing home complex looked like a military installation with scattered flat-top buildings and clumps of trees and the flagpole in the center of the complex.

"Thar she blows," Cliff said.

For a second I didn't know if he was making a nasty reference to Agnes or just being silly. I figured silly. It was just my mood that translated even innocent things into sarcasm.

"I guess you haven't been inside Greenbrier recently," I said.

"Nah, not since that whole debacle a few months ago."

"Yeah, well, I'm glad that's cleared up, but I was there earlier today and there are some strange things happening."

"Like what?"

"Well, old people riding tricycles up and down the hallways and even older people making out in the gazebo."

"Making out? You mean like kissing and stuff?"

"Well, I don't know about the stuff but definitely kissing."

"Ah, it's OK. Old people are just old, not dead."

"I know but it's weird in there. It's like some kind of spell has fallen over them."

"Now you're talking weird. No spell has overtaken the nursing home. Oh, watch your airspeed."

"Right, sorry. I know, but it is weird over there. Agnes said she'll keep an eye on things and let me know if she sees anything else unusual."

I banked the plane and headed back for Hector's Hill.

"How is your sister?" Cliff asked.

"She's OK. They got her on that diet, so she feels a little deprived."

"I'll bet. But is it working?"

"Yeah, I believe it is. Whether she likes it or not, she's losing weight. But the doctor said she'll lose quickly at first and then start to have plateaus when it gets harder."

"I really do hope she gets it under control. It can't be healthy. Doesn't she miss being part of the world—going out, doing things?"

"That's something I never understood. She was always just so content to sit home and pray, watch TV. It was like she wanted to hide from the world."

Minutes later, Hector's Hill was in sight and I lined Matilda up for a landing.

"So what do you say? How about we schedule your pilot's test for next week?"

"Next week is Thanksgiving."

"Oh, that's right. Then the week after."

"I guess. Are you sure I'm ready?"

"I am, but how do you feel? Are you ready?"

The feel of the stick and foot pedals was secure, certain. I enjoyed the way my back pressed against the seat and the sounds inside the plane. Everything about it felt right and good.

"I am," I said. "I'm ready."

I landed the plane perfectly, smooth as butter on toast. Maybe even the best landing of my career.

"Good job, Griselda," Cliff said.

After securing Matilda, Cliff and I headed back to town.

"Are you having Thanksgiving with Nate and Stella?" I asked. Cliff had been living with them until he found a place of his own. But to be honest, I think Cliff enjoyed it on the farm, and Nate liked having Cliff around to help with chores and to have someone other than Stella to talk to.

"No, they're going out of town. Stella's brother is taking them to Bermuda. Must be nice having a rich brother."

"Oh, wow, that will be nice. Looks like we'll all have exotic Thanksgivings."

Cliff walked on ahead and then stopped short. "A what Thanksgiving?"

"Exotic. Ruth is planning a Hawaiian Thanksgiving. That's where I'll be, I'm sure you'd be welcome if you want to come."

"Will Zeb be there?"

"He's supposed to be, but who knows, Cliff? He's acting like a baby. We broke up again."

"Then I'll be there. I mean, that is to say, I'm sorry, Griselda."

"Oh, it's OK. Maybe it's for the best this time. Maybe it'll stick. We've broken up so many times I lose count."

We walked a few more paces as dusk settled over town. "Hawaiian Thanksgiving? What the heck is that?"

"Ruth's idea. It sounds like fun, actually. She saw a picture in a magazine of a pineapple and mango glazed turkey. Started the whole thing. "

"Hey, that does sound interesting."

We stopped outside of the Kincaid's farm. The sun was low at the horizon and looked like a giant nectarine with ribbons of purple and red in front of it.

"The sunset is nice," I said.

"Sure is." He looked into my eyes. "So, OK, I guess I'll see you later."

"Are you going back to the Full Moon?"

Cliff looked at his watch. "Nah, Stella has dinner going by now so—"

This time I caught myself looking into his sky-blue eyes. My heart pumped as I felt a tingle down my spine.

"OK. Tell Stella I said hi."

"Why don't you come in and tell her yourself? I'm sure she'll invite you to supper."

"No, I think I'll just go on down to the café."

"To see Zeb?"

"Something like that."

"You know, Griselda, if it doesn't work out with you two, I—"

"Shhh. I know."

The café was crowded for Thursday night's meatloaf special. Zeb was at his post in the kitchen. I sat at the counter.

"Hey, Griselda," Studebaker said on his way past. "How's it going?"

"Hey, Stu. Not bad." I watched him sit next to Boris Lender. The two of them were always discussing something of importance in Bright's Pond. Boris Lender was our First Selectman—kind of a mayor. He had a paunch that I'm certain made it impossible for him to see his feet while standing, and he always wore gray suits and had misshapen rows of nubby, yellow teeth like corn kernels on the cob.

I saw Zeb poke his head up in the kitchen. "Come on, Dot, I got orders backing up."

"Yeah, yeah, keep your shirt on. I'm getting it."

I wiggled two fingers toward him. "Hi, Zeb."

I saw a smile, but he quickly turned it into a frown. "Hey, Griselda."

Dot came by and took my order. She poured coffee without asking. No need. I always wanted coffee.

"I'll have the meatloaf."

"Everybody wants the meatloaf," Dot said.

I heard some grumbles from Zeb.

"I wish you two would hurry up and work it out," Dot said. "He's more miserable than a bear that woke up too soon for spring."

The meatloaf was as scrumptious as ever. I ate slowly hoping maybe Zeb would come out from the kitchen and talk to me. But once I realized that wasn't going to happen I decided to take the matter into my own hands.

"Hey, Stu," I called across and over the busy restaurant. "I went flying today with Cliff." I glanced at Zeb. His head popped up.

"Yeah, I'm taking my pilot's test in a couple of weeks," I said. "Cliff says I'm ready to solo."

Stu smiled and waved. "That's great, Griselda. You'll do fine."

"Yeah," Boris said. "You'll be flying loop-de-loops over town in no time."

That was when Zeb ventured out of the kitchen.

"No loop-de-loops," he said. "You'll get killed."

"Why, Zeb," I said. "You do care."

"Of course I care. You're the one who doesn't."

"Whoa," Dot said. "This is going to get good. Wait 'til I set these orders down. Be right back."

"What?" I said. "I do so care. I just—"

"Hold on." Zeb grabbed my hand. "Come on. Dot watch the stove."

"Wait a second. I haven't finished my meatloaf."

"Later." He gave a slight tug. "We need to talk."

Zeb took me outside. We stood under the streetlight so I figured everyone in the café could see just fine. Zeb and I grew up together, same schools from kindergarten through high school. We were high-school sweethearts and dated on and off ever since. Zeb was a good-looking man, not what you would call handsome in a movie-star way, but he was cute and if the light shown on him just right I could still see some of the teenager.

"If you care so much, how come you won't marry me?" Zeb said. "I keep asking and you keep turning me down."

"Well, before it was you who kept backing away from getting married. And besides, I never said I wouldn't marry you. I said I wanted to wait." I folded my arms against my chest as a chilly wind caught me. "For heaven's sake, Zeb, I haven't been alone in my own home for a year yet. I just want to know what it's like. I want to get to know me—Griselda Sparrow—better before I become Griselda Sewickey."

Zeb twisted his mouth. "So what you're saying is you will marry me?"

"I didn't say that. Not yet."

"Can we at least set a date—how about next week?"

"No, I'm getting my pilot's license, remember. And I haven't agreed to actually marry you yet. Besides this proposal is not very good. Your others were much better."

He made a noise and kicked at a pebble in the street.

"Fine. You let me know."

"We'll both know, Zeb. In the meantime, can we just go back to dating, hanging out together?"

"OK, Griselda. But it's driving me crazy."

I looked into Zeb's dark eyes. This time I felt a tingle that started at my toes and ran clear through my body like a shock. Maybe I was in love with him.

But before Zeb could kiss me, Mildred Blessing came screaming down the street in her police cruiser with siren and lights. She jumped out of her car.

"Come on, Griselda, I got to get you to Greenbrier. It's Agnes."

I looked at Zeb. He looked at me with that gaze I had seen a dozen times before. Someone else was suddenly more important than him.

"I'm sorry—I'm sorry, Zeb. I . . . I—"

"It's OK. Go. Your sister needs you. Apparently more than me."

He walked back to the café.

I climbed into the police cruiser.

"What's wrong? Is she all right? Asthma?"

Mildred stepped on the gas, and we took off toward Greenbrier.

"Not exactly. Might be a little more serious."

4

Then tell me! What is it?" I asked Mildred. "Is Agnes OK? Is it her asthma? Her heart?"

"No, no, nothing like that."

"Then what?"

"Your sister got into an argument with Haddie Grace."

"For that you come racing into town with sirens blaring and pulled me away from Zeb?"

"Haddie Grace kicked Agnes in the shins and then pulled her hair—made her bleed a little, Griselda. Agnes is awful upset. The police are there, and they want to arrest Haddie Grace."

"Well, what can I do? Let them handle it. Did Doctor Silver check her out?"

"Agnes said she needed you. Said she won't press charges but someone has to figure out what is going on over there. They can't have people getting beaten up."

I think I might have sucked all the oxygen out of the car I had taken such a deep breath. "I can't believe this. This is so stupid. Can't the Greenbrier staff deal with this?"

"They're doing what they can. But Agnes wanted you."

Mildred parked out front of the nursing home. I counted three other police cruisers and an ambulance.

"This is ridiculous."

Mildred and I ran down the hall to Agnes's room. A crowd of residents was gathered outside.

"Step aside, step aside," Mildred said. "Coming through."

"Agnes," I called. "What in tarnation is going on?"

"Oh, Griselda," Agnes called with her arms outstretched. "It was awful. I never seen another person act like that." She put her palm on her chest and panted. "It was so scary. But you're here now. Thank the Good Lord."

I saw Haddie Grace sitting on the visitor's chair flanked by two officers. This tiny woman overshadowed by burly men. It made me sick.

But Agnes had to be my first concern. A nurse I didn't recognize was patching up some scratches on her face.

"What happened?" I asked. "What started all this?"

"Oh, Griselda," Agnes looked at me through teary eyes. "Haddie Grace and I got into a fight. I don't even know how it happened and now they want to arrest her. Don't let them. I said I am not pressing charges. But they said it's up to the nursing home."

I moved toward Haddie who looked as scared as a new puppy lost on the turnpike. "Get away from her," I said to the officers.

Nurse Sally joined me. "See, I knew something was going to happen. They're gonna put Haddie Grace in the booby hatch if we don't figure this out."

"It's OK, Haddie Grace," I said. "It's OK." I patted her hand. She looked at me with wild eyes.

"I want to give her a sedative," Sally said. "But the cops won't let me give it to her. They want to bring her to jail for assaulting Agnes."

"That's ridiculous. Did you call Doctor Silver?"

"He's on his way," Sally said.

I looked at the officers. "Just wait until the doctor gets here. He's the medical director. He'll straighten it out."

"Well, I hope so, ma'am," said one of the cops. "Assault is a serious matter. Don't matter if your nineteen or ninety, you can't go beating people up."

Haddie started to cry.

"What happened exactly, Agnes?"

"It seems that her tricycle is missing. Someone stole it apparently, and she thought it was me. She called me Fatty Fatty Boombalattie and started to kick me. Look at me, my butt would swallow that trike."

The officers laughed. I shot them a look. They stopped laughing.

Mildred motioned for the officers to follow her into the hallway.

"This just isn't right," I said. "Haddie would never act like that. Something is terribly wrong."

"I'll say," Agnes said.

"Did you tell Mildred about what's been happening around here?"

"Yes. She said she'd help us get to the bottom of it. I'm beginning to think someone is poisoning us or something, making us all act weird, maybe piping mind-altering gas in the heating system or putting drugs in our oatmeal."

That was when Doctor Silver arrived. "Someone fill me in," he said.

Sally quickly told him what happened.

He went to Haddie Grace first, and checked her all over. He listened to her heart and asked her to breathe. "Don't worry, Haddie Grace, Sally is going to take you back to your room. Give her 2 milligrams of Valium.

"Yes, Doctor." Sally helped Haddie Grace up and gently helped her settle down into a wheelchair.

"I'm sorry, Agnes," Sally said. "We'll figure this out."

Doctor Silver took a look at Agnes. "She really scratched you up. Are you OK? Any pain? Any chest pains?"

"No, I'm OK, Doc," Agnes said. "I am just so worried about Haddie Grace. What made her get all crazy like that?"

"I don't know. I'm a little concerned too. I have to find out what's wrong with her before I'm forced to put her on the locked psychiatric ward."

"Oh, no, that'll kill her," Agnes said. "She doesn't belong there. It's got to be something else. Something physical."

Doctor Silver spent a few more minutes with Agnes. "Don't worry, I sent the cops away. We'll keep a tight leash on Haddie Grace for a while."

"Did that head shrinker find anything?" Agnes asked.

Doctor Silver shook his head. "No, nothing unexpected. That's why she's still on the floor."

"I'm scared, Doc," Agnes said. "It's not just Haddie acting weird."

"I heard," he said. "And it does have me concerned. But let's just get through this immediate crisis. I think if we find her tricycle she'll calm down."

"Can we just buy her a new one?" I asked.

"Won't work," Mildred said, returning to the room. "She'll know it's not hers. But I'm on it. I'll have the place searched. We'll find her tricycle."

Doctor Silver checked Agnes's blood pressure. "A little high but that's understandable."

"It was like being attacked by a mountain lion," Agnes said. "Who woulda thought that spry little woman could pounce like that?"

Doctor Silver shook his head. "I don't know. She has brittle bones from osteoporosis, but lately, it's like she's a teenager again. I'm ordering some tests to check for a brain tumor."

"I never thought I would say something like this, but in way I hope it is," Agnes said.

Doctor Silver took a deep breath and stuffed his medical tools into a black bag. "I know what you mean. Otherwise, it's BrigaLOON for her, I'm afraid. Get some sleep, Agnes. I'll check in on you in the morning."

"BrigaLOON?" I said once the doctor was gone.

Agnes sort of half-smiled. "Yeah, that's what they call the locked ward. It's a play on that old musical *Brigadoon*. It's a strange mysterious place none of us have ever seen where they stash the hopeless mental cases. Some even call it BrigaDOOM."

"That's terrible," I said.

"I know. But I doubt it's as bad as I hear. It's not a snake pit. Still I wouldn't want to see Haddie forced to go there."

I looked out her window but from there I couldn't see any other buildings. "I'm sure it's not as bad as you think. I'm sure they take real good care of the patients."

Mildred coughed. "I hate to break this up, but I need to organize a search of the compound for the missing tricycle." Mildred was the Bright's Pond Chief of Police—a title primarily honorary since she was the only cop in town. She was an odd bird, a mixture of feminine brawn and adherence to duty. I guess I would compare her to Jane Russell, the 1950s Hollywood sex symbol.

"Sure, sure, you go ahead. I'll call Zeb to come get me."

"You won't mind?" Mildred said.

"Nah, I want to stay with Agnes for a little longer."

Mildred took out a small spiral notebook from her breast pocket. "Can I get a description of the tricycle?"

Agnes laughed and slapped her knee. "Description. Sure, Mildred. It's bright red, with handlebar streamers and a silver bell. But listen, I suspect if you find any tricycle around here, it'll be Haddie's."

Mildred scribbled in her book. "Just want the facts straight. If there's one thing I've learned since moving to Bright's Pond, it's not to assume anything."

"Are you OK?' I asked Agnes once Mildred left the room.

"Yeah, sure. I'm fine. But that little woman packs a punch. She was all over me."

"That must have been scary."

"In a funny, weird sort of way."

"What do you think happened to her tricycle?"

"Don't have a clue. But I suspect someone took it as a joke."

I pushed hairs behind Agnes's ears and looked at the scratches on her cheek. "Some joke."

Agnes pointed to the visitor chair. "Sit. Can you stay a while?"

My mind flashed on Zeb and the kiss I was about to receive before Mildred brought the moment to a screeching halt. "I was planning to. I mean I'm sure the moment has passed."

"Moment? What moment?"

Zeb and I were talking, and he was about to kiss me when Mildred showed up."

"Ah, gee, really. I'm sorry. That stinks. But I was just so frightened and for a minute there I couldn't catch my breath."

I looked away from her and wallowed for a minute in what I suppose was self-pity.

"Look," Agnes said. "Go home and go see him. Rekindle the moment. I'm sure he'll find his pucker again."

"Maybe. He gets so jealous so easily. Like he doesn't want to share me."

"What man does? But if he wants you and loves you then he'll have to understand that you have other responsibilities sometimes."

I took a deep breath and let it out slowly. "I suppose. I just wish he didn't get so upset over this stuff. It's not like I am deliberately doing it. I'm not planning these interruptions."

Agnes reached under her pillow and pulled out a Baby Ruth. "Want some?"

"Sure. Why not?" I said thinking about how easily Agnes recovered from her terrible ordeal.

———∞∞———

I stayed with Agnes for the better part of an hour mostly debating whether to run home to Zeb and waiting for word from Mildred about the fate of Haddie Grace's tricycle.

Agnes's suppertime rolled around and an aide carried a tray into her room.

"Will you look at that?" Agnes said. "More salad. A hamburger patty. Cottage cheese, fruit, and sugar-free Jell-O. It just ain't food."

"It's good for you. And you want to get thinner, don't you? And besides you just ate that candy bar."

Agnes poked a fork into the mound of cottage cheese. "Yeah, but this—this is torture."

Mildred popped into the room. "Found it."

"The trike?" I said. "Really? Where was it?"

Mildred walked farther into the room. "It was out behind the gazebo. Some old geezer was sitting on it and pretending he was on a spaceship bound for Mars."

I smiled. "You shouldn't say geezer, but it is funny."

"Funny? I had to fight him for it." Mildred said, sitting on the edge of Agnes's bed. "Then he took off and skipped back to one of the buildings over there and disappeared."

"Where is it now?"

"Back at Haddie Grace's room. She's still out cold from whatever the doc gave her. Guess she'll see it in the morning."

Agnes looked out the window toward the gazebo. "Something weird is happening. This just isn't right. Folks around here are turning into children."

Mildred made outer space noises. "They're just old and senile—acting out is all."

Agnes waved her hand. "No, no. It's more than that. I tell you, this is not right, and it seems to have started right after the gazebo went up."

That was when I saw the spark in Mildred's eyes. "Really, Agnes? You think something foul is afoot?"

"I do. I just can't put my finger on it. But . . . now don't think I'm nuts but it's like they really are getting younger."

"I still think it's just the holidays," I said. "Bringing out the kid in them."

Mildred said, "Uh-huh, maybe, but I think I should do some investigating. Could be drugs."

"Drugs?" Agnes became excited. "That's exactly what I was thinking."

"That's impossible, Mildred." I said. "Where would they get drugs? And why? Lord knows they take enough drugs already prescribed by the doctors."

"Could be someone is doing it without their knowledge," Mildred said.

"But why?" Agnes said. "Why would anybody want to attack this nursing home?"

"This is nonsense," I said. "No one is drugging or attacking the residents of the Greenbrier Nursing Home."

Mildred peeked out the window. "Still and all I think I'll do some snooping." She opened her little black notebook and scribbled something. "I'll keep it on the Q.T. Ask a few pertinent questions; keep my eye out. Don't want the television news program getting wind of this."

"Or that reporter fella from Shoops—what's his name?"

"Dabs," I said. "Dabs Lemon. He'll be snooping around here like a bloodhound after filet mignon if he catches a sniff of this."

"I hope I can solve this mystery before that happens," Mildred said. "I'll start asking if anyone has seen anyone new or suspicious around the grounds."

"Just the fella that built the Gazebo," Agnes said. "A weird kind of guy. Short, but stocky, you know, strong as an ox. He built that thing all by himself. I think Sally told me his name was Leon . . . Leon—something or other."

"It's a place to start," Mildred said. "I'll go see Sally now."

5

I hope Mildred gets to the bottom of the troubles around here," Agnes said. "I can't take anymore outbursts like that nonsense with Haddie Grace."

"I know." I sat in the visitor chair. "Mildred will figure it out, and Doctor Silver won't let Haddie get into anymore trouble."

Agnes slapped her knee. "Oh, I hate the thoughts of that poor old woman getting locked away in the booby hatch."

"Me too. But let's just pray that the docs can figure out what's causing her odd behavior and take care of it."

"I guess that's all we can do." She lightly touched one of the scrapes on her cheek. "She was truly like a mountain lion, Griselda. She came into my room and . . . pounced on me."

"Well, she's sedated now. She won't be coming back in here tonight."

"Sure could use a slice of pie," Agnes said as she looked out the window. "It's getting dark. My bones are telling me a storm might be brewing."

"I think I heard the weather lady say some rain was moving in."

"Yeah, yeah, that's typical for November around here."

I stayed with her a few more minutes, but my thoughts kept returning to Zeb.

"Listen," I said, "I think I should be getting back to town. I haven't fed Arthur yet today, and maybe I'll try and catch up with Zeb."

Agnes snorted. "Zeb. I wish you two would decide once and for all time if you were getting married or not. My heart can't take all this back and forth. And besides, Griselda, you ain't getting any younger."

"OK, OK. I hear what you're saying Agnes." Although to be honest, I didn't know if I could believe that she really wanted me to marry Zeb. "I just need a little more time," I continued, "and then we'll settle one way or another. Maybe after I get my pilot's license."

"Pilot's license? Are you still going through with that dumb thing?"

I felt a bit insulted by her tone. She made it sound so silly. "Yes, Agnes, I am. And pretty soon I think."

She glared at me. "Well, maybe you just need to get all this airplane business out of your system before you can say 'I do.'"

I didn't know how to respond, except to say, "I guess it's really up to me and if getting my pilot's license is something I need to do before I settle down, as they say, then I guess I better get on it."

"Just don't go crashing into the mountains." Agnes smiled. The little knobs of her cheeks reddened like two cherries. "Seriously, Griselda."

"Nah." I patted her hand. "I just want to fly over them."

It was nearly nine o'clock when I got back to Bright's Pond. The town was still and quiet and illuminated mostly by porch lights and streetlights. Mine was the only vehicle on Filbert Street. Rain started to fall fast and hard the second I reached the café. The lights were on so I reckoned Zeb was inside cleaning up the grill, sweeping, and maybe even making pies. One thing I can say for sure about Zeb, besides the fact that he can be as jealous as all get out, he was faithful—to his business—and industrious. I think he actually loved cooking and baking and handling customers even when he complained. But sometimes I wasn't sure how he would squeeze a wife into his days and nights.

I thought about stopping but a yawn made me realize that it had been a long day. And another argument with Zeb was not what I needed just then.

Arthur was fit to be tied when I went inside the house. He sat in the kitchen near his empty food bowl like a mountain lion—or maybe I should say like Haddie Grace—ready to pounce.

"I'm sorry, Old Man," I said. "Busy day."

The rain fell harder. Large, heavy drops splattered against the kitchen window and blew the curtains. I left the window open only an inch but the rain still came in. I closed it with a bang and Arthur mewed.

"Sorry, Artie."

I dumped Purina Cat Chow into his yellow bowl. I rinsed his water dish and filled it. He was hungry and wasted no time chomping down the kibble. He took some in his mouth and then chewed, all the time keeping an eye on me. I couldn't tell if it was consternation or if he was making sure I wouldn't leave. So I sat down next to him on the floor.

"I hope that poor old woman doesn't have a brain tumor. She's so sweet ordinarily, and who cares if she's riding through the nursing home on a tricycle? And who cares if Clive Dickens and Faith Graves want to get married; they must be in their nineties. Imagine that: getting married at age ninety."

Arthur looked at me and winked with both eyes.

"Yeah, yeah." I rubbed my hand down his back. "I better hurry up and marry Zeb before I'm ninety, is that your opinion?"

Arthur mewed and then yawned.

I yawned. "I should go to bed. Lord knows what will happen this weekend."

Arthur finished his meal and followed me upstairs.

Ruth was banging on my front door the next morning. She woke me from a sound sleep at seven o'clock.

"Ruth," I said when I pulled open the door. "What in tarnation are you doing here?"

"I need you to taste this. I've been awake since four o'clock making it." She held a pot covered with a white dish towel.

"What is it?"

"My stuffing mix. Remember? The macadamia nut stuffing I was planning to make, well, I am just so worried about it. I need you to taste it." She almost pushed me aside and headed straight for the kitchen. A macadamia nut slipped out and landed on the floor.

"Ruth, you're losing your . . . marbles," I said and followed her into the kitchen. "But I didn't even have a cup of coffee yet. Not a single cup and—"

"Oh, you poor dear. I've had six—maybe seven."

Obviously.

"Tell you what. You go on and put some clothes on. I'll make a pot and then you can taste my stuffing. I am just so worried about it. But I wanted to try it. They say you should always try a new recipe before serving it to guests. And so that's what I did. I mixed up a small batch and now—"

I thought she might cry. "OK, OK. Let me put some clothes on. You make coffee and settle down a minute. It's just stuffing."

"No, it's more than that. It's *Thanksgiving* stuffing. It smelled so good early on with the onions and the butter and the celery sautéing, but something happened when I added the spices and the nuts."

Actually, Ruth's turkey stuffing woes were a welcome relief from the events of the day before. I dressed, brushed my teeth, and got back to the kitchen in time to see Ruth trying to persuade Arthur to eat a morsel of the stuffing.

"He won't eat that," I said. "Arthur is picky, and I suspect celery and macadamia nuts are not his choice at seven in the morning."

"Oh, well, you'd think an animal that would eat fish heads would appreciate something else." Ruth said. "But he's just so picky. Now you sit down. I'll pour your coffee."

Ruth set a mug of steaming coffee in front of me, made just the way I like it. Extra cream, no sugar.

I sipped. "Thanks. This is good." I stared at the pot on the table. The stuffing at least smelled good, even over the coffee smell. As a matter of fact, the two aromas kind of complemented each other. I thought that was a good sign.

"Did you hear about what's going on up at Greenbrier?" I asked.

"Greenbrier? Nothing with Agnes I hope."

"Well, not directly, except, of course, Haddie Grace tried to beat her up yesterday."

Ruth fell into a chair. "She what? Agnes? Haddie Grace? That little old woman—older than dirt, with the wrinkles and those little kneecaps that stick out like elbows? I swear that woman's got four elbows."

"She's the one. Only she's not so old anymore."

Ruth looked at me the way Mickey Mantle looks at Ivy when he's confused.

"You mean she died? Well, no one can be surprised I mean she did go to the prom with Moses."

"No, no, she's very much alive. Too much alive. Didn't you just hear me say she tried to beat the living daylights out of Agnes yesterday?"

"I heard that but she coulda expired afterward."

"OK, here's what happened." I sipped more coffee then I told the whole story. At least I told her everything I knew so far about the people, the way they're acting, the gazebo, and the tricycle.

"So I don't know," I said, "if Mildred has talked to this Leon fella yet. I imagine she did."

Ruth poured herself a cup of joe.

"Are you sure you want that?" I asked. "You seem a might . . . jumpy."

"Uh-huh, I get the feeling this holiday season is shaping up to be a doozy, and I'm gonna need to stay awake for it. Now try my stuffing before it coagulates into something unrecognizable."

I lifted the towel off the bowl and there it sat. A mess of cubed-up bread with celery and onions and macadamia and only God knew what else at that moment in time. I'm pretty sure I saw pineapple and maybe coconut. I never liked coconut. But I couldn't say that to Ruth. Not then. Ruth snagged a large tablespoon full of the brownish bread mixture.

"Go on, taste it."

I swallowed another swig of coffee hoping that maybe the coffee taste would linger on my palate and make the stuffing go down easier. I had severe concerns for Ruth's stuffing.

I tasted it. I chewed and chewed. My eyes watered, my nose tickled. I wanted to spit it across the floor, but I managed to swallow. Whatever spices and flavors she had in there were not mixing well. I could have just licked the bottom of a hamster cage and gotten the same effect. I sipped coffee to wash the taste away. "OK, Ruth, what is in that? It's pretty awful."

"I knew it was bad." She looked sad.

"What did you put in it? There's a taste or two that just doesn't make it. Now I did like the one macadamia I crunched into but—"

"Pineapple and passion fruit," Ruth said. "Too much pineapple, too much passion fruit, and then all that sage and thyme and . . . Oh, heavens to Betsy, Griselda, your face is red as a tomato. I hope you aren't allergic."

My stomach rolled.

"Pineapple and passion fruit in turkey stuffing?"

"It didn't sound like a bad idea," Ruth said. "It's all tropical you know. My theme."

"Maybe it isn't the fruit. Maybe it's more about the proportions and the spices you chose and, of course, the coconut. Ruth, I hate coconut."

"How can you hate coconut? You mean you don't like Mounds Bars?"

I shook my head. "Nope."

I took another, small pinch of the stuff off the side of the bowl and closed my eyes praying that God would not let me die a turkey-stuffing death. "Mm, now see, I just a tasted a bit that was not bad, not bad at all."

Ruth tasted it. "I see what you mean. Maybe if I tone it down. Oh, dear, I have less than a week to get everything done. And I wanted the stuffing to be delicious."

"It will be."

"Maybe a shot of rum, you know, just for taste."

I shrugged and sipped my coffee.

"I'm not at all worried about the rest of the meal," Ruth said. "I got everything else under control. Wait until you taste dessert. I'm not telling you what it is. It's going to be a big surprise. A big surprise." She held her hands about four feet apart.

"I can't wait. I know it's going to be great."

"Oh, that reminds me. Can you drive me down to Brisco's on Tuesday to pick up the bird. Mr. Brisco says he has a nice one for me."

"Sure. I said I would, remember? Let's go early though."

Ruth had been getting more and more forgetful lately. Mostly little things. It concerned me, but I chalked it up to getting older and the stress of Thanksgiving. She stayed a few more minutes until I told her that I needed to get to the library. Fridays were not a busy day but I liked to open the doors anyway just in case a kid from the high school needed something.

"Oh, sure, sure. I'm feeling a bit better," Ruth said. "I'll go home and rework this stuffing."

"Good idea. I'll see you later."

"Can I bring another sample over if I need?"

My heart wasn't in it but I said, "Sure. Of course."

"Now if Agnes was still living here," Ruth said on the porch. "She'd know what was wrong with my stuffing right away."

"That's true. But sorry, you only have me. Maybe Ivy can help."

"Ivy," Ruth said looking down the road. "I'll try her."

I watched as Ruth walked down the tree-lined street, fallen autumn leaves crunching under her feet as she carried her ill-conceived recipe home—appropriately hidden under a white dish towel with a turkey appliqué.

The walk to the library was lovely. Crisp fall air with a hint of wood smoke tickled my nose. I passed piles of unburned leaves pushed to the curb and greeted neighbors already outside raking their lawns unveiling that autumn green of the grass just before the first real snowfall. The sun shone bright while wispy clouds like torn lace floated overhead.

"Morning, Griselda, nice day," said Bill Tompkins.

Babette Sturgis was running down the street carrying an armful of books. "Hey, Miss Griselda. I got to catch the bus."

I waved and thought how blessed I was to live in Bright's Pond even though I still nursed a place in my heart that longed for something more, something that I knew was just beyond my reach. Something that started to become attainable when Cliff Cardwell took me up in his plane that first time and I knew with every ounce of my being that I wanted to fly.

The library stood like a grand old lady on a hill just a little ways off the street. She was a fully dressed Queen Anne Victorian with rows of courses and miles of gingerbread, a wide wraparound porch perfect for sitting in the spring and summer and on warm fall days to read and chat. It made me a little sad that more people didn't come to the library to escape into a story now and again. Emily Dickinson said, "There is no frigate like a book, to take us lands away." She was so right.

I turned the key in the ancient lock and pushed open the library door. A breath of cool, bookish air blew out. As usual I set about turning on lights, straightening magazine and newspaper racks all the time wondering if I would see any faces that day. Every time I opened the library I felt the same way, like I was preparing a place of solitude where I felt more in touch with my soul than anywhere, even perhaps, than in Cliff's plane.

After the mail, I always returned books to the stacks with an eye out for misplaced volumes. The students were notorious for shoving books back wherever they wanted even though I told them a hundred times it would be better if they returned the books to the checkout counter. And I was right. I found a copy of *How the West Was Won* tucked on the end of the Microbiology section.

I heard the little bell over the door ring—the bell was new. I asked Studebaker to install it for me so I could hear folks come in no matter where I was in the building. Not that I didn't trust anyone, I was just often in the back rooms or lost among the stacks, and people had been thinking I wasn't there and turning and leaving.

It was Charlotte Figg from the trailer park. I liked the look of her. She wore a dress covered with purple flowers and she carried a small orange purse. Her hair was short, but not too short, manageable I suppose and mostly brown, the color of old oak with strands of gray here and there.

"Can I help you?" I called from the Science section.

She stood close to the door for second and then ventured farther inside.

"You're Charlotte Figg, right?" I asked. I offered my hand. "I'm Griselda Sparrow."

"Nice to meet you, Griselda." She shook my hand. "Ever play softball?"

"In high school, a little. I liked it."

"Well, the Paradise Angels are always looking for players if you want to come out next spring."

"Maybe," I said. "I heard about your team. I think it's pretty neat, you putting the team together and all."

"Ah, they really put themselves together, but thanks. Anyway, my friend Rose—"

"The woman with all the tattoos?"

She nodded and looked at me as if to say, "You don't get many visitors, do you?"

I thought I should back off and let her be. But she kept talking, "That's right, the woman with all the tattoos. Boy, word travels fast in this town. But that's not the issue. Rose said you might be able to help me find some information on . . . " she whispered, "the Fountain of Youth."

"Sure." It was a bit of an odd subject for someone in Bright's Pond.

"I think you can start with the *Encyclopedia Britannica*. It will give you some info. May I ask what exactly you're looking for?"

"Oh, I don't think I know for certain. It's just a hunch, really. Something sparked my imagination," Charlotte said. "I wanted some info on that explorer fellow they claim found it in Florida—Ponce de León."

"Oh, no problem. I'm sure you'll find out all about him in here." I grabbed the book from the shelf. "And if you need more information, there's a whole section on world history over there, lots of books about the explorers."

She took the thick volume and sat at one of the long tables.

"I just wanted to tell you," I said, "that I have heard so much about your pies. Folks are even saying you should open a shop in town."

Charlotte smiled and flipped to the page she needed. "I do like to make pies, and everyone keeps telling me to open a shop—even my mother."

"Maybe you should. There's that empty store down on Filbert Street—across from the town hall and The Full Moon Café."

"There is?"

"Sure. I think it will make the perfect spot."

"Maybe I'll take a look—someday. Maybe next year."

Charlotte looked at the book, and a few minutes later as I passed by again she said, "It says here that Ponce de León never found the fountain. But most people, historians even, claim it's in Florida. Do you think it's possible?"

I shook my head. "What? That the Fountain of Youth is more than a legend, a fairy tale? That water can make you younger?"

"Yes." She was dead serious.

At that moment I looked clear through Charlotte and saw Haddie Grace whizzing down the hallways of Greenbrier and didn't know how to answer her. "How come you're so interested in this?"

"Oh, I'm just thinking, that's all. Folks up at Paradise have been talking about it ever since that Leon Fontaine moved in and started rebuilding the trailer park fountain. Have you seen it? It's pretty near finished and really quite beautiful—in a crooked kind of way."

I smiled. "Leon Fontaine? He's the man who built the gazebo over at the nursing home. It's a little on the crooked side also. But really nice."

"That's him. Weird little man, but I've come to accept weird as normal around here."

I laughed. "Charlotte, I think we're going to be good friends."

Then I remembered. "Say, Ruth told me you and Rose Tattoo are coming to Thanksgiving dinner. I hope you're bringing pie."

"Yes. I mean yes, we're invited and, yes, I am bringing pie."

"Hope it's pumpkin and cherry. Ruth is planning all kinds of tropical stuff."

Charlotte laughed. "I heard. She told me she has a big surprise for dessert."

"Me too, but please, pumpkin pie will be a most welcome sight, I'm sure."

Charlotte patted my hand. "Don't worry. I'm bringing pumpkin and apple and maybe a cherry, since you mentioned it."

That was when I heard the doorbell ring. Mercy Lincoln was standing there holding the copy of *Heidi* she had checked out just a few days previous.

"Mercy," I said. "Did school let out already?"

Mercy Lincoln was one of the backwoods children that came into town for school. She was poor as dirt, usually filthy but always managed to brighten my day. I loved her love for books and stories.

"No, not yet, I reckon. I didn't go to school today."

I ushered her farther into the library. "How come? Not like you to miss a day."

"It was Mama. She weren't feelin' real well this morning and asked me to stay with her."

"How is she now?" I took the book from her hands.

"She's better. That's why I come by, to return that book and get another if I may."

"Of course. You have a look."

I went back to Charlotte who was still reading. "I don't want to interrupt, but do you have a library card? I'll get one ready if you want."

"Oh, that would be so sweet of you. I need a card."

I went back to the checkout counter and wrote out a card for Charlotte Figg. I just put Paradise Trailer Park for her address. I didn't need much more than that.

Charlotte looked through books for another thirty-five minutes or so before she came to the counter. Meanwhile, Mercy had gotten lost among the bookshelves. "I guess I got the info I needed but I think I will check out this book—it's a recipe book on pastries. I think I might make some little tartlets. You know tiny pies, individual pies."

"You could sell them by the dozens if you had a shop."

"Now don't pressure me. I said I'm thinking about it. I got some money, but it's gotta cost a lot more than I got to run a pie shop."

"If you're serious at all, you might want to talk with Boris Lender. He knows about that kind of stuff. He'll help where he can."

"Thank you, I'll keep him in mind."

I checked out her book—*Pies, Tarts, and Filled Pastries.* "Actually that empty store I mentioned used to be a bakery—years ago. It might still have some equipment inside."

Charlotte's eyes grew wide. "Really? In that case, maybe I will take a gander."

Before she reached the door I said, "See you next week."

Charlotte turned. "Aren't you coming to the blessing?"

"Blessing?"

"Of the fountain. Asa Kowalski is planning a big old ceremony when they turn on the fountain Sunday. They're calling it the Blessing of the Fountain Day."

I contained a chuckle. "Oh, good grief. The people in this town will use any excuse to have a blessing or parade. Maybe I will. Can I bring a friend or two?"

"Bring three or more. Heck, bring everyone."

Mercy popped up next to me. "This one looks good."

"Oh, *Sherlock Holmes.* I guess you're ready for it. You like mysteries? Crime stuff?"

"I like figuring stuff out, and it sounds like that's what Mr. Sherlock Holmes is good at."

"Elementary, my Dear Watson."

She looked at me.

"You'll see. I hope your mama is feeling better."

"She will. It's the third time this week she been sick in the morning."

6

It wasn't until after Charlotte and Mercy left that I started to put two and two together and wonder if the new Paradise Fountain, Leon Fontaine, and what was happening at Greenbrier had any connection. It didn't seem possible, but one thing I learned by hanging around Mildred Blessing is that you never let any hunch go unheeded. I dialed Mildred's number hoping she was in her office.

"Chief of Police, Mildred Blessing."

"Oh, good, you're there," I said.

"Who is this? Griselda?"

"Yes. Mildred, I might have some info about that Leon fellow and Greenbrier."

"Really? Because I talked with Nurse Sally and she said that man is just as sweet as can be and claims he doesn't know anything about why the residents might be acting so strange—including Haddie Grace. She said he just came every day, did his work on the gazebo, and left."

"Uh-huh, that may be so, but let me come and tell you what I just thought about."

"OK, meet me at the Full Moon."

That was the last place I wanted to go that morning. I wasn't in any mood to deal with Zeb, but I agreed.

After locking up the library, I went and found Mildred at the café talking with Dot Handy and Studebaker Kowalski. Studebaker and Asa were cousins. I'm sure they might have been discussing the upcoming Blessing of the Fountain. I looked for Zeb out of the corner of my eye and saw his paper hat bobbing around in the kitchen.

"Hey, Mildred," I called with a wave.

"Hey, Griselda," Stu said. "We were just talking about the Blessing of the Fountain. Cousin Asa is pretty excited."

"I figured as much. I just learned about it," I said. "Charlotte Figg came into the library looking for some information, and she told me. I think it's pretty neat they got that old fountain going."

Dot Handy offered me coffee.

"No thanks, Dot. I had enough today. But I would like a glass of water."

"Water?" Mildred said. "Everybody is asking for water today. Must have something to do with that fountain."

"That's right," I said. "That's what I wanted to tell you."

I squeezed into the booth seat. "Charlotte Figg came looking for information on—now get this—the Fountain of Youth."

"Really?" Mildred's eyebrows rose. "You don't say." She took out her trusty black notebook and scribbled in it. Fountain of Youth. Then she drew a great big question mark next to it. "It doesn't exist," she said. "But I wrote it down anyway. A clue is a clue even when it isn't really a clue."

"Everybody knows it doesn't really exist, that's it's just a story," I said.

Dot placed a glass of water in front of me. "Want anything else, Griselda?"

"No, thank you."

"Of course not," Stu said. "Charlotte is just as wacky as the rest of them up there."

"That's not nice," I said. "I think she's very sweet and is really concerned about things. But get this. Isn't it weird that this man, Leon comes to town, rebuilds a fountain and the gazebo and now the people at Greenbrier are all acting so young and—"

"Wait, wait, just a doggone minute," Mildred said. "Are you implying that the Fountain of Youth is in the Paradise Trailer Park?"

I sipped my water. "I guess it does sound stupid. But it seemed uncanny to me that he should get the fountain going and be visiting Greenbrier and now the people are riding tricycles and kissing and skipping and stuff like that."

"Look," Mildred said. "I'll go talk to Leon but I don't think he's got anything to do with Greenbrier. How could he? There is no such thing as water that makes people young or gives them new life."

"I don't know. Just thought I should mention it."

"Anyway," Studebaker said, "are you all coming to the blessing? It should be a lot of fun."

"I haven't been up to Paradise in a long, long time," Dot said. "I'll go."

"Me too," Mildred said.

That was when Zeb came out of the kitchen. "Hey, Hey, everybody." He looked at me. "Hi, Grizzy."

"Hi, Zeb. How are you?"

"Just fine. Just fine."

The tension between us fell like a thick, wool blanket over the café. Everyone felt it. I could tell just by looking at their faces.

"Are you going?" I asked Zeb. "To the blessing?"

"Maybe. Are you?"

"Sure, it sounds like a blast."

"How are you getting there?" Zeb asked. "Flying?"

I looked daggers at him. Every chance he could he said something to jab at Cliff Cardwell.

"No, I'll drive my truck."

"Fine," Zeb said. And he went back to his kitchen.

Studebaker shook his head. "You two really need to work this out. Either get married or break up for good."

"Hear, hear," Dot said. "Make a decision."

My head started to ache. "I just came by to give you that info, Mildred. Do with it what you want. I better get back to the library before school lets out."

❧

I got outside and Zeb was waiting near my truck. He was looking a little guilty.

"I'm sorry, Grizzy," he said. "For making that remark about flying to Paradise. I just get so jealous."

"You shouldn't. I keep telling you that there is nothing between Cliff and me except flying lessons."

We stood toe to toe. He lifted my chin with his fingertips and kissed me. My toes curled as I felt one leg lift off the ground. When he pulled away. A deep sigh bubbled like a fountain from my chest. "Oh, Zeb. Why do we fight?"

"Then you'll marry me?"

I took a step back. "I didn't say that—not yet."

"Then when? I'm going nuts."

"I don't know. Maybe if you just take the pressure off, and we can go on dates and spend time together without all this jealous stuff, and . . . Zeb, I really want to try and get my pilot's license before the marriage license. I know you don't understand, but I need to do this."

"OK, I guess I understand—sort of. And I promise: no more jealousy."

"And no more complaints when I need to see Agnes. I know I run off on you sometimes—" I leaned against the truck. "But how often do you run to the café to check on something or take care of a problem? How many times have you left me at the movie because you needed to check the café?"

"I know, I know. But it's different. The Full Moon is my livelihood. Hopefully one day it will be ours."

I glared at him. "So what you're saying is your problems are more important that mine? I've been taking care of Agnes for years, practically my whole life. I can't just stop."

Zeb kicked at a pebble. "No. Not exactly, but you got to admit that my café is important. And Agnes has other people to take care of her now." He pulled me close to him. "You need to let her go. I can't let the Full Moon go. We can't."

"And Agnes is my sister—" I kissed his cheek. "And if we get married, she'll be our sister."

Zeb backed away. "OK, Griselda. I get it. I guess I can wait, but you got to know how hard it is for me now. I've made up my mind. I'm ready to be married. Really ready."

"I know. I'm almost ready."

"OK. I'll see you later. Right now, I have baloney to fry."

I watched him go back inside the Full Moon before getting into the truck.

"Too much pressure," I said to myself as I turned the ignition. "Why does he have to put so much pressure on me?"

"Who's putting pressure on you?"

It was Cliff standing near the truck. "Is it Zeb? Is he still upset that I'm giving you flying lessons?"

I nodded. "Yeah, he gets so jealous and thinks if I wear his wedding ring I'll stop living or something and that I won't need to fly. But it worries me that even after we're married, he will still be jealous and I'll still want to fly."

Cliff grinned. "I would reckon so."

"I need to get to the library."

"How about later?"

"Later?" I said. "What about later?"

"Go flying. You said you wanted some more flights before your test."

I looked at the café and saw Zeb at the window. "Good idea. I can meet you on the Hill a little after three."

Cliff tapped the car door. "Sounds good."

Then he smiled, my stomach went wobbly and suddenly all I wanted to do was sit next to Cliff in the plane and fly through the clouds.

I wrapped up work at the library just before 3:30. There was only one student who needed a book. I couldn't wait for him to leave and practically shoved him out the door. I headed straight for Hector's Hill. The thought of going flying was the most exhilarating thing I ever experienced.

Cliff waited near Matilda.

"Did you already do the preflight?" I asked.

He nodded. He wore his leather bomber jacket, the one that made him look like he just walked off a 1940s movie sound stage. He had a day's worth of stumble on his face but that only made him more attractive.

"Yep. I did. But I want you to do it also. All part of the test."

I took the clipboard and went through the list. Everything checked out, except I thought the air pressure in the nose tire was a little high.

"What about that tire?" I said.

He smiled. "Good call. An overinflated tire can be just as dangerous as an underinflated one. Let some air out."

I grabbed the tire gauge from the toolbox and let some air hiss out until the pressure was where it should be. "There we go. All set."

Cliff and I went through the check inside the cockpit and all was well. I buckled my seatbelt and planned a course, this time away from Bright's Pond. Away from Greenbrier. I would have flown clear to Peru if I could have that day.

I don't think I will ever get used to or stop enjoying the feeling when the plane first leaves the ground. I leveled her off and set my cruising altitude and speed and headed straight for the Blue Mountains.

"I want to fly over them today, Cliff. Am I ready?"

"You're ready."

It didn't take long for the mountains to come into view. Gee, they were gorgeous in their autumn colors. Brown and rust, purple and gold and green. It was like flying into a needlework sampler. The closer I got, the clearer the scene—the leaves and trees.

"Pull back," Cliff said. "You'll need more altitude."

I pulled back the stick and Matilda climbed like a goose until we were directly above the mountain. I leveled her off.

"This is incredible," I said. "What city is that down there?" I could see an expanse of buildings spread out on a plain. Rows of houses, dotted with taller buildings and spires.

"That's Allentown," he said. "The Lehigh Valley. Isn't she pretty?"

"From up here, yeah. I guess most things are better looking at a distance."

"I agree. Perspective makes all the difference some time. Parts of that town are not so pretty close up. It's only when you get above it that you can see the potential and even see how it fits with the rest of the town."

"Look at you being all philosophical," I said.

"It's true, isn't it? Sometimes it's all about how you look at something. Like Zeb. He sees you wanting to fly as a threat for some reason."

"But if he could see it how I see it. If he could understand why I love it so much, maybe he'd see he didn't need to be jealous or worried."

Cliff and I flew until he told me to take Matilda back. "You better bring her back around and head for home. It'll be dark soon."

I brought her in for a landing with only a slight skip and jump and then stopped with her nose pointing out over Hector's Hill.

"Good job," Cliff said. "Now about that test."

I looked at him and smiled. "Schedule it."

After securing Matilda, Cliff and I walked back to my truck.

"Can I give you a lift?" I asked.

"Sure. Back to the Kincaids. I promised Nate I'd help him with that tractor again."

"I don't know why he just doesn't buy a new one."

Cliff climbed into the cab and closed the door. "Oh, I suspect a man's tractor is a little like a man's airplane. He'll keep it going until she quits for the last time. It's comfortable. Got the seat just where he wants it."

I pulled up to the Kincaid's house. "Are you going to the Blessing of the Fountain?" I asked.

"The what?" Cliff said. "Blessing of the Fountain?"

"Yes, up at Paradise. Some guy named Leon Fontaine, he just moved into a trailer, rebuilt the fountain, and got it running again. They're having a blessing."

"Oh, boy, it sounds . . . boring."

"No, no. It'll be great. Bet there will be some great food and it could be kind of fun."

Cliff jumped out of the truck and closed the door. He leaned into the window. "Oh, I was meaning to ask you since you seem to know everything that goes on around here. Is there any truth to the latest rumor?"

"The one about Greenbrier?"

"Yeah, Stella said the talk is that the residents are getting drugged and acting weird. Nobody really knows what's going on."

"More likely somebody found the Fountain of Youth," I said. "But seriously, yeah, something is going up there. It's weird, Cliff. They do seem to have been bitten by a bug of some sort."

Cliff waved. "Now I've heard everything. The Fountain of Youth in Bright's Pond. Ponce de León is rolling over in his grave."

That was when I saw Stella on the porch. She wore a pair of blue sweat pants and a floppy flannel shirt. She waved. "Stay for supper."

"I can't," I called. "I need to get over to see Agnes."

"OK, maybe another night."

"Count on it," I said.

I found Agnes smack-dab in the middle of another altercation of sorts. It seems this time Clive Dickens and Faith Graves have decided to tie the knot but their family members are making a stink. Over money. It's always over money. Who cares if these two young, I mean old, people are in love?

Agnes, still the go-to person for anyone's troubles, was in between Clive Dickens and his son, Wilfred. It looked a little strange to see the two of them on either side of Agnes's chair. But I figured it was the chair that was keeping them from each other's throats the way they were squabbling and pointing fingers at each other.

"Now, Wilfred," Agnes said. "Don't you want your daddy happy?"

"Happy shmappy," the tall, gangly—and I must say, ugly—man said. His face was so chiseled and pockmarked from acne scars it looked as though he was wearing a plastic mask. He wore Levi's jeans and a striped button-down shirt. Pink and green stripes—thin as thread.

"I can't let you marry that woman, Daddy," Wilfred said. "We'll lose our inheritance to her and her family."

Money, I thought. Why is it always about money?

"But you don't understand," Clive said. "If you'd only listen and care more about us than yourself you'd know, she's got no family left, Willy. She outlived all five of her children. You'd be her kin."

Wilfred backed away and looked out the window.

"Imagine that," Agnes said. "She outlived all her children. Five. I can't even begin to know that pain. And now all she wants to do is get married and maybe have a family again, even for a little while."

"Ah, Daddy, I'm sorry."

"You should be, you dumb-dumb. And I'll have you know that woman, your future mother, is worth more money than three of me."

Wilfred turned around just as his wife sauntered into the room.

"What's going on?" she asked.

"Your husband is being very selfish," Agnes said.

"Wilfred Dickens," the woman said. "What did you do now? If you did anything to lose our mon—" She stopped talking.

"That does it," Clive said. "I have decided to bequeath all our money, mine and Faith's, to Greenbrier and the poor folk in the backwoods."

"But, Daddy. You can't do that," Wilfred said.

His wife grabbed his ear. "Course he can. Why you go shootin' off your mouth? I told you to keep that yap of your's shut. Now we lost everything."

"Well, you didn't exactly help the situation, Irene, now did you?" Clive said. "After the way you been acting. I'm happy the money is going to where it can be best used."

"Sounds like a good idea," Agnes said. "Lord knows the backwoods families can use the aid."

Irene, who never let go of Wilfred's ear, dragged him out of the room. "Wilfred P. Dickens if you ain't the sorriest excuse for a husband."

Agnes slapped her knee. "He's a pip."

"Sure is," Clive said. "I can't figure how that boy got that way. I guess I just made his life too easy for him. Well now, he'll have to learn to stand on his own two feet and work."

"Good for you," I said. "He'll be OK. I have a feeling Irene will see to that."

Clive fell quiet a moment and then said, "Now, Agnes, who do you suppose we could get to perform the ceremony?"

"Boris Lender can do it," I said. "He hasn't performed a wedding in Bright's Pond in quite some time—leastways that I know, but I'm sure he'd be happy to tie the knot for you."

"Whee doggies," Clive said.

Wilfred and Irene came back into the room with their heads hung low.

"Daddy," Wilfred said. "Irene and me been talking. We are terrible sorry for saying what we said. And we understand if you want to give all the money to . . ." He gulped. "Charity. But . . . well—"

"What he's trying not to say," said Irene, "is we would still like to come to yer weddin' and it would be an honor to accept Faith into the fold."

"That's better," Clive said. "Shoulda said that before. But you still ain't getting any money."

I tried not to laugh, but Agnes and I couldn't help ourselves.

Faith shuffled into the room. She stood, all smiles. "Clive, you old dickens."

Everyone laughed at her play on words, which I imagined she used more times than Clive wanted.

"Faith," Clive said. "I want you to meet my son Willy and his wife, Irene. They come for the wedding."

Wilfred glared at Clive and then at Irene.

"Go on now, son," Clive said. "Help your new mama to a chair."

I pushed the visitor chair toward Faith.

Wilfred took Faith by the arm and helped her into the vinyl seat. She was such a sprite of a little thing with translucent skin and gobs of long white hair—not gray, snow white—that cascaded over her shoulders like a twenty-year-old. She wore a robin's-egg-blue housecoat and yellow slippers.

"So," I said, "is everyone OK here?"

Faith grasped Wilfred's hand and then reached for Clive's hand, which she pulled toward her chest. "I'm just fine. Just fine. I got me a family."

That was when Irene burst into several verses of "Oh, Promise Me," and I will admit I needed to hold back from slugging the woman. I knew it was nothing more than a ploy to get her mitts on Faith's money.

I looked at Clive and Faith, and their love for each other was palpable. It seemed some people found love so easily and had no question they had found the right person. But me, I was still floundering around with my feelings like a fish on dry ground, no matter what I told Zeb. The truth was I still wasn't sure I even wanted to marry him—now or ever.

Once Irene finished singing, the Dickens family left. "Thank you, Agnes," Clive said.

Agnes nodded. "I didn't do anything. But I'm glad you found peace."

"So when's the big day?" I asked once they were all safely making their way down the hall.

"I think Saturday. As long as Boris is free, and I can't imagine that man ever missing an opportunity to be in the spotlight."

Agnes pushed herself toward her tray table and poured her own glass of water. I sighed. It was the first time in a long time that she didn't ask me to do it for her.

"You know," she said. "This is quite an occasion here at Greenbrier. I bet that Dabs Lemon would love to do a human interest piece on this."

"Dabs? Really? I suppose. But do you really think he should be coming here with . . . with all the other stuff going on?"

Agnes smiled. That was indeed her plan.

"Sure," she said. "Maybe he can learn a few things about the others. The situation is getting worse. Just this morning Nurse Sally told me she found—"

The sound of a bike bell interrupted her.

"There goes Haddie," I said. "I see she's back to her rounds."

"Yep. I hope Doc Silver gets to the bottom of it, but like I was beginning to say, this morning Nurse Sally found two more residents chasing each other down the hall and three others in the break room listening to that music the kids listen to. She said they were dancing the hootchy-kootchy or something she called disco. Matter of fact, one them requested Greenbrier install something called a disco ball."

I laughed. "No kidding. That's pretty funny, Agnes. This whole place is going crazy."

"But what's the cause?" Agnes said.

I glanced out the window at the gorgeous fall colors. Faith and Clive were in the gazebo smooching. "Look at those two. I think what they have is the real thing and not some drug-induced or hypnotic state. They love each other."

"Maybe Clive and Faith are not related to what else is going on around here."

"Agnes, can I tell you something?" I was going to tell her about Charlotte researching the Fountain of Youth and all but it could wait, especially just after the previous episode of the Greenbrier Soap Opera.

"Sure, you know you can."

"It's about Cliff Cardwell."

Agnes slapped her knee. "I was wondering when you were gonna get around to this. It's about time you faced the truth."

"He makes my stomach wobble whenever I see him. I think about him almost constantly—well, him and Matilda and—"

"Oh, Griselda, my dear sister. I think you have fallen in love with Cliff Cardwell and you don't even know it."

7

For the third time that week my knees turned to mush. Me? In love with Cliff Cardwell?

"No, I don't think so. How can I be? I love Zeb."

"Uh-huh," Agnes straightened her heavy knee, and I heard a loud pop.

"What was that?"

"Oh, it's been doing that sometimes. Doc says it's nothing to worry about. My bones are creaky, that's all."

"Maybe I should take you for a walk around the nursing home. I can push a little while."

"Oh, no, you don't. You can't weasel out of this conversation. I want to hear more about you and Cliff."

I sat on Agnes's bed. "There's nothing to tell, really, except, oh, Agnes we went flying again and this time I flew over the mountain. The same mountain I've been looking at from our kitchen window all these years. It was spectacular. I've never seen anything like it. God's gorgeous creation from on high. It's . . . it's different and wonderful and . . . better. The world is better from way up there."

"Is it creation or Cliff?" Agnes said. "You sure Cliff isn't making you feel so wonderful?"

I couldn't answer her, not then, not directly. "And I told him to schedule my pilot's license test. That's all. That's all that happened."

"You're avoiding my question. Then how come you feel the way you do?"

I shook my head. "I'm not sure. I mean that. I'm really confused."

A nurse carried Agnes's supper tray into the room. "One of these days, Agnes," she said, "you're gonna need to start going down to the day room with everyone else. Can't be eatin' every single meal alone."

"I'm not alone," Agnes said. "My sister's here."

"But not for every meal."

The nurse set her food out and opened some containers.

"Go on, eat," I said. "I think I might be getting back to town."

"Not so fast. Tell me more."

"There is no more. I just wish sometimes that Cliff never landed in Bright's Pond. Maybe all this would be easier."

Agnes cut into her hamburger patty. "Maybe you need to go out with him once or twice. You know. Just to see. Otherwise you might spend the rest of your life wondering."

"That would be awful. But what about Zeb?"

"You're broken up again, right?"

"No. He kissed me again and well, the same thing. I get all nervous inside and I think I love him."

Agnes shook her head and clicked her tongue. "Sister, you need help. You got to decide if you want Cliff or Zeb or neither one."

"I know. I know. I will. I'll figure this out."

"Speaking of figuring things out. Has Mildred gotten anywhere with her investigation into the strange things around here? Honest to goodness, Griselda. This place is going loony.

81

I saw Jasper York riding a broom down the hall like it was stick horse. And if that weren't enough, one of the other men, I don't know his name, had to be pulled out of the creek behind building four. He nearly drowned."

"I don't think she's learned anything new. But did you hear about the fountain up at Paradise?"

Agnes swallowed a bite of her burger. "Paradise? Nope."

"That fella, Leon Fontaine, who built the gazebo, refurbished the fountain, and they're having a Blessing of the Fountain Day—Sunday. I hear Pastor Speedwell is trekking out there and all to pray a prayer and give some kind of sermon about living water and such. The Dixieland Band is going to be there. They're making it a big deal."

"No kidding. Are you going?"

"Sure. I told that Charlotte Figg I would go. She's real nice, Agnes. She came by the library to do some research on the Fountain of Youth."

"The Fountain of Youth." Agnes dropped her fork in her creamed corn. "Why in tarnation would anyone need to do research on that? Unless it was a schoolkid."

"She wouldn't say exactly but I wonder if she's thinking the Fountain of Youth, the new Paradise Fountain, and Leon Fontaine might have something in common."

Agnes slapped her knee. She retrieved her fork and stirred around in her corn before taking a mouthful. "That's just strange, and it can't be true. There's no such thing."

"I know, but sometimes when you have a hunch, you go with it."

"I suppose, but this is laughable."

"It is," I said. "I'm sorry you can't be at the Blessing though. It should be a blast."

"Well, you have fun and maybe you can sneak me a treat. I can't imagine an affair like that taking place without food—and plenty of it."

"I bet Charlotte will have pies. Oh, I told her to take a look at that empty store in town. Maybe she'll open a pie shop."

"Now that's a good idea. But won't Zeb mind?"

"Ah, I'm tired of everything revolving around Zeb Sewickey. He'll still sell enough Full Moon Pie."

Agnes pushed her peas around on her plate. "They never cook them enough. I hate hard peas."

I looked at the clock. It was nearly six. "I should be going."

"OK, Griselda. But think about what I said. Talk to Cliff; figure this out."

The ride home felt lonely even with a billion stars in the sky for company. I rolled the window down and let the cool air filter into the cab. I would never stop loving the mountains or the stars. Yet, I wanted to see more of the world. As I followed the stars home I thought what it would be like to fly up there, at night, with the stars. How close would I come to reaching out and feeling their heat? I knew it was impossible, yet I wanted to know how close I could come to reaching eternity.

I parked Old Bessie in front of the funeral home. I sat for a minute and then took a deep breath, my hands still gripping the wheel. I closed my eyes and imagined I was in the plane, soaring high about Bright's Pond, heading over the mountains. It was a feeling that was all my own—a feeling even Agnes could not imagine. For the first time in my life I had something grand, something that took my breath away.

I climbed out of the cab and started for the house.

"Nice night," I heard from the porch. I recognized Cliff's voice.

"It is." I walked up the porch steps and stopped until Cliff came out of the shadows.

"I was waiting for you. I . . . I needed to see you."

"Is this about the license?" I fiddled with the door key.

"No, no. It's about . . . about—ah, heck, Griselda."

The next thing I knew Cliff had me around the waist. He pulled me near and kissed me long and deep and my knees buckled and my heart pounded. I pushed him away.

"Cliff. What are you doing?"

"Don't you feel it too, Griselda? There's something between us." He took a step back into the shadows. "More than flying lessons. More than friendship."

"You're wrong," I said. "I . . . I love Zeb and—"

"Do you really?"

I took a breath and stepped near the door. Cliff took the key from my hand and held it in his fist. "I have to know if I have a chance."

My heart still pounded. My palms grew sweaty. "Cliff, I . . . I don't know. I can't answer this now. I'm confused. I don't know for sure. I've been with Zeb since high school."

"And where has it gotten you? You haven't married him. That must mean something."

I shook my head. "I don't know what to say. Let me go."

He grasped my upper arm and turned me toward him. "OK. But you can't tell me that when you looked into all those stars tonight that you didn't wonder what it would be like to fly among them."

"You're . . . wrong. I never gave them a thought."

He relaxed his hand. "OK. But, please. I need to know. I love you, Griselda."

Cliff slid the key into the lock and turned it. He pushed the door open, removed the key, and handed it to me. "It's up to you."

I locked the door behind me and waited a few minutes. Then I pushed the curtain aside to see if he was still there. He wasn't. I had never felt anything like this before. Zeb was comfortable. Cliff was something altogether different. Adventure. Stars.

Arthur meowed and looked at me like I had just robbed a bank. I picked him up and rubbed his soft fur against my cheek. "You don't know how lucky you are to be a cat. It's . . . uncomplicated."

The next morning took forever to arrive. I was actually thankful when Ruth Knickerbocker telephoned at 6:00 a.m.

"Griselda, I just don't know if I have everything right. Can you come over here and see my decorations. I keep thinking I'm missing something. But I can't figure out what."

"Don't worry. It's only Saturday. You have until Thursday."

"Oh, it will come faster than you know. Can you come over and go over everything with me?"

"Right now?"

"Unless you got something better to do. But I don't think you have. Now please. Can you? I got coffee."

"OK, OK. Give me a minute to get dressed and I'll be there."

It only took a few minutes to pull on jeans and sneakers and a sweatshirt. I dumped half a can of wet cat food—Seafood Banquet—into Arthur's bowl and left.

"It is so cold," I said when Ruth opened the door. I had chosen to walk the few blocks. My truck would never have warmed up in that short of a distance so it didn't make much difference.

"Come on in and have some coffee. I got a Danish ring also if you want some of that."

"Thanks. Coffee first."

I walked into Ruth's dining room and saw the mess. Bags and bags of luau decorations, grass skirts hanging over the chairs, pineapple flowerpots, fake flower leis piled like colorful snakes on the sideboard. I saw tiki torches and tribal masks. Ruth had managed to assemble every Hawaiian item she could find in the tri-state area—I was certain of it.

"You got enough stuff here to open a store," I said.

"Now why would I want to do that?" Ruth handed me a cup of coffee. She always used cups with saucers and as I stood there, I couldn't figure out what to do with the saucer. Every square inch of the dining room table was taken up by something for the Great American Hawaiian Thanksgiving Day Celebration.

I pulled out a chair and sat. "What's the problem? It looks like you have everything. Except the turkey, of course, and we're getting that Tuesday."

Ruth snapped her fingers. "The turkey. I almost forgot. You won't let me forget, now will you?"

"Nope."

"Let's see," Ruth said. She started opening bags and looking inside. "I got after-dinner mints in here, you know those Andes mints everyone likes, and look—" she pulled out little tiny paper umbrellas. "I thought it would be fun to stick one of these in everyone's drinks. I'm making Hawaiian Punch—not that stuff that comes in the can, you know from the commercial? How would you like a nice Hawaiian punch? And then the guy punches someone."

"I know, slow down. How much coffee have you had?"

"Two—pots."

"Oh, Ruth you know you can't take caffeine. Not like a human anyway. It makes you crazy like you are right now. Promise me no more coffee, especially Thursday."

She ignored me and grabbed another bag. "I found this darling turkey platter." She showed me a platter shaped like a large Tom Turkey. "I thought I'd arrange a lei or two around the plate and set the turkey down on a bed of green grass—fake of course. What do you think?"

"Sure, Ruth. That will be fun."

And so it went for the better part of an hour. Ruth opened every shopping bag and showed me all the items she got for the holiday. I could appreciate her nervousness and I didn't want to make her feel bad so I complimented each item even though deep inside I worried that something was going to go terribly wrong with this Thanksgiving.

"The decorations are special," I said. "But make sure you have everything you need for the dinner—the actual meal—and let me know. We'll get it Tuesday when I drive you into Shoops for the turkey—you did order it?"

"Of course. I did a lot of shopping by bus and the driver kept looking at me like I was a nut job when a bag broke and all those leis dumped out on the bus floor and then the Tiki torches got caught on the stop buzzer wire and it rang for like three minutes and then I accidentally knocked off some woman's wig with the turkey platter on account of it being so big."

I laughed. "You're not a nut job. Just a little enthusiastic and the woman with the wig is probably better off."

"Well, it's the first time I've entertained for Thanksgiving. I want it to be perfect."

"It will be," I said. "Are you coming to the Blessing of the Fountain tomorrow? I think it will be good for you to get away from all this."

"Is that tomorrow, already?"

"Yes, tomorrow is Sunday. It will be fun. Good for you to get away from the Thanksgiving festivities." I repeated it in case she didn't hear me.

"I guess, Griselda. What time is the Blessing?"

"After church. We'll just drive on up right after the service. I think the actual blessing is scheduled for one."

"Speedwell doing the blessing?"

"Uh-huh. In a way it's kind of nice that they got that old fountain flowing again."

"I guess. But why does a trailer park need a fountain?"

"Why does a turkey need a lei?"

Ruth smiled. "Thanks for coming over."

"Now look, tomorrow is your day off. Tuesday we get the turkey. I'll come over Wednesday and help you get everything under control and even help you cook and stuff Thursday."

"Thank you, Griselda. Thank you so much."

I hugged my friend and held her an extra second. Her heart beat like the Dixieland Band. I had never seen her so nervous over something that should be so simple. It was just dinner.

After I left Ruth it occurred to me that Ruth's anxiety was actually a blessing. I had not thought about Cliff or Zeb the whole time I was with her. It wasn't until I passed the town hall that I realized I was standing at a crossroads. One way leads to the café, the other toward the Kincaid farm and Cliff. At that moment, I didn't want to see either one of them. But when Studebaker happened by all in a tizzy, the decision was made for me.

"Griselda," he called. "I was just up at your place. We have to have an emergency Yuletide Committee meeting."

"What's going on?"

"It's about the parade. The marching band from Roosevelt High can't come and neither can the Shoops Moose Lodge, and they come every year. We have a huge hole to fill or Santa will arrive too soon and—"

"Slow down, did you find everyone else?"

"Just have to get Ruth. I was on my way to her place."

"You know what? Let's leave Ruth out this time. She's got her plate pretty full right now."

"Whatever you say."

"It was one thing to be short one marching band but to have the Shoops Moose Lodge not show up—that was different." Every year the Moose, which was an organization dedicated to helping children with disabilities, collecting old eyeglasses and books, presented Boris Lender with a check that went a long way to keeping the parade afloat and buying new books for the library.

As usual for Saturday, the café was crowded. Folks were waiting outside for booths. But Studebaker made it sound like it was a matter of national security that the Yuletide Committee got a table. This did not make a couple of truckers very happy and I thought the situation might come to blows before Boris arrived with the key to the town hall. I was extremely gratified. I would not have to see Zeb unless he moseyed over to the meeting, which was doubtful on a busy Saturday morning.

It didn't take long for the entire committee, minus Ruth, to assemble. Even Nate Kincaid, who wasn't known for attending every meeting, made an appearance. We sat at a long rectangular table with so many dings and dents and scuffmarks it was hard to imagine what it once looked like. But that was OK. I liked all the wear and tear on it. I wondered for a second, as I waited for Boris to bring the meeting to order, how many decisions were made around that hunk of wood.

"OK, OK," Boris said. "Let's get started. Now what seems to be the trouble?"

Dot Handy had her trusty legal pad out and pencil poised to start taking minutes.

"The Shoops Moose Lodge has pulled out of the parade," Studebaker said.

Gasps filtered around the table.

A quizzical look fell over Boris's face. "Did they give a reason? Did they make a formal petition to be released from their contract? They can't just do this. There's legalities involved in this."

"It's just a Christmas parade," I said. "How serious can it be?"

Studebaker pulled a piece of paper from his jacket pocket. "It says here that the Shoops Moose—or is the Mooses, Moos-i—will not participate because," he took a breath "because of the nefarious doings at the Greenbrier Nursing Home, and since Greenbrier is technically within the town limits of Bright's Pond they cannot associate with us until the matter is cleared up. It's a matter of morality, and they will not have their good name besmirched."

"Besmirched?" I said. "Who's besmirching their name?"

"Matter?" Boris said. "What's the 'matter' they're talking about? Somebody better clue me in on this. Here I am the First Selectman and I don't have a single clue about what in jumpin' blue heck is happening."

Mildred Blessing stood. "I can tell you, Boris. And it's not very pretty but for right now anyway it looks like . . . drug activity, or so it seems."

I thought Boris Lender was going to have a stroke right on the spot. His eyes bugged out like two Ping-Pong balls. He swallowed so hard he could have swallowed his teeth. "Drugs? In Bright's Pond? That's not possible."

"Can someone please tell me what is happening?" Studebaker said. "Where is this drug activity supposedly taking place? At the high school?"

I put my hand up in hopes to quiet the table down. "Not at the high school," I said. "At Greenbrier Nursing Home."

It took a minute or two after that but they simmered down and I explained everything I knew.

"And so you see," I said, "with the residents acting so strange, it's no wonder some people think there is something going on. If you all could have seen Haddie Grace and even Jasper York, you'd think they were children again."

Dot Handy was busily taking everything down while she made noises and clicked her tongue in both derision and surprise.

Boris banged his gavel on the table. "This is just the most ridiculous thing I have ever heard. Why would the residents take drugs and where would they get them?"

"That's the issue," Mildred said just taking her seat. "Sorry I'm late I was up at Paradise."

"Paradise?" I said. "Did you speak with that Leon Fontaine?"

Mildred nodded. Boris slumped back in his chair. Studebaker put his head in his hands, and I watched Dot draw a picture of a cube.

"Paradise?" Boris said. "What in jumpin' blue heck does the trailer park got to do with Greenbrier and who is Leon Fontaine?" He looked at Dot. "Make a note, Dot, that from now on I am to be made privy, part and parcel, to everything that is going on in this town. I will not be brought in on the tail end anymore."

Dot busily scribed on her legal pad.

"Leon Fontaine. Isn't he the fella that rebuilt the fountains and the gazebo?" Stu asked.

"I remember him now," Boris said. "I wrote out construction permits for him. Didn't think nothing of it at the time. He had all his licenses and everything in order."

"That's right," Mildred said. "Did a beautiful job too. The gazebo is a might crooked but it's still very nice."

"So you think he's giving the Greenbrier residents drugs?" Studebaker said.

"I never said that," I said.

"No, no. Doesn't seem like it." Mildred pulled out her trusty black notebook and flipped through the pages. "I can't find anything to hold him on, nothing suspicious. Course I haven't talked to him yet. Can't seem to get a hold of him. He's slipperier than an eel. Every time I get to where he's supposed to be someone tells me he just that minute left."

"Well, did you run a background check on him?" Boris asked.

"Clean as the day is long," Mildred said. "Not even a speeding ticket on account of there's no record of him ever having a driver's license, leastways not in Pennsylvania. It takes a little time to hear from the federal agencies. They got other problems to tend to. Our little town don't matter much, but I got to say, Fontaine made me feel kind of odd. Like he was hiding something."

Boris nodded along with everyone else. If there was one thing for certain about Mildred Blessing, she had good instincts.

"I guess you better keep your ears and eyes open, Mildred," Boris said.

"Oh, I plan to," Mildred said, "and I'm asking all of you to do the same. Something is afoot up at the nursing home."

"We must get to the bottom of it," Boris said. "We can't afford to upset the Shoops Moose—Moosesses."

The group grew quiet for a minute until the door swung open. It was Ruth Knickerbocker. She stood in the doorway and cried. She was dripping from head to foot with what smelled and looked like cranberries.

"Ruth," I said. "What happened?"

"Oh, Griselda, I was practicing one of my recipes for Thanksgiving dinner: cranberry guava passion fruit kiwi sauce. I had it all in the blender and then—" she made a noise like an explosion, "cranberries, guava, passion fruit, kiwi— everywhere. The lid popped off for some reason and . . . and my kitchen is a mess." She sobbed harder.

"Come on," I said. "Let's get you home and cleaned up and see what we can do."

I looked at the Yuletide Committee sitting there with their mouths open and eyes wide. Ruth did look a sight. Her hair was dripping with goo. It ran down her face and off the tip of her nose. She had managed to clean two small circles on her glasses so she could see.

"I will say this," I said. "It smells really, really good."

Ruth attempted a chuckle. "Thank you. But that's hardly the point. I didn't come for you to have a taste test. And I promise you, I cut back on my coffee intake just like you said."

I directed my attention to the committee. "You all figure this out. I mean we can't make the Moose Lodge march in the parade but maybe if we solve the mystery soon, they'll reconsider."

"I agree," Boris said with a tap of his gavel. "Make this your number one priority, Chief Blessing."

"Yes, sir," she said. "I think I'll head back to the nursing home and do some more snooping, ask a few questions, keep my eye out."

Studebaker stood. "Hold on a second. I know everyone is concerned about Greenbrier but we have a Christmas Fest to plan. It's less than a month away and this year's Santa Claus has not been decided, the parade route I would assume will be the same as always. Nate is taking care of the floats, and we need to purchase the candy canes and—"

"You do it," Dot Handy said.

"Me?" Stu said. "Do what? Buy the candy canes?"

"No, play Santa. It's your turn."

"Dot's right," Boris said. "I'd do it but I have to ride with the grand marshal."

"And that's another thing," Stu said. "Who is this year's grand marshal?"

"I thought somebody asked Cliff Cardwell," Nate said. "He seems to think he's grand marshal."

"Good choice," Boris said. "He's as close to an actual hero as we got."

"I am not big enough to play Santa," Stu said. "It should be Frank Sturgis—especially this year. Have you all seen the belly he has now? He's just gone to pieces."

"Then you ask him," I said. "I got to go with Ruth."

"Fine," Studebaker said. "But we really need to have another meeting, and soon."

Studebaker loved the Christmas Fest more than anything in Bright's Pond. The man loved Christmas and would do pretty much anything to make the annual parade and pageant a success.

"Let's meet Monday," Boris said.

Ruth started to cry. "Please, Griselda, I got to get home. It's such—" she sucked back a sob, "a mess."

"Let's plan on Monday for a lunch meeting at the Full Moon," I said. And with that everyone got up. I was, of course, first out the door followed quickly by Mildred, who practically jumped into her squad car and took off for Greenbrier with a fresh priority assignment.

"Where's she going?" Ruth asked.

"Oh, Ruth, you won't believe it when I tell you."

I wiped red sauce from her cheek. "But let's get this mess fixed first."

It didn't take as long as I thought it would to wipe down the counters and mop the floor. Ruth scrubbed the stove and took a quick shower.

"You shoulda seen it," she said.

"Seen what?" I asked.

"The tub, it ran red with all the sauce coming out of my hair and off my body. I scared myself a little. It made me think of that movie *Psycho*."

I shuttered. "Oh, Ruth, don't even kid. That was the scariest movie I ever saw."

"I'm sorry, but it's true. You shoulda seen my tub."

I moved toward the door. "Tomorrow should be a good day. You are still going to the Blessing of the Fountain, aren't you?"

"It's right after church, isn't it?" she said.

"Yep. Just like I told you. And I hear they're having food and everything up there."

"Sounds good. I just hope some of this red is gone by tomorrow."

"Me too, Ruth. But even if it isn't, so what?"

Ruth looked at me with that squirrely look she could get from time to time. "I'll never try that again. Do you think folks would mind if I just opened cans of cranberry sauce?"

"Not at all."

I looked around the kitchen and dining room. It still looked like a hurricane had blown through, especially the way the plastic palm trees lay on their sides.

"We'll get this under control in plenty of time. Now why don't you just take it easy. Make the things you know how to make and don't worry about getting too fancy."

"Maybe," Ruth said. "But I'm still planning on making my special dessert. It's going to be spectacular. Something that will just about knock the socks off of everyone."

"Oh, Ruth, don't get too ambitious."

"I need to do something extra special. Something no one will expect. Something that will set this Thanksgiving apart from all the rest—not that Thanksgiving at your house wasn't always good. It was. The best but—"

"I can't wait," I said. "Now I need to be going."

"Where you off to? Maybe see Cliff?"

"Ruth, you know better than that. No. I actually was thinking it's a nice day for a walk in the woods with Zeb."

8

I passed Ivy's house on my way to the Full Moon. She was on the porch with Mickey Mantle.

"How's it going?" she called. "I saw Ruth running past here a while ago. I thought she'd been shot."

"Cranberry sauce," I said.

Ivy laughed. "That woman is a pip. Where you headed?"

I looked into the clear blue sky. "Oh, it's such a nice day, I might see if I can talk Zeb into taking a walk in the woods."

"Ohhh, sounds romantic."

"Maybe. That's up to Zeb."

Ivy stood up. "What's wrong, Griselda? Zeb giving you a hard time again?"

"Not really. Well, no more than usual. It's me this time. Have you ever been in love Ivy?"

Ivy looked at me for a long minute. "Me? Well, I never told no one, but yeah, I was in love, long time ago."

"How do you know?"

Ivy let air escape her nose. Mickey Mantle sidled up next to her. "As much as I hate saying this, the answer is . . . you just do. It's a feeling, but it's more than a feeling. It's like an allergic reaction."

"Do you lose your appetite and feel all scatterbrained?"

"Yep. Is that what Zeb does for you?"

"Used to. Not so much anymore. Zeb and I have been going together for so long the feelings are more like the feeling of slipping on a pair of old, comfy sneakers. You know how they fit you just right."

"That's love," Ivy said.

"But am I IN LOVE?"

"Then who is making you feel all squishy and lose your appetite?"

I didn't say anything. I just looked into her eyes until she saw the truth.

"Cliff Cardwell. Why Griselda Sparrow, you have fallen head over heels in love with that aviator fella."

"I'm not so sure." I patted Mickey Mantle's head.

"Sounds like he got your engines started."

"That's just it. Maybe I'm love with the aviator, the flying, not the person."

"You better figure this one out. And with Christmas coming? Whee doggies, Griselda, Christmas is way too romantic and wonderful to spend it with the wrong fella."

"I know."

I gave Mickey Mantle one final pat. "I'll see you later."

The air felt crisp and turned steadily chillier the closer I got to the Full Moon. It was after the lunch rush, so Zeb should have a little time. I had no clue what I was going to say to him. I just wanted to see him and hoped with all my heart that nothing would interrupt us this time.

I was right; Zeb was sitting at a booth eating a sandwich. It wasn't too often I saw Zeb eating any of his food.

"Hey, Zeb," I said.

"Grizzy, join me. Hungry?"

"No, not really. I just wanted to stop by and say hi. I just came from Ruth's. She had exploding cranberry sauce."

Zeb laughed. "Exploding cranberry sauce. I'm not even going to ask."

"Ah, she's just so excited about Thanksgiving. She's trying all these crazy recipes."

"Oh, boy. It should be interesting."

"You're coming, right?"

Zeb took a bite of his sandwich. Swallowed and looked me square in the eyes. "That depends. Is Cliff coming?"

"I don't know. And . . . and why should it matter?"

"It just does."

Dot passed by. "Coffee, Griselda?"

"Maybe just water."

"Suit yourself."

"Zeb," I said. "I want to be honest with you. I think I'm feeling confused or something. I like Cliff, I'm not going to lie about that, but not in the way you think, at least I don't think so. He just makes me feel different."

"Different?"

"It might just be the flying. I really love to fly that airplane."

Zeb finished chewing his sandwich and then gulped down a glass of milk. "Are you in love with him. Just tell me. I can't stand being on the outs like this."

My eyes closed for a breath. Then I looked at him and then I looked away. Dot placed my water in front of me.

"I'm not sure," I said. "Maybe. Maybe not."

Zeb tossed his napkin into his plate and stood. "Then I guess I won't be coming to Thanksgiving."

My heart started to race. "I'm sorry, Zeb. I just want to be sure."

"I doubt you'll be sure by Thursday."

I went to church that Sunday but my heart wasn't in it. Pastor Speedwell was talking forgiveness in such a way that I think he made everyone in the room feel guilty. Even me. Mostly I felt guilty about Zeb and Cliff. I sat in the pew and prayed through pretty much the entire service. I asked the Good Lord to help me figure out my feelings. I prayed that God would make my choice so clear that I couldn't possibly be wrong.

Ruth, who was sitting next to me, grabbed onto my hand. Sometimes I think the woman had a sixth sense. She held on tight and whispered in my ear. "You'll get it figured out." We held hands for almost five minutes, and I appreciated the comfort it brought.

After the service, Ruth and I headed up to the Paradise Trailer Park for the Blessing of the Fountain. I had not been in Paradise since Ruth and I went up there to watch one of the Angels softball games. Charlotte Figg was not only a tremendous pie baker, but she was also the Angels coach and nearly coached the team to a championship. From what I understood, she had moved to Paradise after her husband died. She started the team because she didn't think there was enough community spirit in the trailer park. Apparently it worked because ever since then everything I hear about Paradise is positive and sweet.

I couldn't help smiling when I drove under the Paradise Trailer Park sign. There was something totally endearing about the place. I enjoyed seeing all the colors of the trailers—everything from bland gray to turquoise. Now I don't mean no disrespect but trailer parks do seem to attract a different kind of people. They are their own culture. And Paradise was, of course, no different. But I suppose the strangest thing in the park was the giant concrete hand that Rose Tattoo had in her front yard. It was there that she and some of the other residents went to pray—safe in God's hand.

Studebaker told me that he and his cousin Asa rescued it from a defunct amusement park. They hauled it back to Paradise, and Rose immediately set it up in her front yard. Then, Stu says, she proceeded to paint the names of every individual in the park on the hand. Stu said it was a physical manifestation of the Scripture that tells us we are all safe in God's hand and that our names are written on his palm and nothing and no one can pluck us from it.

I've seen the hand only the one time, but I will admit that that day I wondered if maybe some time in God's giant palm might help me think through my quandary.

"Maybe I'll do it," I said.

"Do what?" asked Ruth.

"Oh, I'm sorry. I'm thinking out loud. Maybe I'll sit in that giant hand they got here and pray about Cliff and Zeb."

"Couldn't hurt," Ruth said. "And while you're up there, Pray for my Thanksgiving."

We drove a little farther down the road. People were walking toward the center of the park carrying lawn chairs and blankets and covered dishes.

"Looks like they're gearing up for the festivities," I said.

I parked the truck against a curb between a black Oldsmobile and a yellow Duster. I haven't seen such a gathering since the night Studebaker unveiled the welcome sign to honor Agnes Sparrow and the supposed miracles she was performing. The sign was wrong in many ways from spelling to purpose and the festive feeling failed. Now that was the debacle to end all debacles and in my opinion was far greater than what was happening at Greenbrier. I caught a glimpse of Asa making his way to the front of the crowd.

Asa was himself quite a character. He was missing his right arm. The story goes that he blew it off playing with dynamite when he was teenager. I saw children carrying American flags. And every so often a firecracker would go off. Studebaker said Asa had gotten his hands—or I should say hand—on some real fireworks, and they were planning on setting them off after dark.

I sailed a silent prayer that when the fountain was revealed, nothing would go wrong.

The Paradise folk gathered in a small crowd near the fountain. From where Ruth and I were it was hard to get a good look unless we could stand on something. But I didn't see anything that would accommodate us.

"Come on," I said grabbing her hand. "Let's get closer."

I saw Rose Tattoo standing next to Ginger Rodgers, the little person who played shortstop on the Angels softball team. I never met her before, but I watched her play in a couple of games. She could run like greased lightning. Next to her was a tall woman, skinny as a rail with long hair tied in a ponytail that hung down her back and reached to her waist. I didn't recognize her. But next to her was Charlotte Figg holding what had to be a pie.

"Let's go stand with Charlotte and her friends."

"You think it's going to be all right?" Ruth asked. "I wouldn't want to intrude. It is their fountain."

"Oh, don't be silly, they won't mind. Come on."

"Hi, Griselda," Charlotte said. "I'm glad you could make it. Do you know my friends?"

"Of course she does," Ruth said. "I told her all about them. This here is Rose, the woman with all the tattoos."

I shook Rose's hand and noticed green, scraggly tattooed vines encircling her wrist and one finger. I tried not to pay it any attention. But she smiled into my eyes like she knew the best secret in town.

"Nice to meet you," she said. "We've heard a lot about the Sparrow sisters."

"And this is Ginger Rodgers. She's a Little Person. They don't like being called midgets."

"Nice to meet you too," I said to Ginger.

She shook my hand seemingly unaffected by Ruth's remark. I will admit it was a little like taking the hand of a child.

Ruth swallowed about a dozen times trying to get her bearings. A tattooed woman and a little person might have been a little much for her to introduce all at once. She became a bit rattled and starter to sputter her words. She was like an outboard motor having trouble getting started. Or she fibbed and has been sucking down coffee like wild again.

"This is my friend Ruth Knickerbocker," I said. "I don't believe you and Charlotte have met."

"Ruth," Rose said. "Are you Vera Krug's sister? The woman on the radio?"

"In-law. Sister-in-law."

"Oh, well, anyhoo, I saw her earlier. She's probably gonna report about the blessing on tomorrow's show."

"Dandy," Ruth said.

One of those silent, awkward pauses passed through our little group until Ruth blurted out, "I'm just so excited that you're all coming to Thanksgiving dinner."

"I was meaning to ask," Rose said. "Would it be all right if Asa came along? Otherwise he'd just be here by himself."

Ruth's table was going to need another leaf, or we were gonna have to rent out the town hall to get everyone accommodated.

"Absolutely. I just hope my turkey is big enough," she said looking at Ginger Rodgers. "But I don't suppose you eat much now—"

I elbowed her spleen.

"Don't let my size fool you," Ginger said. "I can eat like a lumberjack."

"How . . . delightful," Ruth said.

The crowd continued to grow and then all of a sudden music blared through the PA system. "The Stars and Stripes Forever." Some folks clapped but most grew quiet. I noticed a few men take off their hats, placing them over their hearts in a silent meditation.

The music faded off and so did the noise from the crowd. Asa stood on a homemade podium that seemed a skosh crooked to me. "Leon must have made it," I whispered to Ruth.

Asa spoke into a microphone and his voice was transmitted over the speaker system. I figured they could hear him clear to Scranton.

"Welcome," he said. "Welcome to the Blessing of the Paradise Fountain."

A cheer went up through the crowd.

"Some have said that the fountain would never flow again. But they were wrong."

Another cheer, but smaller and shorter.

"Thanks to our new friend, Leon Fontaine, the waters flow again." He indicated for Leon to join him on the podium. Leon had been sitting up front in one of the wooden folding chairs arranged for the VIPs. I saw Pastor Speedwell and Boris Lender also.

Leon, a little troll of a man with a long crooked nose, long curly hair, and a chin the size of a Granny Smith Apple, stood to a resounding round of applause and cheers. Then he sat back down.

"He must be shy," Ruth said.

"Leon didn't want to speak today," Asa said. "We are all so appreciative of his great effort and skill. Thank you, Leon Fontaine."

Leon stood and took a deep bow, swiping the ground with his hand.

Another cheer and then Boris Lender stood near the huge tarp that hid the fountain from view.

"It is with great honor and excitement that I now ask First Selectman Boris Lender to unveil our Paradise Fountain."

"Thank you," hollered Boris. And he gave a great yank on a cord and . . . nothing happened. He pulled a second time and still the tarp held fast.

"Oh, dear," Asa said. "Just a moment, folks."

Asa ducked behind the tarp and we heard some rustling and cursing until he popped back out. "Now, Mr. Lender, drop that tarp."

BAM! The tarp fell; the cheers rose to the heavens and then stopped as all eyes gazed upon the wonder that was the Paradise Fountain. A peach-colored brick wall, six courses high encircled the area. Inside that wall was another square red-brick enclosure with small gargoyles perched on each corner. The gargoyles looked handcarved from chunks of granite. They were skinny and weird with arched backs and wings. But not too unfriendly.

The actual fountain was inside the circle. I saw one large pipe and three smaller ones.

"Would you look at that," Ruth said. "What are those little creepy things on the corners? They look kind of like bats."

"Gargoyles," Ginger Rodgers said.

"Yes, they're actually traditional and were used as waterspouts on rooftops to drain away rainwater," I said.

"Um," Ruth said. "Librarians."

Asa moved to the podium again. "And now with no further ado, Leon Fontaine will turn the water on."

Leon moved to a small, crooked shed with a crooked cupola behind the fountain. He disappeared inside and then seconds later the water flowed in great gushes and spurts and seconds after that the water ran from the gargoyles' mouths into the square section of the fountain which began to fill and then recede.

"Well," Rose said. "I must admit that it is . . . spectacular. Almost makes my giant hand pale."

"Don't you ever talk like that," Ginger said. "It's no comparison. Not at all. What you got is the Hand of God."

Pastor Speedwell walked to the podium next. "I stand in awe and wonder today at this magnificent sight. A sight that will not only bring joy and beauty to Paradise but a sight that will remind us all of the Living Water available for each and every one of us to drink. Namely, Jesus Christ our Lord and Savior. Let us pray."

It took a second or two but Pastor was off into one of his Holy Ghost–raising prayers that made you afraid to open your eyes for fear you'd see the spirit of God moving through the crowd.

All at once, a woman I didn't recognize burst into an *a capella* rendition of "There Is a Fountain". "There is a fountain filled with blood," she sang, "drawn from Emmanuel's veins; and sinners plunged beneath that flood lose all their guilty stains."

She completed three of the four verses and then sat down with tears streaming from her red face. But then cheers and calls went out through the crowd as this tiny trailer park community united in a common theme of joy and identity made possible by a strange little man with a funny nose and a funny name that for right now, at least, was Bright's Pond's number-one suspect.

9

The next morning, Monday, I drove Old Bessie up to the top of Filbert Street near Hector's Hill and tuned in to radio station WQRT. Rassie Harper, the biggest jerk on planet Earth as far as I'm concerned, did the morning talk show. Ruth's sister-in-law Vera Krug had a small spot on the show called *Vera Krug's Good Neighbor News*. She mostly reported on what was happening in Shoops but often stuck her nose in the business of Bright's Pond.

I waited a few minutes listening to Rassie go on and on about political nonsense. He was still harping on about the war in Vietnam that nobody understood. Rassie hated Richard Nixon's guts and was thrilled as peaches and cream the day the president resigned.

"And now," Rassie said, "let's spend a few minutes with that friend to you and me, that lovely lady of the radio. Here she is, that winsome woman of the airwaves, Vera Krug here with your *Good Neighbor News*."

"Thank you, Rassie," Vera said. "Vera Krug here with your *Good Neighbor News*, for Monday, November 25, the Monday before Thanksgiving. I hope you all got your turkey ordered from Brisco's Butcher Shop, your shop for the tastiest, tenderest, meats in town. Mr. Brisco says there's still time to order your turkey, but do it today or you are out of luck."

That reminded me that I promised Ruth I would take her into Shoops the next morning to do just that—get the turkey. For once, I was grateful for Vera Krug.

"And speaking of Thanksgiving," Vera said. "The folks up at Bright's Pond were at it again. Well, the Paradise section of the town, you all know that funny little trailer park they got up there with all them pretty-colored trailers? Well, guess what? Now they got themselves a fountain. A real fountain that flows water and everything. I was up there yesterday—" she paused and coughed and it sounded like she took a sip of something—"yesterday for the Blessing of the Fountain. It was a nice time, except I got to tell you folks that the odd little man that built the fountain, a man they call Leon Fontaine, is one strange fella—looks a little like the gargoyles he carved for the fountain."

I laughed right out loud because she was right. Leon Fontaine did look a gargoyle.

"And not only that," Vera continued. "But am I the only one that smells a rat in Paradise? I mean it, really, Leon Fontaine. Isn't that just a little too convenient a name for a fountain builder? I looked it up. Fontaine is the French word for fountain and wasn't that explorer fella, who was looking for the Fountain of Youth named Leon? Leon Ponce a Tawney or something?"

"Ponce de León," Rassie broke in. "The explorer was Ponce de León."

I think my heart might have stopped beating for a second or two. I hadn't taken notice, but bless her soul, Vera was right. Mildred was right. The deck was quickly getting stacked against the man and the sooner Mildred or somebody figured it out the better.

I turned up the radio. "And that ain't all," Vera said. "I hear there are some strange doings up at the Greenbrier Nursing Home. I've had reports that some of our octogenarians have been acting quite a bit odd—riding tricycles and pitching woo like they was teenagers. Woo hoo, Bright's Pond is going nuts."

"What?" Rassie cut in. "When did all that start?"

"Don't know for certain but my sources tell me that ever since that Leon Fontaine, if that's his real name, and I'm betting it's not, came into town and started working up at Greenbrier the people have been acting weird, all young and all."

"And you think he found the Fountain of Youth?" Rassie said.

"Now I didn't say that, Rassie. I just said I see some coinky-dinks that are kind of hard to swallow."

"You keep your reporter's nose to the air," Rassie said. "We'd all like to know what's going on up there."

"I bet you would," I said to the radio. "You just love digging up dirt."

I turned off the radio and the windshield wipers. For some reason the station always came in better if I had the wipers going. I headed straight for the town hall. I needed to talk to Mildred Blessing about all of this. I hoped she had learned something more.

But before I could drop the gear shift into drive there was a tap on the window. It was Cliff Cardwell.

"Hey, Griselda, what are you doing up here. Looking for me?"

"N-N-No, Cliff. You startled me in fact."

"I'm sorry. It's hard to creep up on a person without scaring them."

"I came up here to listen to the morning show. Vera Krug's show."

"Oh, yeah, I heard about her. She's a pip from what I hear."

"Yeah, she is. But maybe smarter than we give her credit for."

"Um," Cliff looked into my eyes. "I still think you are the prettiest woman in Bright's Pond."

"Cliff, I told you. I'm not interested—"

He put his head through the window and kissed me.

"You were saying," he said.

I took a breath and swallowed. "I was saying that I need to be going. I got something to do and then I have to open the library and tomorrow is turkey day and then it's Thanksgiving and Ponce De Leon is in town and—"

"Slow down," Cliff said. "You're a little rattled."

"I'm sorry. But I really need to go."

"OK. I have to fly to Binghamton this morning and pick up a package for someone in Shoops. Want to come?"

"No, Cliff. I just told you I have things to do."

He tapped the door. "Right. Things." He stepped away from the truck as I pulled away. When I figured I was out of sight, I banged the steering wheel. "I am so mad. I hate the effect he has on me."

But I pushed that thought aside and made my way straight to the town hall. Mildred Blessing had a small office inside. I parked next to her cruiser and dashed up the steps and through the door.

"Mildred," I called even before I got to her door. I looked inside. She was sitting there looking through a stack of papers.

"Mildred."

She looked up. "Oh, Griselda, morning. Why do you look so flushed? Been seeing that sexy pilot fella again?"

I shook my head. "No, now listen." I sat in the leather chair. "Did you listen to Vera Krug's show this morning?"

"No," she said still looking through papers. "I was going to but I had to come here instead."

"She reported about the fountain blessing and—"

"So, what's that got to do with anything?"

"It might have everything to do with what is happening at Greenbrier. I just can't figure out how. The connection I mean."

Mildred's eyes brightened. "Ohhh. You got something, Griselda. So there is a Paradise connection?"

"Not sure. I mean I don't have any evidence. I don't have any facts. I only have what Vera Krug said."

Mildred laughed. "So you got nothing. Just the babbling remarks of a postmenopausal busybody with nothing to live for but rumors."

"Now that isn't nice."

"OK, I take it back. I'm just in a mood."

"Is it your time?" I said. "Have a little visit from Aunt Flo?"

"Aunt Flo? Oh, I get it. No. That's not it. I just lost some permits I was supposed to have and if I don't find them I could be in a heap of trouble."

"That might have to wait. Listen to this." I told her about the Blessing of the Fountain and then about what Vera said.

"Ponce de León? Fountain of Youth? Leon Fontaine? Um. It does sound fishy."

"What should we do?"

"What can we do?" Mildred continued to rifle through the stacks on her desk.

"Can I help you?"

"I'm looking for three papers, stapled together."

I started to stack the papers one by one.

"What are you doing?"

"Organizing. You just need to organize your papers better."

"Well, says you, Miss Dewey Decimal System."

"Don't knock it." I looked on the floor and there they were. "Look, Mildred. Is this what you need?"

She grabbed the pages out of my hand. "Yes. That's them. I thought for sure Boris was gonna take my badge. I have to get recertified every year so I can carry a gun."

"That's nice. Now do you want to take this seriously or not? I think that gargoyle is up to something."

"Gargoyle?"

"Oh, you had to be at the blessing yesterday. Leon Fontaine. He looks kind of like a gargoyle."

She chuckled. "Yeah, I guess he does—kinda. But he can't help that. And unfortunately ugly is not against the law."

"I think you should talk to him."

"I've been trying. I can't catch up with him and until I have some cold, hard evidence I can't even put out an APB on the man."

"OK, Mildred. I understand you've been trying. But there's got to be way to get a hold of him."

"It's gonna have to wait now."

"Wait, until when? He could be drugging the people at Greenbrier."

"Well, it's Thanksgiving and I am meeting my brother in Wilkes-Barre. He came all the way from Florida."

"Why Wilkes-Barre?"

Mildred snorted air out of her nose. "Even I need a day off now and again. Not that I ever take one, but this time I thought for once—besides, Boris is giving me a hard time. Says it's in my contract and if I don't take a day off now and again I'll be in breach."

"Ah, he's only looking out for you. But now? I don't think it's the best time."

"OK, look. What say we mosey up to Paradise and have a talk with the man before I leave. That is, if he's anywhere to be found. But we'll need to go today."

"What do you mean we? You want me to go along?"

"Sure. You know more about this than I do, apparently. We'll take the cop car."

"Ohh, can I run the siren?" My sarcasm annoyed even me.

⚬⚬⚬

The Paradise Trailer Park was just on the other end of town and down a side street that wound around the mountains a bit. We passed under the neon rainbow and flamingo sign that blinked Paradise.

"I want to check out that fountain before we leave," Mildred said. "See what all the hype is about."

"The fountain? Why? Shouldn't we be looking for Leon?"

"If you are saying that it's the Fountain of Youth then I want to see it at some point."

"I didn't say it was the Fountain of Youth, Mildred."

"Still, I need to check out all the leads. And I guess I'm a little curious about the gargoyles. I mean who would have thought that Bright's Pond would ever have gargoyles. Aren't they supposed to be on churches in Europe?"

"Yes. But they're in Paradise now."

Mildred parked near a blue and white trailer with striped awnings and flower boxes hanging from the windows. Whoever lived there had a rush on Christmas as lights were already strung from one end to the other and a large plastic Santa Claus stood in the yard.

"That's a pretty little place," I said. "I can sort of see the appeal of trailer life."

"Not me. But I hear since that Fergus Wrinkel, the previous park manager, got his just deserts that things around here are improving. Asa Kowalski, you know, Studebaker's cousin, is doing a great job managing the place."

"And with just one arm," I said. "I don't know how he does it. He did a great job emceeing the blessing yesterday."

"I wish someone would have told me about that Fergus character before it got so out of hand. I would have fixed his trolley. No man has a right to beat up his wife. Not in my book anyway."

"Guess they didn't think you could do anything to stop it."

We climbed out of the vehicle. Cool air swirled around and I took in the aroma of burning leaves. I could see puffs of smoke down the street a bit. "What is it about burning leaf piles that seems so rustic and primal?"

"Makes me sick to my stomach," Mildred said. "Can't stand it."

"Maybe I should speak with Asa, first" Mildred said.

"Sounds like a plan."

We started down the street. It was pretty much vacant except for a couple of women out hanging wash on the line.

"Even in this cold weather they hang their wash," I said.

"Still easier than hauling everything to a laundromat to use a dryer."

"Maybe we'll run into Charlotte Figg," I said. "I like her—a lot. I really hope she does decide to open a pie shop in town. And she kind of got me started thinking about this whole Fountain of Youth thing."

"I heard something about that," Mildred said as she offered a wave to one of the women. They were eyeing us like we were invaders from Mars. "A pie shop would be a great idea. At least we'd have some place other than the Full Moon to go to."

"Over there," Mildred said. "A sign says manager."

The manager's trailer sat on a small incline. It was bright yellow with a blue stripe. No awnings but a small wooden deck was attached near the door. A small neon sign that blinked manager hung over the door.

Mildred knocked. She waited a few seconds. She knocked again.

"Guess Asa's not here," she said.

"Now what?"

"We stroll."

"Stroll?"

"Around the park. How hard can it be to miss a one-armed man? We'll find him."

She was right. Pretty quickly, we found him talking to Rose. She was wearing a long, heavy brown sweater. "Oh, he's with Rose Tattoo. I met her yesterday. She has tattoos. That's why she wears that sweater."

"Her business," Mildred said. "Did you know I have a tattoo?"

"No. Where is it?"

"My business."

"I don't know any of the details of Rose's story except that something happened that caused her to get herself covered with tattoos—arms and neck mostly from what I hear." I needed to pick up my pace to keep close to Mildred. "And I hear they all have some religious significance. And I would be lying if I said I didn't want to see them one day. All I've seen so far are some wiggly vines."

Mildred removed her cop hat and tucked it under her arm. "Excuse me," she said as she approached the two. "Can I have a word?"

Rose Tattoo wrapped her sweater tighter around her. Asa took a step forward seeming to protect the woman.

"Hi, Griselda," Rose said.

I smiled. "Great blessing yesterday. The fountain is beautiful."

"It sure is," Rose said. "Leon did a great job even if it is a little crooked."

"I'm thinking crooked is his trademark," I said. "Hey, Asa."

"Hey, what's up?" Asa said.

Mildred made a noise.

"I'm sorry," I said. "This is Chief Mildred Blessing. She's here on official business."

"Official business?" Rose said. "What sort of official business?"

"Rose," I said bringing my voice to almost a whisper. "I'm worried about that Leon Fontaine fella. I think he might have something to do with what's going on up at Greenbrier."

"Greenbrier. I heard all that nonsense about what's going on up there—people acting younger and riding tricycles, but what in the world could he possibly have to do with it?"

"Well, I was listening to the Rassie Har—" I was just about to tell them what Vera Krug said when Mildred jumped into the conversation. I figured she didn't want me spilling the beans too soon.

"That's why I'm here," Mildred. "About this Leon Fontaine. What do you know about him?"

"Leon?" Rose said. "All I know is he's new to Paradise. A nice fellow. He rebuilt the fountain and got her running again. It's a real sight—not the Trevi Fountain or anything but still romantic and—"

Asa touched her arm. "How come you want to know about him? Is he in any trouble? Is he wanted by the police?"

Mildred shook her head. "No, no, I'm just asking questions."

"Like Rose already told you," Asa said. "He seems perfectly normal and natural. A good, hard worker. Skilled at stone-work, let me tell you, those Italian men are naturals."

"So he's Italian," Mildred said. She wrote it down in her little black notebook.

"What difference does that make?" I asked.

"None," Mildred said. "Just keeping facts straight."

Asa looked past us. "We were on our way somewhere if you have no more questions."

"Do you know where I can find Mr. Fontaine?" Mildred asked.

"Probably at his trailer or down by the fountain," Asa said. He pointed with his only arm.

"He really is a nice fella," Rose said. "Maybe a little quixotic, but I kind of like that." She reached her hand to Mildred and I saw a part of her tattoo on her wrist. "My name is Rose Tattoo, by the way. We weren't properly introduced. Not that I'm blaming anyone under the circumstances."

"Nice to meet you, Rose," Mildred said. "Thank you for your time. We'll just mosey around and see if we can find Mr. Fontaine."

"OK," Asa said. "But really. He's a good guy."

Mildred smiled. "I never said he wasn't, Mr. Kowalski."

We walked away from them and Mildred said, "It's a little hard to believe that Asa and Studebaker are related. They seem so different."

"But you can see the family resemblance. They both have the same mouth."

"That's true. I did notice that, but Stu is so much more out-going. Now what did Rose mean by 'quixotic'?"

"Well, I'm not entirely certain, but I guess she means he thinks he's a little like Don Quixote."

"You mean that fellow who lived in fantasy world and tried to kill windmills?"

"That's him. But he also wanted to help the poor and defend the downtrodden."

We walked a little farther and I saw the fountain. "Wow, it is pretty."

"I'll say," Mildred said. "That Leon Fontaine has some talent. I hope he's not guilty of any wrongdoing."

We approached the fountain. "I think he carved the gargoyles all by himself," I said. "They're so—gothic."

"Look," Mildred said. "That one resembles Eugene Shrapnel with the ugly bulbous nose."

"It does. But I have to admit, it's a work of art."

"Like it?" came a voice from behind.

We turned and there stood the funny-looking little man tapping his large chin.

"Are you Leon Fontaine?" Mildred asked.

"At your service," he said with a sweep of his arm.

"Mind if I ask you a few questions?" Mildred asked.

The man looked first to me and then back to Mildred. "Why certainly, my dear, but why would an officer of the law want to speak with Leon Fontaine—master stonemason, an ar-teest, a man of many crafts."

"Uh-huh," Mildred said. "I understand you built the new gazebo at the Greenbrier Nursing Home."

"That I did, but aren't you forgetting something?"

"What's that?" Mildred asked.

"You haven't introduced me to your lovely companion."

I reached out my hand to Leon, who I already thought was a hoot and couldn't possibly be doing anything nefarious in Greenbrier. "My name is Griselda Sparrow."

"Sparrow?" Leon said. "You're that lovely woman Agnes's sister. I've never really spoken to her but she's all the talk at the nursing home and yes—" he turned to Mildred—"to answer your question I was indeed the carpenter that made the gazebo, with my own two hands and lots of lumber and nails and a wee bit of magic."

Mildred's eyes lit up. "Magic?"

"Of course, that's the artistic part, you know. The actual look of the thing. You must admit it's not your usual gazebo."

"No, no," I said. "It reminded me of the fairy tale about the man who built the crooked house."

"Yes, yes," Leon said. "And what did you think of the . . . the steeple for lack of a better word. Bit much?"

"No, no. It's charming. It's a work of art. Even if it's crooked."

Leon smiled and grabbed both my hands. "A fellow admirer of all things artistic."

I chuckled. "I . . . I suppose."

"Then you must love my fountain."

"Yes, it's wonderful. I was at the blessing yesterday. I especially like the gargoyles."

"Ah, yes. The gargoyles. Carved them myself I did. Took quite a bit of time but an artist never worries about trivialities like time."

Mildred cleared her throat. "Mr. Fontaine, can we get back to my questions, please, sir?"

"Sir, indeed," Leon said. "I am not a sir; I have yet to be knighted. Nor am I a duke or a prince. I am Leon Fontaine, master builder, stonemason. An ar-teest extraordinaire."

"Yes, yes," Mildred said, "you've said that. Now I can't help thinking you are trying to confuse the issues."

"Why Officer—" he looked her up and down.

"Blessing," Mildred said. "Chief Blessing."

"Ah, that you are. A blessing to the community, I'm sure."

Leon was either everything he claimed or he was, as Mildred suggested, skirting the issues. I tended to think he was a little of both.

"Uh-huh," Mildred said. "Now, Mr. Fontaine, there have been reports of strange things happening up there—at the Greenbrier Nursing Home—ever since you arrived and built that . . . that—"

"Gazebo, Chief Blessing. Gazebo. An interesting word— one whose meaning no one is certain of. It probably means 'handsome sight.' And that it is, a gazebo I mean, a handsome sight."

It was at this point I thought Mildred might arrest him for committing some kind of double-talk speech crime. She reached into her shirt pocket and retrieved her little black notebook. "Mr. Fontaine," she said. "I will need your name, address, telephone number, and date of birth, please."

"Why in the world would you require that information?" he said with a step back. "Are you arresting me? Am I suspect of a crime? Was a crime committed here in Paradise—lovely name for a trailer park don't you think."

"Mr. Fontaine," Mildred said with force. "Please."

I couldn't contain a smile. I liked Leon Fontaine.

"Oh, yes, yes, sorry," he said. "My address is, of course, here at the park. I am a resident now, been so for over three months. And I have no telephone so I don't have a number. I . . . I answer only to . . . to the wind."

Well, OK. Now he was getting a bit weird.

"I go where I am needed. A hero of sorts, that's what they call me. Now if you will excuse me I am expected elsewhere."

I half expected to see Leon Fontaine mount a skinny horse and ride off with a lance toward the nearest windmill.

He turned on one foot and set off in the direction of the trailers.

"What in the heck just happened?" Mildred said. "That is one strange little man."

"I like him. Did you learn anything new?"

"No. Not one blessed thing, except I'll tell you this: I'm keeping my eye on Mr. Leon Fontaine and his fountain. When I get back from Wilkes-Barre, of course."

"Of course."

10

The Tuesday before Thanksgiving at Brisco's Butcher Shop was a little like Kresge Department Store the day after Thanksgiving when the Christmas sales begin. The butcher shop was crowded with lines of mostly women, waiting to get their holiday birds. Even though Ruth and I left early enough, we still ran into quite a group. I saw a few folks from Bright's Pond, including Edie Tompkins and Janeen Sturgis standing in line holding their tiny triangular number papers.

"Griselda," Edie called. "How are you, dear?"

Janeen waved.

I waved back.

"I was just thinking about you this morning," Edie said making her way toward us. "I was wondering how Agnes was getting on what with the holidays approaching and all."

"She's doing fine," I said. "Ruth and I are here for our turkey."

"Ruth?" Edie said. "But aren't you having Thanksgiving at the funeral parlor like you do every year?"

That turned a few heads and raised a few eyebrows.

"No, not this year," Ruth said. "I'm cooking and we're gathering at my house."

"Oh, that's nice," Edie said. "But what about Agnes? Will she be . . . forklifted back to town?"

"No," I said. My annoyance growing. "We'll be visiting Agnes at Greenbrier."

Janeen clicked her tongue. "Greenbrier. Well, I heard that something was going on up there, something that might even be illegal," she said. "I heard the inmates are—"

"Residents," I said.

"Yes, of course, residents," Janeen said. "I never know what to call them. But it doesn't matter. I heard they're all taking drugs and climbing trees and riding tricycles."

I looked at Ruth who had just pulled a number from the number machine near the counter.

"We got twenty-seven," she said. "Not bad."

Edie stole a glance at her ticket. "I got number thirteen. Lucky thirteen."

"Good for you," I said. "And nobody is taking drugs at Greenbrier."

"That's not the scuttlebutt," Edie said. "I heard that the police are investigating the possibility of"—she leaned in close to whisper—"illegal drug activity up there. Imagine that. All them old and sick people getting drugged."

"It's just a rumor, Edie," I said. "And do you really believe the residents would do something like that?"

"Oh, well, I didn't mean to imply that they had any knowledge," she blustered.

"Well, something is happening to cause all the attention," said Edie. "I even heard Vera Krug talking about it on her morning show. She said the folks up there are acting strange. And then she said something weird."

"Weird?" Ruth said.

I hadn't told Ruth what Vera said about Leon Fontaine and how she connected him with the Fountain of Youth.

"Yeah, she made noises that some fella—what was his name, Janeen?"

"Leon Fontaine," Janeen said who went back to shaking her head and clicking her tongue.

"That's right, Leon Fontaine," Edie continued. "She seemed a might suspicious about him. Said he found the Fountain of Youth or had some sort of relationship to Ponce de León? You know that explorer fella who discovered Florida?"

"Not exactly, Edie," I said. "She just intimated that Leon's name was similar to Ponce's and that his last name meant fountain in French or Italian or something." I tried to wave the subject away, but Ruth lit up.

"Vera," Ruth said. "Why, that little busybody. She just has to stick her big, fat nose in everything that happens around here—even when nothing is happening—even when we don't know what is happening. And who is she to draw correlations between that man and a dead explorer, I mean what in tarnation do you make of that?"

Mr. Brisco called number eleven.

"Oh," said Janeen, "I guess we better move up in line. I sure hope he got us a good turkey this year."

"Brisco's turkeys are always good," Ruth said. "It's all in how you cook them. I'm planning something different."

"Different?" Janeen said. "Are you sure that's a good idea? I mean, what is wrong with a traditional turkey dinner? Why, my Frank would never stand for anything other than a good old-fashioned turkey. He loves to carve."

"I'm planning a Hawaiian Luau Tropical Thanksgiving," Ruth said, so proud I thought she'd bust.

Edie snickered into her hand, as did a few other people. "Did you say Hawaiian? What do they know about Thanksgiving? It's not like the pilgrims landed in Honolulu."

Janeen smirked. "Are you planning to stuff the turkey with a pineapple?"

"As a matter of fact," Ruth said.

Mr. Brisco called number twelve. And we moved closer to the display case filled with meats and sausages.

"As a matter of fact I am making a wonderful stuffing with macadamia nuts and passion fruit and—"

Edie and Janeen laughed.

Ruth stopped talking.

"Oh, we're sorry dear," Edie said. "We just never heard of a tropical Thanksgiving. I mean, what is the point?"

"I only wanted to attempt something fancy. Anyone can roast a turkey. But it takes real cooking finesse to make it . . . spectacular."

Edie looked at me. "I imagine all the regulars are invited, but what are you going to do about Agnes? This must be her first holiday away from home."

"We'll be taking dinner to her up at Greenbrier," Ruth said.

"Do you think you should?" Edie asked. "Isn't she on a strict diet?"

"Diets don't count on Thanksgiving," Ruth said.

I was glad when Mr. Brisco called Edie's number and she moved forward to claim her fresh turkey. It was so big it took the two of them to carry it out the door.

We waited a bit longer while other customers received their orders. Most people walked away with turkeys but others also left with sausage and ground beef. Finally, he called our number.

"Good morning, Ruth," Mr. Brisco said. "I got your bird all ready for you. Picked you out a nice one, nice and young. Should be tasty."

"Thank you," Ruth said. "Your turkeys are always the tastiest."

"And how are you, Griselda?" Mr. Brisco asked. "Don't see you in here much since Agnes moved to the nursing home."

"I know," I said. "Seems I don't eat much meat these days."

"And how is your sister?" he asked as his helper handed over the turkey to Ruth.

"She's doing well," I said.

But it seemed that even Mr. Brisco was not resistant to rumors. "So tell me, Griselda." He leaned over the counter. "Any truth to what I hear is happening up there. I mean the talk is pretty scary. Mildred Blessing's been snooping all over town, getting folks nervous."

"The truth is no one knows what's happening. Probably nothing more that the residents feeling a little happier than usual."

"I think it's just that the holidays are coming," Ruth said.

"Could be. Could be," Mr. Brisco said. He handed Ruth some change. "Thanks for your business as always. And happy Thanksgiving."

I was quite glad to be out of the shop but not thrilled when Ruth suggested another visit to Madam Zola's.

"I need more nuts," she said. "I used them all up in my experimentation phase."

"Well, I'll wait in the truck. You can go in yourself."

"Ah, you won't make me do that, will you?"

We drove down the street and found the last parking spot anywhere near Madam Zola's. "Come on," I said. "Let's go get your nuts."

"Ah," Madam Zola said when we walked into the store. "I had a vision you vood be returning."

"Yeah, right," I whispered. "Just tell her to give you the nuts and let's get out of here. It gives me the creeps."

Madam Zola stepped closer to us. She still dragged her left leg behind her.

"Your nuts," Ruth said. "I mean I would like some more of your macadamia nuts, please. Just one jar this time."

"But of course you do. Top shelf, dahling."

I reached up and grabbed the jar. "Quick, pay for them."

It took Madam Zola a little too long to reach the cash register. But she finally made it. Ruth paid for the macadamias, and I thought we were out of there until Madam offered to read Ruth's palm. Ruth looked at her palm.

"I don't get it," she said. "How can these lines tell you anything? It's a bunch of malarkey, ain't it?"

Madam Zola's eyes grew wide and maybe a touch wild.

"Come on now, Ruth, before she puts a curse on us or something."

On the way home, Ruth said, "Can you believe those two?"

"Who?" I said. I was still seeing Madam Zola's angry eyes in my brain.

"Edie and Janeen. If they aren't the biggest buttinskies in town. And what about that sister-in-law of mine? She's got no right reporting about Greenbrier when nothing's been proved. And what could that weird little man have to do with Greenbrier?"

"Oh, she just likes to stir up trouble when she can. Her audience likes it."

"I suppose so, but all those people up at the nursing home have no way to defend themselves."

"You're right about that. But let's just hope there is nothing to defend and Mildred or someone, maybe Doctor Silver, gets to the bottom of it soon."

"I hope so," Ruth said. "For Greenbrier's sake." She thought a moment. "But tell me the truth, Griselda, do you think that fella, Leon, has anything to do with it—I mean really?"

"No, I don't think so. Mildred and I went to visit him at Paradise. He is a bit—eccentric," I said. "But I don't get the impression he's doing something to hurt people. He just loves what he does—even if he might be a little overly impressed with himself."

"Really? You talked to him?"

"Mildred and me. I got a little worried after Vera's radio spot that she might be onto something. I mean it is strange—his name, the fountain, the folks at the nursing home turning into children and teenagers."

"Uhm, uhm, uhm." Ruth shook her head. "I just can't think about all of this now. I got to get ready for my big day. Thanksgiving is just two days away."

"Now you're sure I can't help with anything?" I said as I turned onto Hector Street. "I can make sweet potatoes with those little marshmallows and maybe a three-bean salad."

"Three-bean," Ruth said. "I got a six-bean salad planned. "It involves pine nuts. Ever hear of pine nuts? They come from actual pine cones."

"Nope, never tasted pine nuts. Are they good?"

"You'll see soon enough. Like I've been telling everyone. Just bring your appetites."

"And your sense of humor," I said.

"What?"

"Nothing, Ruth. I'm just being facetious."

I pulled up out front of Ruth's house. "Are you coming to the next Yuletide Committee meeting?"

"Oh, sure, certainly, Griselda. I wouldn't miss it. When is it again?"

"Monday, at the café."

"I'll be there. I'm planning on sewing the shepherd costumes again and the sheep. I just love to make the robes. I wonder who will be Mary this year. Seems like all the girls are getting too big or are too young and we might have more sheep than we need."

"Oh, we'll find someone, and Babette will always do it, you know. She's eighteen now but that won't matter."

"Well, it is the church children's pageant."

"I know. But when you need a Mary, you need a Mary."

───── ∞ ─────

I was driving down Filbert toward the funeral home when I noticed Charlotte Figg standing outside that empty store. She appeared to be waiting for someone and I decided that what she was doing was much more intriguing than going to the library, particularly since everyone's been talking about her opening a pie shop.

I pulled over and parked the truck.

"Charlotte," I called as I walked across the street.

"Hello." She waved.

I felt a wide smile stretch across my face. "Are you considering renting the space?"

She shielded her eyes with her hand and peered into the large window. "I thought I'd take a look. No reason not to—take a look I mean."

"I think it would make a fine pie shop. I can just see it. Charlotte Figg's Pie Shop in big bold neon lights."

This time a smile appeared on Charlotte's face. "Neon? Really? That does sound nice."

Charlotte tilted her head slightly. She was an attractive woman with graying hair—but not completely—broad shoulders, but not big—and her high cheekbones were a bit flushed.

"It just seems like such a huge undertaking. Something my dead husband would never approve, but like Rose keeps telling me, he's not here to boss me anymore."

"I think most folks can do whatever they set their hearts on. Look at me, I wanted to fly an airplane and now I'm this close," I held my thumb and index finger an inch apart, "to getting my pilot's license."

"You are? Well, I think that's just amazing. I didn't get my driver's license until I was close to forty, and Herman wasn't even too happy about that."

"Like Rose says, he's not here and you need to be your own person—even if it means opening a pie shop."

She shielded her eyes and looked inside again. "It would be nice. I can see it now, a long counter with a glass case filled with pies and maybe a couple of tables with pretty yellow tablecloths and flowers in the center where folks can sit and eat pie and drink tea or coffee and talk their cares away."

"That does sound nice."

Charlotte looked down the street in both directions. "I am looking forward to Thanksgiving. And so are Rose and Ginger."

"I am too. It should be a great time."

"I plan on bringing apple pie and maybe a berry or two, pumpkin, of course. You think that will be OK?"

"I can't wait. I think your pies will be the only normal food there—well, your pie and Zeb's—if he comes."

"If he comes?"

I looked at my feet and wondered if I should say anything personal to this woman. I hardly knew her but there was something easy in her countenance and body language that invited me to speak. Agnes always made me feel drawn out, like chewing gum, when we spoke.

"You know he's my—gee, what would you call him—boyfriend? It sounds so high schoolish to say."

"I didn't know that. I only ate at the café once, maybe twice. I'm not sure if I ever met Zeb."

"He'd be the one with the paper hat. The chief cook and bottle washer as he calls himself."

"No, sorry. I don't remember. But I hope he comes." Charlotte looked down the street. "Boris Lender was supposed to meet me. Guess that's why I seem so . . . distracted."

"He'll be here. I've never known Boris to miss an appointment."

"Oh, good. Anyway, is everything OK—with Zeb and you?"

I shook my head. "Not really. He's very jealous."

Charlotte took a step back. "Jealousy is never a good sign. It's sad when a man can't let a woman be herself without going all nuts. Tread softly. And just be very sure."

That was when Boris arrived, wearing his usual gray suit with the striped tie. He carried a thick cigar cradled between his middle and index fingers.

"Afternoon," he said flicking the ash in the gutter. He looked first to Charlotte and then me. "Are you with Charlotte, Griselda?" he asked.

"No, no I was just saying hello."

I touched her arm. "I guess I'll see you Thursday."

"Looking forward to it."

"Be ready for anything," I said.

"Well, Charlotte," Boris said. "Shall we look inside? I have a good feeling you will soon be our newest shop owner."

I headed back across the street with Charlotte's words, "tread softly" ringing in my ears.

11

Thanksgiving morning I woke early, 5:00 a.m. No matter what Ruth might have said, I knew she was going to need some help. So I fed Arthur his Thanksgiving meal and headed over to Ruth's. It was cold and icy, as frost had etched the windows and my truck wouldn't start. But that was OK. I walked the few blocks to her house.

I pushed open the front door. "Ruth," I called, first in whisper and because I thought there was a small chance she was still asleep. But then I heard a crash, like pots and pans falling from a cabinet in the kitchen and went running. "Ruth. Are you all right?"

She was sitting in the middle of the floor, sobbing.

"What's wrong?" I said.

"If I ever say I'm making Thanksgiving again, just hit me over the head and put me out of my misery. I just plain didn't think that cooking for eight people, nine including myself, ten, including making a plate up for Agnes would be so cotton-picking hard."

"How can I help?" I took her hand and lifted her up.

"Well, for one thing I really don't know what to do with that bird. How long it takes to cook, and that six-bean tropical salad I was making has been demoted to three beans. And I can't find my macadamia nuts."

"They're probably still in your handbag. That's where you put them Tuesday."

"Oh, that's right. I hope they're still there."

Ruth looked around her kitchen. "Have you ever known me to make such a mess? I don't understand."

"It's a lot to do, Ruth. Don't worry. You have plenty of time, and I'm here to help now. Just tell me what to do."

"I appreciate that but I don't really have plenty of time. Folks are arriving at three o'clock. Must take ten hours for a bird that big to cook through."

"No, no, it will take half the time. You don't need to even pop him into the oven until ten o'clock or so. You'll want him to set a while after cooking."

"Will you do it? Will you take care of the turkey? I think I can handle the rest—especially mashed potatoes. Now *that* I know I can do."

"You mean you're making regular mashed potatoes? The white kind?"

"Well, yeah. I thought about it and I just don't have the skills needed to make something exotic. I keep trying and I keep falling flat on my face."

"I'm sorry Ruth. Maybe we can do a little traditional mixed with a little exotic."

"That's true. It certainly doesn't mean we still can't use all the decorations and hand out leis, and I'm still making my pineapple upside-down cherry surprise cake."

"What's the surprise?"

"I ain't gonna tell you. It wouldn't be a surprise if I did."

I tied a yellow apron with white trim around my waist and washed my hands in the kitchen sink. "OK, Ruth," I said drying my hands on a terry towel. "What can I do?

Ruth looked around at the mounds of food and bags and cans scattered on the countertop and the small round kitchen table. "I don't rightly know. It's early to prepare the veggies, and the hors d'oeuvres can wait.

"What about the turkey? I can get him stuffed and into a pan and ready for the oven."

"Oh, would you? Thank you."

It didn't take me too long to get old Tom ready for roasting. After stuffing the breast with Ruth's exotic mixture, which I must say smelled kind of tasty, I laced him up and plopped him into a roasting pan. Then I slathered his skin with butter and salt and pepper.

"Say good-bye, Ruth."

Ruth turned from what she was doing with the pineapple. "Good-bye, Tom. Roast well."

And then I got busy preparing the vegetables for cooking and even mixed up dough for biscuits. Almost before we knew it the kitchen had taken on that Thanksgiving aroma that had the capacity to warm even the coldest hearts. That nutty, brown, spicy smell with just enough savory to make your mouth water.

Later in the day, Ruth was busy making her pineapple surprise when the first guests arrived. She was up to her elbows in some kind of yellowish mixture in the stand mixer, even had a streak or three of it in her hair. The first to arrive were Charlotte, Rose, and Ginger Rodgers. I greeted them at the door.

"Welcome. Come on in and get comfy. Dinner will be about an hour or so."

Charlotte was carrying some kind of fancy pie-carrying bag. It was white with tiny red roses all over it. Embroidered on the bag were the words, "Nothing Like a Warm Pie Fresh from Our Oven to Your Affair."

"It's not mine," she said when she noticed me reading. "Herman brought it home for one day. Never did tell me where he swiped it from. Where would you like me to put these?"

I looked around. Just about every spare inch of table and counter surface had been occupied.

"I'll just take them into the kitchen."

Fortunately, I was able to set the pies on top of the refrigerator.

"Happy Thanksgiving," Ginger said when I returned to the living room. "And thanks for inviting us." She sat on the long blue sofa. Her feet barely reached the edge of the seat cushion.

"Sure thing," I said. I took their coats and hung them in the closet.

"This is a very nice house," Rose said. "Very spacious—and what are those? Palm trees?"

"Yes," I said. "These old Victorians have lots of room—and yep, palm trees. Ruth wanted a tropical Thanksgiving."

"Oh, how cool," said Ginger. "And look, I see tiki torches in the dining room. Is she going to light them?"

"Oh, I hope not," I said. "I don't think the fire department would appreciate getting called away from their Thanksgiving to put out the fire."

That was when Ruth came from the kitchen. She was wearing an orange apron with a giant pumpkin appliquéd on the front and she carried a large mixing spoon.

"Hello," she said. "Happy Thanksgiving."

"Hi," the three women said at the same time.

"I'm so glad you all could come," Ruth said walking just a little ways into the living room. "Please make yourself at home. Griselda already brought out the hors d'oeuvres as you can see." She indicated the crowded coffee table. "We got those tiny sausages in tiny rolls, pigs in a blanket they call them, and some veggies for dipping, and I made a tropical dipping sauce also with honey and yogurt and chili powder."

"Take your time," Rose said.

"And oh, I have iced tea also. Made it fresh this morning— nice and sweet. Just the way my hubby used to take it. Oh—" she put her hand over her heart. "I miss him so much around the holidays."

"That sounds so nice," Charlotte said. "Thank you."

"You'll need to excuse me," Ruth said, "but I have to get back to my pineapples and cherries. But help yourself to some hors d'oeuvres."

"Yes, yes," I said. "We have everything Ruth mentioned along with cheese and crackers and cheese puffs with bacon and—you can see what else."

"Oh, and Griselda," Ruth said poking her head back into the living room. "Aren't you forgetting something?" She nodded toward the den.

I looked and then I remembered. "The leis."

"What?" Ginger said.

"Of course," Rose said. "We should all be wearing a lei."

"I have a pretty flowery lei for each of you to go with our tropical Thanksgiving theme," Ruth called.

Everyone but Rose who joined right in on the spirit of things choked back a chuckle as I went to retrieve them. I handed one to each. Ruth told me I was supposed to kiss everyone on the cheek also, but I vetoed that idea pretty quickly.

"This is nice," Charlotte said looking around. "It does look like a picture of a Hawaiian luau I saw in a magazine once. 'Course I never been. Herman was though, once. On a Fuller Brush Salesman Convention."

"I'd like to go someday," Rose said. "I think going down inside a volcano must be so thrilling. I hear you can get a tour to do that over there."

The conversation quickly died after that.

"So," I said. "Anybody want to watch football?" That was when I noticed Charlotte swiping tears away from her eyes. Then she blew into a yellow hanky. I noticed she looked a bit shell-shocked as I draped the flowery necklace over her shoulders but I didn't say anything then.

"Are you OK, Charlotte?" I said. "The holidays can be rough, I know." Charlotte wore a pretty blue dress with dainty white trimming.

"I'm sorry," she said. "It's just . . . just that it's been a long time since I had a Thanksgiving like this."

I put my arm around her. "Well, we're just so happy you're here. Now how about enjoying some snacks before the men arrive and wolf them all down." I whispered in her ear, "But I suspect it's your pies that will be the hit of the day."

"Thank you, Griselda," she said. "It does smell good in here. But not exactly traditional although you can never mistake the savory aroma of Bell's Seasoning."

"You'll see," I said. "I think it'll be a little of both."

"Griselda," Ginger Rodgers said, "could I trouble you for a glass of water?"

"Certainly, be right back."

I went into the kitchen and grabbed a water pitcher that was on the kitchen counter right next to a bowl of Ruth's Ambrosia Salad—a mixture of shredded coconut and chunks of pineapple, mandarin oranges, marshmallows, pecans, and two cans of fruit cocktail folded into whipped cream.

"How's it going Ruth?" I asked. "Need any help yet?"

She looked up from her work. She was dropping cherries into the centers of pineapple rings. "No yet, but the turkey will need to be checked soon and then I guess we get the vegetables on the table."

The doorbell went off again. "That's probably the boys," I said. "I'll go let them in."

I poured Ginger a glass of water and brought it to her.

"Thank you," she said.

I opened the living room door. Boris, Studebaker, Asa, and Zeb stood on the other side. My heart began to pound as I looked past them just in case Cliff had decided to come—invited or not. And I wouldn't put it past Ruth to have invited him—just for the fireworks. I honestly had not expected to see Zeb and it was hard to hide my surprise.

"Zeb? I . . . I didn't expect you."

"I know. I . . . Stu talked me into it."

"OK, I hated the idea of you spending the day alone, anyway."

"Me too." He smiled wide.

"So . . . happy Thanksgiving," I said. "Come on in. I'm not sure who knows who so you can make your introductions as needed."

That accounted for all the invited guests except Ivy Slocum. She was often a hit-or-miss guest. Ivy marched to her own drum and if she woke up that morning feeling sour or sad or just plain bored with the whole thing, she would stay away.

Zeb hung back. He grabbed my hand. "Are you glad to see me, Grizzy?"

I looked into his chocolate eyes. "Sure I am. I've been missing you."

"That's good. I've been missing you." Then he gave me a quick peck on the lips.

Soon the conversation was flowing as the three guys found seats. Zeb and Boris got into a discussion about a needed stoplight on the corner of Filbert and Main. Studebaker had a hard time keeping his eyes off of Ginger. She seemed amused by it. I glanced out the window again half expecting to see Cliff.

The aroma of the turkey drifted into the living room. I went to the kitchen to baste the bird. It was nearly ready and smelled heavenly. The skin was golden brown and crispy. I drizzled juices over it.

"Smells good," Ruth said. "How much longer?"

"I think it might be ready." I checked the meat thermometer and sure enough it was perfect—one hundred and sixty-five degrees. "I think I'll take it out so it can settle while we mash the potatoes and get everything else on the table."

I lifted the turkey onto the stove top.

"Whatcha doing?" Zeb said. He had come into the kitchen. "Come on." He took my hand. "Come and join the group. We were just talking about the fountain up in Paradise."

"OK. Just a few minutes."

"Well, don't take too long," he said.

"Go on," Ruth said. "Join the others. I got everything under control out here."

"No, no, that's not right."

"I'd love to help," Charlotte said. "I heard you talking and thought I'd see what I can do."

"Go on," Ruth said. "Spend time with Zeb. Charlotte can help."

"OK. As long as you're sure."

She looked at me and twisted her mouth.

"OK, OK," I said.

Zeb and I rejoined the group in time to hear Asa say, "It was exciting. When that water turned on and everything worked and the water went where it was supposed to and everyone cheered it was almost as though I had made it myself."

"I still can't believe that strange fella built it," Ginger said. "He worked almost day and night for weeks. Sure was noisy, but worth it."

"Where is Leon Fontaine?" I asked.

Asa shook his head and exchanged looks between him and Rose.

"I heard he was spending the day at Greenbrier," Ginger said. "He said something about helping to serve Thanksgiving dinners to the residents who have no family today."

My heart sank as I was reminded of Agnes. Rose seemed to sense my sadness. She patted my hand. "Your sister will be all right," she said. "You're going up there later."

Tears gathered in the corners of my eyes. "I know. It's just that this is the first Thanksgiving we haven't spent together—all day long. It's weird."

"Try not to fret, Grizzy," Zeb said. "Agnes is a grown-up. She must understand the predicament she put you in."

"*She* put me in." I know I sounded incredulous. "It wasn't her fault. What Agnes became—I mean. She couldn't help it—leastways not early on. Not when there was all that bullying and talking going on."

"Calm down, Honey," Zeb said. "That might be true but you got to admit that she did have some say as she got older."

I took a deep breath and decided that Thanksgiving was not the day to air the Sparrow family laundry. "OK, it will be nice to see her later."

"Sure it will," Ginger said. "And believe me, with Leon Fontaine making the rounds up there, well—he'll keep them all happy." She sipped her water. "There's just something about that man."

Studebaker looked at Boris like the two of them knew something the rest of us didn't. I figured Mildred had told Boris all about the Fountain of Youth thing and what Vera Krug had said. And if Boris knew, then Studebaker knew.

The doorbell rang. "That must be Ivy," I said.

Sure enough, Ivy was here wearing a perfectly hideous Thanksgiving sweatshirt with a giant cornucopia on the front. But that was Ivy for you. She held Mickey Mantle's leash. He was sitting like a reasonable gentleman.

"Hey, should I take Mickey Mantle out back?" Ivy asked.

"That's probably best."

"OK, I'll see you inside in a minute or two."

I rejoined the festivities.

"Excuse me," Ruth said coming into the living room. "But, Griselda, could you help me get food on the table, please? Dinner is almost ready."

"Oh, boy," Studebaker said. "I am hungrier than a bear in spring." He rubbed his belly. And then he playfully rubbed Boris's belly. "But you, my friend, could live off the fat of the land for a while."

Boris pushed his hand away. "Just try and keep me from that turkey and the mashed potatoes—my favorite."

Ruth and I placed all the various foods Ruth had prepared on the table. Her table looked wonderful with the bird of paradise centerpiece and little paper umbrellas in all the drinks and in the yams and potatoes. Everything was in place except the turkey, which I imagined she wanted to carry in after everyone was seated. And speaking of seats, I said, "Ruth, you're missing two chairs."

"Oh, oh, would you ask Zeb or Boris to run up to the attic and get two folding chairs."

"Sure."

"I'll go," Asa said.

"No problem," said Zeb.

I went back into the kitchen just in time to catch the gravy just before it boiled over onto the stove. I poured it into a white gravy boat and placed it on the table near Boris's seat.

Finally, everything was ready, and Ruth called the guests to the table.

She stood at the end, closest to the kitchen. It took her a moment to regain her composure. Her face was red, her hair a mess with streaks of flour and glop I couldn't recognize. She took a deep, shaky breath. "Welcome," she said as a tear ripped down her cheek. "Now for the star of the show."

I watched as everyone looked around the table at the fancy dishes Ruth had prepared. Asa turned his nose up at the Ambrosia. You'd think he was looking at a pile of horse manure the way he stared at it.

"Now I don't know if I ever seen a dish like that," he said. "What do you call it?"

"Ambrosia," I said. "It's got coconut, which I don't care for, and pecans and whipped cream and other things. Ambrosia is the food of the gods."

"Not for me," he said. "I hate coconut."

"Oh, boy," Ivy said. "I love Ambrosia. Anything with coconut."

Boris, who looked uncomfortable in his lei, teetered his burned-out cigar on the edge of his bread plate. An act that caused Ginger Rodgers to come painfully close to biting his leg. "Get that off a there. Where did your mama raise you?"

Boris snatched the stogie and dropped it into his suit pocket. "Didn't mean to upset you."

Charlotte finally reappeared from the kitchen carrying a large serving bowl of mashed potatoes. They were piled high like a mountain.

"Ohhh," Rose said. "My favorite. I could eat mashed potatoes every single day of my life."

Then Ruth carried out the turkey on the large turkey-shaped platter she purchased at Kresge. She had stuck little tiny paper umbrellas all over him, he wore a lei and little pink paper booties on his legs. Everyone cheered as she placed him on the table.

"Now that," Studebaker said, "is the happiest roasted turkey I ever did see."

"My, my," Asa said. "That's what I call an excellent bird." And for a second or two I tried to envision Asa carving the holiday bird with just his one arm.

"Let's join hands," Ruth said. She took a breath. "And Rose will you pray for us?"

Rose smiled. "Dear Lord, We thank and praise you for this day. I never imagined I would be part of such a festive Thanksgiving Day meal. Thank you for this, thank you for everyone around this table and for Ruth who so lovingly prepared it all and for those who came alongside to help. We ask you to bless each one here, and remember those who are far from us this day. We ask your blessing on this food and that our time and talk bring glory to you, for you, Lord, are worthy of our praise and thanksgiving."

Everyone said, "Amen."

Zeb continued to hold my hand or maybe I continued to hold his. It was hard to tell but I think we were both imagining a Thanksgiving celebration in our own home someday. Then the thought made me so angry I dropped his hand. Why did he have to be acting like such a big jealous jerk? I sailed my own silent prayer. Help me figure out my feelings, Lord.

Ruth took the big carving knife and the big fork and stood. She stared at the bird who looked more like the Big Kahuna than Tom Turkey. "Zeb," she said. "Would you come and do the honors?"

Zeb squeezed my hand. "I certainly will."

"Carve him good," Ivy said. "And I got dibs on the gizzard."

While Zeb carved, the food was passed around the table. I watched as folks bit into their first bites of the tropical surprise food. I think Ruth sneaked a little bit of the islands into each dish. Charlotte surreptitiously pulled a piece of mango out of her mouth that she had found in her three-bean salad. She looked at it and tucked it on the side of her plate.

Boris was confused by the little white nuts in the stuffing.

"What in the heck are these little white ball things in here, Ruth? Are we supposed to eat them?"

"Sure, they're macadamia nuts express from Hawaii. I got them at Madam Zola's shop in Shoops."

The sky outside grew dark as night fell over Bright's Pond but the spirit inside was bright and cheerful. Ruth turned on teeny lights she had strung from the ceiling that reminded us all of stars. She lit candles that cast dancing, wondrous shadows on the walls and table as Don Ho sang "Tiny Bubbles." Ruth Knickerbocker had pulled off her tropical Thanksgiving dinner.

But it was the final course that stole the show. After we had gathered dishes and brought most of the food bowls and what was left of the Big Kahuna into the kitchen, Ruth unveiled her pineapple, mango, passion fruit and raisin, pineapple upside-down cake. The four-layer cake sat on a large silver platter with plastic lei flowers tucked all around it. I think the dessert must have weighed thirty pounds.

"Oh, Ruth," I said. "It looks—amazing."

"You ain't seen nothin' yet." She squeezed lemon juice into a small cup of what smelled like brandy. She sprinkled it onto the cake.

"Ruth," I said, "what are you planning?"

"Just watch. Help me get this to the table."

It took the two of us to carry it and hoist it onto the table. Everyone cheered, even if they did appear somewhat dismayed—or scared.

Then Ruth pulled a book of matches from her apron pocket. "Are you ready? Here goes."

She struck the match and touched it to the cake and WHOOOOSH! Flames shot straight up as everyone recoiled and cheered at the same time. I made sure I knew where the phone was just in case I had to call the fire department. The cake burned for a few more seconds as the flame turned to a pretty, almost purple glow.

"Now they say you should cut into it while it is still flambé-ing," Ruth said. "So here goes."

The cake cut nicely and soon everyone had a small piece of Ruth's dessert flaming in front of them.

"This is so much fun," Charlotte said. "I never ever thought to flambé one of my pies. But you've inspired me, Ruth."

Ruth blushed. "Thank you, Charlotte."

"As a matter in fact," Charlotte said after a few bites of the odd cake. "This is so tasty I am going to include it on the menu at my pie shop. It would be a special order but—"

"Really?" Rose said. "You didn't tell me. You're definitely opening the shop?"

"That's exactly so," Boris said. "She signed the lease yesterday."

Ruth sunk back into her seat as though the wind had been knocked out of her sails. I know Charlotte didn't mean to steal her thunder and she was actually paying Ruth a huge compliment but still, I understood what if felt like to be suddenly overshadowed by someone else's greatness.

⊶⊷

The party broke up at seven o'clock. A little later than I had hoped but I couldn't very well tell people to stop having fun on account of Agnes. It seemed I had done too much of that. But I finally had to say something.

"Listen, everybody. I promised Agnes I would bring her a plate of food and some of Ruth's now famous flaming pineapple upside-down surprise. I know she would love it if you all came along."

Boris leaned back in the recliner and patted his bulging belly. He had already loosened his belt. "Oh, not me, Griselda. I'm bushed."

Studebaker joined Boris's sentiments as did Asa and Rose and Ginger, who I think really wanted to come, but she declined too. Not so much out of tiredness, but embarrassment, perhaps. It surprised me. I watched her shake her head toward Rose when the offer went out. Rose grabbed her hand and squeezed it. "Don't worry," I heard Rose say.

Charlotte said she was anxious to get into the shop the next day and get started on some cleanup. "The place is a mess. But I've had some experience cleaning up messes." She smiled at Rose and Asa.

But Zeb surprised me. "I'll come."

Ruth touched my arm. "The man loves you. He's making an effort."

"That would be great, Zeb. I just need to pack a plate for her and—"

"I'll help," he said.

Ruth conspicuously left us alone in the kitchen. Zeb sliced turkey for Agnes as I packed bowls with potatoes and vegetables and ambrosia. I cut her an extra-large piece of Ruth's surprise cake.

"Now I need to be sure and bring whatever it was that made that cake catch fire. I think Agnes will like it," I said.

"You think that's a good idea?" Zeb asked.

"Sure, it'll just be a little flambé. A small flame and then she'll blow it out—like a birthday candle."

Zeb shook his head. "I hope you know what you're doing."

I assembled everything into a picnic basket. After I closed it, Zeb put his hands on my shoulders. I turned and we stood nose to nose. He said nothing, but held my chin with the tips of his fingers and kissed me and that time my toes curled and my knees buckled. I was all caught up in the moment, feeling full and happy and maybe even a little struck by the magic of the little white star lights and electric tiki torches that shone around the table.

"Let's stop playing games, Griselda. Tell me you'll marry me."

I took a step back and felt my racing heart. Maybe it was the moment or the holiday. I could have blamed it on many things, but I followed my heart. "I will, Zeb."

But apparently nothing in Bright's Pond is very private and just as I said the words the crowd cheered, especially Ruth.

"I knew it," she said. "I knew she'd say yes."

"Wait," I said. "You knew Zeb was going to ask me again tonight?"

Ruth looked at her feet. "Sorry, Griselda."

"How in the world did you keep that secret? You are a lousy secret keeper."

"Oh, gee, it was hard," Ruth said. "I just had to keep myself busy the whole time. I wanted to tell you that Zeb told me he was coming and that he was gonna get you to say yes this time. But I held my tongue. I let him surprise you."

"That he did." I looked in Zeb's quiet eyes. "That he did."

"Let's set a date," Rose said. "I love weddings."

"Me too," Ginger said. "I can be the flower girl."

Everyone laughed except Charlotte. It was like this kind of news didn't faze her at all. "Tread softly," she had told me. "Tread softly."

12

Needless to say, the evening ended with quite a bit of fanfare and excitement. Asa even had some firecrackers left over from the Fountain Blessing, which he exploded in Ruth's backyard in honor of Zeb and me. Unfortunately, Mickey Mantle was tied up against the fence and started barking and howling louder and louder with each explosion. And that brought nasty Eugene Shrapnel out of his lair. Eugene was, of course, the town curmudgeon. Every town has one.

Eugene, who somehow knew everybody's business, came banging on Ruth's door around seven o'clock.

"What's all that racket?" he said, the instant Boris opened the door.

Eugene was surprised to see Boris. "What are you doing mixed up in this kind of tomfoolery?" Eugene asked.

Boris laughed. "It's Thanksgiving, Eugene, and Zeb and Griselda just got engaged. We're celebrating."

That was when Ruth pulled the door open farther. "Come on in, Eugene, have some pie. Charlotte made it."

Eugene was short with a crooked back that necessitated he walk with a cane. He had a bulbous nose with icky purple veins running through it and smelled like a combination of Lysol and wet wool.

"I . . . I can't," he said.

"Oh, come on," everyone else called. "There's plenty."

Eugene sheepishly stepped into Ruth's house, and for the first time, I saw something other than derision on Eugene's face. "Thank you. I can't stay long."

"However long is long," Asa said. "I got more fireworks in the truck."

It was the twinkle in the old rooster's eyes that told Asa to go get them and before we knew it Eugene had struck the final match that set off the final colorful explosion that blasted from the canister on the ground into red and green screamers and hot streamers in the sky.

Zeb and I stood arm in arm. Eugene and Ivy stood closer together than ever and I smiled when I saw Eugene scratch Mickey Mantle behind his ear. The others watched, and it was Ruth who burst into a spontaneous version of "The Star Spangled Banner." Everyone joined in. It had been a spectacular ending to the best Thanksgiving ever in Bright's Pond.

Zeb placed the picnic basket into the truck after we said good-bye to everyone. Ruth stood on the curb looking like she had just been hit by a train.

"You all right?" I asked.

"Sure, sure, but if you don't mind I think I'd like to not come to see Agnes. I know I said I would, but I am just plumb tuckered out. And there is just so much cleanup yet to do."

"Don't you worry about that. I'll be by tomorrow to help clean up. Maybe you should just go to bed. You do look bushed."

"Griselda's right, Ruth. You take it easy for the rest of the night."

Zeb climbed into the driver's seat, which I will admit caught me a little off guard, not that he never drove before but I guess I was expecting to that night. I got into the passenger side.

"I hope she's not thinking we forgot about her," I said. "I was expecting to be at Greenbrier two hours ago."

Zeb pulled away from the curb. "She's OK. I'm sure they have stuff going on up there to help pass the time."

"But still, I can't imagine a worse place than a nursing home on Thanksgiving—or any holiday."

Zeb reached his arm out for me to snuggle close to him as we drove the short distance to Greenbrier.

"Ruth did a great job," I said.

"She sure did. But next year, Grizzy, it's you and me. We'll be hosting Thanksgiving in *our* home."

I pushed my head into his shoulder and felt his warmth tingle through my body. "It will be nice."

The nursing home was all lit up when we got there. It looked like every light in the place was on. The parking lot was still pretty full so we had to park a little ways away from the building.

"I'm glad so many people at least visit their loved ones."

Zeb grabbed the picnic basket, and we headed for the front door. The wind had kicked up like it usually did that time of day. Breezes seemed to blow down from the mountains as night fell. The sky was dotted with stars as a half-moon shone with a halo around it.

"Doesn't a halo mean rain?" I asked.

Zeb looked to the sky. "You mean around the moon? I think that's what they say. Maybe rain tomorrow."

Zeb pulled open the door.

"Have you ever been to Agnes's room?"

"Nope. First time here."

And well, I suppose Zeb couldn't have chosen a worse time to get a first impression of Greenbrier because just as we walked a few steps down the hall, Haddie Grace came whizzing down the hallway on her tricycle, ringing her bell and laughing as Nurse Sally gave chase.

"What in tarnation?" Zeb said, jumping out of Haddie's path.

"Haven't you heard about what's been happening here?"

"I heard some talk, but I didn't pay it much attention."

After Haddie came a woman I didn't recognize until she got closer. It was nasty Eula Spitwell on skates. She whizzed by with a great big, "Hellooooo."

"Oh, dear," I said. "I think it's getting worse."

"What is?"

"It seems the residents are acting strange. Like children many of them, others like teenagers and young lovers."

"Young lovers?"

"Yep, Faith Graves who is ninety years old is fixing to marry Clive Dickens this Saturday—he's just eighty-six. Boris is officiating."

"No way."

"Yep. It's true. That why Mildred has been spending so much time up here. She thinks that fella, Leon Fontaine, has something to do with what's going on."

"Leon? The fountain fella. The guy who built the gazebo?"

"Agnes told me they call it Lover's Hideaway," I said. "On account of that's where the folks go to make out and stuff."

"Eww," Zeb said. "That's not right."

"I know. I know. But until somebody figures out what in tarnation is going on, there's not much anyone can do except keep them safe."

"I bet. Should old people be on roller skates?"

"Probably not. But you can't stop them. Doctor Silver has already treated two broken hips and one heart attack."

Zeb shook his head.

"Come on," I said. "Agnes is down the hall."

We passed the common area where families were visiting residents. I saw some folks holding hands with visitors whispering, laughing. Others were crying. And one small group looked to be praying off in a corner.

"I really hate this place," I said. "All these lives coming to an end together. And then others in various states of limbo. They're too sick or disabled to do anything except sit around here and—"

Zeb stopped me. "Shhh, let's just enjoy the day."

We found Agnes sitting in her room. She was peering out the window toward the gazebo that had been lit up with what looked like a thousand small light bulbs. It looked magical.

"Agnes," I said. "Happy Thanksgiving."

She turned her chair. "Griselda. You finally made it."

"Sorry. I had a little trouble getting away from Ruth's."

Zeb put the picnic basket on Agnes's tray table. "Happy Thanksgiving, Agnes."

She merely harrumphed at him.

"I thought Ruth was coming. And the others. You said you'd bring the party."

"I know, I'm sorry. Everyone got tired and full. You know how it is after a turkey dinner."

"I suppose," Agnes said, eyeing the picnic basket. "What did you bring me?"

"Oh, boy, lots and lots of goodies. Turkey, vegetables, mashed potatoes, gravy, pie. Everything."

"Good-o," I am starving. "If you coulda seen that meal that they tried to pass off as Thanksgiving dinner! It was awful. Gravy should never have lumps like that or other gelatinous goo floating around in it. And the potatoes tasted like wall-paper paste. I think they coulda been used to glue just about anything."

I set out the food and Agnes ate, happily making yummy noises with nearly every bite.

"So," I said. "It seems the folks around here are still acting weird."

"Oh, Griselda, it's getting worse. Every time I turn around something else is happening. People on skates, bikes. Two of the men built a teeter-totter outside with two rain barrels and the bench seat. One of them went flying and is in the hospital." She chewed her turkey leg. "Someone better figure this out—and soon."

Zeb tugged my sweater sleeve. "Tell her our news."

"Oh, yeah, sure. Agnes, Zeb and I are getting married."

She dropped her turkey into her plate. "Really? Just like that? Wow."

"Not just like that," Zeb said. "We've been talking about it for a long time."

"I know," Agnes said. "Well, when did you decide this?"

"Tonight, after dinner. Right in Ruth Knickerbocker's kitchen," Zeb said.

Agnes mixed peas into her mashed potatoes. "Well, I guess congratulations are in order." But she wasn't pleased. It was hard not to hear the confusion in her voice.

"Aren't you happy for us?" Zeb said.

"Sure, I am. It's just that I know you two have had your ups and downs and—"

"It's only up from here," Zeb said. "I'm going to make your sister very happy."

"I hope so. The two of you have had more breakups than a box of Mrs. Stumpnagle's Peanut Brittle."

Then all of a sudden, we heard a mighty crash and yelling and screaming.

"What was that?" I said.

Agnes, who seemed unmoved and not even a little bit startled by the sound, said through chews, "Haddie Grace probably had another accident. From the sound of it, I'd say she slammed into a medicine cart."

"Oh, dear," Zeb said. He went out to investigate.

"Griselda," Agnes said once Zeb was out of the room. "What are you doing? Are you really fixing to marry that man? Are you sure?"

I looked at my feet. "It happened so fast. We were all happy and Don Ho was singing "Tiny Bubbles" and then we flamed the cake and then he asked me. Well, actually he told me. He said we should stop playing games, and I think he's right. It's time to settle."

Agnes swallowed whatever she was chewing hard. "Games. He's the only one who was playing games."

"I know, Agnes, but what can I do now? I already said—"

"Said what?" Zeb came back into the room.

"Said Ruth's dessert was amazing and I can't wait for Agnes to try it."

"You were right. That crazy old woman took a spill and slid right into the cart. Nothing happened. The nurse took her back to her room."

Zeb and I watched Agnes finish her Thanksgiving meal. She and Zeb barely made eye contact, and I could tell Zeb was nervous. He sat in the visitor's chair and twiddled his thumbs.

"Never took you for a twiddler," Agnes said finally.

Zeb looked up. "What?"

"A twiddler," Agnes repeated. "Your thumbs."

Zeb looked down and saw that his fingers were intertwined and his thumbs were rolling around each other like root beer barrels in a gumball machine.

"And speaking of dessert," I said.

"We weren't," Agnes said.

"We are now. Are you ready for something spectacular?"

I took Agnes's slice of Ruth's surprise from the wicker basket. "I need a match, Zeb."

Zeb reached into his pocket and handed me the book of matches. I set the plate on Agnes's table. "You might want to lean back as far as you can."

I doused the cake with some of the Brandy lemon juice mixture and then struck the match, touched it to the surface and the cake went up in flames.

"Yee ha!" Agnes said. "That's wonderful. Look at it go. How do I eat it?"

"You can blow out the flames," I said.

"I hate to do that, it's so pretty."

But at that moment I heard someone in the hall holler FIRE! FIRE! And then we heard people scrambling and running. "Oh, dear," I said. "I better go tell them—" It was too late. The next thing I heard was the fire alarm. And once the alarm had sounded there was no stopping an evacuation.

I ran to the hallway and tried to find someone in charge. I saw Nurse Sally. She was issuing orders to the orderlies and nurses. "Get everyone outside. Outside."

"No, no," I called. "It's a false alarm."

No one paid me any attention. I tried to make my way to Sally but my path was blocked as an orderly pushed two people in wheelchairs toward the doors. "Sally," I called over the confusion. "It's OK."

By the time I had gotten to her, I saw Zeb pushing Agnes down the hall. "What are you doing?" I hollered.

"They made me do it," Zeb said.

Agnes was laughing so hard I thought she'd split a gut. It was clear by then that I couldn't do anything else, and so I joined the group outside. There we all stood waiting in the cold autumn air for nothing. Waiting for the fire company to arrive.

"It was just cake," I whispered to Sally. "I brought Agnes a slice of pineapple surprise cake and, well, we flamed it. You know, flambé?" I gave a little sweep of my hand.

Sally looked daggers at me. "You what? This is a false alarm?"

"See any flames? Smell any smoke?"

"No, but, but now we are obliged to wait for the fire company to get here. The fire marshal must give the all clear before I can get all these cold, tired, and soon to be angry people back indoors."

"I am so sorry." I suppressed a smile. "But you gotta admit it is an exciting way to finish off the evening."

Sally grinned. "It was pretty exciting."

"Too bad Asa isn't here with his fireworks," Zeb said.

"Oh, please, that's all we need," Sally said. "These people are already pretending to be nine years old. Can you imagine—" She stopped talking and hollered, "Jasper York, you get down from that tree this instant!"

But when the fire truck arrived with screaming sirens and flashing lights, the "children" in the crowd rushed toward it. I heard Jasper York holler, "I want to ring the bell. Can I ring the bell?"

The firefighters made their way into the building as Sally and me and whoever else we could enlist snagged people off the truck and attempted to keep everyone quiet.

Fortunately, the firefighters didn't take long to complete their inspection. One of the officers came out of the building carrying the jar of the flammable liquid I brought. He was walking toward Sally.

"Are you in charge here?" the officer asked.

Sally cracked up. "Yes, yes, sir, I am. I mean for tonight. Doctor Silver is the medical director."

I couldn't help it and laughed right along with Sally and Agnes and Zeb.

"We found no fire. But we did find this—are you aware this is a flammable liquid?"

I laughed harder. "Yes." I managed to say through tears and laughter. "I brought it so I could flame Agnes's pineapple surprise."

The fireman looked at me like I was the worst criminal on the planet. "You what? Flame what? Pineapple what?"

"Surprise," I said. "Kind of like cherries jubilee only it's pineapple mango upside-down jubilee or something like that."

The officer handed me the jar. "You could have created a serious situation here, Ma'am."

"Yes sir," I said. "I won't do it again."

"Happy Thanksgiving," he said. Then he called his men to the truck. "And get those people off my truck." And off they went.

———— ✦ ————

It took a little longer to get all the residents back into the building and into their rooms than it did to get them out. Sally had to take an inventory and make sure every person was accounted for. Zeb and I helped as much as we could.

"That was fun," Agnes said when we arrived back at her room. "I can't believe how fast you got me out of here, Zeb."

"You're getting lighter, Agnes."

In a way it was nice. Nothing like a good old-fashioned false alarm fire drill to make people friends. Impending disaster was great for soothing old wounds.

I was still laughing as Agnes finished her cake. "At least they didn't confiscate your cake."

"It's good," Agnes said. "I got to hand it to Ruth. Make sure you tell her how much I enjoyed it."

Zeb stood near the window looking out at the gazebo. "That's quite a piece of craftsmanship. I wonder why he makes everything so crooked."

"Because he's a crooked little man with a crooked nose and so he makes crooked things," Agnes said. "He might even be a little cross-eyed."

"I don't know," I said. "I think it's awfully suspicious. I think he has something to do with the people acting so weird around here."

"Ah c'mon," Zeb said turning around, "what could he possibly have to do with it?"

"Ever hear of the Fountain of Youth?" I asked.

I thought Agnes was going to choke on her cake. "Are you kidding?"

"I don't know what to think," I said.

Zeb pulled me in for a hug. "Let Mildred and the folks in charge of Greenbrier figure it out. We have a wedding to plan."

Agnes choked again.

"Rrr-right," I said. "The wedding." I buried my face in Zeb's shoulders as a shiver wriggled down my spine. A *wedding*.

My mind was just not on my work at the library—which wasn't all that invigorating—I restocked books, dusted, opened mail, and read a magazine.—After I finished, I decided a long walk home might be the ticket. All I kept thinking about all day was Zeb and planning a wedding. I had no clue where to even start. I just figured we'd invite folks to the church, pastor Speedwell would do his thing, and then it'd be done. But as I leafed through some of the women's magazines— including *Modern Bride*, my hands got sweaty and my heart pounded. Cake, flowers, reception, music. It all sounded so daunting and not the least bit enjoyable. But maybe it had less to do with the work involved and more to do with Zeb. I was feeling so mixed up I was driving even myself nuts over it. But I couldn't help feeling like something was missing between us.

One of the magazine articles said something about speaking with the pastor before the ceremony. That might be important. As weird as I thought our pastor was, he was still our pastor. He would still be the one to do the pronouncing, so I'd ask Zeb to make an appointment.

As I straightened up and made sure windows were locked and shades drawn, I remembered that Clive and Faith were set to tie the knot the next day. "I bet they didn't plan some huge affair," I said out loud. "I bet they just got a license, scheduled Boris, and paid him ten bucks to do it." Short. Sweet. And to the point. I hated rigmarole.

The day was cold but nice. Winter was definitely in the air and I thought I even smelled a hint of snow in the air as I started down the library steps. I heard a rustle in the bushes. "Mickey Mantle," I called. "You come out of there."

I waited, but he didn't show. So I spread apart the branches and much to my surprise saw my little friend Mercy Lincoln. "Mercy. What in tarnation are you doing in those bushes?"

She pushed her way out. "Just playin', Miz Griselda. I was hidin' from that Mickey Mantle, but he took off long ago and hasn't come back to find me."

I helped her onto the pavement. She was only wearing a little blue windbreaker and thin pants. "Where's your heavy coat? It's downright cold today."

"Mama didn't get one big 'nuf. I done outgrew my other."

"Oh, Mercy. OK. I'll get you a coat. Now you run back home and I'll get it to you. Don't want you catching a cold."

"Oh, no, I won't catch no cold. I never catch cold. Not like some of the other children. Some of them been coughing something fierce."

"OK, Mercy. I'll ask Doc Flaherty to stop by and see if he'll check out some of the families."

"Thank you. But . . . I was wonderin' something, too."

"What's that?"

"I was wonderin' if I could get me another book ta read. I plumb read all I got."

"You finished *Heidi* and *Sherlock Holmes* already?"

"Oh, yes'm. That Mr. Holmes is one right smart fella."

"Where's the book?"

"It's ta home."

"Well, the library is closed right now so—"

But Mercy had a way of looking at me that pierced my heart every time. And besides, a short visit in a warm place might do her more good than sending her back to the hovel right away.

I opened the door and in she ran straight for the radiator. She warmed her hands like it was a fireplace. "It's so nice and warm in here. A body could live in a place like this. With all the books. Then I'd never run out."

"I can't let you do that, Mercy. But let's go find you a new book."

A few minutes later, I checked out a copy of *Moby Dick* for Mercy.

"Now it's a big book, with lots of adventure and lots of stuff about whales."

"Oh, I know that. I heard of this here book."

I locked up and turned off the lights. "Now you go straight home. No more chasing Mickey Mantle."

"OK, Miz Griselda. Now that I got a new book to read."

And off she ran toward the backwoods where she lived with just her mother and a few chickens. Most of the families in the backwoods were poor as dirt and relied on others to keep them in clothes and sometimes food. The Society of Angelic Philanthropy was great at keeping the little ones in shoes and the adults when they could. I planned to tell Tohilda Best, this year's current president of the SOAP that Mercy Lincoln and her mother needed warm coats and some looking after.

I still felt like walking and made my way toward Hector's Hill. It was a special place for me and probably for many of the folks in town. The hill overlooked the town on one side and the mountains always seemed closer on the other. It was where we flew kites as kids and where Cliff Cardwell made his emergency landing a few months ago. He kept Matilda, his airplane, parked there.

Boy she looked nice, Matilda I mean. Cliff kept her clean and in excellent running order. I stood there looking at her like she was a long-lost friend and imagined flying solo, dipping my wings as I passed over the town. I imagined soaring over the Blue Mountains and turning right at the first star I see and flying straight on 'til morning.

My reverie was broken by Cliff's soft, leading-man voice.

"Hey, Griselda, you looking for me, kid?"

I turned. The sun glinted off his bomber jacket as the light breeze rippled his hair.

"Cliff. No, I was just taking a walk and came by here."

He walked closer. "I understand congratulations are in order."

"Congratulations?"

"Yeah, silly, you and Zeb. Engaged. To be married." He held up his left hand and pointed to his ring finger.

"Oh, yeah. Word gets around fast."

"I was just at the Full Moon. Zeb is on cloud nine. So is Dot Handy. It's all everyone is talking about. This is going to be some wedding. I bet every single person in Bright's Pond and Paradise will come out."

My stomach wobbled as I swallowed what seemed like a large, sour lemon drop.

"Oh, yeah? That's . . . great. It will be fun—the wedding I mean."

Cliff walked right up to me. "Why don't you seem so happy?"

"Oh, I am." I looked away from him. "I guess it's normal to have some nerves."

"I thought the guy was supposed to be the one with cold feet."

"It's not that. I'm sure I'm ready to get married. I'm only wondering about the changes it will bring. I lived with Agnes so long and now I'm finally on my own—mostly—and now I'll be living with : . . a husband."

"I'm gonna hate myself for saying this but you and Zeb belong together. It's one of those marriages made in heaven. It just took you both some time to see it."

I smiled. "Are you taking her up?"

"Yeah, I have to fly into Wilkes-Barre and pick up a passenger and take him to Philly."

"Philly? That's a long flight."

"Kind of long. Don't usually like those flights. But the money is good."

"He sounds important."

"She. And I don't know anything about the situation. I just fly them where they want to go. But it's not unusual for a business person to hire a private pilot when they have an important business matter."

"I suppose so." I rubbed the wing again. "Have a good flight."

I started to walk away. Cliff grabbed my elbow. "Griselda. I really am happy for you." He looked into my eyes. "If this is what you want, that is. I know what I just said and all but . . . but are you sure he's the one for you?"

"He is, Cliff. It's just a lot to get used to."

He let go and I walked back toward the street, fighting the urge to look back. When I got to the street, I waited until I heard the engine start and watched Cliff take off into the clouds.

13

Monday after I shooed the last of the students out of the library I headed for the café. The Yuletide Committee was meeting. At our last meeting, we learned that the Moose had decided to pull out of the parade unless the mystery of Greenbrier was resolved. I couldn't blame them, not really. They were, after all, a group dedicated to civic duty and pride. A drug scandal would not be something they'd like to be associated with.

Everyone was there this time, which for a Bright's Pond committee of any sort was a rarity. Dot Handy sat with her handy dandy notebook, Studebaker and Boris were yakking about something. Ruth was sewing something on her lap. Mildred was standing up, leaning against the counter like she was poised to dash out the door in case of emergency. Even Nate Kincaid showed up. Nate was our best carpenter and generally saw that the floats were assembled in time.

He usually kept them on his farm property. It was the only place in town big enough. The Bright's Pond Christmas Parade was a sight and well worth it to stand in the cold night air and watch her go by. The parade was always held at night on account of the lights. And that way, mothers and daddies could get their kids home and straight to bed after the festivities.

This year we scheduled the parade for Monday, December 23, and as usual, it would start at the Kincaid Farm on account of that's where the floats were and travel down Filbert into the town square and then head east toward the church and the town limit. Then the whole shootin' match would be turned around, regrouped, and paraded back down Filbert, past the town hall and up toward Paradise.

It was Studebaker's job to organize the parade and the order in which the participants walked or drove or marched. At various places along the parade route, the entire thing would halt while the onlookers enjoyed a performance.

"And then," Studebaker said, "that is where the high school choir will sing a few carols, and Miss Almira's Dance Academy will do their usual tap dance to 'Jingle Bells.'"

Boris hung his head. "I hate tap dancing."

We all knew that. He said it every year.

"But those girls dance their hearts out," Ruth said. "There. All finished." She held up a long, brown robe. Only three more to go. We got some tall shepherds this year. I've had to alter them all. Must have been a mass growth spurt. I still got the sheep to mend. But they're easy."

The sheep were always played by the little kids—the toddlers, and invariably one of the sheep, would lose his way during the play and need to be brought back into the fold. The sheep costumes were simply white sweatshirts with cotton balls glued and sewn all over them. The sheep heads were hoods with sewed-on ears. Every year some of the cotton got lost or crushed and needed to be replaced, and an ear or two would need fixing.

Dot coughed. "Who is driving the Grand Marshal, and—by the way—who is the Grand Marshal this year, and what will they be driving?"

"Didn't you hear?" Zeb said. "They were thinking about making Cliff Cardwell the Grand Marshal on account of him being a pilot and all. Course they didn't ask the committee."

I swallowed. "Really? But—" I looked around the group. It was useless to argue, but I asked the question anyway. "When was that decided?"

"Oh, Nate and Stu and Boris were down at Personals Pub the other night and got to talking about it," Zeb said. "Cliff seemed a natural choice—to them. I wasn't too hepped up on it when they told me."

"I think he's a great choice," Nate said. "We never had a bona fide pilot in our parade before. The kids will love him."

"Yeah, he can hand out red buttons and licorice," Dot said. "The kids love them, and they love him, and isn't that why we have the parade every year? for the children?"

"Yes, of course," I said. "But this committee does operate by a democratic process. It's not right that you all went off and made the choice without consulting the rest of the committee."

"Oh, don't be such a stick in the mud," Stu said. "Cliff is the best man for the job. Who else is there?"

I looked at Zeb. We were both thinking the same thing. It wasn't really about Cliff being the right choice for Grand Marshal. We were upset because it was Cliff and neither one of us really wanted to work with him. But Nate would take care of it, and hopefully Zeb and I would only have to wave as he passed the reviewing stand.

Boris banged his gavel on the table. Zeb winced. "I wish you wouldn't do that to my table," he said. "Just tap your water glass, for corn sake."

"Sorry, force of habit," Boris said. "I am a judge, you know. So it's decided. Cliff Cardwell is this year's Grand Marshal."

"Looks that way," Zeb said. "Has anyone told him?"

"I did," Nate said. "He's happy to do it. Thought it might even be fun to tow Matilda down the street. What do you all think about that? Maybe Santa can arrive in Cliff's airplane instead of that rickety old sleigh you pull out of Ivy Slocum's garage every year. That thing is older than the hills, and it's a wonder it doesn't just crumble away."

"That's a great idea," Boris said. "The kiddos will love it. Santa in an airplane. What a hoot."

I looked at Mildred who had been very quiet through the whole meeting. "Any problem with towing an airplane down the street, Mildred?"

She looked up from whatever thought she was deep into. "No, no. I think it will be OK."

"Uhm, hum," Zeb said, obviously wanting to divert the attention away from Cliff. "Now what about food? I suspect we'll have the usual pies and soft drinks, coffee, hot chocolate."

"Yep," Dot said. "I got the church ladies on it."

Our dear friend Cora Nebbish had always been in charge of food. This would the first year without her. She died several months ago. I knew it was still hard on Zeb. She had been his waitress for many years and they were very close friends. It would be sad to get married without Cora.

"OK, good," Stu said. "You can set the tables out as usual right near the town hall. Just make sure none of the Sterno pots get tipped over this year. Don't want the paper snowflake doilies catching fire again."

"I'll keep an eye out, Captain," Dot said with a salute.

"Don't make light of it," Mildred said. "Fire is serious business. The food tables must be manned at all times."

"They will be," Dot said. "All I do is serve food."

"And what about the ice skating afterward? Will the pond be frozen enough?" Studebaker asked. "I tested it just yesterday and I got to say I'm a little concerned."

"Let's just call the skating off," Boris said. "We can schedule a town skate sometime in January."

"Works for me," Zeb said. "We can do a weenie roast out there and build a bonfire."

"I move we cancel ice skating this time around," I said. "We don't want any kids slipping through the ice this year."

"Second," Ruth said. She liked to second. It was like her main job in the committee. That and sewing.

The meeting went on for another hour or so before all the questions had been answered and schedules planned and floats named. Nate said he had six on his land, including the Frost sisters' annual *O' Holy Night* tractor, complete with nativity, and Zeb's Full Moon Café entry. It was pretty much the same every year—a small flatbed pulled by one of Nate's tractors. A giant full moon hung over a replica of the café counter. Bill Tompkins usually rode on it dressed as a snowman and handed out lollipops.

"That reminds me," I said. "What about the pageant? The kids' play. Has anyone found a Mary?"

Glances were exchanged around the table.

"Guess it'll have to be Babette again," Ruth said.

"Well, I have a suggestion. How about Mercy Lincoln?"

"You mean that backwoods girl you're always telling me about? The little girl who comes to the library?" Ruth said.

"Yes. I ran into her a little while ago. She's cute and curious and smart. I think she'll be perfect and love the chance to do it."

I watched as more glances and raised eyebrows were passed around the table. I figured everyone would agree that it was a good suggestion except maybe Nate Kincaid. I was correct.

"Isn't she a Negro?" he said just as blatant as a wart on a thumb.

"Yes, but why should that matter?" I said.

"Mary was not . . . colored," Nate said. "It . . . it wouldn't be right."

"But that's not the point," Studebaker said. "Jesus was born for all mankind, not just the white folk. I say Mercy Lincoln should be our Mary. All in favor say aye."

All hands around the table shot up lickety-split. All except Nate who reluctantly and only after a nudge from Stu. His hand raised just slightly.

Nate shook his head. "I'll go along with it because the majority rules, but I want to go on the record as saying I was against it."

"Did you get that written down, Dot?" I said. "Nate Kincaid is prejudiced."

"I am not," he said. "I was just trying to keep the play . . . authentic."

"Uhm-hum," Ruth said. "This from a man who raised an orange pumpkin like it was his own kin."

Boris laughed so hard I thought he might swallow his cigar, which thankfully was not lit. The man just couldn't stand to be without a cigar in his hand. It was his trademark, kind of like George Burns, only George Burns was funny.

"I'll ask her today," I said. "Just think of it. Maybe some of the other families back in the woods will come out. Could be a good thing."

"Yes indeedy," Ruth said. "The SOAP ladies have been trying to get some of them families out to church for years. But they stick so close. It might not be as easy as you think to have Mercy play the part. Some folks back there could get up in arms about it."

"Thanks, Ruth. I'll be sure and speak with her mama."

"Just don't go alone," Zeb said. "Those woods can be dangerous."

"I'll be fine," I said. "The Society ladies go back there all the time."

"As long as she's with Mercy, no one will bother her," Ruth said.

And she would know from her work with the SOAP. Those women knew their way around the backwoods, and more important, they knew the proper protocol when it came to calling on one of the families.

Stu looked over his clipboard. "I think that about wraps up all that was on the Yuletide Committee agenda. If there are no further remarks or questions, I move the meeting be adjourned until December 19 at 6:30 p.m. at which time we will discuss any last-minute issues that arise. Other than that, I say we're good to go."

"I second the motion," Ruth said.

"Meeting adjourned," Boris said with a rap of his gavel. "Now, on to more serious business. Mildred," he said turning in her direction, "any progress on Operation Greenbrier?"

Mildred straightened up. All the men smiled as she pulled herself up to her full height. "I have a little news to report. But not much. It's still a mystery, but as you all know I am investigating a Mr. Leon Fontaine."

"The man who built the fountain?" Boris said.

"That's correct, sir. There's some scattered reports that Leon claims the water in that fountain has certain . . . properties."

"Properties?" Boris said. "What in tarnation are you saying?"

"She's saying that people are thinking it's Fountain of Youth water, near as we can ascertain," I said. And with those words the entire committee lost control and laughed so hard I thought they'd all split a gut. Well, all except Ruth, who kept right on sewing the ear on a brown sheep hood.

When they quieted down I spoke. "We know it sounds silly, but what if he's convinced the residents up there that it is the Fountain of Youth and he's giving them water and—"

Boris banged his gavel. "Griselda, you've slipped a gear. There is no such thing as the Fountain of Youth, and even if Leon Fontaine is giving people the water and claiming it's got youthful properties, it doesn't work."

"I know. I know," I said.

Zeb came to my rescue. "Maybe we should let Griselda finish saying what she has to say."

I smiled at him. "Thank you."

Studebaker chuckled. "Should that be, 'thank you, darling'?"

"I will admit that Leon is a little weird," I said, choosing to ignore Stu's comment. "And the odd behavior did start after he got to town. But we can't go arresting him on trumped-up charges. There's no proof he's really done anything wrong."

"Still no such thing as the Fountain of Youth," Boris said.

"Why are you defending him?" Zeb asked me.

"I kind of like him. He's like a knight in shining armor or something. Out to save the world."

"But he's a shyster," Zeb said. "Plain and simple."

"Not really. He believes all this. So that makes him more, I don't know, unstable, but still, I don't see any need to go off and arrest him," I said. "Maybe it's just the power of suggestion. Maybe the folks are doing it to themselves. He's just making the suggestion."

"Power of suggestion?" Nate said. "You mean like hypnosis? That's mind control, and in my book it's just as bad as the power of drugs or that wacky weed the kids smoke."

"No one is smoking wacky weed at Greenbrier," I said.

"Yeah. I'd a smelled it," Mildred said. "Can't miss that aroma."

"Maybe you better get out there and see what you can find," Boris said. His voice took on a decidedly authoritarian tone. Every so often he liked to show off that he was, after all, Mildred's boss and kind of the town mayor, even though it wasn't official. "Ask some questions of them old people. Look for signs of goofy water being sold or drank or . . . something. Lord knows we don't need anyone getting hurt out there on account of whatever it is Mr. Leon Fontaine is up to."

"Heading out there today, sir," Mildred said. She didn't let Boris get to her. She knew he was mostly bluster and had very little bite. But she did like to treat him with the respect a man in his position deserved even if the rest of the town didn't.

Ruth continued to tug and pull at the sheep head costume. She had seemed oblivious to the whole conversation about Leon. It became obvious that she was when she lifted her head and spoke. "I think Mercy Lincoln will make a very nice Mary. Only trouble is, since the family never goes to church, how am I supposed to fit her costume? I'd be afraid to go out to her home with Mary robes. I could get my rump filled with buckshot. Most of those folks have very definite opinions about God."

"It's a sheet," Stu said. "Just pin her up on the night of the pageant."

Ruth clicked her tongue. "That's not how I do things. Maybe I will just mosey back there—into the woods—and see if I can get her fitted. She's playing Mary for heaven's sake. If God were ever gonna protect me that would be the time. Will you go with me, Griselda?"

"Might not have to. She comes to the library a lot. Why don't I call you the next time I see her and you can run on up and do your fitting then? That is, of course, if I get her mama's permission to put her in the play."

Dot Handy was still scribbling on her legal pad. "Do it soon, Griselda," she said. "I got to get rehearsals in, and I need a Mary. Can't possibly have a Christmas pageant without a Mary."

"If she doesn't get to church," said Nate, "how can she be in the children's Sunday school play?"

"Because it's the right thing, Nate."

"Yeah," Zeb said. "You think Jesus would turn her away?"

Nate looked at his coffee cup. "I . . . I suppose not."

I squeezed Zeb's hand and whispered in his ear, "I am so proud of you."

The meeting broke up with another one planned for the following Monday.

"You all have a good day," Mildred said. "I'm going up to Paradise and see what I can figure out."

"Mind if I tag along?" I asked. "I'd like to talk to Rose Tattoo. I was hoping she might help paint some of the scenery for the play. I hear she's an artist."

"I hear she's a nut," Boris said. "Ever see her tattoos, and what's with that giant cement hand in her yard and all those paintings on her trailer?"

"Like I said, she's an artist."

"Yeah, so is Leon Fontaine," Mildred said. "A con artist."

"No, no," I said. "He's an ar-teest. There's a difference."

Mildred laughed. "Come on, let's go." Mildred popped her cop hat on her head. I slipped on my coat and zipped it up.

"See you all later," I said. "Good meeting."

Zeb pulled me aside. "I was thinking I'd like to see you tonight. Can I come by your house later, around eight?"

"Sure, that would be nice."

He kissed my cheek.

"See you then."

The first words out of Mildred's mouth when we got into her car were, "You know, for someone who just got engaged you sure don't act like it."

"What do you mean?"

"Ah, gee, Griselda. You can hardly look at him and you didn't seem all that happy to see him tonight. Shouldn't you be all giddy and hanging all over him?"

I didn't say anything at first. For at least a mile.

"It's just . . . just—"

"Cliff Cardwell?"

"No! Not Cliff—not exactly. I love Zeb. I really do. But I worry about him being a husband. He can be so—so jealous."

"Ah, all men are like that. He'll settle down."

"You think he will?"

"Sure. I was talking to my brother when we were in Wilkes-Barre for Thanksgiving. He said that Cliff sounds like adventure, but Zeb seems more secure. My brother is a businessman like Zeb."

"I get that," I said. "Zeb is more secure than Cliff. But it really isn't about that. I don't love Cliff."

I let another mile go by without a word. Then Mildred said, "Are you sure, absolutely positive, you aren't in love with Cliff?"

I looked out the window. The once colorful trees had lost most of their leaves. Another storm would bring them all down. "Not him. Just his airplane."

Mildred laughed. "Then you have no problem. Maybe it would help if you told Zeb your concern. Get it out in the open—now—before you say those vows."

"I think he already knows. But how do I get him to stop being jealous of an airplane? Of me just wanting to be . . . me . . . me with wings."

"You know something. As a police officer I pride myself on being a pretty good judge of character and I would say Cliff is a good man, not very industrious but a good man, level-headed. But Zeb? Now he's a good man, too, but if I were to stake my badge on who would give you the best life, you and your children? It'd be Zeb."

"Children? But I'm too old to have babies, and we never talked about it."

"Even so. Anything can happen."

<hr />

We drove under the Paradise Trailer Park sign and saw Asa right away near the entrance. He was burning a large pile of leaves. Large fingers of gray and brown smoke swirled above him and drifted into the park. Mildred stopped near him and rolled down her window, "Howdy, Asa. I'm looking for Leon."

Asa looked away for a second—obviously annoyed. "Ah, I keep telling you that man is not up to anything. He's a good guy. Little eccentric but—"

"Please," Mildred said. "Have you seen him?"

"I don't know. I haven't seen him today. You could try his trailer. It's the last one on Mango Street. Three down from Charlotte. It's got orange awnings, can't miss it."

"Thanks," Mildred said. She pulled slowly away taking the speed bump with caution.

"Charlotte Figg is a nice woman," I said.

"She is. I've only talked to her once, but I liked her well enough."

"She's opening a pie shop in town. Across from the town hall. In that old bakery. Kind of ironic, don't you think?"

"Really? That's great. But how does Zeb feel about that? Isn't his Full Moon Pie king of the pie hill?"

"He's actually OK about it, which surprises me. He likes Charlotte's pies."

"There it is," Mildred said. "Leon Fontaine's trailer."

Leon's trailer was white with the orange awnings Asa mentioned—pumpkin orange. It sat back from the road a bit, and a narrow wooden path led from the street to his front steps. His trailer had one of the makeshift porches tacked onto it. I noticed a windsock flying from his roof, a telescope in the front yard, and several baskets of hanging flowers from his roof.

"Uhm, wonder what he does with that telescope?" Mildred said.

"Looks at the stars, I suppose. He seems the type that would stargaze."

"Why, because he's so moonstruck? Or is he looking into the windows of his neighbors' trailers?"

"That's not nice. Were you this suspicious as a child?"

Mildred turned off the ignition.

"Should I stay or go find Rose?"

"No, stay, sometimes two sets of eyes and ears are better than one."

Mildred approached Leon's door. She knocked several times. No answer.

"Guess he's not home," I said.

"I'll just check out back," Mildred said.

She moved like a stealthy cougar around his trailer. I decided to follow—just out of curiosity. And, no, I didn't strike a stealthy pose. I just walked.

Leon's backyard was filled with little sculptures of gnomes, mushrooms, and angels. I counted five of those gazing or butterfly balls. I saw four tall sculptures made from tin cans and tires, bicycle handlebars, and all manner of random and loose objects. I also saw several acetylene torches and a welder's mask.

"He is weird," Mildred said.

"He's an ar-teest. A lover of art and apparently a sculptor."

"Sculptor? It's scrap metal and garbage welded together."

I stood near one that resembled a conquistador and a skinny horse. "Look, I thought he reminded me of someone. Don Quixote."

"That's Don Quixote?"

"Sure. It's a self-portrait or self-sculpt. He fancies himself a hero."

"Goes with the pathology of a psychopath," Mildred said.

We continued to look around the yard when the thought occurred to me, "Are we allowed to be snooping around the man's property?"

"I won't tell if you won't."

Mildred made her way to a small shed. The lock was open. She opened the door slowly like she was expecting Leon or a jack-in-the-box to pop out.

"Well, what have we here?" she said.

14

W hat?" I called. "What did you find?"

"Looks to me like about a hundred or so little . . . bottles, containers. They're all shaped like teardrops like he somehow got his hands on a thousand perfume bottles."

"Bottles?" I nearly ran to the shed, tripping over a gnome.

"Well, I'll be darned. What do you suppose Leon Fontaine is doing with those?"

"Can't say for 100 percent certainty, but I have a suspicion he's filling them with something."

"Water?"

"Uh-huh. That'd be my first guess. Have you seen any bottles like these at the nursing home?"

"No, but I wasn't looking and even if I did I probably would have just figured it for perfume."

"He's a crafty one."

Mildred poked her head inside further. "Wonder what else he has in here."

All of a sudden, we heard a noise at the front of the trailer.

"It's him," Mildred said.

"Come on. Let's get out of here before he catches us."

"Shhh, it's OK. We'll just go have a talk with him."

She pocketed one of the bottles and closed the shed door gingerly. And then indicated with her head for me to follow. Leon Fontaine was in the front of the house. I saw him grab what looked like a bag of groceries from his car—a very beat-up Buick, maroon with a white stripe and more dents than the moon. Today he wore a brown vest and a brown fedora with a half a peacock feather.

"Why, hello there," he called. "Fancy meeting you here. Come to admire my artwork, I see."

"How you doing, Mr. Fontaine?" Mildred called. "Mind if I ask you some questions?"

"Leon Fontaine never turns down an officer of the law's request for an audience."

Mildred whispered, "I want to see inside his trailer somehow—see if we can take a look around."

"And Griselda Sparrow," Leon said. "It's most definitely a pleasure to see you too. Let everyone in the world halt, unless the entire world acknowledges that nowhere on earth is there a damsel more beautiful than—"

"Cervantes," I said. "And he was talking about Dulcinea."

"Ah, you are quick," Leon said. "But none the less beautiful."

"Would you mind if we came inside for a few minutes, Mr. Fontaine?" asked Mildred. "I just have a few more questions."

"My home is yours fair lady, although I must tell you that . . . well, housekeeping is not one of my strengths. I would much rather be engaged in the service of others."

I watched Mildred's eyes roll around in their sockets.

Leon pulled open the screen door and then pushed open the metal door to his trailer. It opened into a small foyer and then a larger room that divided into a kitchen. I assumed bedrooms were down the narrow hall.

"If a man's home is his castle," said Leon, "then welcome to Inverness."

Mildred walked right in and stood in the middle of the living room with her arms folded across her chest as though she were waiting for a classroom of children to settle down.

"Nice place," I said as I looked around at all the oddities. Jars of strange goo, about a million books in bookshelves and stacked along the walls, piles of magazines. I saw the entire *Encyclopedia Britannica*, a skull with emerald eyes, several snakeskins nailed to the wall, a framed picture of Albert Einstein, and a copy of *Don Quixote* under glass.

"It was always one of my favorites, also," I said, indicating the book.

"God, Who provides for all, will not desert us; especially being engaged, as we are, in His service," Leon said. His eyes twinkled.

"What?" Mildred said. "What's he talking about?"

"He's quoting the book."

"Oh, well, now, let's get down to the facts, please," Mildred said.

"Facts, dear lady," said Leon, "are the enemy of truth."

"The book," I whispered to Mildred. "It's the book."

It was at that point quite clear to me that Leon Fontaine fancied himself a kind of man from La Mancha, a Don Quixote, and I will admit that I had grown even more enamored and intrigued with him at that moment.

"Now then, Mr. Fontaine," Mildred said pulling her little notebook from her shirt pocket. "Just a few questions for the record first."

"Record? Record," said Leon. "Why keep records on me? I am but a poor man, an ar-teest and a do-gooder as it were. Nothing more nor less nor somewhere in between."

Mildred sucked in a deep breath. "What was your previous address before coming to Paradise?"

"Ah, Paradise, such a lovely name, don't you think? I came here only after my services were no longer needed by her lady Francesca DeLaRue."

Mildred rolled her eyes. "Now look, you have got to come clean and just tell me the truth."

"Truth? I perceive everything I say as absolutely true, and deficient in nothing whatever, and paint it all in my mind exactly as I want it to be." He raised his eyebrows in a kind of smirk and sat down on a stool with a red velvet seat cushion.

"Oh, he's good," I said.

"OK, look, I'm just gonna come right out and ask. What are you doing with all those bottles in the shed out back?"

Leon looked at me as though I could help him. "Is it customary for people around here to go snooping in another person's shed? Seems to me there should be a law about such things otherwise we could have mayhem—people going about walking into their neighbor's homes like they were theirs."

"The shed was open. I saw a lot of empty bottles, Mr. Fontaine."

"Is it a crime to keep empty bottles in a shed?"

"No, of course not. But why would you need so many?"

"Well, one can never have enough empty bottles, dear lady, and I for one simply like them. They—are useful here and there."

"Where is there?" I asked trying to decipher his strange answers. It was possible that "there" could have meant Greenbrier.

"Ahh, there is but a question and only I know the answer."

"That does it," Mildred said. "You're under arrest."

Leon backed away. "Arrest? You cannot arrest me. On what grounds?"

"Failure to cooperate with a police officer and just being an all-around nut job."

She unhooked her handcuffs from her utility belt. "Come on, Mr. Fontaine. Maybe we'll have better luck in jail."

"You can't do that," I said. "He hasn't done anything. Why are you doing this?" I was starting to feel just a wee bit angry that Mildred had lost her patience with Leon. The last place he belonged was jail.

Not surprisingly, Leon had something to offer, too. "Even Aristotle couldn't comprehend if he'd come back to life just for that purpose."

"I just think I'll have better luck getting the answers I need if we went into town," Mildred said. "It's cold outside, Mr. Fontaine. Do you have a jacket?"

"No, no, my heart is warm and therefore all of me."

Mildred helped Leon in her cruiser. He seemed almost happy to be going to jail but then again, it is part of the story. Don Quixote was imprisoned. I figured this arrest only empowered Leon.

"I think I'll stay here, in Paradise," I said. "Maybe I can learn something. And I still need to speak with Rose about the scenery."

"Suit yourself," Mildred said. "I need to get him processed. Honestly, I think he likes this."

"He does. But, Mildred, take it easy with him. He's really not out to hurt anyone. Don Quixote wanted to do chivalrous things, defend the poor, help damsels in distress."

"Yeah, yeah, and the Easter Bunny is real, too."

I watched them drive off and then headed out back to take a closer look at the bottles. From what I remembered of the book, Don liked to mix potions and such. It wasn't difficult to believe that Leon Fontaine, if that was really his name, was mixing up something for the folks at Greenbrier. I knew I was invading the man's privacy, but I really wanted to help. I was hoping to find something that would get him off the hook.

I searched through boxes and found small pieces of paper and some black markers. And then I found the most damning bit of evidence.

"Oh, Don," I said. "You're in trouble now, I think."

That was when Asa sneaked up behind me.

"What are you doing? This is private property."

I spun around on one foot knocking a case of bottles to the ground.

"Oh, Asa," I said. "I'm glad to see you."

"I don't understand. Why are you going through Leon's shed?"

"We didn't expect to, Asa. Mildred—you know who I mean—Mildred Blessing, Chief of Police in Bright's—"

"Yeah, I know her."

"Well, she thinks Leon is responsible for what is happening up at Greenbrier. We came up here to ask a few questions. He didn't answer his door so we came out here looking for him and found this." I pointed to the boxes of bottles.

"So what? It's bottles."

"And I found this, just now." I handed him the funny label.

"It says Fountain of Youth Water. I still don't get it."

"Isn't it obvious? Leon Fontaine has been bottling water from that fountain he built and selling it to the residents of Greenbrier as water from the Fountain of Youth. The man thinks he found the secret of longevity, right here, in Paradise."

Asa took a step back. "Ohh, so that's why—"

"They're all acting so crazy. They really think Leon Fontaine found the Fountain of Youth in Paradise. And so does he. He really believes it—I think. Unless this is his thing, going from trailer park to trailer park building fountains."

"Oh, man, I knew the guy was a little off his nut, but I never pegged him for a fraud or a con artist."

"Ar-teest," I said. "And in all fairness to him. He's not a fraud. Leon really believes this—that's probably why the residents at Greenbrier believe it. He can really sell it because I think he's convinced that water from the fountain over there is magical."

"So what now?"

"Not sure. Mildred arrested him and—"

"Arrested him? For what? Giving people water?"

"Nah, she got frustrated. You know how he talks circles around you. She took him down to the jail just to scare some answers out of him—I think. Although, I doubt she'll get any further."

Asa looked into the shed and scratched his head. "I had no idea he had all this stuff. I knew about all the garbage he collects for his sculptures, but that's his business, long as he keeps it to himself. But this, maybe he is the problem."

"It's really pretty sad, but yeah, it looks like Leon is creating the problems over there."

"How's it going up there anyway? Are they still all—" Asa turned his index finger in the air and made the universal crazy gesture.

"Not sure about that either. Maybe we just leave them alone for now. Wait until Mildred gets some answers, then I guess she'll talk to Doctor Silver."

"OK, but in the meantime, maybe I should turn the fountain off."

"Nah. I wouldn't. He's not hurting anyone—well, one broken hip and a bloody lip but you really can't blame him."

"I don't know, Griselda. I think you need to go right to the head of the nursing home and tell him. As manager of

Paradise—I still enjoy saying that—I can't just let it go. What if someone decides to sue us?"

"It's not Paradise's fault."

"But now I know about it. Well, I am at least going to speak with Hazel Crenshaw."

"Who?"

"Hazel Crenshaw. She owns Paradise. She lives down the road a piece. She'll know what to do."

"I guess you have to do what you have to do. But I'd hate to see Leon go to jail or get kicked out of Paradise for this."

"Nah, he ain't the devil. Just a little—misguided," Asa said with that calm tone I had come to expect from him.

"He thinks he's a hero, a knight in shining armor come to help people," I said. "He'll probably just move on after all this settles down. It's how he lives."

"Oh, he's helping all right," Asa said.

"Gotta admit, it's a great fountain."

"That much is true, at least."

"Well, I drove up here with Mildred, but I actually came to see Rose. Have you seen her?"

"She's one of two places, I reckon. Her trailer or Charlotte's."

"Thanks. Which way—"

"Rose's trailer is just down that way. You won't miss it. It's the one with the giant cement hand in the yard."

Asa looked at the bottles and shook his head. "I still can't believe this."

"It's not as bad as all that. It will get figured out and all will be well again."

"I suppose you're right," Asa said. He closed the shed door. "And listen, I can drive you back to town after your time with Rose if you'd like."

"Oh, thanks, Asa, that would be great."

"Just come by the office. I need to go into town anyway and see Stu."

"OK, I shouldn't be too long. I want to ask Rose if she'll help paint the scenery for the Sunday school Christmas pageant."

"Oh, she might do it. Long as it can be done up here."

"This way?" I pointed to the east.

"Yep. Just go to the corner, turn right and then about half-way down. You'll see the hand."

And he wasn't lying. A block or so down the road I saw it, the famous giant hand. It stood about eight feet off the ground with a rickety-looking ladder leaning against it. Part of me wanted to climb on up and see what it was like up there.

The rest of Rose's property was what I'd expect for an eccentric artist. The trailer was bright, sunflower yellow with images painted all over it—like one giant mural. She had hanging baskets of flowers and colorful pinwheels and whirligigs poking out from what amounted to a bed of weeds.

I knocked on her door and waited. No answer.

"She must be with Charlotte."

Fortunately, I knew where Charlotte's trailer was nestled amid the others, and I headed in that direction. But first, I couldn't fight the temptation anymore and climbed up the ladder and into the giant hand. I felt comforted right away if maybe a little damp from a small puddle of water leftover from the last rain. I lightly touched all the names so carefully painted there.

Now I will admit that I felt a little silly, but after a quick peek around and seeing that no one was looking, I sailed my own prayer. A prayer about Zeb and me asking for God's clear direction. I sailed a prayer for Leon and all the folks at Greenbrier, and I sailed a prayer for Mercy Lincoln as she came to mind. Such a sweet child living in such deplorable circumstances. But I knew God had her name written on his palm also.

After another quiet minute I climbed back down. "Uhm," I said to myself. "I think I'll come back here."

It still seemed remarkable to me that I didn't see any of the other trailer park residents as I walked toward Charlotte's. I smelled cooking though, onions frying, maybe bacon, barbecued chicken for sure. But the only life I saw was a stray kitten drinking water from a birdbath in someone's yard.

When I turned onto Charlotte's street I saw the long red car first, a convertible with several yards of gray duct tape on the convertible roof. "Must have sprung a leak at one time."

Charlotte's wooden walkway was slightly reminiscent of the one Nate Kincaid built for last year's Spring Dance. We had a Western theme and everyone dressed like cowboys and cowgirls. Except Cliff Cardwell, who was dashing enough in his bomber jacket. But I smiled at the memory of Nate wearing a skinny bolo tie with a silver clasp.

Charlotte's trailer looked old and out-of-date compared to some of the others I passed, but I did like the hanging baskets of autumn wildflowers she had dangling from the makeshift porch roof. I knocked on the door and then I heard a dog bark. Then I heard Charlotte. "Lucky, come on boy. Let me get the door."

The door opened.

"Griselda," Charlotte said. "What are you doing here? Come on in."

I stepped over the threshold and into another world. Charlotte's trailer was very much a trailer on the outside, but inside it was like a regular home with regular furniture and carpet, curtains, and the cutest little kitchen I had ever seen.

But how she made all those pies in that space was beyond me. Charlotte Figg was truly a pie genius.

"I was here with Mildred and actually came to see Rose. But she wasn't at her trailer so I took a chance that she might be here."

"I am," Rose said coming out of the bathroom. "How are you, Griselda?"

"I'm fine. I was just telling Charlotte that I came with Mildred but I was really looking for you."

"Is she still after Leon?" Charlotte asked showing me to a sofa. "Sit. I can make coffee, and I have pie."

That was when I noticed the large silver trophy on a long side table.

"Pie?" I said. "Do you have cherry?"

She smiled. "Uh-huh."

"Charlotte always has cherry pie," Rose said. "It's become her signature." And that was when I noticed Rose was not wearing her usual brown sweater. I could see all her tattoos plain as day. The stories were correct. That woman had the entire gospel played out on her two arms and clear up to her neck. I saw a shepherd and a tomb and three empty crosses among other images that were difficult to make out depending on how she bent her elbows.

I supposed we could have gotten into big old conversation about the reasons she had the picture made, but it wasn't my business—not then. Maybe one day.

"Yes," I said bringing myself back to the moment. "Mildred came to speak with Leon, but I came to speak with you, Rose—about our annual Sunday school pageant."

"Me? What can I do for the pageant?"

"Well, I hear you're an artist."

She nodded. "I like to paint, if that's what you mean."

"Well, yes, I know. I saw the pictures on your trailer. They're beautiful."

"Thanks."

"Anyway, I was hoping you might consider painting the scenery for the play. Not much, just a manger scene and maybe a shepherd's field, some stars in the sky, that sort of thing."

She looked at me for a long few seconds, almost like she was trying to look right through me and I felt a little uneasy. I thought I might have offended her sensibilities but if she had all those tattoos then . . .

"Why not?" she said. "It would be fun. But, can I do the scenes up here? I'd feel better than going into town."

"I don't see why not. Asa and Stu and probably Nate Kincaid can haul them down to the church when you're done."

Charlotte returned with a Christmas-y tray with pie and coffee on it.

"Help yourself," she said. "And Rose, I think that sounds like a fabulous idea. About time you used your talent outside of Paradise."

"It does sound like fun," Rose said chewing a bite of cherry pie. "But you're gonna help me, Charlotte."

"Me? I can't paint."

"If you can work a brush you can paint sky and grass. I'll add the details."

It was as though Rose had already imagined the entire scene. She knew exactly what she was going to do.

"I'll get started right away," Rose said. "But I need some materials."

"I'll have Nate bring you the stuff. He has these giant rolls of paper."

"Good and thick, I hope," Rose said.

"Yep. He gets leftovers from the printer in Shoops."

We finished our pie and sipped coffee and enjoyed a bit of small talk about Christmas and such. Charlotte was looking forward to the parade.

"Do you know I have only seen Christmas parades on the TV? I never been to one for real. Not a single one. Herman always said parades were stupid and he didn't want to stand out in the cold watching a bunch of idiots parading around like they were better than everyone else."

"Geeze," I said. "I'm sorry you missed out. I think you'll enjoy this parade. We do it every year and it's always a lot of fun."

That was when I spied the trophy a second time and an idea popped into my head. "Charlotte," I said. "I have a grand idea. Why don't you not only watch the parade but be in it?"

"What? In the parade? But why?"

"You and the Angels can ride on one of the floats. Maybe even have your own."

Rose looked at Charlotte and the two of them burst into huge smiles. "Oh my goodness," Rose said. "That is a great idea. What do you say, Charlotte?"

"I love it. The Angels will all be there—in our uniforms!"

"We never had a softball float," I said.

Charlotte sniffed and I think she might have wiped tears from her eyes. "I love it here. I never felt so at home in my life."

Rose poured me more coffee. I also asked for another slice of pie—a sliver. The conversation lulled for a minute.

"How's the pie shop coming along?" I asked

Charlotte laughed a little. "Oh, that will be a while. I thought I might have it up and running for Christmas, but it doesn't look like it. Asa says it needs a lot of work to get it up to code—

whatever that means. So I'll just take my time. I'm in no rush. Maybe by spring."

She handed me a yellow plate with a perfect slice, more than the sliver I asked for of cherry pie. It could have been in a picture in a magazine.

"How do you do this?" I asked. "I can't make pie to save my life. Crust is so hard."

"It is tricky, but I had so much practice. My dead husband loved his pie."

"I'm sorry for your loss." I took a bite of pie.

Charlotte sat in her rocker across from me. She held a slice of pie on her lap. "Oh, thank you, for your concern," she said. "But don't be sorry, I mean—gee, that sounds terrible—I'm sorry he died and all and I guess I still grieve for him in ways, but it wasn't a happy marriage."

"Is that why you said what you said?"

"What did I say?"

"You told me to tread softly with Zeb the other day."

"Oh, I'm sorry, I didn't mean to rattle you. And here you are all engaged and everything. I'm just a little leery of—men."

"So your husband, did he—"

"Let's just say he was a bit domineering."

I swallowed more pie. "Oh, Zeb isn't domineering. He just gets so jealous whenever I try to do anything on my own—fly an airplane for instance."

"Fly an airplane?"

"Yeah, that pilot fella, Cliff Cardwell, they talked about him at Thanksgiving, he's been giving me lessons."

Charlotte nodded her head. "Oh, and Zeb is jealous."

"Uh-huh."

Charlotte looked at me for a long few seconds. "Should he be?"

I finished my pie. "Cliff likes me and all, but I just like his plane. At least I think that's all I like."

Charlotte clicked her tongue. "You better make certain. Make very certain Zeb's the right choice."

"How can I tell?"

"Ha! That's the question for the ages. I was sure when I married Herman. But then it all went wrong. And I let it fester for years and years. It would still be festering if he hadn't taken that stroke."

"Stroke? Yikes."

"Dropped him like a sack of potatoes."

"Wish someone could tell me if I was making the right decision."

"Pray about it first. And, then, I think you need to talk to Zeb about your concerns. Tell him—now."

───⊗⊗⊗───

Charlotte was correct, of course, so I decided that I would tell Zeb my feelings that night. I felt good about it too. I had agreed to marry him but there was still time to be sure. And it would seem to me that of all the decisions I needed to make in life, certainty about marriage rated pretty high.

Charlotte ended up driving me back to town. We let Asa know first and he was fine with it. Rose went along because she wanted to go into Shoops and get some paint she would need for the scenery.

"Just give me the receipts and I'll get the church to reimburse you."

Rose waved her hand. "Nope. It's on me. All part of my tithe."

"As long as you're sure," I said.

JOYCE MAGNIN

They dropped me at the town hall. I liked riding in her convertible. It was sleek and fast. Not like Old Bessie, who drove like . . . well, a truck.

"I hope Leon isn't in any trouble," Charlotte said before I opened the door.

"Me too. I kind of like him, and I really don't think he's trying to hurt anyone."

"Leon? No. He's just weird is all," Rose said.

"Thanks for the ride and the talk."

———∞———

The jail was little more than a locked room with no windows in the basement of the town hall. We didn't even have one until Mildred came to town. She insisted on it.

"Got to have a place to lock the perpetrators up," she had said. "I can't be driving them all to Shoops all the time."

I don't know why she thought Bright's Pond had a crime problem, but her jail was voted on and passed. Nate and Studebaker put the heavy-duty lock on the door and declared it the Bright's Pond Prison. Even hung a sign on the wall outside the room. Harriet Nurse embroidered it with big block letters but the tiny rosebuds seemed to take away from the seriousness of the place. I had only been in the basement a couple of times, usually to look for something missing from one of the town celebrations. It was where they kept the town nativity and Santa Claus decorations.

Mildred was sitting outside the room reading a newspaper.

"What's up?" I said.

"If he isn't the most exasperating little man on the planet. I can't get a word out of him that makes sense. He just talks in circles and repeats things. I figured I'll let him stew in there for a while, then maybe he'll talk."

194

"Ah, let him go. I really don't think he's doing anything. Did you ask him straight out about selling water?"

"Claims he isn't selling it."

"Did you ask if he was giving it to them?"

"That was when he started that double-talk gibberish. I even checked up on him. Called Dabs Lemon, the reporter fella and asked him to do some checking. Waiting to hear."

"So why are you keeping him?"

"Mostly, Griselda, because he's annoying. And it isn't like he's being treated like a prisoner. Heavens to Betsy, Harriet brought him a basket of food, and he's had three bathroom breaks already. He's having a good time."

"How did Harriet know you were holding him?"

"I have to tell her. Boris makes me tell the jail committee whenever I lock anyone up so they can see that the prisoner is properly attended to. Boris is always on the lookout for a possible legal situation. And besides, Harriet likes to bring them a basket, like he's a prisoner of war and the rules of the Geneva Convention apply." She yawned and stretched. "I just put up with it."

"Leon hasn't committed any crime. Come on. Let him go home. You might get more information if you kinda followed him around, staked out his trailer or something."

"Oh, all right."

Mildred opened the door. "What in jumpin' blue heck?" she said. "That's not possible."

"What?" I looked in the room and giggled. Leon Fontaine had flown the coop.

"What the—" Mildred said. "Where is he? This is impossible. The door has been locked the whole time. I only left for a few minutes to call Dabs. I only brought him to the latrine and Harriet Nurse was his only visitor."

"He figured out a way," I said. "Seems to me that Leon Fontaine is not only part Don Quixote but maybe he's also a little bit of Houdini."

"That tears it," Mildred said. "Leon Fontaine is guilty, and I'm gonna get him. Mildred Blessing always gets her man."

I laughed. I had a feeling Mildred might have met her match in Leon Fontaine.

15

That evening, Zeb came by my house around six. We had made plans earlier to go to dinner in Shoops. Nothing fancy, we decided just a burger and then maybe we would take in a movie.

"Arthur," I said as I was getting dressed. "I really wish I hadn't told Zeb I would marry him."

Arthur mewed loudly.

"I don't know why I did. I just got all caught up in the moment."

Never one for fashion, I wore a simple, brown wrap skirt and a striped blouse. I tied my hair in a ponytail and this time secured it with a ribbon instead of just a rubber band like usual. As I looked at myself in the mirror, I thought maybe, just maybe, I could learn to like the woman I saw, but I couldn't expect Zeb to make that possible. I needed to like me for me.

"Maybe that's the problem," I said, scratching Arthur behind the ears. "Maybe I'm blaming Zeb's jealousy for what could really be my problem." I looked out the bedroom window and I could see the nearly frozen-over pond in the distance. The old fishing boat was lying upside down on the grass, and I remembered my father and how he would take me out to catch fish. It wasn't the fish that mattered. It was time we spent on the water. My father always made me feel secure even when the boat rocked a little. I remembered how he would put his hand over mine and help me reel the fish in and land him.

"That's a good one, Griselda," he used to say. "He's a keeper."

As I looked out the window I could still see my father out on the water in his little boat. He always said he felt closest to God on the water fishing and knowing which ones to keep and which ones to throw back.

I had my answer.

The doorbell rang. "That's him. Wish me luck."

Arthur meowed.

I opened the front door, and Zeb was standing there with a bouquet of yellow roses and a funny grin on his face.

"Come on in. I just need to get my coat." I took the flowers. "I'll put these in water first."

Zeb waited in the viewing room while I went to the kitchen and found a vase. I arranged the roses and carried them into the viewing room and set the vase on the coffee table. "They're beautiful," I said. "Thank you. Yellow roses are my favorite. I just need to get my coat."

"Grizzy," he said. "Before you put on your coat I got something to say."

"Oh, is everything all right?"

"Yes." Zeb got down on one knee. He took both my hands in his and looked up at me. "I don't think I did this proper before so here goes. Been practicing all day. Dot helped me—"

"Zeb, I—"

"Shhh. I got to get this out. Griselda, I love you. I've loved you for a very long time. I want to spend the rest of my life with you. Will you—" he swallowed—"marry me?"

A tear trickled down my cheek.

"Zeb, I—"

"Oh, Griselda, don't say no. You can't. You already said yes. I just wanted to make it proper."

Oh, dear, here was my chance to back out. I could say, "No, I changed my mind." But all my doubts had melted away and disappeared like wood smoke as I gazed into his eyes. My heart pounded, my palms went sweaty, and I said, "Yes, I'll marry you." I had been fighting my feelings and the truth. Zeb was the man I had been meant to marry. I could see it in Zeb's eyes, and I could see it through my father's eyes.

Zeb stood and kissed me as my heart pounded. I melted into him like a big pat of butter on warm toast.

"I really do love you," he said.

"I love you, too."

He kissed me again.

"Now look," he said. "About dinner, I . . . I have some place special in mind."

"Aren't we going for burgers in Shoops?"

"Nope." He took my hand. "Come on, but promise me you won't laugh or say anything for at least five minutes after we get there."

"OK. I promise, but—"

"Nope. Just come with me. I borrowed Studebaker's Caddy."

Zeb often borrowed Stu's car for special occasions like funerals. He never bought a car of his own.

"How about that burger joint on the Boulevard, Zips or Zaps?" I said.

"I said I have a place."

"OK, I'm sorry."

We drove toward the center of town. Oh, no, he was taking me to the Full Moon. Of all the places we could have gone that night, he had to go to the Full Moon. But I had promised him I wouldn't say anything.

He parked the Caddy. There were no cars in the lot and all the lights were off in the café except the large neon moon that hung over the roof. Zeb ran around the car and opened the door for me.

"Now you promised. Not a word."

"OK, but it's dark."

He took my hand and led me up the steps and pushed open the café door. He flipped the light switch and a thousand tiny lights went on. They looked like stars. The only other light was the neon clock that glowed against the wall above the pick-up window. It was dark but light enough to see.

"Have a seat," Zeb said. "In the first booth."

I followed his instructions and squeezed in. He sat across from me.

A Full Moon Pie sat in the center of the table next to two plates, two forks, and two napkins.

"Is this dinner?" I said.

"No rule about having dessert first," Zeb said.

He cut into the pie with a triangular server and gently placed a large slice on my plate. Then he did the same for himself.

"Go on, eat some. What better way to celebrate our engagement than with a Full Moon Pie?"

To be honest, lemon meringue was the last thing I wanted that evening. I had my taste buds all set for a juicy cheeseburger and fries and maybe a chocolate milkshake.

I bit into the slice, chewed, and swallowed. Zeb looked at me like he was waiting for me to explode or something.

"Go on, have some more." OK, now I was suspicious. I cut off another bite and put it in my mouth. That time I felt something strange, hard, and rough.

"What's this?" I said trying to pull the offending object from my mouth in a ladylike fashion. But yeah, I was surprised when I uncovered a diamond ring.

"Zeb. You . . . this . . . wow!" I sounded like an idiot. I wiped it off with my napkin. "It's beautiful."

"It's been in my family for generations."

He gently took it from me, dipped it into a glass of water he had waiting nearby, dried it with a napkin, and slipped it on my finger. "I hope it fits. I would have gotten it to you sooner, but I needed to have it sized."

"It fits perfectly."

"Really? That's amazing. It really was meant for you."

Then he leaned across the table and kissed me and as he did the jukebox turned on and the bright café lights burst on and I heard cheers from outside.

"What the—" I said.

"I planned it, Grizzy. It's a celebration. Everybody's here. It's a party—for you. For us."

I needed to swipe more tears. Zeb opened the door and friends piled in. Ivy, Bill and Edie Tompkins, the Sturgises, even Eugene Shrapnel came out to celebrate. Ruth arrived laughing.

"You knew about this?" I said to her.

"Uh-huh, the whole town knew Zeb's plan."

"And believe me," Edie said, "It was not easy to keep the secret."

"I can't believe you all managed to keep it under wraps. This has got to be a first in this town."

"Zeb said he'd stop making sandwiches and move the Full Moon to Canada if we told," hollered Dot from the back of the café.

I had never been so happy in my life. And the best part? I didn't even miss Agnes. I thought about her, but I pushed the thought aside. This was my night, mine and Zeb's.

Zeb, of course, did the only thing he could do that night that seemed appropriate. He fired up the grill and started turning out burgers and fries and fried baloney sandwiches. Everyone ate and everyone smiled. It had been the best night of my life.

I never did get a chance to finish a burger that evening, but that was OK. Afterward, Zeb and I went back to my house and for the first time in a long time were able to spend an evening alone, without interruption.

"So should we set a date?" I asked.

"Sure, I was thinking around Christmas." Zeb and I were sitting on the red velvet sofa watching the fire in the fireplace.

"This Christmas?" I said. "That's just in a couple of weeks."

"I know. Why not? We don't need a big wedding or anything fancy, do we? Why should we wait? It's not like we're kids."

I looked into the dancing flames. "No, I suppose not. But we'll need to do some planning. Invite guests and have a cake and all."

"Well, yeah, but I thought we'd get married in the chapel and have a small reception in the town hall. It's been used for weddings before."

"We could do that but—"

"What, Grizzy? But what?" His voice took on a different tone. Annoyed?

"No, it's not that big a deal, I don't think. But what about Agnes?"

"What about her?"

"How will she get to the chapel?"

Zeb was quiet a few moments. "I don't know. The forklift again?"

I shook my head. "I can't ask my sister to be carried into town on a forklift. Not again."

"Then what do you suggest? Maybe we should just elope. Go see the justice of the peace in Shoops and get it over with. That way we can tell Agnes that nobody was invited."

That idea didn't help. Not really.

"I'm sorry. But how can I get married without Agnes? She's my only family."

Zeb got up and poked at the fire. He tossed on another log. "I'll get more wood in a few minutes."

"Not sure how much is left," I said. "I need to split some more."

He sat next to me again. "Just think, Grizzy, now I'll be chopping your wood."

I smiled. "I can't wait."

He pulled me close, and we avoided any talk about Agnes for the rest of the night—at least until he was about to leave. We stood near the front door saying goodnight. My thumb kept nervously fidgeting with my engagement ring. It would take some time to get used to.

Zeb held my hand. "Don't worry about Agnes. We'll figure something out. I want you to be happy."

⸺◦⸺

I lay in bed thinking, not sleeping even though I was more tired than I had felt in a while. I thought it was mostly emotional exhaustion. Getting a surprise engagement party was tiring. I kept holding my pretty little ring up to the light on the bedside table, admiring its beauty and clarity, looking at all the facets. I thought for a minute about the other women who had worn it. I knew that I would now forever be connected to them through this ring. I only actually knew Zeb's mother, Mabel. She was a good woman with a good heart. Little did I know when Zeb and I were children running in and out of her house—eating the delicious pies she baked and getting told countless times to wipe our feet and wash our hands—that I would one day wear her ring. But God knew. And for the first time in my life that night I felt part of his plan.

⸻

The next day arrived cold and typically gray for late autumn in the mountains. The air smelled clean with hints of wood smoke from the many chimneys in town. I made my way to the kitchen, fed Arthur, and plugged the percolator in. I would need to go to the library, but I also wanted to get out to Greenbrier and show Agnes my ring. My thumb continued to fidget with it like it was a missing tooth.

I was engaged to be married—and in just a couple of weeks. Zeb wanted a Christmas wedding. I sat at the kitchen table thinking about this. A Christmas wedding would be nice. But where? The church would be the obvious place but how in tarnation would I get Agnes down the aisle? I wanted her to be my maid of honor, as unpractical as that might have been.

But I didn't daydream very long. I was not one of those little girls who dreamed of my wedding day. Maybe Zeb had the right idea. A quick drive into Shoops; visit the justice of the peace; let him say a few words; and sign the license. Just a quick one-two-three wedding. Then I wouldn't have to worry about Agnes. I would just tell her after the fact.

Arthur mewed as though reading my mind again. "I know, I know. She'd be terribly upset, but she'll get over it and I won't have to finagle some way to get her to the church."

It seemed my sister was always in my life's path.

⸻

I dressed and headed for the library in my truck. It was early enough for me to catch the *Rassie Harper Show* and see if Vera Krug had any more tidbits to share. I couldn't imagine that news of my engagement to Zeb would have spread that quickly, and why would Vera care? The better news was, of course, Leon Fontaine's disappearance from Mildred's jail, although I didn't suspect Mildred would have told anyone. It was a mystery how he managed to escape, but I had a sneaking suspicion it had something to do with Harriet Nurse and her picnic basket.

The drive was short and I parked at the very top of the hill with a view of the town, the mountains, and of course, Matilda. The sun glinted off her wings as a frosty mist gathered on the ground giving the plane a romantic look, like something out of *Casablanca*. "Here's looking at you, kid," I said.

I tuned in the station and heard Rassie's voice. He was talking about football and then about Christmas. Rassie Harper was always complaining, and that morning he even found reason to complain about Christmas.

"It's too commercial," he was telling an on-air caller. "What happened to peace on earth? Not that I would balk if someone wanted to leave a gift of, say, a Harley Davidson under my tree—hint, hint, Harcum Motors. And speaking of which—"

Rassie went into a thirty-second advertisement for the largest "Harley Davidson dealer in the tri-state area."

"You are so full of it, Rassie," I said to the radio. "You complain about how commercial Christmas is and then sell motorcycles."

I listened to a couple more Rassie-styled rants before he introduced Vera. "And here she is, that winsome woman of the airwaves, your good neighbor and mine, Vera Krug." This time for some reason he added a cowbell to the end of the segue.

"Good morning," said Vera. "This is Vera Krug with all your Good Neighbor News for Wednesday, December 4. Not much to report today, except, of course, for the big sale down at Kiddie City in Shoops Borough. They got specials on all the favorite toys this season. So come on out all you mothers and dads. Save Santa some running around. If you get there before noon today, they have a sale on that Easy-Bake Oven all the little girls are gaga about."

I took a breath. "Come on, Vera, get to the good stuff."

"And now for the news of the day. From what I hear strange things are still happening up at the Greenbrier Nursing Home. Ninety-two-year-old Faith Graves and eighty-six-year-old Clive Dickens got themselves hitched the other day. Imagine that. Love senior-citizen style. Well, I wish them all the luck in the world. And speaking of weddings—"

Uh oh, I turned the volume up.

"I have it on good authority that another wedding in Bright's Pond is in the planning stages. It seems that Griselda Sparrow and Zeb Sewickey—owner of The Full Moon Café— are engaged. No word on a date yet, but I can't imagine those two will wait very long. Leastways they better not. From what I hear that relationship has had more ups and downs than the Wildcat Roller Coaster in Dorney Park."

Sheesh. How does she know this stuff? It must have come from Ruth. But Ruth always promises me that she never speaks to Vera. I guess it really didn't matter, except I hated having my personal business on the airwaves. And, as I looked at my pretty little ring, I felt proud. Why not? "Go ahead, Vera," I said. "Shout it from the rooftop. I am getting married."

"Hold on a second." Rassie Harper cut in. "Isn't she the sister to that fat woman up there? Agnes Sparrow. The supposed miracle maker?"

"One and the same," Vera said. "Looks like she's produced yet another miracle. Griselda ain't no spring chicken, and Zeb Sewickey was not what you would call the marrying type."

"Well, I want an invitation to that wedding," Rassie said. "I guess Agnes would be the maid of honor. Now how much satin and crinoline would it take to wrap that woman up?"

My stomach churned. The nerve that man had. He took every opportunity to deride people, and Agnes had been a standing target of his for a long time now.

"And, not only that," Vera said, "but there's news out of Paradise, that little trailer park they got up there, you know the one, don't you, Rassie?"

"I sure do, Vera. Didn't they just have some kind of thing up there?"

"Oh, you mean the Blessing of the Fountain. Now ain't that the strangest thing you ever did hear? It seems the fountain was rebuilt and turned on and that created the need for a clergy blessing on the waters, I suppose. But my sources tell me that all might not be kosher with the Paradise Fountain. It seems there might be some funny business afoot. I'll keep my eyes and ears open and report back as soon as I learn more."

One of these days I was going to find her sources. I couldn't imagine who in town was filling her head and her notebook with information. Ruth never liked Vera very much. It had to be someone else.

I turned off the radio and started down the hill but I only got a few hundred feet when I saw Cliff heading up. Probably going to the plane.

I stopped and waved. He waved back and picked up his pace toward me.

"Good morning," he said when he got close to the truck. He leaned on the opened window. "Congratulations. I hear you and Zeb have finally made it official."

"We did." I held up my hand and wiggled my ring finger.

"Well, look at that. I'm very happy for you." He kissed my cheek. "Zeb is a very lucky man."

"Thanks, Cliff. And thanks for understanding."

"Ah, look. The better man won. But say, this doesn't mean you're gonna give up flying, does it?"

"No way."

"You still need to test for your license."

"I know."

"How about this Saturday? We'll fly over to Scranton and get you tested and get your license."

"Saturday? I think that will be all right."

"Good. Meet me here around nine in the morning."

There were days when I hated my library routine. And this was one of those days. Maybe it was my engagement, but whatever it was I had to really argue with myself to stay and open the mail, restock books, et cetera. But as I went about my business, I found myself thinking differently than I ever had about the library. I mean I loved the place, the building, which was actually an old Queen Anne Victorian. I knew every angle, every nook and cranny, every floorboard that creaked, but for the first time I wondered if it was still the job for me.

I had been the librarian for twenty years, and now I was thinking it might be time to turn the job over to someone else. Maybe getting married would make it possible for me to quit working. Zeb and I never discussed it, but I actually liked the idea.

The SOAP women filed in around eleven o'clock. The Christmas season meant extra duty for them. They doubled and tripled their secret acts of charity. People usually gave more money at the Thanksgiving SOAP offering at church. Once a month they took a special offering but Thanksgiving was always the largest.

"How are you, Griselda?" asked Tohilda Best, president of SOAP. "I hear congratulations are in order."

I felt my face blush. "Yes. Thank you."

"He's a fine man," she said

"He is, Tohilda. Thanks."

"Well, we best be getting to our business. So much to do this time of year. So many needy folks. We're planning a toy drop for the backwoods kids in a couple of weeks. Studebaker Kowalski is going to be our Santa Claus."

"Oh, that's terrific. He'll make a good Santa."

"We could use all the help we can get for our wrapping party at the church if you'd like to help."

"Oh, maybe. But I'm so busy right now."

"Of course," she said, "You have a wedding to plan."

"But I was wondering if you ladies had Mercy Lincoln and her mother on your list of charitable giving. They really need some help."

"Yes, yes we do. But Griselda," Tohilda said. "I heard you were planning on asking the girl to play Mary this year."

"That's right. I'm hoping she comes today so I can discuss it with her."

"Are you sure that's a good idea? Some of them backwoods families have strict ideas about fraternizing with the town folks."

"I know, but her mother lets her come to school and the library. I thought it would be worth a shot. Babette is getting too old. Mercy will do a good job—if her Mama lets her."

"Don't be surprised if she doesn't," Tohilda said.

The SOAP ladies stayed for another hour. They made their Christmas giving decisions, mapped out the routes they would take through the woods, and then left in silence, as was the custom.

I closed up the library and headed to Greenbrier. I would need to discuss the whole maid-of-honor / where-to-have-the-wedding conundrum with Agnes. She might have an idea or two. I just hoped she didn't get to feeling all sorry for herself and say something stupid like, "It's OK, Griselda. You can get married without me."

When I got on the main road to Greenbrier, my thoughts turned to Leon Fontaine. I still hadn't had the opportunity to track down Mildred and see if she figured out how he broke out of her jail. I figured it was probably something obvious. The man was after all a man and not really magical even if he did kind of fit the bill of having a bit of leprechaun in him. I suspected Harriet Nurse had something to do with his escape.

Agnes was in her room eating her lunch. It didn't look all that appetizing, and I couldn't blame her when she complained. "What I wouldn't do for a decent tuna sandwich," she said when I walked into the room. "I can't eat this slop, Griselda."

"I'm sorry, Agnes. But the doctors say your health depends on you losing weight. And don't you want to feel better and move better and look better?"

"I know, I know, but why should a diet be so . . . so not delicious? Please Griselda bring me a sandwich, even just the tuna salad with no bread. I need something to tickle my taste buds."

"Well, you just had all that Thanksgiving food."

"I know but . . . but geez, this is awful." She dipped her soup spoon into the bowl of broth and let it run off the spoon back into the bowl. "Dishwater."

"At least eat the peaches and the cottage cheese and the hamburger patty."

She snorted. "I got to eat, I know it, but really."

"Go on," I said. "Besides, enough about your food. I have news."

She perked up. "Oh, I hope it's good news. Did you all figure out what in tarnation is going on around here? The folks are going crazier and crazier. They got residents climbing trees and skating and staying up well past nine o'clock playing cards in the Sunshine Room."

"Is that so terrible?"

"No, I guess not when you think about it, but it ain't normal for Greenbrier."

"Well, no, I haven't any news about that but—" I held up my left hand. "Look."

"At what?"

"My hand."

"Yeah."

"My ring finger. Look."

She pulled my hand closer to her face. "Oh, oh, a ring. An engagement ring. Who's it from?"

"Agnes."

She laughed as she dug around in her cottage cheese like she was looking for a sausage. "Well, it could have been Cliff."

"Don't be ridiculous. Zeb gave it to me. It's been in his family for years and years. He gave it to me in a slice of Full Moon Pie."

"No. Really?"

"Yep. It was kind of sweet and romantic. He decorated the café with flowers and hung little twinkling lights from the ceiling like stars. Then he served me pie. I took a bite of it and found this."

"Ah, that is sweet. Sort of."

"It was. I wish you could have been there, Agnes. They had a party for us after he gave me the ring and we kissed and all. Everybody was there. It was so much fun."

"I'm sorry I missed it." She sounded sad.

"That's why you got to stick to the diet and lose weight. So you can participate in . . . in life again."

I moved to the window and saw the funny-looking gazebo. "Has Leon Fontaine been around?"

"Haven't seen him since yesterday. He's been visiting some of the folks—or so I hear. He hasn't been to see me."

"Yesterday? Yesterday afternoon?"

"Yeah. He was flitting around here like a butterfly. Why you so interested?"

"Uhm, because get this, Mildred arrested him yesterday. Even though she really had nothing to hold him on. She put him in that locked room in the town hall basement. But guess what."

"He escaped!"

"Now how did you know that?"

"I didn't," she bit into her hamburger patty. "This is awful."

"Come on, tell me how."

"I didn't know, not for certain. I just figure a tricky guy like him would find a way."

"I think Harriet Nurse helped him get away when she brought him his picnic basket of food and goodies."

"Ha, good old Harriet. She is a sly one."

"But no one's seen him since, except you, if you say you saw him here."

Agnes slapped her knee. "Ha. He's a pip."

I kept looking at the gazebo and then it struck me. Just like that. Just like lightning. "Agnes. We can get married out there. In the gazebo."

"Who can?"

"Me and Zeb. We were talking about the wedding and figured it would be hard to do at the church on account of how we would get you there."

Agnes closed her eyes. "Ah, it's me again. I'm always causing trouble."

"No, no, don't think that way. This is cool. We'll get married in the gazebo. And Agnes, will you be my maid of honor?"

Agnes slapped her knee again. "Why, Griselda Sparrow, you know I will, but . . . but are you sure? I mean what will I wear? Don't think they make many bridesmaid dresses in my size."

"Ruth can sew anything. I bet she can alter a dress for you."

"Ah, she'd need to alter six or seven dresses to get one to fit me."

"Why are you doing this? Don't you want to be my maid of honor?"

Agnes closed her eyes and leaned her head back. "Yes, yes, of course, I do. It's just . . . just embarrassing."

"Agnes, you've never been embarrassed by your weight—ever."

"That's where you're wrong." She pushed her plate away. And then moved it back. She wolfed down the cottage cheese. "I've always been ashamed. I . . . I just didn't know what to do about it," she said between chews.

"But, Agnes, this is different. It's my wedding."

"I know. I'm sorry. But it'll be mighty cold out there. Could snow."

"We'll make it a quick ceremony. Snow would be nice. I'll talk to Ruth. We'll figure something out." I felt the excitement build in my chest. But then deflate.

Sure it seemed simple enough to me. Talk to Ruth, sew a dress large enough for Agnes to wear, something to make her look and feel pretty on the most important day of my life. It was becoming about Agnes again.

"You know what, Agnes," I said. "I just remembered. I had an appointment."

"Appointment? You sick?"

"No, nothing like that." I kissed her cheek. "I'll get with Ruth. Don't worry we'll figure something out. I want you in my wedding."

I made my way down the hall practically tripping over Haddie Grace who came whizzing around the corner on her tricycle. "Hello, Haddie," I said. "How are you?" She didn't say anything but kept riding around the corner toward the Sunshine Room ringing her bell.

That gave me an idea. Maybe we could just get married in the Sunshine Room. Agnes could be wheeled down in her chair and even just wear a pretty housedress. I mean what did it really matter if she wore a real bridesmaid dress or not? I still didn't even know what I wanted to wear and we were getting married in just a couple of weeks.

16

I drove home from Greenbrier that day wondering and worrying about what I was going to wear to my wedding. The idea to drive into Shoops and look at some dresses crossed my mind but what also crossed my mind was that dress shopping was something I should probably be doing with Agnes. But that was impossible. I had no choice, though, than to shove the notion away and find someone else to go with.

Ruth came to mind first, but then I saw Ivy and Mickey Mantle walking along Filbert Street. I hadn't seen Ivy since the engagement party and we didn't really get a chance to talk. So I thought this would a good opportunity to catch up. I pulled Old Bessie against the curb and got out.

"Ivy," I called.

She waved. "Hey, Griselda. Congratulations."

"Thanks. But say, are you busy right now?"

"Nah, just walking."

"Feel like a ride into Shoops? I need to find a wedding dress."

"Oh, did you set a date?"

"Zeb said he'd like to get married at Christmas."

"You mean on Christmas Day?" She clapped her hands when Mickey Mantle became sidetracked by a trashcan. "Come on Mickey Mantle, stay away from that."

"Nah, not Christmas Day. I don't know which day he has in mind."

"OK, I'll go but I don't know anything about weddings or dresses."

"Me neither."

We took Mickey Mantle home and headed into Shoops.

"I guess you heard about what's going on at Greenbrier," I said as we pulled onto the main road to Shoops.

"Sure. I think it's funny. Everyone says that man from Paradise is behind it. Any truth to the rumor?"

"I'm not sure, but it sure looks like it." Then I told her about the bottles and how Mildred arrested him even though she had no real evidence and how he escaped.

"Good for him. Personally, I don't get the big deal. And that Mildred can be quick on the draw. No one is getting hurt, are they?"

"Not really. A broken hip. Some falls. Some of the residents are doing some pretty crazy things that they are really too old to be doing."

"Ah, I think it's good for them."

We chatted a few more minutes about Greenbrier and then about my upcoming wedding and Agnes.

"Just get yards and yards of pink satin and wrap her up in it. No one will notice. Besides, it's your day, and you're more worried about her than yourself."

"Look, I don't care," I said as I pulled into a parking place out front of Oppenstainers' Department Store. "I'd get married in blue jeans."

"So why don't you?"

I pushed the gearshift into park and opened the door. "Ah, I don't know. Maybe I really do want a dress, you know the whole thing."

"Really?" Ivy pulled open the store door and held it for me. "After you."

"Thank you."

The store was large, and we had walked right smack dab into the ladies' shoe department, which was right next to the perfume and makeup counters where they sprayed you whether you wanted them to or not and insisted that they test your skin type. I hated the idea that we would have to walk through there. It was like entering a mine field as far as I was concerned.

"Let's just ask someone where the dresses are. Aren't sales-ladies supposed to help you with stuff like this?"

I shrugged. "Beats me. I never bought a wedding dress before. Look there's a directory."

Dresses were on the second floor. "Come on, Ivy." I took a deep breath as we stepped onto the escalator. It was like diving into a deep dark pool. The whole thing made me anxious. Maybe in a good way. Maybe not.

I saw a friendly looking saleslady arranging a rack of blouses. "Let's ask her. She looks nice."

"Excuse me," I said.

The stylish, young, and thin woman turned and smiled. "Can I help you?"

"I'm looking for a dress and—"

"Oh, certainly. Did you have anything in mind? What kind of dress were you thinking?" She looked me up and down. "Walk this way," she said. We followed her through a maze of clothing racks and displays. I had to smack Ivy when she put her hand on her hip and wiggled her hips like our saleslady.

Kind of dress? "Well, actually, it's to get married in."

"Married. You're looking for a wedding dress?" She stopped walking. "This isn't a bridal shop."

"Oh, do I need a bridal shop? Can't I just get something pretty?"

"Sure, but most brides want a wedding gown, you know with a veil and train and everything."

"A train? No, no, nothing like that. I just want a dress."

"OK, then you want formal wear. Over here."

The next thing I knew, the saleslady, who said her name was Mavis, had shown me three dresses. I hated all three until she found a dress that I thought would be perfect. It wasn't your traditional wedding dress, and that was fine with me. It was long, dark blue like the sky just before the sun completely dropped behind the horizon, and had the tiniest white dots on it like stars. It made me think of the night Zeb gave me his mother's ring.

Mavis helped me into it and zipped it up the back. "Now that's gorgeous on you," she said. "I particularly like the scoop neckline and wide sleeves."

"It does look nice, doesn't it?" I said looking at myself in the long mirror. "I've never owned anything so pretty."

"I wouldn't call it a wedding gown, but for a Christmas wedding, I think it's perfect," Mavis said. "With the right hat, maybe a little pillbox with veil and corsage made from red poinsettias. Gorgeous."

"It's very nice," Ivy said.

"Now you'll want to get your hair done and maybe even your makeup," Mavis said.

"Hair? Makeup? I hadn't thought about those things."

"Of course. We have a wonderful beauty parlor right here in the store. You should make an appointment to come in the morning of your big day. Tell them you want Mr. Frederick. He's the best."

"And they'll take care of it?"

Mavis smiled again. "Yes. They'll take care of it all. Now, what about your bridesmaids? How many and what are they wearing?"

I glanced at Ivy. She shrugged.

"Oh, it's just my sister. She's my maid of honor."

"Oh, how adorable," Mavis said.

Ivy chuckled.

"Actually," I said as Mavis lifted the dress over my head. "Maybe you can help with that. She's a bit of a problem case."

"Problem?" Mavis hung my dress on the hanger. "What kind of problem?"

"Well, she'll most likely be in a wheelchair."

Mavis clicked her tongue. "Oh, I'm sorry. Is it one of them diseases that folks get that makes their muscles stop working?"

"No, no. She's . . . she's . . ."

Mavis kept looking at me, and I couldn't bring myself to say the words.

"Fat," Ivy said. "Griselda's sister is . . . large."

"That's not a problem. We have dresses for plus-size women."

"More like quadruple plus," I said.

"Triple X?" Mavis said. "Still . . . I—"

"Larger than that," Ivy said. "Have you ever heard about Agnes Sparrow?"

Mavis swallowed. "You mean the woman that was supposed to do all them miracles? I heard about her last year sometime, on that Rassie Harper show."

"That's her."

"My, my," Mavis said. "I never dressed a celebrity before. Maybe she should come in and—"

219

"She's not a celebrity, and she can't just come in." By then I was annoyed and just wanted to pay for my dress and leave. "It's OK," I said. "We'll figure something out."

"No, no," Mavis said. "Look, maybe I can bring a few things to her and—"

I shook my head. "That won't work either."

"OK, but let me know if I can help. Should we ring this up?" She took my dress and walked toward the cash register. I paid cash for the dress and Mavis wrapped it in a clear bag, which she zipped along the bottom.

"Now be sure and make that appointment downstairs, basement level, with the beauty parlor before you leave today. And don't forget about shoes. A pair of open-toe sandals would work well with this."

"Thank you," I said. "You've been very helpful."

Ivy and I walked through the dress department to the escalator.

"Maybe I should make that appointment, except I don't know for which day."

Ivy shook her head. "I suggest you get that straight. Then make the appointment. And then worry about Agnes."

When we got to the bottom of the escalator, Ivy said, "What are you going to do about Agnes?" as though the problem had just dawned on her. "How will she get to the church?"

"We're not getting married in the church." We walked toward the exit, right past the women's shoes. I'd worry about that later.

"No? Where?"

"Greenbrier. In the gazebo."

Ivy laughed. "Oh, you can't be serious. It's cold, especially out there. The wind whips around like a mad man."

"We'll make it work. Just the ceremony in the gazebo and the reception in the Sunshine Room out there. Folks can wait in there if they don't want to sit out in the cold. God is out there in the wind too. Not just at church."

"OK, OK. You made your point. It's fine with me. Not my wedding."

"My biggest problem is getting a dress for Agnes to wear."

"I'd talk to Ruth. She can sew anything."

"I had already thought about that, but you know how she can get. She's already sewing all the pageant costumes."

"Oh, right, well, she'll be done with them soon. The pageant is next Sunday. Did they ever get a Mary?"

"I suggested Mercy Lincoln."

"The little girl from the backwoods? She'd be perfect."

"Some of them balked at the idea."

"Why?"

"Because she's . . . you now . . . a Negro." We got into the truck and I backed out of the parking spot. "I know it doesn't make any difference but—"

"So who got upset? As if I didn't know?"

"Nate Kincaid."

"Why, that little bigot. I'll fix his wagon."

I started down the road to Bright's Pond. "Oh, don't fret over him. He can't do anything about it. Majority rules on the committee. He'll get used to it."

"A black Mary? I don't know," Ivy said. She clicked her tongue.

"Like I said, it's not up to Nate Kincaid. But what if some people in the audience don't like it?"

"Who cares? Let them get upset."

"Well, I still have to ask her and get permission from her mama. That might be a problem."

"Yeah, some of them woods people don't like us townsfolk."

"I know, but Mercy's different. I hope her mama is too. I figure I'll ask her next time she comes to the library."

"You better hurry. Time is running out and you would look pretty silly playing Mary."

"I'll have Mercy at the next rehearsal."

"I bet you will."

"Say, did you hear about the animals?" I asked.

"You mean all those little kids dressed up like sheep?"

"Nope. We got us a real live camel for the show."

"But how? There are no camels in Bright's Pond."

Ivy rolled down her window a couple of inches. The cold December air felt good on my face. I said, "You know that artist fella, Filby Pruett?"

"Yeah, sure."

"Well, he apparently knows someone with a traveling animal act, and he got this person to lend us a camel and a sheep."

"That's amazing. We never had real animals—well, except the time one of the Frost sisters' pigs got loose and rampaged through the scenery." Ivy laughed.

"I remember that. They treated that pig like a dog."

"Yeah, but they should never have let it off the leash during the play."

I pulled up out front of Ivy's house. "Thanks for coming with me."

"Sure. But pick a date—today. And then make that appointment and talk to Ruth about Agnes."

"I will."

I pulled away from the curb and headed toward home. With only nineteen days before Christmas there was a lot to do. This was one of those times I resented Agnes for being so huge and helpless and incapable of helping me. I knew she couldn't help it but that didn't mean it still didn't hurt to know that once again I would be doing all the work to make her look and feel good and that somehow I would fade into the background.

17

A Yuletide Committee meeting had been called for that evening. A final decision had to be made about the Shoops Moose and about Mary. It wasn't important to me if the Moose marched in the parade but allowing Mercy Lincoln to be our Mary this year was.

So I hung my wedding dress in my closet and went to the library. School would be letting out soon, and I needed to open the library anyway just in case some of the kids needed to do research or check out a reading book.

On the way, I saw Charlotte near her new store and it was at that moment that I remembered we still needed some kind of wedding cake. There needed to be something traditional about my wedding.

"Charlotte," I called. "Can I talk to you?"

"Oh, sure," she said. "I was waiting for that plumber fella to come by. Supposed to help me with the appliances and such, not to mention the toilet in there. It's a mess."

"I guess you heard by now that Zeb and I are getting married around Christmas."

"Yes, I did hear. Rose Tattoo told me. A Christmas wedding does sound nice. You can do so much—themewise. And as long as you're certain."

I thought a moment. "I'm sure. I think all that confusion over Cliff and Zeb had more to do with me wanting to feel a little freedom for a while. I'd been stuck in the house with my sister for years and years. It felt nice to be on my own."

"Sure it did, Griselda. I remember feeling a similar way when Herman died. Oh, I was sad and all but after a while I started to enjoy being on my own."

Charlotte turned her key in the shop door lock. "Have you been inside?"

"No."

"Come on, I'll show you around. Not much to see yet, but I have designs in my mind."

The shop was nothing more than a few broken down stoves and a big empty space with wires hanging from the ceiling and pipes sticking up through the black and white checkerboard floor.

"I know it looks a fright but the inspectors have insured me that it's basically sound."

"From what I know of Bill Tompkins and Claude Hastings the plumber they won't steer you wrong. This place will be churning out pies by the new year."

"I hope so. I am kind of looking forward to opening day. Think we could have a blessing of the pies?"

"Absolutely. And speaking of which I have a little predicament I thought you might help me with."

"Me? Sure. What's up?"

"Zeb and I want to be married around Christmas—which day exactly I don't know—but . . . well, we need a cake and—"

"Oh, I don't make cakes. I wouldn't know how to make a wedding cake. I could make a wedding pie but—"

"Uhm, that's OK. There must be a bakery in Shoops that can do it."

Charlotte brushed dust off a narrow counter with her palm. "You know, Griselda, does it have to be cake?"

"Well, I kind of wanted—but what are you thinking?"

"I could probably construct some sort of wedding pie, you know with tiers that go out like this." She spread her arms about three feet wide. "And then stack them in layers to form a kind of cake-shape and we could decorate the pies with Christmasy flowers and ornaments, make kind of a Christmas Pie Tree Wedding Cake."

I took a breath and let it out slowly. Thinking. Imagining. I had no idea if the picture in my mind matched the image in Charlotte's, but I said, "OK. Why not? But can you make something like that in your trailer?"

Charlotte looked a bit dumbstruck. "Uh-huh. I sure can. Leave it to me—except what flavors?"

"Cherry, of course, and apple."

"Maybe a coconut cream to represent the snow on the ground. Oh, my, my, Griselda, that's it. I'll make a tier of coconut cream and then start stacking pies like this and like that—" she moved her hands from side to side. "I'm sure Asa can build me a pie stand that would work."

"Sounds good to me as long as you think you can. Course I don't like coconut but don't worry about that. I like the idea of it."

"As long as you're sure . . . and oh, I just had a thought. We'll top it all off with one of Zeb's Full Moon Pies."

"Sounds good. Thank you, Charlotte."

The shop door opened.

"Oh," I said. "There's Claude. I need to get to the library anyway."

"Hey, Claude," I said.

"Congratulations, Griselda," Claude said.

"OK, Griselda," Charlotte called as I walked out the door. "We'll talk."

———— ∞ ————

By the time I made it to the library a small group of students were waiting on steps.

"Hey, Miss Griselda," called one of the boys. "We thought you weren't gonna open."

"I'm sorry. I got tied up in town. Just need a minute to get the place open."

I unlocked the door and flipped on the lights and the kids piled in and then scattered like roaches all over the library. I kept my eyes open for Mercy. She usually moseyed in toward closing time. It was important that she went home to help her mama after school. I remembered I needed to ask if Doc made it back there to check on Charlamaine Lincoln. She had been sick, according to Mercy.

After restocking a couple of books and laying out the latest copies of *Scientific American* and *Hunters Digest*, I sat behind the counter waiting for the kids to clear out for home and supper.

Mercy showed up about ten minutes before closing.

"You got any books about the Civil War, Miz Griselda?" she asked. "I need to do a report on Robert E. Lee."

"Sure, Mercy. Right over here."

I showed her three books and then decided to pop the question. "Mercy," I said. "Have you ever come to the Sunday school Christmas pageant?"

She shook her head. "No, Ma'am, I never."

"Well, you do know the story of baby Jesus, don't you?"

"Oh, sure. Everybody knows about the baby Jesus being born on Christmas Day and all. I read me the story straight from that Bible you got over there."

"Good. Good, well, every year the children at the Bright's Pond Church put on a play about that day. They have shepherds and Joseph and Mary and the innkeeper and angels and sheep."

"That sounds nice. I never seen anything like that in all my born days."

"This year they are looking for a little girl to play Mary, and I thought you might like to do it."

"Me, Miz Griselda?" She pointed to her heart. "You want me to play-act Jesus' mama? Well, I can't do that. She's awful holy and all and I'm . . . not holy. No way. I mean I like Jesus and all but pretendin' to be his mama?" She shook her head.

"I think you would make a perfect Mary. And God won't mind you doing it. In fact, you'll make him proud. "

She looked around the library. "I'll need to ask my Mama, first."

"Good. You do that. But do it tonight. You'll need to be at the church Thursday at seven o'clock."

"Will you be there?"

"I sure will."

"I'll go straightaway home and ask Mama. Imagine that, me play-acting Jesus' mama."

"OK, so you'll come to the church then, Thursday. You know the way?"

"I do. I can get there all by myself."

I closed up the library and headed down to the café. The committee meeting was scheduled, but first, I was hungry and I kind of wanted to see Zeb, tell him about the dress and the Christmas Tree Pie Wedding Cake.

Dot Handy greeted me first. "Hey, Griselda, how's tricks?"

"OK, Dot. But I am hungry. What's good tonight?"

"Oh, you know it's all good. Zeb is a fine cook."

"Yeah, makes me wonder who will do the cooking in the family."

"Oh, this is strictly business. Believe me, you'll be the chief chef."

"OK, well, how about a burger tonight with fries."

Zeb stuck his head through the pick-up window. "Hey."

I smiled. "Hey, yourself. Make me a good burger."

"Let me see it," he said.

"See what?"

He held up his hand.

"Oh, oh, the ring. Right here. Right where you left it."

He smiled and went back to cooking and singing "Jingle Bells."

"I don't know when it was worse," Dot said. "When you two were on the outs or now. He's like a child back there. Never seen him so happy."

"He is cute."

Dot poured coffee in my cup.

"Are you coming to the meeting tonight?"

"Yep. Zeb is closing up early so we can have the place to ourselves."

"Good. Then I'll just stay here until everyone arrives."

Dot worked the counter and waited tables. She had gotten pretty good at handling the job. I could never do it. I would have everything so messed up and confused.

"I don't know how you do it." I said, as she placed a turkey platter in front of a customer.

"Do what?"

"Keep it all straight."

"Oh, you mean waitressing? Ah, it's nothing."

"I couldn't do it."

"Yeah, but I couldn't fly a plane. We all have our specialties."

Zeb's rendition of "Jingle Bells" came to a stop. "Plane?" he said. "Did you go flying with Cliff today?"

"No, not today, but I'm planning on flying to Scranton with him Saturday. Going to take my pilot's test."

"You still need to do that?" Zeb asked with his head and practically his whole body through the window.

"Yes. I told you. I'm getting my pilot's license."

"Uh-oh," Dot said. "Here we go again."

"No, no, Dot," I said. "It's all right. Isn't it, Zeb?"

Zeb was silent.

"Isn't it?" I said louder.

"Yeah, yeah. It's just fine."

Then all of sudden Zeb was standing in front of me. "I just worry about you—up there. It's dangerous."

"Cliff says it's safer than driving a car or truck."

"But you can survive a car crash."

"Don't fret. I'll be fine. We're getting married. God isn't going to take me home this close to my wedding day."

"You don't know that," he said.

"And speaking of days. What day are we getting married?"

Zeb grew quiet, as did the whole café.

"Yeah," called Harriet Nurse. "When is the big day? And are we all invited?"

"Sure, the whole town is invited. And how about it, Zeb? Want to make it a real Christmas wedding and get hitched on Christmas Eve?"

"Awwww," Dot said. "That's nice."

"I bought my dress today and arranged for a cake—well, sort of a cake, more like a Christmas surprise."

Zeb shook his head and rubbed the back of his neck. "Gee, Griselda, I hadn't thought about the exact date."

"You getting cold feet now?" Dot said.

"No. Fine. Christmas Eve it is. At the church. One o'clock in the afternoon."

I didn't say anything. If I did he'd just get all bothered that once again Agnes was getting between us. But I knew I had to tell him that we should probably have the ceremony at the nursing home.

Zeb went back to his kitchen and resumed singing.

Dot leaned close to me. "You know I was thinking. What about Agnes? How in the heck are you gonna get her to the church. Can't expect them to knock a wall down again to get Nate Kincaid's forklift through."

"I know," I whispered. "I have a plan, but he's not going to like it."

"And what do you mean by 'sort of a cake'?" he called.

18

Zeb had all the customers served and out the door by six o'clock—all but the members of the committee who had come in for dinner. We waited for Nate and Boris to arrive. Mildred would be late as usual. But Ruth was there. She brought her sewing along.

"I finished all the shepherds and Joseph, but I have two more angels to finish—my goodness but them girls shot up like weeds this year—and of course, Mary, but I can't do Mary until I know who's playing her."

I sat at the booth Ruth was at. "I'm hoping it will be Mercy Lincoln. I asked her today and she got really excited about doing it, a little dumbstruck at the notion of playing Jesus' mother. But she said she'd talk to her mama."

"Mercy Lincoln would be a great Mary," Dot said. "And I say we let her have the part in spite of Nate's protests. The old blowhard."

"OK," I said. "Now I know this is Boris's job ordinarily, but I think there are enough of us here to make a quorum. So with a show of hands, all in favor of Mercy Lincoln taking the role of Mary."

It was unanimous. Now I just had to pray that Charlamaine Lincoln would approve.

Boris and Nate arrived. They squeezed next to Studebaker. We only had to wait on Mildred.

"I sure hope she has news from Paradise about what's going on," Boris said. "I'd hate to lose the Shoops Moose. They provide a lot of revenue for us with advertising."

"While we wait," Nate said, "maybe we can move on to other business. I just want you to know I finished building the manger set. It's a doozy this year. And yes, Griselda, I got the inn finished also. It looks great. Stella helped me nail it all together."

"Boy, I haven't seen Stella in a while," I said. "How's she doing?"

"She's doing good, Griselda. She's been spending time with her brother. He's taking us to Bermuda this Christmas."

"Didn't you just go there for Thanksgiving?"

Nate nodded. "Yep, but we want to go back. It's fabulous. I might just move there some day."

Dot and I shared a knowing glance. That ended the possibility of Agnes getting forklifted into town. Nate was the only person in town who owned a forklift.

"And just so you know, Griselda," Nate said. "Stella and I brought the scenery out to Paradise for that woman to paint."

"Thank you, Nate," I said. "That's great."

"Honey," Zeb said. "Hold up your hand and show everyone."

"Oh, the ring. Yes, isn't it pretty?" I let everyone get a look at my diamond.

"It's very nice," Stu said. "A little small but . . . nice."

"Been in the family for generations."

"Congratulations," Boris said. "When's the big day?"

"Christmas Eve," Zeb said. "At the chapel."

Dot elbowed me. "You better say something," she whispered.

"Later," I said.

Fortunately Mildred came in. "Sorry I'm late, everyone. But I was out at Greenbrier interviewing the residents.".

"Did you learn anything," Boris asked. "Is it drugs?"

Mildred grabbed one of the lose chairs and pulled it close to the meeting. "No. Not drugs. Not exactly."

"Now what in jumpin' blue heck does that mean?" Boris asked. "We have to get this mystery solved."

"OK, OK," Mildred reached into her jacket pocket. "I found five or six of these in Haddie Grace's room." She placed a bottle on the table.

"What is it?" Boris asked. "A bottle?"

"Oh, it's more than a bottle. It's the Fountain of Youth."

"What?" Nate said.

"I don't understand, Mildred," Boris said.

"It's simple. That kooky Leon Fontaine thinks he discovered the Fountain of Youth up in Paradise."

Dot Handy cracked up. "That's hysterical."

"Hysterical?" Boris said. "It's criminal. Is he selling the water to those poor people."

"Nope," Mildred said. "He just gives it to them."

"And they believe him?" Studebaker said.

"Well, if you'd ever talked to Leon Fontaine you'd understand why," I said. "He fancies himself a kind of Don Quixote, defending the poor, doing good deeds. He thinks he's a kind of modern-day knight in shining armor."

"Then he's crazy," Boris said.

"Maybe," Mildred said. "He's certainly delusional. But I just don't know what to do with him."

"Did you talk to Doctor Silver?" I asked.

"Not yet. Going up there in the morning."

Boris looked both pensive and aghast. His big round eyes became slits. "I don't know if this will satisfy the Moose. They're pretty clear on what they condone and what they don't."

"It's water," Zeb said. "Plain, old-fashioned water."

"Leon just convinced some of the people out there that it'll make them younger," I said. "And they believe him."

"Power of suggestion," Dot said. "My, my, but it's powerful. I heard of cases where doctors gave sugar pills to people and cured them of their ills—all because the patient believed it."

"Mind control?" Boris said. "You're talking about some kind of mind control. I don't know what's worse—drugs or mind control."

"No, no," Mildred said. "Leon isn't doing anything but telling people that they can be younger if they drink his special water. They believe it and voila!"

"Voila!" Stu said.

"You should go see for yourself. It's quite a sight."

"Trouble is," Mildred said. "I'm not sure what to do about it."

"Arrest him on fraud charges," Boris said.

"Oh, stop it Boris," I said. "The man is harmless. I say we let Doctor Silver decide. He's the medical director out there."

"OK, OK. I'll inform the Moose Lodge of your findings, Mildred, and hopefully they'll agree to be in the parade. Silly little moose antlers and all."

"So it's all settled then," I said. "We have our Mary, and the mystery of Greenbrier has been solved."

"Floats are ready, scenery painted," Nate said. "Mary? You mean that Negro girl?"

"Yes," I said.

Nate took in the glares that were sent his way. "OK, OK. Just asking."

"My goodness," Ruth said. "I don't remember a time when we were more prepared for a Christmas Festival."

"It is in good shape this year."

"And don't forget about the camel and sheep," Ruth said,

"Hold on a second," Boris said. "Camel? Sheep?"

"Yep, we're getting live animals for the pageant. Isn't that just so wonderful?" Ruth said. "And maybe they can march in the parade too."

"We can't have live animals in the church," Stu said. "They'll . . . they'll mess all over the place."

"Oh, don't be such a fussbudget, Stu," Ruth said. "They'll walk on, stand there while the children say their lines, and then walk off. Filby said his friends will take care of the whole thing."

"Well, they better," Boris said. "And they better not bite any of the children. Our insurance doesn't cover camel bites."

"Don't worry, none of the children will get hurt. In fact, they are really excited about it."

Boris banged his gavel. "All right, all right. If there is no other business then I move that the meeting be adjourned and we meet at the Kincaid Farm next Saturday at 6:00 a.m. to kick off the Bright's Pond Christmas Parade."

We all cheered. As much trouble as it was to carry off, the parade was the highlight of our year. I think the whole town came out for it and maybe even a few folks from Shoops. They had their own parade, but there was just something special about a Bright's Pond Christmas Parade. It brought cheer to all and ignited the Christmas spirit.

Everyone got up to leave. Zeb grabbed my hand. "It's early yet. Want to go for a walk or sit by the fire at your place—soon to be our place?"

"Sounds nice," I said.

"Ah, you two are so cute together," Dot said.

Zeb turned off the lights and pulled the café door closed. He locked it and checked the handle twice. "OK, let's go."

"Zeb," I said. "We have to talk."

"What now, Grizzy? Don't tell me you changed your mind again."

"Not about us. But—and I know you're gonna get angry—but it's about Agnes."

"Agnes. I knew she'd get in the middle again."

We walked a few steps holding hands. "Maybe I'll explain after you get the fire going."

———— ❧ ————

A little while later the fire was blazing, and I made warm cider for Zeb and me.

I kissed him and then I said, "There's no way we can get married in the chapel."

"Ah, Griselda, I told you it was important to me to get married in church."

"There's no way to get Agnes there. I can't get married without her."

"Why? Don't you think she'd understand? You dedicated your whole life to her. It's her turn to give up something for you."

"Zeb, I understand. But she's all the family I have. I keep thinking about what it would be like to know that I got married without my sister looking on, without her being there with me. I . . . I don't think I can live with that."

"But what about what I want? I don't have any family, since my mother died. I guess it's the town, Bright's Pond is family, my customers, the regulars who I know more about than their doctors."

"I understand that, too, but I know that if you think Agnes's presence comes between us a lot, well, I'm afraid what this absence could do."

Zeb poked at the fire. "Then what do you suggest, the nursing home? I don't want to get married in a smelly old nursing home surrounded by sick people and—"

"How about at the nursing home, but outside? In the gazebo."

"That crazy monstrosity that loony Leon Fountain—"

"Fontaine."

"—built?"

"Yep. We can wheel Agnes out in her chair. She can sit right at the foot of the little steps. It could be so romantic. You and me and Pastor Speedwell in the gazebo with—say, who is your best man?"

Zeb looked at me with a funny grin. "Oh, I hadn't even thought about it."

"You need a best man."

He poked at the embers and a giant spark jumped onto the hearth. He stamped the tiny molten pool with his boot. "Like I said, I never gave it a thought."

"What about Studebaker?"

"Stu? Maybe. I'd say Nate but he'll be in Bermuda."

"Boris?"

"For criminy's sake, no! He'd insist on wearing that ugly gray suit and that striped tie and probably want a cigar in his lapel."

"There must be someone."

"Do I really need a best man?"

"Someone has to hold the rings."

"OK, Grizzy, I guess it'll have to be Stu."

"Stu it is. But you better tell him soon. Or I should say ask him soon."

"We should have just eloped," Zeb said.

"Oh, Zeb, no, I want a wedding. It will all work out. You'll see . . . I hope."

"Could be pretty cold outside on Christmas Eve," Zeb said. "Not like we can wear overcoats on top of our wedding clothes."

"That's doesn't matter. Our hearts will be warm."

"Oh, Griselda, that's—"

"A little much?"

Zeb pulled me close and kissed me. "I wish we were already married."

I sighed. "Me too. But soon."

19

The next morning arrived with rain and cold. It was the kind of rain that started as ice pellets and then turned to rain once it hit the ground. I could hear it pelting the windows and roof. Arthur never liked this kind of rain. I think the noise bothered him, and he stayed underfoot all morning. I tripped over him twice.

"I'm going to hurt you if you don't watch out," I said. "Crazy, paranoid cat."

After breakfast, I made my way to the town hall hoping to catch up with Mildred. She was planning on meeting with Doctor Silver. I kind of wanted to be in on the conversation. I walked because the roads looked a little slippery, and it could be worse by the time we finished at Greenbrier. Mildred could just drop me at home afterward.

"Nasty weather," she said when I saw her in her office.

"Yeah. I'm worried about the kids' rehearsal tonight. I hope Dot is able to still hold it. And I hope Mercy Lincoln comes out."

"Oh, that's right. Well, they're calling for rain on and off all day and turning to ice. Not a great day to be on the roads. I might have to close the highway in and out of town later."

"Oh, that won't matter so much. Most of the kids can walk."

"Good." Mildred searched through papers on her desk. "So are you ready to go?"

"Yep. I'm hoping the doctor decides to let it go. Maybe just tell Leon to stop coming around and then he can get the place back to normal."

"I'm hoping he decides to pop Leon Fontaine in the loony bin."

"Ah, that isn't nice. He's harmless."

"For now, but one day . . . he could snap and shoot up the trailer park."

"Nah, they got one wacky guy up there already. That's his job."

"Oh, yeah, I remember. The old war vet who shoots trash cans and raccoons. Haven't heard much from him lately."

She pulled her office door closed, and we headed for the car.

Mildred drove a little slow, maybe a little too slow, all the way to the nursing home. "I'd much rather drive on snow than this stuff," she said. "I don't like not being able to feel the road under my tires."

"I appreciate you going up here today."

"Need answers, Griselda. The law doesn't take a holiday."

That time I tried real hard not to roll my eyes but sometimes it was all a person could do.

She pulled into the parking lot. It was pretty sparse that day. "Looks like some folks might have taken the day off."

"It's the smart thing to do," I said.

We saw Nurse Sally first.

"Don't you ever leave this place?" I said half joking. "Doesn't your family miss you?"

"No. I spent the night last night on account of the weather. I knew a lot of people would call in sick. Someone had to be here."

"Is Doctor Silver here?" Mildred asked.

"He called. He'll be in a little late. Maybe an hour."

"Oh, geez," Mildred said looking around the place. "That's OK, mind if I interview some of the other residents?"

"No, just be careful like before. We don't want blood pressure spikes and heart attacks on a day like this."

"Let's start with Agnes," Mildred said.

"Agnes? But she hasn't taken any of the magic water."

"I know, but she might know something."

We headed down the hall toward Agnes's room. I noticed Christmas cutouts taped to the walls—ornaments, Santas, trees, and candy canes. Some of them looked homemade and cut from construction paper with glitter and ribbons, while others were definitely store-bought.

"She would have told me if she knew anything," I said.

"Yeah, but still, let's go visit. Sometimes a trained interrogator can ask just the right question to jar a person's memory."

Agnes was still in her bed. The home was short on aides so there was a good chance she could stay in bed all day. When I saw her lying there I imagined Ruth trying to wrap enough pink satin around her to make a suitable bridesmaid dress. I didn't know whether to laugh or cry.

"Morning, Agnes," I said. "Look who's here."

"Mildred Blessing," Agnes said. "How are you?"

Mildred removed her cop hat and walked over to Agnes's bedside. "Hi, Agnes. It's good to see you. You're looking chipper, and I think maybe a little skinnier?" She put a question mark on the end of the sentence.

"Yeah, they say I'm losing but I can't tell. I still have enough blubber to keep Anchorage in lights for a year or more."

"Now, Agnes," I said. "What did we decide about you putting yourself down?"

"Oh, I've just been feeling upset since our last talk. You know about the wedding and the dress and all."

I helped her with a sip of water. "I have good news about that," I said. "We're going to get married right here at Greenbrier. Out in the gazebo."

"No kidding, really? Zeb agreed to that?"

"Sure did. I figure we'll wheel you out and you can sit in your chair while Pastor Speedwell does the deed."

"Does the deed," Mildred said. "You make it sound like an execution."

"Oh, stop," Agnes said. "It sounds lovely. When?"

"Christmas Eve."

"Christmas Eve? Wow. But what if it snows?"

"No matter, we'll still do it."

"But what about a dress?" Agnes asked.

"Ruth Knickerbocker is working on it."

"She's sewing me a dress?" Agnes said. I thought I saw a spark of interest. She pulled herself up on the trapeze bar. "That's so sweet of her."

"Yep." I knew I was rushing the truth, but I also knew that when the chips were down Ruth was the woman you wanted in your corner.

"Agnes," Mildred said, "mind if I change the subject?"

"Course not. What's on your mind?"

"It's about Leon Fontaine and the way people are acting."

"Oh, I suppose you want to talk about that supposed Fountain of Youth water."

"You heard about it?" I said. "Why didn't you tell me?"

"It was just the other day, and you haven't been here for me to tell. Haddie Grace showed me one of Leon's bottles. Cute."

"Do you know anyone else he might have given it to?" Mildred asked.

Agnes smiled and her eyebrows rose. "Just look around. Plenty of people acting a little . . . peculiar."

"Did he try to give you any?"

"No. Not sure why. Maybe he was afraid of me. I could crush him, you know."

Nurse Sally poked her head in the room. "Excuse me, but Chief Blessing, Doctor Silver has arrived a little earlier than he thought. I told him you wanted to speak to him."

"Oh, oh, thank you," Mildred said. "Now look, Agnes, you just keep getting skinny and don't worry about Leon Fontaine. I'll get the little con artist on some charge."

"I ain't worried about him," Agnes said. "I'm just wondering why everyone is making such a big deal about it."

"People could get hurt," Mildred said.

I kissed Agnes's cheek. "I'll be back before we leave." I looked out the window. "And from the looks of that sky and the sleet falling it better be soon."

———∞———

Doctor Silver was tall, young, and handsome with Al Pacino hair. He wore his white doctor coat with two pens sticking out of the top pocket. His name, Dr. Richard Silver, was embroidered under the pocket in blue thread.

Mildred spoke first. "Good morning, Doctor Silver, Chief Mildred Blessing, Bright's Pond Chief of Police, I was hoping you could shed some light on what is going on around here."

He looked up from his desk work. "Morning. I wish I could. All I know is what you know, and I also wish someone would put an end to it and soon. These people should not be carrying on the way they are."

"Then you know about Leon Fontaine?"

He nodded. "I do. And I told Haddie and Clive and the others, especially Jasper York, to stop taking his water. They call it the Elixir—did you know that? The Elixir of Youth."

"Can't you force them to stop?"

"It's water." Doctor Silver stood up and walked to a small table that held a coffee carafe. "Oh, please, let Sally have filled this thing this morning."

"Are you OK?" I asked.

Doctor Silver poured the carafe. "Ah, hot coffee. Yes, I'm fine. A bit busy." He returned to his desk. "I think you'll need to ban Leon Fontaine from coming around here," Doctor Silver said. "Slap some kind of restraining order on him."

"Will you swear that he's a detriment and harming people?"

The doctor nodded his head as he sipped coffee from a green mug. "Yep. Just give me the papers."

That was when we heard Haddie whiz past the office.

"She is going to kill herself," Doctor Silver said. "That woman's bones are as brittle as tree bark. One good crash and—SNAP!"

I shuddered.

"OK," Mildred said. "I'll round him up today and put an end to these shenanigans."

Doctor Silver doodled something on a white pad. "You know, it really has been something though. I've seen people who haven't gotten out of bed in weeks suddenly get up and move around like they were ten years younger."

"Then what's the big deal?" I asked.

"It's dangerous, Miss Sparrow, this kind of mind control."

"Mind control?" I said. "Are you serious? It's just a little— well, a lot of—persuasive salesmanship."

"Just stop him, please. Before something happens. It's hard to examine people on tricycles and hanging from trees."

"I will," Mildred said. "You can count on—"

BAM! CRASH! The sound of falling objects rang through the room.

"Oh, no," Doctor Silver said. He nearly leaped across his desk. We followed after.

Haddie Grace was lying in a twisted heap near her tricycle.

A resident who was standing with his back against the wall like he had been stapled there said, "I jumped out of her way and she swerved and crashed into the medicine cart. Is she . . . dead?"

Doctor Silver knelt beside Haddie. "No, she's unconscious, and from the looks of it I'd say she has a broken hip and God knows what else."

"That tears it," Mildred said. "He's under arrest now. Come on, Griselda. I got to get to Paradise and find him, if you're coming."

I looked at the spare little woman. "Coming, Mildred."

∞

It was a rare occurrence but also one of Mildred's all-time favorite parts of being a cop: she flipped on her flashing lights and siren and off we went to Paradise in hot pursuit of Leon Fontaine.

"Do you think he's on to us?" Mildred said as she took a curve like a racecar driver. I thought we might flip over for a second.

"N-n-no," I said hanging on for dear life. "He doesn't know he's doing anything harmful."

"I can't let him keep giving them people that water," Mildred said.

"I think he'll be reasonable. If you just talk to him. And Mildred, I'd like to wear the dress I bought to my wedding and not a body cast. Slow down."

"Oh, sorry," she said and then added, "civilians."

The weather turned nastier and nastier the closer we got to the trailer park. Ice and sleet pelted the windshield. No one was on the road but us and what smelled like a manure truck up ahead. Dark, almost black, snow clouds hung overhead, bottom-heavy and ominous.

"Did you hear anything about snow later?" I said. "Sure looks it."

"No, but that's fine with me. Rather have snow than this . . . stuff. I hate ice."

"All the more reason to slow down."

I saw the Paradise sign all lit up and flashing against the gray sky. "Oh, good, almost there."

"I think this is gonna be harder than you think," Mildred said. "We can't even get him to admit that he's giving the water to the people, let alone get him to stop."

"I know, but I think maybe if you put a little scare into him, that might work."

Mildred chuckled. "Are you kidding? That man's a nutcase. I don't know how to get through to him. Might have to arrest him and bring him out to Greenbrier—to that psychiatric ward of theirs and let them deal with him."

"Brig-a-LOON," I said. "Oh, don't do that. He'll crumble in a place like that. Leon thinks he's a hero, a knight in shining armor saving people."

"But what if Haddie Grace dies?" Mildred said.

"We'll pray she won't. But even then, I doubt the reality of the situation will sink in. Leon is convinced he's Don Quixote or something."

"All the more reason to lock him away."

Mildred pulled against a curb in front of a green trailer and pushed the gearshift into park. I caught my breath. "Mr. Toad's Wild Ride."

"What?"

"Nothing. Let's find Leon."

"I want to find Asa first. We might need his help."

Mildred pushed open the door and stepped out. She plopped her cop hat on her head. This time it was covered with a shower cap. I smiled at it.

"Regulations," she said. "If I ruin another hat, Boris will have my hide."

We approached the manager's trailer. Mildred knocked three times. We waited. Finally, Asa opened the door.

"Ah, geez," he said. "What in the world are you two doing out in this weather?"

"Official police business," Mildred said. "Can we come in?"

Asa stepped aside. "Sure. Come on in."

Asa's trailer looked comfortable enough with its pale blue walls and a kitchen counter that jutted into the living room. "Oh, that's a good idea," I said. "It's like a bar, a counter you can eat at without needing to take up space with a table."

Asa looked at me with raised eyebrows. "Now I know you didn't come to see me about my kitchen."

I watched as he pinned the empty sleeve to his shoulder. "Don't need mice running up my sleeve," he said. And then smiled.

"I'm here to arrest Leon Fontaine. I'd like you to come along, Mr. Kowalski, if you don't mind."

"Me? Why? What can I do?" He took a few steps backward.

"I hope you don't have to do anything, but if that little weirdo tries to escape I might need your help, and besides, you know the park. You know where he could run."

Asa shook his head. "I don't like this but—"

"Asa," I said. "One of Leon's regular customers had an accident. It's pretty serious."

"Oh, no," he said. He pushed his feet into a pair of black leather boots. "I'm sorry to hear that. But they do know it's just water. Not like the man drugged them—well, not with actual drugs."

"I know," Mildred said. "But he endangered people's lives. He needs to be stopped . . . now."

"I guess you should try his trailer," Asa said.

We walked the short distance to the trailer in the now driving rain and sleet. There wasn't a soul stirring on the streets. The trailers appeared battened down for the duration with shutters closed and curtains drawn. Lawn furniture tethered to porches, flags removed from their posts. It was kind of creepy—like a ghost town.

"You better make this snappy," Asa said. "They'll be closing the roads."

"I'm a cop, Asa," Mildred said. "I always get through."

Asa and I grinned at each other.

"So," Asa said when we approached the trailer. "Want me to knock or—"

"No, I'll do it," Mildred said. She walked up the three steps and rapped on the screen door. We waited. No answer. Mildred pulled open the screen and knocked on the wood door. No answer. She tried the knob. It wouldn't budge.

"You a got a key?" Mildred called to Asa.

Asa shook his head. "Look, I have spare keys to all the trailers, but I can't let you use it. Not without a warrant."

"Ah, come on," Mildred said. "I just want to see if he's hiding in there."

"Nope, sorry. I can't do it. Taken me a while to build trust around here. I won't do it, Mildred."

Mildred walked down the steps. "Mind if I check out back?"

"Go ahead, but I doubt he'll be out there. All the sane people are holed up somewhere waiting out the storm."

"Could be in that shed mixing up another batch of magic water."

I laughed and stayed back with Asa.

"I don't know who's crazier," Asa said. "Leon or Mildred."

"She's just doing her job, and you know Leon needs to be stopped. I mean, what if Haddie dies as a result of his actions?"

"He didn't force her to drink the water. She did it of her own volition. But yeah, I get it."

Mildred returned. "He's not there. All I found were bottles."

"I told you," Asa said. He folded his arms across his chest. "It's cold. Can I go home now?"

"Any idea where he might go?"

"Look, Mildred, I'm the manager not the babysitter. I have no idea. He's over twenty-one and can do what he wants."

We headed back to the car. Asa took off in front of us.

"Now what?" I said.

"He has to come home sometime."

"You aren't planning on sitting here all day? I got to get home."

"No, no, not today."

We arrived back at the car. The radio was squawking when we sat inside. Mildred picked up the receiver. "This is Mildred, go ahead."

"Mildred, it's Boris. I'm patching a call through from Greenbrier."

"Ten-four. Go ahead."

"Can he do that?" I asked.

Mildred shushed me.

"Chief Blessing, this is Nurse Sally."

"Copy that, go ahead."

I heard Nurse Sally suppress a laugh. "I just wanted to let you know that Haddie has been taken by ambulance to County. Richard—er, Doctor Silver says her condition is serious."

"Copy that. Keep me posted."

"Ten-four," Sally said. I could hear her sarcastic smile through the airwaves.

Mildred hung the receiver on a little hook.

"Oh, dear," I said. "This doesn't sound good."

"We have to find Leon—and soon. Before someone else gets hurt. Or Haddie dies."

20

Where to?" Mildred asked as we approached the town square.

"I guess home. Not much we can do but wait until Leon comes out of hiding."

"Hiding," Mildred said. "Where could he be? He's like an . . . what do they call it? An enigma."

"It's a very Don Quixote thing to do. I worry what he'll do if he finds out that Haddie had an accident."

"Oh, I kind of think Leon will be just fine." She pulled against the curb. "See you later."

I pushed open the door and Arthur met me, mewing like he was angry. "I know, I know, I haven't been around a lot. Bet you're hungry."

My cat was not a fan of dry cat food but sometimes it was just easier and less smelly than canned. I dumped about a cup of kibble into his bowl. He looked at me like I had some nerve to serve it to him, but he ate it anyway.

Sometimes, especially on stormy days, the house was too quiet. It made me look forward to having Zeb move in even if I was still a little nervous. As I looked around the house, I tried to imagine him sitting in an easy chair by the fire, watching TV while I puttered away in the kitchen preparing meals. The kitchen, it hadn't changed since my mother cooked in there for my father and Agnes and me. Well, except for some new curtains and minor repairs. The table was the same one our family used, long and rectangular full of dings and dents now that I always covered with a tablecloth.

My stomach growled as I stood peering out the window over the sink. The sleet had turned to mostly snow now. I could see the large flakes falling at a more leisurely rate as the wind had died down. But I could still see snow blowing over the street like dust.

Arthur leaped onto the counter and meowed deeply. I chased him off. "You know you're not allowed up there."

My thoughts turned to Leon as I watched the snow. He was out there. Somewhere. Mostly likely snug in his trailer on a night like this. But then again, he could have been or gone anywhere. It was entirely possible that we would never see him again.

"Where could he have gone?" I asked Arthur, who had nothing to say on the subject. "There are no windmills in Bright's Pond or Knights of the White Moon for him to battle or pigs—"

Oh, dear. Pigs. I remembered that Don Quixote had a run-in with some pigs. Leon could have gone to the Frost Sisters' pig farm, expecting to be trampled. It's possible that word got to him about Haddie and he had gone out to harm himself now, just like Don Quixote would.

I searched through my address book and found Charlotte Figg's number. I dialed.

"Charlotte," I said. "This is Griselda Sparrow."

"Oh, hi," she said. "Terrible storm, eh?"

"Yes, terrible, but have you seen Leon Fontaine today?"

"Leon? No, I don't think so. But I haven't been out much today. Why?"

"Oh, just a hunch. I can't explain now."

I hung up and dialed Mildred's office number. She answered and I told her my theory.

"Pigs? But that's crazy," she said.

"Mildred, Leon is not the sanest member of the group, now is he? I think we can all agree that he seems to have a few screws loose."

"Yeah, I know, but pigs? Are you certain?"

"It makes sense, given everything else."

Mildred made a noise like she was tapping the receiver against her forehead, considering things. "I guess I better ride back out there."

"Or you could call the Frost Sisters."

"Oh, right. I'll do that first."

"Let me know what happens."

"Ten-four," she said. "I'll be in touch."

There was no way I was going to drive out to Paradise, so I decide to just wait it out by the fire. It would give me time to think about my wedding. I grabbed a notepad and a cup of tea and settled on the red sofa near the fireplace. I had nice dry kindling and plenty of wood, so getting the fire roaring took no time at all.

"Now then, I should make a checklist."

I started with the dress and checked it off. Next I listed, shoes, cake, Agnes's dress, rings, music, and reception. Reception. I supposed we could hold it in the nursing home Sunshine Room but we would sure as shootin' need to provide the food. Oh, dear. Food—sit down? buffet? pizza? Maybe Zeb could handle that. No, he's the groom.

The night seemed to go quickly after that, and I was happy to be going to bed. The next few days were sizing up to be on the bumpy side.

∞

Haddie's condition that Thursday morning remained unchanged. She was still serious and unconscious. And Leon was still nowhere to be found. Fortunately, the weather had cleared, the sun shone, and the temperature was supposed to reach near fifty degrees. The ice had made for some slick spots on the sidewalks and roads but by eleven o'clock or so it would be clear, easy to get around.

"I need to see Ruth," I told Arthur. "I mean, it would be nice if I told her she was making Agnes's dress, don't you think?"

He looked at me as if to say, "No problem, Griselda, she has less than a week. Plenty of time." My cat meowed and then licked his paws like he had said his piece and that was that. Now it was my problem. As I scratched under his chin, I wondered how he would feel when Zeb moved in.

Ruth was home and still busy at work trying to finish all the Christmas pageant costumes.

"One more sheep head to go," she said. "Then I can take a break. No more sewing. Not that I mind all that much, but the tips of my fingers are raw from pushing needles through that thick sheep material."

I smiled and raised my eyebrows at her. Well, satin would be easier to work with.

"Griselda, you got something on your mind?"

254

"I do," I said. "But how about some lemon squares and coffee. I can smell the lemon. How'd you find time to make a batch?"

"I needed a change from thread and pins and needles, and speaking of which, my bottom is full of them from sitting so long."

"What?"

"Pins and needles. A stretch will do me good."

"Good, let's go in the kitchen and have a snack."

"Griselda Sparrow. You definitely have something percolating around in that brain of yours. And it must be big, from the looks of you."

"You could say that."

We sat at her kitchen table and enjoyed a lemon square or two.

"That was some storm yesterday, huh?" she said.

"Yeah, I was out with Mildred. Which reminds me, did you hear what happened to Haddie Grace?"

"That little old lady on the red tricycle?" She stirred her coffee.

"Yes, she took quite a spill and is in the hospital, unconscious and in serious condition."

"Oh, dear me," Ruth said. "I hope she'll be OK."

"Me too. Mildred is looking for Leon Fontaine. She's going to try and slap charges on him and have him arrested, especially if Haddie . . . if something happens to her."

"Oh, don't say that. But what did Leon do? He gave her water. Riding the bike was her idea."

"Mildred said he endangered her life, and apparently that's against the law."

"It'll never stick."

"I'll check on her later. And I hope Leon, wherever he is, finally decides to show up. For his own sake. The longer he hides the worse it looks. I thought he might have gone to the Frost Sisters' pig farm."

"Pig farm. Now why in the heck would he do that? Pigs don't need Fountain of Youth Water."

"Oh, it's a Don Quixote thing."

"Oh, then, I, of course, could never understand." Her sarcasm apparent.

"Oh, Ruth, I didn't mean to make it sound like you couldn't understand. I'm just tired of thinking about it, and I have a huge favor to ask—I mean huge." I spread my arms out wide.

"Uh oh, now what? I am not playing Mary in the play." She smiled.

"No, no, Mercy Lincoln is still our Mary, but speaking of Mary, well, marry actually, I want Agnes to be my maid of honor."

Ruth patted my hand. "Of course you do. My feelings aren't hurt. She's your sister. We're just friends."

"Thank you, Ruth. But what I need is for you to make a dress for her."

She swallowed and a piece of lemon bar got caught in her throat. She coughed and choked. "A dress? A whole dress? For Agnes?"

"Yep, something pink and maybe a wide-brim hat."

She shook her head. "Pink? For a Christmas wedding? No, it's got to be red. Bright, Christmas red with a red sash around a wide-brim hat."

I thought a moment. The image was stunning.

"Can you do it? By Christmas Eve?"

"Sure, but I'm gonna need to get out there and take some measurements."

"Fine. We can do that today."

Ruth picked at the remaining lemon bar on her plate. "I guess I can do it. Gonna need a lot of fabric and maybe some elastic, lots of elastic."

"Well, Shoops is the elastic capital of the world."

"Oh, yeah, that factory is down there."

"I guess I could get a pattern and alter the pattern. I'll need two, no make it three patterns, and I'll piece them together to make one huge dress."

"This sounds complicated," I said.

"It is. But I'll do my best, and look, if worse comes to worst, we'll just wrap the fabric around her."

"I had thought of that, but Ruth, she's feeling a bit sensitive about it so if we can find a way to make her look and feel pretty—"

"Don't fret. I'll do something. But what about you? Are you going to feel pretty?"

I looked past her out the window. "You know, as silly as it sounds, I've actually been feeling pretty already—even in blue jeans—ever since Zeb gave me the ring."

"Ah, that's so sweet. Now when do you want to get out there? I think I should get started right away. This is a big operation. And then, I'll need to go into Shoops to the fabric store down there and buy the patterns and pins—Oh, good grief—I'm gonna need a lot of pins and . . . and help, Griselda. I'm gonna need help."

"I'll help as much as I can."

"And green ribbon," Ruth said. "And thread, lots of thread. Might need a spare bobbin or two and maybe some more machine oil. It's been sticking . . ."

I listened as Ruth meandered on about the dress, and for the time being, at least, Leon Fontaine's troubles took a backseat to my wedding plans.

Ruth pulled on a heavy blue coat and slipped into a pair of ankle-high rubber boots with zippers up the instep.

"At least the weather is cooperating," I said as we climbed into the truck.

"Yeah," Ruth said. "I'd hate to be driving to Shoops in all that sleet and ice—but I'd still do it, you know. This is an emergency."

"Thank you, Ruth. You are a really good friend."

And that was when it dawned on me that Ruth should have been my maid of honor.

"Are you happy?" Ruth asked. "Really and truly happy to be marrying Zeb?"

"I am happy. At first I wasn't even sure I wanted to. But after I got to thinking about it I realized that I love Zeb with all my heart. I've loved him for a long time and that's why, at least I think it's why, I wasn't having all those in-love symptoms. I already did all that, long time ago."

"I guess that makes sense. But I got to tell you, I was worried that you were gonna run off or fly off with Cliff Cardwell. I had visions of you two soaring off into the clouds and I would never, ever see you again."

I turned onto the street that headed straight to the nursing home. "To be honest. There was a time there when I thought I might also. But that's all over."

Ruth was quiet a minute or two. "I'm glad you didn't. Zeb's the right fella for you."

"I know. But don't get worried if you see me flying over Bright's Pond with Cliff on Saturday."

"Saturday? What's happening?"

"I'm taking the test for my pilot's license."

"No fooling? You still think you need that?"

I ignored the snippet of annoyance that crept into my mind. "Yes. I still need to do it—for me."

"OK, just asking. Now tell me, did you get a cake?"

I told her about Charlotte's Christmas Pie Cake idea.

"Oh, goodness gracious that sounds like fun. So . . . unique, kind of like my Thanksgiving."

―――∞∞∞―――

We arrived at the nursing home in time to see Mildred walking toward her police cruiser.

"Wonder what she's doing here?" Ruth asked.

"Still looking for Leon, I would imagine. He's a slippery one."

"Any ideas?"

"Nah, he probably doesn't even know anything is wrong or that anyone is looking for him. But I did tell Mildred that he might have gone to the Frost Sisters' pig farm."

Mildred spotted my truck and waved me over. I stopped just near her. She leaned on the open window. "Morning."

"Hey, Mildred. Any news?"

"Just that there is still no change in Haddie Grace and Leon is still missing."

I shook my head. "No one has seen him?"

"Nope. But I posted some spies inside the nursing home to keep a lookout, and I confiscated seventy bottles of that wacky water."

I couldn't help laughing.

"You do know it's just water." Ruth said.

"But they don't," Mildred said. "And that's the trouble."

"So, just tell them." Ruth leaned over me to get a better look at Mildred. "Just tell them."

"Doctor Silver doesn't think that's a good idea just yet. Might be too jarring for some of them, and he also said that a few people like Jasper York are doing pretty well—lower blood pressure and such."

"That is just amazing," Ruth said. "Makes me think about my Hubby Bubby, maybe if Leon Fontaine was here back then he might have been able to convince Bubba he didn't have that tumor."

I looked at her like she had completely lost her mind. "But he still would have had the tumor."

"Anyway," Mildred said. "Keep your eye out and report back to me if you see him."

"Did you go to the pig farm?"

"I called the sisters. They hadn't seen hide nor hair of him and said their pigs were all accounted for and doing just fine."

"That's good. I just thought I should mention it. Now, if I do see him, should I say anything to him?" I asked.

"Nope. Just tell me his location."

"Ten-four," I said.

⸎

The nursing home felt a bit subdued when Ruth and I entered. Oh, a few folks were bustling around and there was a lot of chattering going on among residents, but it still felt different, like maybe the magic had worn off. I saw Jasper working on a puzzle with another old man.

Nurse Sally greeted us.

"Is Haddie doing any better?" I asked.

"No, I just got off the phone, and the doctor at the hospital says she's still unconscious. I'm going to try to contact her family today. I hate doing that. They live in Missouri."

"I'd a thought you would have done that by now," Ruth said.

"I tried," Sally said. "I have one phone number and if no one answers the phone there is nothing I can do."

"Telegram?" Ruth said.

"That would be next, but if they aren't home to answer the phone then they wouldn't be home to sign for a telegram."

"Are you OK?" I asked. Sally seemed a little short on patience. Not that I could blame her.

"Oh, yeah. I'm OK. Just tired. Been working a lot of hours."

Ruth appeared pensive a moment and then she tugged on Sally's sleeve. "Oh, oh, I just had a thought." She sort of half-laughed. "Maybe you should get Leon to go to the hospital and talk to Haddie. Maybe she'll listen to him. Maybe she'll wake up for him if he has so much power over these folks."

Sally and I looked at each other like we had both seen the same lightbulb snap on at the same time.

"That is not a bad idea," Sally said. "It couldn't hurt."

"It is a good idea except there is just one problem."

"What's that?" Sally asked. "I'm sure Rich—er, Doctor Silver would allow it."

"Leon Fontaine is missing," I said. Mildred has been looking for him. "No one has seen him. We've been looking all over town."

"Oh, that's why she's been wandering around here like a bloodhound. Sometimes I think that woman doesn't like me. She never talks to me."

"Well, look," I said. "We have to find Leon now. He could be Haddie's only hope."

"That's all fine and dandy," Ruth said. "But if I'm gonna build a dress for Agnes to wear in your wedding I need those measurements—today."

"Don't worry. We'll do that first."

Agnes was up and in her chair. She actually looked kind of happy and my first thought was that she had gotten hold of some of the Fountain of Youth water, but Agnes didn't believe in it. And you had to be completely sold for the water to work.

"Morning," I said. "Look who I brought."

"Ruth," Agnes said and then smiled as wide as I have ever seen. "It is so nice to see you. Come give me a hug."

Ruth wrapped her arms around Agnes as well as she could and kissed her cheek. "How are you, Agnes? You're looking and feeling skinny."

"Oh, go on. I'm still fat Agnes."

"Now, Agnes, you got to stop thinking of yourself that way. After all, it's not all your fault you got so . . . like this. Now we're here on business."

"Business?" Agnes said. "What kind of business. I haven't seen Leon Fontaine if that's what you mean."

"No, not Leon. Remember I told you Ruth is making your dress? Well, she needs to take some measurements."

"Just three or four or five, maybe six," Ruth said. "I want to be certain the dress fits you right."

"Oh, just dye a horse blanket pink and wrap me up."

"No, no," I said. "And we decided that you should wear red with white and green trim—more like Christmas."

"Oh, dear Lord," Agnes said. "I'm gonna look like a giant tree ornament or Christmas piñata."

"Agnes," I said with my fists on my hips. "Do you *want* to be my maid of honor or not?"

"Of course, of course. Just don't want to be all embarrassed in the process."

"Don't worry about that," Ruth said. "I'm gonna make such a pretty dress. You will feel so nice rolling down the aisle."

Ruth unsnapped her purse and dug deep inside. She pulled out a lipstick, two hankies, a pincushion, three nickels, and lint-covered butterscotch Life Savers, all of which she piled on Agnes's tray table. Then, finally, she pulled out a long tape measure.

"Now don't get upset, Agnes, but I had to string together two tape measures into one, so's to reach all the way around."

Agnes only closed her eyes a second like the words might have stung. I patted her hand.

"OK, let's start at your . . . um . . . bosom. Griselda will you take one end of the measure and just kind of start where you can. And Agnes if you could sit up as straight as you can that will help, and maybe lean forward so I can reach this tape—" she brought the tape measure around her back where I grabbed it. "There, that's it."

"OK," I said. "I got it. Looks like—"

"No, no," Agnes said. "I don't want to hear the number. Just write it down."

And so it went the next several minutes as we took six different measurements including the length of her arm and distance around her bicep.

"All done," Ruth said. "Now I just need to go into Shoops and purchase the fabric and elastic and a wide-brimmed hat and—"

"Hat?" Agnes said. You mean I gotta wear a hat too?"

"Sure," Ruth said. "Don't worry. It'll be so pretty."

Ruth shoved the tape measure and everything else she had fished out of it back into her purse.

"Have you heard any news on Haddie?" Agnes asked.

"Just that she's still unconscious," I said.

"They're looking for Leon Fontaine," Ruth said. "I bet he can call her out of her sleep. You know whisper in her ear. I bet she'll hear him."

Agnes's eyebrows rose. "That might work."

"Except no one can find him," I said. "He just disappeared."

"Oh, he's got to be somewhere. Everyone is somewhere."

"Well, if you see him, let Sally or Mildred know."

"I will."

I smiled into Agnes's tiny eyes. "We should head into Shoops. Lots to do before the wedding, and I haven't even talked to Pastor Speedwell yet."

"Maybe Zeb can do that much," Agnes said.

"I think we should talk to the pastor together," I said.

"That's better yet." Agnes smiled. "I am really happy for you."

"I know you are."

"I just wish I felt better about this whole project. I mean sewing shepherd costumes is one thing but this is a whole other kettle of fish," Ruth said when we got to Old Bessie. "I'm gonna need a lot of fabric, scads of fabric, to make her dress. It might not turn out right. I can't do fittings, and Lord only knows if they make a dress dummy that big. I don't think that they do."

I pulled open the passenger door for her. "You can do it. Just think of it as making quadruple the recipe for lemon squares."

"Maybe, but sewing isn't the same as baking. I thought Thanksgiving was hard enough and now this."

"I was thinking maybe some holly on her hat," I said.

"Ohhh, yeah, that would be fun. Little sprigs of green holly with red berries. I guess I can find plastic holly."

"Why plastic? We got that big old holly tree in the backyard."

"We can do the cutting a few days before the wedding because holly stays pretty well."

When I got on to the main road leading into Bright's Pond, I passed Mildred in her cruiser. She was headed in the direction of Paradise and seemed in a hurry.

"I wonder if they found Leon."

"That poor man. You know he means well."

"Yes. He does, but I suppose he can't just keep doing what he's doing. Not when people are getting hurt."

As we approached the church, I asked Ruth if it would be all right if I took a minute to see if Pastor Speedwell was there and to set up an appointment with him.

"Oh, certainly, Griselda. You go right ahead. I'll just sit here and think on making this dress."

I parked and then walked up the steps and into the church. It was very cold inside, but that wasn't unusual. Pastor Speedwell only kept heat in his office during the week. It saved the church members a boatload of money.

"Pastor," I said with a light rap on his opened office door. "Excuse me, Pastor?"

Pastor Speedwell looked up from his studies. He always reminded me of Abraham Lincoln. Long, square horse face, tall with slightly exaggerated limbs like he just walked off a Norman Rockwell painting.

"Oh, Griselda," he said. "Come on in. Have a seat."

"I can't stay, but I was hoping to set up an appointment for Zeb and me."

"Zeb and you?"

"Guess you're the only one in town who hasn't heard. We're getting married—Christmas Eve—and we'd like you to do the honors."

He stood a moment staring like he was trying to solve a riddle. "That's marvelous. I can see you Monday morning, but Christmas Eve? I don't know. We have the service here at seven o'clock and the singing and—"

"The wedding will be early, around noon if that works."

"Oh, yes indeedy, much better."

"OK, then. I'll . . . Zeb and I will see you Monday."

I turned to leave, but he stopped me. "Griselda, is there anything particular you'd like to discuss?"

My heart quickened. "No, not really, unless, do you ever talk about jealousy?"

He smiled. Wry. Like he instantly understood. It was the first time in all the years that Milton Speedwell has been my pastor that I thought he understood me.

"Oh, and I guess we should discuss the ceremony."

"Of course, Griselda." His voice like velvet now. He folded his hands in front of him. "Good day to you."

I turned to leave. He stopped me again.

"Congratulations," he said.

"OK," I said climbing back into the truck. "That's all set. I need to tell Zeb he wants to meet Monday morning."

Ruth seemed lost in her dressmaking calculations.

"I can do it," she said. "I think just a simple skirt with an elastic waistband. I'll make it so it looks fluffy. And a blouse, no buttons, just a pullover with just a bit of a scoop neckline. That way it'll be two pieces. Much easier to dress her. You can pin a big corsage of poinsettias on her."

"Sounds good."

The Shoops Dry Goods store was located on the same block as the Pink Lady Café. I've eaten there often with Ruth and Zeb. You could usually get a decent hamburger. In good weather they had dining *al fresco* on little bistro tables. In winter the patio was barren except for dried leaves congregating in the corners and remnants of snow and ice that lingered in the shadows.

"I love going to the Dry Goods," Ruth said. "All that fabric and sewing notions. It's like a wonderland to me."

"Not me," I said. "You're looking at the girl who sewed the zipper into the *armpit* of the dress she was making for home ec."

Ruth laughed. "You have other gifts."

We walked into the store and Ruth swooned. "Nothing like the smell of fresh fabric."

To me it was nothing more than miles of bolts of fabric. The Christmas material was up front. "How do you decide which one?" I asked.

"Oh, that's simple. The satin is over there. And maybe some netting for underneath or a crinoline."

An hour later, we left with fabric, enough elastic to make a circuit around the Bright's Pond pond, pins, thread, and three copies of the same McCall's skirt and blouse pattern.

"I don't think we should waste any more time here. I want to get right directly on this."

"That's fine. I'll get you home as long as you're sure there's nothing else you need."

"Nope, got everything," Ruth said as she rolled down the window. "It's almost warm out today."

"It's nice. Sunny."

The corn-stubbled fields looked so barren as we drove past. Hard to believe anything would ever grow on them again. But it would. The fields needed the cold, the rest, before the spring planting season.

I pulled up to Ruth's house. "Now you let me know if you need anything. But not tonight. The children's pageant rehearsal is tonight and I need to make sure Mercy gets there."

"Oh, dear me, that's right. I have to be there also. I need to fit the costumes."

"Maybe I can help with that."

"Um, I don't know. Look, I'll just do the best I can but if I don't get Agnes a dress by Tuesday, you'll just have to understand."

"I know, and I will. We'll wrap the fabric around her and be done with it."

"Did you just tell me Mercy is playing Mary?"

"Yep. She told me her mama said it would be OK."

"She's just a little thing. I can get her Mary outfit done in two shakes of lamb's tail."

"You're a good friend," I said.

21

That evening, before heading to the library to pick up Mercy, I stopped at the town hall looking for Mildred. She was in her office poring over stacks of papers.

"Is there that much paperwork?" I said instead of a customary, "Hey."

She looked up. "Reports, Griselda. I have to fill out reports on everything. Even jaywalking. They all get sent to Harrisburg, and if one is missing or incomplete, I'll hear about it."

"Don't suppose you found Leon."

"Nope. And it's really starting to make me angry. I've searched everywhere. I suspect he left town and only the Good Lord knows where he is."

"Well, the Good Lord can bring him back if he's meant to talk to Haddie Grace."

"That's true. That's true."

"Did you ever figure out how he escaped? I'm just curious."

She looked at me, embarrassed. "I sure did. It was Harriet Nurse. Did you know that woman has a spare key to the jail?"

"Ha, that's funny. How'd she get that?"

"Boris gave it to her. Since she feeds the perps, he figured she should have it in case no one is there to let her in."

"That could be dangerous," I said.

"I know. I know. I took the key right away from her. She was madder than a wet cat, but I had to do my duty."

"Good work."

"I was heading to the children's pageant rehearsal. Let me know if you hear anything or find him."

"I will."

My next stop was the Full Moon to see Zeb. I kind of missed him after not seeing him for nearly a full day.

"Hey," I said with a wave. I saw his paper hat moving around in the kitchen.

He poked his head through the pick-up window. "Hey, yourself." He smiled wide.

"Just came by on account of I missed you," I said.

"That's good to hear."

Dot wiggled past me. "Oh, isn't that sweet?" she said in a baby voice. "Kissy, kissy." Then she laughed.

"Thanks," I said.

"Hey," Zeb said. "Don't forget I can fire you." He pointed his finger at Dot.

Dot waved her hand at him. "Oh, go on. You need me more than I need this job. I just do it for kicks. And I always look for a chance to say, *Oh, kissy, kissy.*"

I sat on a counter stool. "I can't stay. I have to go get Mercy and then go to the play rehearsal."

"So Mercy is going to be Mary?" Zeb said.

"Yep."

"Ah," he said. "She is so cute."

Dot looked at me with raised eyebrows. "Sometimes the man surprises me. Wouldn't know it by looking at him that he could be so tenderhearted."

"You big softy," I said. "I better go get Mercy."

"See you later?" Zeb called.

"Sure."

—⚬⚬⚬—

Mercy was waiting on the library steps petting a calico cat so skinny I could see its ribs.

"Hey," I called. "You ready?"

Mercy ran toward the truck. "I surely am, Miz Griselda."

The cat looked dejected and then bolted into the bushes.

"She looked like a nice kitty," I said when Mercy climbed into the truck.

"Oh, she is. She comes around me a lot. I asked Mama if we can keep her, but she said she has 'nuf trouble feeding our two mouths; can't possibly add another."

"She knows what's right," I said.

"I reckon so, but I sure wouldn't mind having that soft kitty to play with."

We drove toward the church. It was cold and a little windy but no snow or rain. The sky had turned that gunmetal gray as the last of the sun disappeared behind the mountains.

"Are you excited about being in the play?" I asked.

"I thought it was called a pageant, I like the sound of that— it's royal, and yes, yes I am very excited. Imagine me, play-acting Mary—Jesus' mother. Land o' Goshen!"

"You'll be perfect. Now Miss Ruth will be there to help with your costume. She might need to do some sewing on it to make it fit just right."

"Oh, that's fine. I'll stand real still for her."

I parked the truck out front of the church, and Mercy and I quickly found the other children and some parents in the basement. Dot Handy was already there with her clipboard. Dot always directed the play. She loved doing it and one time told me, in confidence, that she had wanted to be an actress when she was a young woman. I think she would have been very good. Dot had a kind of Bette Davis air about her.

"What's she doing here?" I heard one of the boys say. "There ain't no Negros in Bethlehem."

I saw the boy's mother grab him by his collar. "You shut your mouth, Kyle, we don't say Negro in polite society."

Then the other walked toward me. "Um, excuse me but, just why is that little girl here?"

"I'm Mary," Mercy said. "Mother of Jesus Christ himself, our Lord and Savior Almighty, Amen."

"What?" said Kyle's mother. "YOU are this year's Mary?"

"That's correct," Dot said. "Mercy Lincoln is our Mary this year. Jesus did die for all men, not just those of a certain color—now isn't that right?"

"But ain't she . . . from the backwoods?"

"She sure is," I said. "Isn't she just so sweet and pretty?"

The mother moved quickly away. "Come on, Kyle. I don't think your daddy would approve of you being in this play anymore."

"But, Mommy, I want to be a shepherd. I'm shepherd number one. Number *one!*"

All we heard was the shuffling of feet and the basement door slam shut.

"That is such a pity," Dot said. "He was a good shepherd."

"Too bad his mama isn't," I said.

Mercy slipped her hand in mine. "Is it OK, Miz Griselda? Am I still Mary?"

"Of course you are."

Dot climbed onto the stage and spoke loudly enough for everyone to hear. There must have been at least twenty children, and I counted nine adults.

"Let's start from the beginning," she said, "with the angels singing their angel song, 'Away in the Manger.'"

Nine little girls climbed onstage and burst into song as Sheila Spiney played the piano. They did sound like angels as their voices lifted and swirled around the cold church basement.

"Beautiful," Dot said. "OK, I need Mary, Joseph, and the innkeeper onstage."

Mercy clung to my waist.

"Go on," I said. "That's you."

"Oh, but I don't know, Miz Griselda. I don't want to go upsetting the apple cart."

"You aren't upsetting anything. Go on. Miss Dot will tell you exactly what to do and say. You just listen to her, not any nasty children—or adults."

Mercy climbed the two small steps onto the stage. She stood close to Dot. I watched Dot instruct her and give her a sheet of paper with her lines. Rose and Nate had done another marvelous job with the scenery. It was like being in Bethlehem. Mary and Joseph stood out front of the inn—a house that reminded me of a gingerbread house without the decorations.

Joseph rapped on the door. The innkeeper, played by Brady William Trout, opened the door. "How can I help you?" he said.

I moved away and sat at a table and watched the rest of the rehearsal from there. Mercy caught on quickly, as I knew she would. But the highlight of the rehearsal was when we heard the sound of the basement door open and the bleating of a sheep. Then the grunts of a woman wearing denim overalls as she led a recalcitrant camel into the room.

The children went a little wild, laughing and pushing and falling all over each other to get to the animals.

"Lookee there," called Brady. "A horse with lumps."

Darlene Milligan punched his shoulder. "That ain't no horse with lumps. It's a camel. Ain't you ever been to the zoo?"

"No," Brady said. "I ain't never seen a camel, so how's I suppose to know?"

I helped Dot call the kids off, but they weren't listening very well until the man in the blue denim overalls spoke.

"They'll bite if you rile them up," he said in a booming voice.

The children backed away. Parents reached out for their young ones.

"Filby said you were having your dress rehearsal tonight," said the woman, "so we thought we'd bring Bruce and Debbie down so they could rehearse also."

"Oh, boy," said Hanky Frankel, "do I get to ride the camel? I am Balthazar. They rode camels, didn't they?"

"No, no," Dot said pulling Hanky away from the camel. "You can walk beside him, if it's safe."

"It's plenty safe," said the man. "By the way, my name is Ford, John Ford and this is my wife, Karen."

"Pleased to meet you," Karen said.

I decided to keep my distance and let whatever was about to happen, happen.

"Well, gee whiz," Dot said. "This is great, you bringing the animals down and all. Let's get them where they'll be during the play."

That was when Mercy jumped off the stage and threw her arms around Debbie the sheep. "Ain't she just the fluffiest thing you ever did see?"

"She'll be standing with the shepherds," Dot said. "Debbie, not Mercy. Over there." She pointed to the far right of the stage. "But not yet. Not until the second act when the star appears and the angels tell the shepherds about the baby Jesus."

"OK," Karen said. "I'll just stand over here with her and wait until you call us."

"Fine, fine," Dot said.

I sat back and watched as Dot directed the children and the animals for a little over an hour. She was like a miracle worker, the way she got everyone organized and kept what had the potential to turn into play pandemonium to a peaceful time of telling the story of Jesus' birth.

Ruth arrived just as Dot had the children cleaning up for the night. The Fords gathered their animals and left by the basement door.

"That camel stinks," said one of the wise men, I forget which, it might have been Caspar. "I don't want to stand near no smelly camel."

"It's all right," Dot said. "It'll only be for a few minutes. Can you imagine what it must have been like for the real Joseph and Mary? Pretty stinky."

"I'm sorry I'm late," Ruth said, "but I got started on Agnes's dress and lost track of time. Is there still time to fit Mary, er, Mercy?"

I glanced at the clock. "It's only 8:30. I think you can work with Mercy."

"It won't take but a minute," she said.

"Mercy," I called. "Come on over here." She was still next to the cradle rocking it back and forth. The plastic baby doll representing Jesus was still there.

"Too bad we don't have a real live baby," she said.

"It's OK," I said. "As long as we have a real Mary. Now come on over here so Miss Ruth can fit your robes."

"OK. I'm coming." Mercy left the stage and joined us.

Ruth slipped the robe over Mercy's head and then tied it around the waist with a wide and colorful sash. "Now don't you look darling? I don't think I have to do much, maybe a six-inch hem and a tuck at the shoulders."

"Oh, I like this costume just fine," Mercy said. "I'll wear it everywhere. Even to school."

"Oh, no, sorry," Ruth said. "You have to return the costume to me after the play. I'll save them for next year."

Mercy looked at me.

"That's right," I said. "They're just for the play."

"Ah, but I like wearing this robe. I wish we wore robes all the time."

Ruth inserted a pin here and a pin there. "OK, all done."

Mercy raised her arms and Ruth slipped the costume off.

"OK, everyone," Dot said still holding her clipboard like the Statue of Liberty holds her book. "It's time to go home. If you're waiting for a parent please stand by the basement door. Your parents were told to come to the back door." She looked at me and whispered, "I bet some of them still try to get in through the front door."

"Oh, well, human nature. It is what it is."

By 8:45, all the kids were gone and just Dot, Ruth, Mercy, and I remained to lock up.

"Can I give you a lift?" I asked Dot.

"No, I'll walk. It's not far. And to tell the truth, I can use the fresh air."

"That camel did stink to high heaven," Mercy said. "Worse than the outhouse in August."

We all laughed, and Dot locked the door.

"I can drive you home after I drop Mercy off," I told Ruth.

"Oh, that'll be fine."

The three of us climbed into the truck and I headed toward the library. "Mercy, I can't let you out at the library. You can't walk home through the woods in the dark and cold. I'm gonna have to go with you."

"Oh, but Miz Griselda," Mercy said, "you can't rightly drive this truck to my house. I can walk the woods at night. Done it a million times. I'll be all right. I got a flashlight."

"Oh, that's great, but I wouldn't feel right letting you walk this late at night."

"But I said I'll do OK. It's not far from the library. Honest. Not far at all."

"Still, I need to go with you."

I stopped the truck at the curb and we all got out. But first I grabbed my flashlight from the glove compartment.

"Now come, Mercy, you lead the way."

"Well, OK, but like I said, I can go by myself."

We walked into the woods and after just a few yards everything went so pitch black I couldn't see my hand in front of my face until Mercy clicked on the flashlight. "My house is just over there." She pointed the light through some sycamores.

"OK. Keep moving," Ruth said. "It's a little scary."

A few yards later, I smelled wood smoke and the unmistakable smell of burning trash. Mercy showed the light through the trees. "My house is right there. You can go back now."

"No, we'll see you to the door," I said.

I turned on my light and directed the beam in the direction Mercy pointed. It landed on a small shack with a slanty roof and a tiny porch. I saw a dim light through a small window.

"Is that your house, Mercy?" I asked.

Mercy stopped walking. I showed my light near her feet. "Is it?"

"I'm sorry, Miz Griselda."

"For what?"

"For lying to you. My Mama never told me it'd be OK to play-act Mary. I never told her. I told her I was going to the library just to do homework. She'll be awful sore if she finds out where I was. Mama said God is no God if he can let us live the way we do—eating canned beans one night and going without the next. Mama says God don't play fair. She said God would never give me such a bad daddy if he was a good God, and now we got nothing but what the Society ladies bring us from time to time."

"But, why, Mercy? Why did you lie?" I asked.

"On account of I just had to play-act Jesus' Mama. I thought that would make him happy, you know, and maybe he'd help us more if I did it real good, real sweet you know. I figured God would have to love me and Mama then."

I swallowed. At that moment I had no idea what to say. "It's OK. I won't tell her." I gave her a little nudge. "Now you go on but be sure and come back Sunday, five o'clock for the real thing. I won't tell," I said wondering if I was doing the right thing.

Ruth and I watched until Mercy was inside the ramshackle dwelling.

We walked silently with only the crunch of dead leaves underfoot, until we reached the truck. I think both Ruth and I held our breath the whole time. It was one scary walk even with the flashlight.

"Come on, come on," Ruth said. "Let's get out of here."

"We're safe."

"Now what?" Ruth said. "Are you gonna let Mercy do the play without permission?"

"I'll do it. Get permission, I mean."

The dark seemed a little darker that night, and I drove off a little quicker than usual and was thankful Bessie didn't complain.

"You know," Ruth said when we reached her house. "It's too bad that Leon Fontaine doesn't have some potion, some power of suggestion to give Mercy and her mama. Something that would make them rich."

"No, that's impossible. Leon is selling what amounts to a lie, even if he believes it with all his heart. What Mercy and her mama need is the truth."

"Best thing you can do is help the mama stop hating God. Find a way to show her that God loves her, even if her circumstances don't say so."

22

Saturday. My big day. Well, my second big day. I was supposed to meet Cliff Cardwell at Hector's Hill bright and early. We were scheduled to fly into Scranton where I would take my pilot's license test. I was a nervous Nellie. I couldn't eat and could barely get a cup of coffee down.

I pulled on a pair of blue jeans and a turtleneck sweater. Then I fed Arthur, who I believe thought I was crazy for going out on such a cold, cold day—only twenty-seven degrees that morning, cold even for Bright's Pond standards. I wondered if we could even take Matilda up in such conditions. I figured Cliff would let me know if we had to call off the test.

Old Bessie didn't want to start that morning. She complained three or four times and then started. "There you go," I said patting the dashboard. "Don't fail me now."

There wasn't a soul on the streets, but the Christmas lights that hung from the posts and the wires and hedges and trees still lit my way. I arrived at Hector's Hill and saw Cliff standing near Matilda.

"Hey," I called.

He waved but from the look on his face I thought we might not be going.

"Everything all right?"

"Oh, Matilda's fine, but I'm not."

"What's up?"

"I have to fly into Binghamton, right now, first thing and pick up a sales rep for some rug company."

"Oh, no, so we can't—"

"Sorry, Griselda. How about next Saturday or one day during the week?"

"No, that won't work. We'll have to forget about it for now. I have so much to do to get ready for the wedding. It's in less than three days now. And the parade is Monday night, and we still have some details to figure out—"

Cliff twisted his mouth. "Looks like next year."

"I guess so. I was really looking forward to this."

"Me too," Cliff said. "But don't worry. Think of it this way: next year when you go for your license you can use your married name and you won't have to worry about switching it."

Seemed a miniscule consolation. "That's true."

I watched for a minute as he did his check, but the cold air got the best of me. "I'm gonna get going."

"I'm really sorry, but I need this job and—"

"I understand. Next year."

I started to walk away but then turned. "Hey, are you coming to the wedding? It's Christmas Eve, Tuesday at noon at Greenbrier. The gazebo."

"What about Zeb. Think he'll mind?"

"No. He'll be all right."

Frankly, I was a wee bit relieved that I didn't have to take a solo flight that day. My mind was not exactly on flying and flying alone to boot. I kept thinking about Mercy and Leon. One second I was worried about Mercy and the next I was thinking about Leon and trying to figure out where in the heck he could have run off to. And that made me think about Haddie Grace in the hospital, unconscious. Then my mind switched back to my wedding and I worried about the details and Ruth. My mind was spinning in a hundred directions.

I went to the café where Zeb prepared me breakfast—eggs and scrapple. I didn't tell him that my plans got canceled. I was banking on the notion that he had forgotten.

"Weren't you supposed to go to Scranton today?" he said as he placed a plate of food on the counter.

"You remembered?"

"Sure, Grizzy. I remembered."

"Cliff had to cancel. He's flying to Binghamton. Work."

"Oh, too bad," Zeb said. "I was getting ready to tell everyone that I married a pilot. She really does have her head in the clouds."

"That's sweet. Well, maybe next month or maybe in the spring."

"Spring gets my vote," Dot said. "Whooeeee, I was not looking forward to watching you get married with two broken legs or something. And maybe by spring you'da forgotten all about it."

"I would not have crashed," I said. "I am a pretty good pilot, you know."

"OK, OK, Miss Amelia Earhart," Zeb said. "What else are you going to do today?"

"Not sure. I thought I'd check on Ruth. She's making Agnes's dress for the wedding, which reminds me, did you talk to Studebaker about—"

"Yes. Stu said he'd be proud to be my best man. Wants to throw me a bachelor party."

I laughed. "Sure. That sounds nice. I can see the two of you now."

"Now hold on. I got more friends."

"OK, OK, but after a couple of hours at Personal's Pub you'll all be asleep."

"Don't you count on it. We can get wild."

"Wild for you is putting food coloring in your meringue."

"Or horseradish in the meatloaf," Dot said.

Zeb kissed my cheek. "I got potatoes to fry."

Dot wiped the counter next to me. "So Ruth is really making a dress for Agnes?"

"Yep. I can't wait to see it."

"Me neither."

"Oh, Zeb, I almost plumb forgot. We have to go see the pastor Monday morning."

"Milton Speedwell? How come?"

"To talk about the ceremony and, I don't know, don't they always talk to the bride and groom before the hitching?"

"Yes, I suppose, but we are not teenagers. We know what we're doing."

"I know, but we still need to see him and we need to get a license. I think Boris can handle that."

"Oh, yeah, I already talked to him. You need your birth certificate."

"I do? I'm sitting right here. Do I really need to prove I was born?"

"Yep. We can go down to the town hall Monday, too, and get the license."

I finished my breakfast. Zeb was such a good cook but I had a feeling once we were married that I'd be doing the cooking at our house. I was a fair cook but nothing fancy. As long as he didn't expect much more than meat and potatoes and tuna salad we'd do fine.

"By the way," Dot said. "Any news on that poor old woman that slipped her trolley?"

"It was a tricycle," I said. "And, no. I also need to check on her today. I just wish we could find Leon Fontaine."

Harriet Nurse, Filby Pruett, and the Tompkinses came into the cafe just as I was leaving.

"Oh, Griselda," Edie said. "I haven't received my invitation, or am I not invited? I told Bill that, of course, we were invited. I'm sure it was just an oversight."

I snapped my fingers. "Invitations. Edie, I never sent any out—to anyone. I just assumed you all, I mean everyone, knew you were invited."

"Well, of course, dear but how can we know what time and where. I assume the church but—"

"No, no. It's at Greenbrier. We're getting married in the gazebo."

"The what?" Edie's voice smacked of incredulousness. "The gazebo? Where is that? I don't remember there ever being a gazebo out there."

"It's new. You won't have any trouble finding it."

"In the cold? What if it snows or ices or sleets?"

"Don't worry, Edie. It will be fine. Just fine."

I dashed out of the café. I had not even thought about invitations. Now what? There wasn't time. I jumped into the truck. She complained again but started. I headed to Ruth's. Fortunately, I saw Ivy Slocum walking Mickey Mantle.

I parked the truck and then waved her down. She waited until Mickey Mantle finished watering some weeds and then headed in my direction.

"Griselda, where have you been? I haven't seen you in days."

"I know it. I have been busy with—well, with everything."

"The wedding, I would imagine."

"Yes, and today I found out that I plumb forgot invitations."

"Do you need them? Just get the word out. You know how stories fly around here—quicker than flies on manure."

"I know, but don't you think I need something more . . . formal. Fancy?"

"How many do you need?" She pulled on Mickey Mantle's leash. "Come on boy. Just sit a minute."

"I don't know, fifty or sixty?"

"Um, it would be a stretch but how about if we buy some of them blank postcards and just handwrite them. And I guess Mickey Mantle and me and maybe Studebaker can pop them in everyone's mailbox—Pony Express."

"Really? You think we could? I mean you'd do that?"

"Sure. How hard can it be. Just write out the information."

"You mean like Mr. and Mrs. So and So invite you to . . ."

"Not that exactly, what with you and Zeb being adults and all."

"OK, I'll write it down and drop it by your house. I can't tell you how much I appreciate this."

"I have to walk Mickey Mantle anyway, easy enough to drop a card in the mailboxes. But I suspect most people already know, and well, you know Bright's Pond. They'll invite themselves."

"I suppose but, boy, getting married is complicated."

"No, it's just all the stuff around it. Keeping everyone happy. Weddings tend to bring out the best and the worst in people. Everybody wants a slice of the pie."

"And I feel like a great big Full Moon Pie right now."

"It will be over soon and you and Zeb will be happily married. Imagine that, Griselda Sewickey. Has a nice ring, don't you think?"

"I suppose it does. I'm kind of partial to Sparrow, but Sewickey has a nice sound, too."

"You'll get used to it. I'll head on down to the five-and-dime and buy the postcards and then get the stamps from the mailman next time he comes past."

I hugged Ivy. "You're the best."

As I walked to Ruth's house, I was struck with a sudden wave of melancholy. I missed my parents even though they died when I was just a youngster. Who would walk me down the aisle? There was no *Mr. and Mrs.* to invite anyone anywhere. I guess, even at my age, I wanted a daddy to give me away.

I sighed deeply and pushed open Ruth's yellow door. "Yoohoo," I called. "Ruth?"

"In here. The sewing room."

I found her under a mountain of bright red satin and crinoline.

She looked a fright, like she had been up all night. Her hair was mussed with two pencils sticking out of it, her glasses hung low on her nose like she was simultaneously trying to look over and through them. And she had kind of a wild look in her eyes.

"Ruth, are you OK?"

"Mm-hmm," she said with pins in her mouth.

"Take the pins out before you swallow them."

She poked seven pins into a small tomato-shaped pincushion with a little green stem coming out the top.

"I'm trying to get this done so we can take it out there and fit it on her."

"How much longer do you think?"

"Oh, not long. What do you think?" She held out a long red skirt with fancy crinoline underneath. "I'm still sewing the elastic into the waistband."

"It's gorgeous," I said. "I think you're going to make Agnes look very pretty."

"Good. I still have to make the blouse and then assemble the hat. Don't forget to cut me some sprigs of holly. Griselda, do you realize you're getting married in three days?"

"I know. It's a little scary."

"Now tell me about your flowers."

"Flowers?"

"Of course. All brides carry a bouquet when they walk down the aisle. You need something to toss to the single women in the crowd."

I sat with a thud onto an overstuffed chair. "Oh, criminy, Ruth. Flowers, invitations, music, dresses, license. This is getting out of hand."

"Every bride deals with this. That's why you have a maid of honor. She can help you with this stuff, unless, of course, your maid of honor is—well, you know."

Oh, boy, was Ruth just telling me that making Agnes my maid of honor was a mistake? I knew I should have picked Ruth. She would be a much better help than Agnes. But I couldn't disappoint Agnes.

"I've been thinking, Ruth," I said after the pregnant pause lifted. "Is it OK to have two maids of honor? Double maids? Comaids?"

"Don't know." She continued to push material through her sewing machine. The rhythm was soothing. "Don't see why not."

"Then Ruth, will you be my second maid of honor?"

"I never thought you'd ask. Of course."

"Good, you and Agnes can wear matching dresses."

"Uh-oh, that means I'll need more fabric."

I smiled. This idea was the first one that actually made me happy right down to my toes. Ruth was such a good friend and who cares if we were throwing convention out the window? Probably Agnes.

23

At around five o'clock Sunday evening I received an irritated phone call from Dot Handy. I was at home preparing to go to the Christmas pageant. My plan was to pick up Ruth and Ivy and we would meet Zeb later. He needed to close up the café and suggested he might not make the first part of the play. Then I would meet Mercy at the library.

Best-laid plans are often interrupted, but I have never been interrupted by a runaway camel.

"Griselda," Dot said into the phone "That camel broke off its leash and is running around out back of the church like a banshee."

"Did you call the Fords?"

"No answer. What am I gonna do? The kids will be arriving in fifteen minutes and I'm afraid someone is going to get hurt."

"I'll call Mildred. Maybe she can do something."

"Thank you—uh oh!" CRASH!

"Dot," I said. "Dot?" No answer. So I hung up and headed outside in time to see Dot Handy racing down Filbert Street followed closely by a two-hump camel harboring some kind of grudge.

"Oh, dear," I ran after her not knowing what I would do if I caught the camel. His leash was dragging behind him. It was metal and was creating sparks as he ran.

"Stop! Stop!" But the camel ignored me and was heading for the center of town. Next thing I knew doors were flinging open and folks were coming out onto their porches. Fred Haskell took off after the camel.

"Stop!" he hollered.

I saw Dot duck onto Eugene Shrapnel's porch. Now that was a good decision. Eugene hated everyone and everything. I doubted a camel named Bruce would put a smile on his sour puss.

It didn't take long for a stream of men to be chasing Bruce clear to the town hall. I passed Dot and waved. "You stay there."

The poor animal got cornered by Mildred's cruiser and Studebaker's Cadillac and stopped running. But not for long because he leaped, or tried to leap, over the police car. Unfortunately, his leash got caught on the wheel and Bruce nearly choked.

"Don't get close," Studebaker hollered to Mildred who was standing there with her hand on her gun. "And don't shoot him either."

Studebaker inched closer.

"Watch it," I called. "They spit. And bite."

Stu waved his hand at me. "I know. I know. But if I can just grab onto his leash."

"Wish I had a tranquilizing gun," Mildred said. "I'd take him down with one shot."

"He's just scared," Stu said. "Something must have spooked him."

That was when a pickup truck screeched to a halt about forty yards away from the police car. It was the Fords.

"Bruce's owners are here," I said.

"Good," Stu said and he started to back away. Meanwhile, the camel was tugging and pulling and choking and spitting. His eyes were so big they looked like something otherworldly. His lips were curled, and I could see his yellow, ugly teeth.

"It's OK," John Ford called. "Everybody back away. Give him a minute to calm down."

John crept slowly toward his camel. He managed to untangle the leash and get Bruce calmed down. "There, there, boy," he said. "It's OK now. Nobody's chasing you."

Bruce allowed John to lead him slowly up the street toward the church. But that was when Dot started to get riled again. "I can't allow that wild animal to take part in the pageant," she said. "What if he breaks free and goes on a rampage with all the children around?"

"He won't" John said. "As long as Debbie is with him."

"Debbie?" Dot said. "Is that how come he got spooked? I had Debbie inside the church when all this started."

"Oh, dear," John said. "Bruce needs to see Debbie all the time or he gets . . . upset."

They started walking again. The camel stood about seven feet tall and walked with a swagger like John Wayne.

"Still and all," Dot said. "Maybe we should forget about having live animals in the play."

"Your call," John said.

I caught up with Dot who was still catching her breath. "Are you all right? He didn't hurt you, did he?"

"No, no but I have never been so scared in my life. I never had a camel bust out like that before you know. First time for everything. He just went crazy until he broke his chain and then started running."

"He couldn't see Debbie."

"That's crazy," Dot said. "So now what? I'm too nervous to allow the animals onstage. But everyone was so excited to have them."

"Like the man said, it's your call."

"I'll decide in a minute. Right now I got to get the stage set up and people in place. I'm sure the children are arriving."

"Oh, I need to go get Mercy. I sure wish there was a way we could get her mother to come."

"Ask her."

"I think that would upset Mercy. She hasn't even told her mother she's in the play. Mama isn't fond of God."

"Oh, dear," Dot said. "I can't help with that. But maybe you can come up with an idea."

We reached the church, and I walked across the street and climbed into the truck. If only there was something that would lure her out of that shack. You'd think watching your daughter in a play would be enough but Mrs. Lincoln had some deep, deep hurts.

Ruth was waiting on the porch. She held Mercy's costume.

"Come on," I said. "Sorry I'm late, but I was chasing a renegade camel."

"What?" Ruth said as she closed the truck door.

I explained on the way to get Ivy. She also was sitting on her porch wearing blue jeans and a Christmas sweatshirt with a tree and holly and the words Merry Christmas embroidered underneath. Ivy was pretty much her own person, rarely swayed by what was going on around her.

"Sorry. Runaway camel," Ruth said.

"I heard. What a riot."

We drove up to the library, but Mercy wasn't there. My heart sank. "Oh, dear, you don't suppose she changed her mind." I said.

"Or her mother changed it for her," Ruth said.

"I need to go check." I got out of the truck and leaned on the open window. "Maybe you guys should stay here."

"Will you be OK?" Ruth asked.

"Yeah. I'll be fine. But if you see her, grab her."

I made my way through the woods to Mercy's home. Smoke poured from the chimney. I walked onto the porch and rapped lightly on the door. No answer. I knocked again. Louder. By now my heart pounded as I worried something was terribly wrong.

The door opened. Mercy stood there.

"Are you coming?" I said. "Tonight's your big night."

Mercy glanced behind her into the one-room shack. "Mama said I can't go."

"Really? Did she say why?"

"Like I told you. She don't like God very much."

"I'm glad you told her. Do you think she'd talk to me?"

Mercy shook her head. "Don't know. Probably not."

I pushed the door open a little more and got a clear view. Her mama was sitting in a rocking chair moving back and forth, back and forth.

"Hello?" I called. "Mrs. Lincoln?"

"Go away. Get on now. We don't need no visitors."

"But Mercy is in the church play. She has to come. She's the star."

I dared to take a step inside. Mercy moved aside. The cabin smelled from rotten wood and leaves and burning garbage. There was a worn and dirty couch pressed against a wall, the rocker Mrs. Lincoln was sitting in, a small table with two chairs and one lamp that looked so out of place it almost made me laugh. Mercy must have trash-picked it. It was brass with a figure of a cherub in the middle. A filthy lampshade with tassels hung crooked. A small fire burned and smoldered in a rickety woodstove.

"Mrs. Lincoln, please."

"Don't need no daughter of mine pretending to be the mother of God when God don't exist."

Mrs. Lincoln pulled an oversized, orange sweater she wore around her thin frame. Her hair was matted and frizzy. She never looked at me.

"But Mercy has to come. She has a responsibility and . . . and she won't get paid if she doesn't do her job."

Mercy looked at me. "Paid? What's that Miz Griselda? You gonna pay me for play-acting?"

"Yes." I lied through my teeth. But I hoped that if money was involved that her mother would allow her to come. I had no idea just then how. But it would be worth it even if I paid Mercy out of my own pocketbook.

"Money?" Mrs. Lincoln said. "That's another story—long as it's work she's doin'."

"Then I can do it?" Mercy said. She ran to her Mama and flung her arms around her. Charlamaine Lincoln pushed her away. "Just see to it you bring me that money—all of it. Every penny."

"Yes, ma'am, I surely will." Mercy got to her feet.

"Don't matter none. Just bring me the money."

Mercy and I started through the woods. She slipped her hand in mine about halfway through.

———— ❧ ————

Mercy had to sit on Ivy's lap as we traveled back to the church.

"Glad you could make it," Ruth said. "I got your costume all ready. You are going to be so pretty."

"How much money they gonna pay me?" Mercy asked.

I saw both Ruth and Ivy look at me. "Not sure, yet, honey," I said. "But you just pay attention to being Mary. You'll get paid after."

I parked the truck in front of the house and we walked across the street together. Ivy went through the front but Ruth, Mercy, and I needed to go in the back. The children were gathering in the basement. People would make their way down the steps into the fellowship hall where rows of chairs were set up.

"There you are," Dot said. "I was beginning to get concerned."

"I'll explain later."

"Come on, Mercy," Ruth said. "Let me get you into your robe."

Sheila Spiney, Edie Tompkins, and Harriet Nurse were also on hand to help.

"I need to go speak with Pastor Speedwell," I said. "But I'll be in the front row, Mercy."

On my way through the room, I saw Debbie and Bruce chained together on stage. The camel looked calm enough chewing his cud. But the smell, well, that was a different story. Some folks had already gathered and were sitting waiting for the show to begin.

Pastor was in the sanctuary lobby instructing people to make their way to the basement. I had no idea if it would help but I needed to ask him.

"Pastor," I said. "Can I speak with you privately?"

"Of course, Griselda. Of course." He shook one more hand and excused himself. "Just make your way to fellowship hall," he said as he led me into the sanctuary. I explained to him what happened with Mercy and her mother hoping he would have a solution.

"I'll pay her myself," I said. "But I was hoping the church might be able—"

"You are the church," he said.

"Right, OK. Soooo—"

"Don't worry, Griselda. Mercy and her mother will be provided for."

Several minutes later the fellowship hall was packed with proud parents, cousins, and neighbors and enough after-pageant treats to feed the entire backwoods' population for a month. Lemon squares were always a huge hit as were brownies and chocolate chip cookies. I saw the usual Lime Jell-O Macaroni Surprise that Darcy Speedwell always contributed. Even in a pretty red and green Christmas bowl it looked unappetizing. The hall smelled like Christmas with butter cookies and pinecones.

I found seats up front that Dot had reserved for Ruth and me. Ivy sat in the back, but that was fine with her. She never liked to sit up front.

Pastor Speedwell stood at the front. "Welcome. Welcome. Let us begin our pageant night with a song. 'Hark! the Herald Angels Sing' as the children make their entrance."

Sheila began playing and everyone stood on cue. Voices lifted high and seemed to bounce off the walls. The children in their costumes walked by twos down the center aisle and onto the stage to the admiring oohs and ahs of the audience. The sheep, always the littlest children, toddlers, bleated and baaed their way onstage. One of them veered off course when he saw his mommy and daddy. They were followed by John Ford who led Bruce and Debbie down the aisle and onto the stage. Bruce wore a lovely jeweled halter-type collar that wrapped around his snout—I was happy to see that. The animals were met with slightly more rambunctious appreciation. John needed to pull on Bruce's chain a couple of times to keep him controlled.

The song ended and all the children and animals were behind the stage curtain. I heard some rustling of papers and moving of props. One long baaa from Debbie but all in all the procession went smoothly. I sailed a silent prayer that Bruce would behave himself.

Pastor invited everyone to sit. "Christmas, such a marvelous glorious occasion. The occasion of our Savior's birth. The greatest gift of all. Although we have never taken an offering at our Christmas pageant, a need has arisen among our people that merits our favor and attention. I need to ask you all to dig deep and give from your hearts as the baskets are passed. There is a child in need, and what better time to give from our hearts to this blessed child of God than on a day when we celebrate the birth of God's own Son?"

Sheila Spiney burst into "Angels We Have Heard on High" as the ushers passed the baskets. Being in the front, I couldn't see how much money was collected, but I did know that this time of year most folks were a little short of extra funds. But I also knew the congregation always gave from the heart—well, most of the time.

The room grew quiet once the offering had been taken. Dot took center stage. A small spotlight illuminated her. She looked especially lovely that evening in a pretty blue dress dotted with snowflakes. "Merry Christmas," she said. "And welcome to the Annual Bright's Pond Church of Faith and Grace Sunday School Christmas Pageant."

Applause and cheers filled the windowless room. Edie Tompkins stood on account of she had a niece in the play this year. And a few other scattered parents rose to the occasion also.

"So without further ado. I give you—*The Greatest Gift.*"

The curtains opened on the inn. Mary and Joseph and Bruce stood outside the inn door. They said their lines beautifully. Mercy was made for the part. The innkeeper shouted, "You are welcome to stay in the stable."

"With the mules?" Mercy said. "But, sir, I am to have a child this night."

The innkeeper shook his head. "I am sorry."

The curtain closed to applause and after a couple of minutes opened on the manger scene. The sheep were there and the angel choir was singing "Away in a Manger." I will admit it was so sweet that tears pooled in my eyes. Unfortunately, the exiting of the sheep didn't go so smoothly as the lead sheep lost an ear off his head and it was stepped on by the other sheep creating quite the laugh fest for the angels and the three other still-intact sheep.

After a couple more songs, the curtain closed and reopened on Mary and Joseph kneeling at baby Jesus' cradle. Mercy looked so proud to be there. She spoke her lines clearly and with force. Joseph was not quite so demonstrative but did a fine job nonetheless.

But when it came time for the offstage narrator to recite Luke's account of the birth of Jesus the stage fell into a nervous silence. He couldn't go through with it. Then Mercy jumped to the rescue and stole the scene. She moved to the front of the stage and began:

"And there were in the same country shepherds abiding in the field, keeping watch over their flock by night." She gestured toward the shepherds and Debbie. "And, lo, the angel of the Lord came upon them, and the glory of the Lord shone all around them." A bright light illuminated the shepherd field.

"And they were very sore," Mercy continued as the audience grew increasingly quiet.

"And the angel said unto them, Don't you shepherds be afraid because I got good news. Tidings of great joy, which shall be to all people. For unto you is born this day in the city of David, a Savior, which is Christ the Lord. And this shall be a sign unto you; Ye shall find the babe wrapped in crumpled-up clothes, lying in a manger. And suddenly there was with the angel a multitude of the heavenly host praising God, and saying, Glory to God in the highest, and on earth peace, good will toward men."

Then she knelt back down and looked adoringly at the baby Jesus. I was so proud of her—even if she did steal someone else's lines. The rest of the play went pretty well, with Dot and Ruth ushering children on and off the stage. The kings and Bruce arrived with the kings appropriately singing "We Three Kings." Then Dot asked for the sanctuary lights to be dimmed as the angels helped light the candles everyone held. Sheila began to play and we all joined in singing "Silent Night, Holy Night."

All in all, it was a tremendous evening. A total of one hundred and twenty-two dollars and seventeen cents was collected for Mercy. After I dropped Ruth and Ivy home, Mercy and I headed for the library.

"I can't wait to show Mama how much money I made."

"Maybe you can buy some food."

"Maybe. So did I play-act Mary good?"

"You did a great job. In fact, I think you were the best Mary ever."

"Really, Miz Griselda, you mean that?"

"I do." I parked the truck, grabbed the flashlight from the glove compartment and got out with Mercy.

"It's OK. You don't have to walk me clear to home."

"No, I insist."

The walk had become familiar by then and we made it to the little house quickly. Smoke still poured from the chimney and one light illuminated the front window.

"Mama might be sleeping. She's been tired lately."

"It's OK if she's asleep. I still want to see you all the way home."

Mercy pushed open the door. It squeaked like a chipmunk. "Shhh," Mercy said. "That door always makes such a ruckus."

Charlamaine Lincoln roused from sleeping under a worn blanket on the sofa.

"That you, Mercy?"

"Sure, Mama. I'm home and I got paid just like they said."

Charlamaine sat up and rubbed her eyes. "How much you got, girl?"

"One hundred twenty-two dollars and seventeen cents."

"Hand it to me."

Mercy reached into her pocket and gave her mama all the money.

"I'm gonna say good night," I said. "You did a great job, Mercy."

I waited for Charlamaine to acknowledge me, but she never looked my way.

24

It was now officially Christmas week. The day before my wedding. Two days before Christmas and Bright's Pond was dressed in her holiday best. The weather had turned consistently cold with flurries nearly every day. The walk to the town hall or café had become brisk, and I traveled it quicker because cold mountain air could slip right through even my warmest jacket.

Lights had been strung across the streets from light pole to light pole. The shops and businesses along Filbert Street were decorated with multicolored lights and Santa and snowmen. Holly wreaths adorned the doors and even Charlotte Figg had placed some lights around the window of her new shop even though it wasn't scheduled to open until January, and it didn't have any distinguishing signs on it, except for the one hand-painted by Rose. It was rectangular with a deep-dish cherry pie in the center and the words SOON TO BE CHARLOTTE'S PIE SHOP encircling it.

But I suppose my favorite of the Bright's Pond Christmas traditions was the loudspeaker atop the town hall that blared Christmas carols into the air. Most folks did their Christmas shopping in Shoops but the five-and-dime had a nice selection of gift items. Mr. Gleason always managed to find someone to play Santa for the children. This time I think he snookered his wife for the job. For me that year, my best gift was waiting at The Full Moon Café. It was still a little hard to believe that Zeb and I were actually getting married.

But we were, and that Monday we had a meeting scheduled with Pastor Speedwell to discuss the particulars and maybe a few of the personals. I pulled open the café door and saw Zeb standing there like a deer in headlights.

"You OK?" I said.

He looked at me after a few seconds. "I . . . I guess. Now, how come we need to speak with Milton Speedwell?"

"I told you already. Just to get some facts straight about the ceremony. Are you nervous? You look nervous."

Dot happened past. "Of course he's nervous. He's a man ain't he?"

"I'm not nervous," Zeb said.

"Then we better get to the church." I took his hand. "Come on, honey. Let's go."

"How come we're walking?" Zeb asked.

"Just thought we would," I said. "I think the cold air will do you some good."

Pastor Speedwell was in his office just where I expected to find him.

"Come in," he said as he stood. "Welcome."

Zeb didn't say anything.

"Morning," I said. "That was some pageant last night."

"It sure was. And that little girl—Mercy, you called her— she did a fine job."

"Thank you for taking the offering. She and her mother were very happy to receive it."

"I'm glad we can help."

Zeb finally took a breath. "Hello, Pastor."

"Hello, Zeb. How are you?"

"Fine. Just fine."

There was a much-too-long silence before Pastor Speedwell spoke again. It gave me time to notice his divinity school diploma on the wall. I guess it looked legit enough. I also saw a picture of his family: his wife, Darcy, and their four boys, Matthew, Mark, Luke, and John. Next to that on his desk was a picture of an older woman I took to be his mother. She also resembled Abraham Lincoln.

I was glad that the pastor did not bring up that whole jealousy issue. I didn't think Zeb was in any shape to hear it and for all of his lackluster ways, pastor seemed to catch on also. Instead we went over the vows, the order of things and the pastor's fee, which he said, he always donated to the Society of Angelic Philanthropy.

"I guess I understand the need to be married at Greenbrier, but outside? In the cold?" Pastor said.

"It works best," I said. "I thought about the nursing home Sunshine Room, but I didn't want the place crowded out with residents who weren't . . . you know family or friends. Maybe it's selfish."

"No. It's not. But I think we'll make it short and sweet. I can dispense with the usual sermon since it'll be difficult for folks to hear."

The whole meeting took less than thirty minutes although from the look on Zeb when we left we could have been in there for hours and the pastor could have performed a lobotomy on him.

"Why are you so nervous?" I said when we got outside.

"I'm . . . not nervous."

"You sure? You still want to get married?"

"I do."

"Remember those words Tuesday afternoon. Now I got another question," I said. "How come you didn't make it to the church pageant?"

We walked toward the café.

"Oh, I'm sorry about that. I just got busy at the café. Had some orders to put in and paperwork and the evening got away from me. I'm sorry."

"I guess it's OK. Mercy Lincoln did a great job. And get this, Pastor Speedwell collected an offering for her. I have never seen such poor people, Zeb. It was awful."

"What was?"

"I went to Mercy's house, if you can call it that."

"Oh, pretty poor, huh?"

"Yeah, and her mother is mean. Terrible mean."

"Poverty can do that to a person."

"I suppose, but to be that mean to your own daughter. I just don't get it."

After a few more steps toward the café, Zeb tugged my hand and stopped walking. "Grizzy, I got something to say."

My stomach went a little wobbly. "Sure. What is it?"

He took a deep breath and looked away from me. "Listen, I got to know. Do you really want to marry me or . . . or did you just settle for second best? Are you sure you don't want Cliff Cardwell and airplanes?"

My first inclination was to snicker. After all the rumination I had gone through. If he only knew. But instead, I took hold of both his hands, which I figured were about as cold as his feet. "I love you, Zeb. And yes, I am absolutely certain I want to marry you."

He let the breath he was holding out. Now you can believe it or not, but I think his breath formed a little heart when it hit the cold air.

"That's all I need to know," he said. And then we kissed and my toes curled and my kneecaps turned to pudding.

—∞∞—

We were standing out front of the Full Moon when Mildred drove past.

"Is she still looking for Leon?" Zeb asked.

"I think so. I haven't talked to her in a couple of days but I'm thinking she still hasn't found him." I shivered as a cold wind kicked up around us. Zeb put his arms around me.

"Are you sure you want to get married outside, on Christmas Eve, in a gazebo?"

"We have to. For Agnes."

Zeb looked into my eyes. "Someday I hope you stop letting Agnes control your life. Now I have to get inside and get ready for the lunch rush."

"I guess I'll see you at the Christmas parade tonight?" I said just after he kissed me.

"Are you sitting in the grandstand?"

The grandstand was nothing more than a set of bleachers Stu and Asa would move in from the high school football field. It would stand right in front of the town hall.

"Yep."

"OK, I'll meet you there."

—∞∞—

Christmas week was always a week off from the library whether I was getting married or not. It was great to have the whole day to myself. At least until five o'clock when I would be expected at the town hall to help get the parade off. I decided to check in on Ruth.

She was still at work on Agnes's dress. "Just fixing the sleeves," she said when I walked into the sewing room. "Then I think we should go out there and try it on her in case I need to make alterations."

"OK, but what about your dress?" I was suddenly beginning to feel like a nervous bride wanting everything to go right. "And I still need to head out to Paradise and check in with Charlotte to see how she's coming with the Christmas Wedding Cake Pie."

"Well, if you'd rather just take a chance that the dress will fit Agnes we can just forget about going." She sounded annoyed.

"Are you mad at me or something?"

Ruth looked at me. "No. Not really. I just feel like I am working my fingers to nubs and Agnes will still get all the glory just like at the pageant."

"Pageant? Agnes wasn't at the pageant."

"No. I mean Dot Handy. I worked just as hard as she did and I didn't get a bouquet of flowers. Agnes and I are co-maids of honors, maid of honors? Whatever, and she'll steal the show. Probably from you too."

"Oh, Ruth. This isn't like you. Pride has never been one of your faults."

Ruth ended the hem she was making and snipped the red thread. "I know. I'm sorry. Look over there, how do you like the hat?"

I saw the hat on the couch. I picked it up and looked at it from all angles. It was a wide-brimmed straw hat but you couldn't really tell—not with all the holly and berries and that big red scarf tied around the crown. It had a long tail that would flow down over Agnes's shoulders.

"It's beautiful. You do such nice work. You're like an artist. I can't do anything like this."

"Sure you can. Just have to take your time and think about it."

"Nah, you could scrape a dead raccoon off the road and turn it into a lovely centerpiece. I can't even wrap my own Christmas gifts."

"You're too hard on yourself."

I watched Ruth finish up the other sleeve. She then spread the dress out on the floor. The dress was large and red and absolutely stunning with the holly corsage and little holly leaves and berries sewn into the shoulders. Ruth had pinned a large plastic poinsettia on the front.

"We can always switch the poinsettia for a real one if we can. But the plastic isn't too bad."

"Like I said. It's lovely."

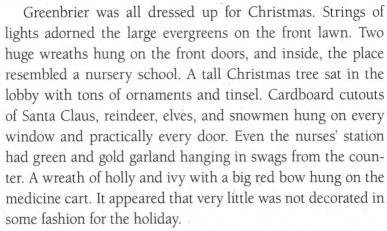

Greenbrier was all dressed up for Christmas. Strings of lights adorned the large evergreens on the front lawn. Two huge wreaths hung on the front doors, and inside, the place resembled a nursery school. A tall Christmas tree sat in the lobby with tons of ornaments and tinsel. Cardboard cutouts of Santa Claus, reindeer, elves, and snowmen hung on every window and practically every door. Even the nurses' station had green and gold garland hanging in swags from the counter. A wreath of holly and ivy with a big red bow hung on the medicine cart. It appeared that very little was not decorated in some fashion for the holiday.

"There are no gifts under the tree," said an old woman sitting on one of the hard visitor chairs. "There are no gifts under the tree."

I couldn't tell if she was sad or mad. But the place did have a decidedly different sense to it. Before Leon disappeared the people were happy, jovial even, and seemed to move with a lot more intention and energy. But now as I looked around, the faces were glum, their movements slow and rigid. Greenbrier had gone back to being old Greenbrier.

My first stop was when I saw Nurse Sally talking with Doctor Silver. They seemed to be discussing something of a personal nature. I think they were in love but weren't letting on. They made a cute couple and would have beautiful children.

"Excuse me," I said.

"Oh, hi, Griselda," Sally said.

"Hello," said Doctor Silver. He looked at Sally. "So you'll take care of that . . . matter," he said.

"Yes, Doctor, just as soon as I can."

I figured that was code for, "I'll meet you in the parking lot the minute my shift is over."

"I was wondering if there was any news on Haddie Grace," I said.

Sally's eyes grew wide. "You mean you haven't heard?"

My stomach sank as I immediately thought the worst. "No. What happened? Did Haddie—"

"Oh, dear Lord," Ruth said.

"No, no, it's good news. Haddie is awake and responding to treatment. She should be back by the New Year."

"Really? Wow. That's amazing."

"Yeah, considering . . . "

"Considering what?" I asked.

"Boy, were you on vacation or something? The rumor is that a funny little man visited her. Then she got better."

"Leon," Ruth and I said together. "Leon Fontaine."

"That's the story," Sally said. "Except no one has seen him since. The hospital called Mildred, but by the time she arrived, he was splitsville."

I laughed. "That Leon. He's a pip."

<hr />

Agnes was in her usual spot, looking out the window from her wheelchair. I wondered if she ever left the room. There were activities and such she could participate in if she wanted, but I had never seen her or heard from the nurses or doctors that Agnes ever went anywhere. The nursing home room had become an extension of the viewing room at the funeral home. But, hopefully, that was about to change. She would get out into the world again, feel the fresh air, sunshine, and the chill breeze against her skin. I hoped it would be invigorating.

"Agnes," Ruth said as we entered the room. "I got your dress all ready for a fitting."

"Fitting?" Agnes said. "You mean you got to try it on me?"

"Hey, Agnes," I said. "Ruth would feel better if she knew the dress fit you correctly."

"Yeah, it wasn't easy to make it. I had to piece together three patterns and—"

"But how are you gonna do it? The aides have enough trouble just getting me into a housedress in the morning let alone a bridesmaid dress."

"Well, what did you think?" I said with irritation building. "You were gonna wear a housedress in my wedding?"

"No, of course not," she said.

My goodness, but it seemed everyone had a case of sour grapes that day.

"Now come on," I said. "Let's try the dress on."

Ten minutes later, we had somehow managed to get the pretty dress slipped over Agnes's head. She looked like a giant beefeater tomato, all red and puffed out.

"It would be easier if you could stand up," Ruth said. "Can you?"

"Not without help," Agnes said. "It usually takes two people."

"Well, I haven't forgotten how," I said. "Remember I used to walk you back and forth to the bathroom a few times a day."

"And you're lighter," Ruth said.

"OK, but don't hurt me," Agnes said.

I reached under her armpits and pulled as she lifted herself out of the chair. Ruth held tight to the chair that wanted to move even with the brakes on. "One, two, three," I counted, and Agnes was standing.

"I need my walker."

Ruth grabbed it and placed it in front of Agnes. She held fast to the walker. The dress flowed down nearly to the floor. The crinoline puffed it out. Ruth straightened the skirt, the sleeves, the pullover blouse.

"It looks good," Ruth said. "I think it fits you well."

Agnes looked at herself the best she could. "I'll have to take your word on it."

"Wish we had a full-length mirror," Ruth said.

"You look nice, Agnes," I said. "And with the hat you'll be the prettiest maid of honor."

Agnes took some steps toward the window. "There's that stone pathway that leads to the gazebo," she said. "I wonder if I can make it down—walking."

"You think?" I said.

"I'd sure as shootin' like to try. Maybe Ruth or someone can follow behind with the wheelchair in case I need to sit."

I looked at Ruth.

"Sure. I can do that. We'll decorate your chair with some holly and poinsettias and maybe hang a few ornaments from it—you know Christmas it up."

Agnes laughed. "Let's do it."

"Now Agnes," Ruth said as she tugged on the right sleeve. "This sleeve feels a bit snug. I can fix it."

"No, no it's fine. Don't worry about it."

"You sure? I suppose we'll need to make arrangements with the nursing staff to have you dressed and ready for the wedding."

"True," I said. "I'll tell Sally to have her ready by eleven o'clock."

"Good, that will be plenty of time."

"What time is the wedding?" Agnes asked.

"Noon," I said. "I originally wanted to get married in the evening but Zeb and I decided it would make more sense with some warmth from the sun."

Ruth and I got Agnes out of the dress and back into her purple housecoat. She looked a bit red in the face and tuckered out from the ordeal but happy enough.

"Agnes," I said. "I asked Ruth to be my second maid of honor. So it's good that you two will be walking down the aisle together."

"Oh, really? You did that?"

"Sure."

"This way," Ruth said, "I can be the maid of honor that does stuff."

Agnes looked away.

"Ah, gee, I'm sorry," Ruth said. "I didn't mean to hurt your feelings but you need to face facts sometimes."

Ruth looked at me. "I know. It just makes me so mad—"

"At me?" Ruth said.

"No, at me. If I wasn't in this—" she slapped her thigh—
"this predicament I could be a proper maid of honor."

"I'm not worried," I said. "It's just how I want it to be. Say,"
I said in an effort to change the subject, "did you hear that
Haddie Grace is up and doing well? It seems that Leon Fontaine
paid her a little visit."

"No kidding," Agnes said. "You think he might have actually had something to do with her recovery?"

I shook my head. "I can't say for certain, but it is uncanny."

"Uncanny," Ruth said.

"Is Mildred still out to arrest him?" Agnes asked.

"Yeah. She's been searching everywhere. But every time she
thinks she caught up with him, he disappears."

"I think he's got a bit of leprechaun in him." Ruth folded
Agnes's skirt neatly and placed the blouse on a hanger.

We talked a few more minutes about Leon and the Fountain
of Youth. Agnes even remarked how different everyone was
now that Leon hadn't been visiting.

"It's like a nursing home again," she said.

I looked at the clock after a while. It was nearing twelve
o'clock. I needed to be at the town hall to start getting things
ready for the Christmas parade.

"It starts at six o'clock sharp," I said.

"Who's Grand Marshal?" Agnes asked.

"Cliff Cardwell," I said. "They thought it would be exciting
to have an actual pilot in the parade. He'll wear his bomber
jacket and his flight wings. The kids will love it. He's like a
hero or a movie star to them."

"Wings?" Ruth said.

"Yeah, silver wings. It's like a brooch. All pilots have them."

"Except you," Agnes said.

"Oh, I'll get my wings one of these days."

"You OK with Cliff leading the parade?" Agnes asked.

"Sure. I'm all over him. I was just in love with what he represented. Zeb is comfortable. I thought being in love meant having big feelings, no appetite, you know getting into minor accidents and such. But then, I realized that *in love* could mean being content. Zeb makes me feel content."

I looked out the window toward the gazebo, "And in a couple of days, I'll be Mrs. Zeb Sewickey."

"All content and happy," Agnes said.

"Right," I said, just as Cliff's plane flew over the trees.

25

By 4:30 that afternoon, Filbert Street was lined with Bright's Pond residents awaiting the start of the annual Christmas Parade. "Silver Bells" blared from the speaker as light flurries fell onto the grass and streets. I waited on the town hall steps with Zeb for the participants to file past so I could check them off my parade list. It was nearly dark and so cold I thought my nose might freeze and snap off. Zeb kept his arm around me and encouraged me to keep moving.

Large oil drums with warming fires had been placed at careful intervals so people could warm their hands and, as I had seen many times, roast a marshmallow or two. Some folks brought lawn chairs but most of the people stood holding hands with children or locked in the embrace of a spouse. A twelve-foot Douglas fir tree cut from the woods and hauled by Nate Kincaid stood proudly in the center of town. Nate told me he strung four hundred lights on it. The tree was topped with a huge gold star that twinkled against the night sky. It was a warm sight on a frosty evening.

Cliff showed up in a 1942 Packard driven by Claude Monroe. He owned the largest Plymouth dealership in Shoops and never passed up an opportunity to advertise. A long red banner with the words "Monroe Plymouth—Have We Got a Deal For You" in bold letters hung from the doors.

Cliff looked handsome enough in his jacket and jeans. His wings had been polished and he certainly brought his best smile. He waved at Zeb and me.

Also in the car with him was Boris Lender along with the Mayor of Shoops and Asa Kowalski, manager of the Paradise Trailer Park. Mayor Yost was a large man with broad shoulders and, like Boris, had a penchant for fat cigars. The acrid smoke swirled above their heads. Every so often Cliff waved it away.

"Where's the marching band?" I asked Zeb. They're supposed to step off first—before Cliff.

"They'll be here. Probably staying warm until the last minute."

"I hope so. The Moose Lodge will follow Cliff and then the characters." I held a clipboard and had been checking floats and people off as they arrived. The SOAP Float was always somewhere in the middle, and they collected donations along the parade route in coffee cans, which seemed to surprise everyone since they liked to do their charitable giving in secret. I supposed collecting didn't need to be so private.

The Paradise Angels softball team led by Charlotte Figg arrived in a truck driven by one of the Frost sisters. They assembled in their float, which was parked off to the side. It was a flatbed truck with a smallish softball field on it made from fake grass. A scoreboard constructed from plywood and painted by the high school art club stood on one side. The Angels looked cold in their uniforms. But everyone seemed good-natured and in the Christmas spirit. A speaker on the float blasted "Take Me Out to the Ballgame."

I was relieved when I saw the band line up. "Oh, good," I said. "They're here."

At precisely five o'clock the Bright's Pond High School Marching Band stepped off playing their version of "Jingle Bells." If you listened real close you could make out the tune. The Bright's Pond High School Marching Band never won a competition or garnered invitations from the big cities like the Shoops High School Band. The gathering crowd cheered and applauded as the parade participants made their way down Filbert Street toward the church and the town limit. Zeb and I followed the parade on foot.

Cliff waved and tossed candy canes and lollipops to the children while Boris acted like they were best friends. He was followed by Frosty the Snowman, three reindeer including Rudolph whose nose blinked red. There was a gingerbread man and a Christmas tree, also battery-operated and blinking thanks to the ingenuity of Nate Kincaid.

The characters were followed by the nativity float. I managed to talk Charlamaine Lincoln into allowing Mercy to play Mary again. Mercy looked so proud. She smiled wide, but I will admit it seemed just a little strange to see the mother of Jesus handing out candy canes. Next came cheers for the Paradise Angels. Dressed in their uniforms, they held bats and tossed a ball around and, of course, tossed more candy canes and ribbon candy to the crowd. The team looked pretty chilly. Charlotte nearly busted her buttons she was so proud standing there with her almost championship team.

Except I couldn't help feeling a little disturbed when I heard one of the teenagers along the route call out that Ginger Rodgers would have made a better elf.

A big red tractor spouting black smoke pulled the Society of Angelic Philanthropy. They were all dressed in green dresses with red hats, even Ruth who reluctantly agreed to ride along.

Then came the Safety float headed up by Mildred Blessing. She tossed candy but also Christmas tree safety tips to the parade goers. She waved as she passed by, but I could tell even from where I sat in the grandstand that Mildred had her eagle eye out for Leon Fontaine.

Forty minutes later, Santa Claus arrived last in a sleigh pulled by two live reindeer borrowed from the Shoops County Zoo. The children loved it and cheered and cheered as Santa tossed out small packages of candy and gum and mints and games of jacks and pick-up sticks.

An hour later the streets were empty except for leftover trash, candy wrappers, and cups that once held steaming coffee or hot chocolate. It was tradition that, after the parade, everyone gathered at the pond for ice-skating, but that had been canceled this year. So folks gathered their children and headed back to their homes, tired and happy.

"So, how about it, Grizzy? Wanna slap on the skates and twirl with me anyway?"

I folded my arms against my chest. "It's really cold. And I'm tired. And besides, don't you have your bachelor party tonight?"

"Yeah, but that can wait. I'm just meeting Stu and Boris and a few of the boys at Personals. I don't care if I go or not."

"You have to go. They planned this for you."

"I guess. I'd really rather spend the night with you."

I looked into his eyes. He kissed me and then pulled me into a warm embrace as the flurries thickened around us.

"OK," I said. "You better get going. I'm going home to finish up some last-minute stuff before the big day tomorrow."

We walked hand in hand toward my house.

"You know," Zeb said. "There is one thing we haven't talked about."

"What's that?"

"The honeymoon."

I walked another step or two. "Oh, you're right. Are we that settled that we haven't even thought about where we would go?"

"Uh-huh. But I've been thinking, and well, you know how I don't like to spend money."

"Everyone does."

"How would you like to go up to Jack Frost for three nights? I called and got us a package deal. We'll get one of them honeymoon specials they have up there. You know the room with the giant champagne glass bathtub that shoots water out in all directions."

"Champagne glass?"

"They got round beds, too, Grizzy, perfectly round. Or you can get a heart-shaped tub. And a TV with a remote control, Grizzy. Imagine that. Remote control. We can watch TV from the champagne glass."

"What's the point of that?"

"That's just it. There is no point. We'll just think about having fun. We can ski or sit by the fire in the lodge and drink hot chocolate and eat some of the best food in the Poconos. I checked and The Velvet Fog is headlining."

"Mel Tormé? You mean Mel Tormé is going to be at Jack Frost?"

"Yep. What do you say?"

"I love Mel Tormé. And I hear when he knows a couple is on their honeymoon he always says something to them and invites them backstage."

"Yeah, so it sounds like a plan then?"

"Let's go." I flung my arms around his neck. "I really do love you. And not just because you're taking me to see Mel Tormé."

We walked a few more paces and finally reached my house.

"And guess what else?" Zeb said.

"What?" I couldn't imagine anything more exciting than a champagne glass tub and Mel Tormé.

"I already asked Stu and he's letting us take the Caddy. We will ride in style all the way."

"Oh, Zeb. Its sounds wonderful. Just us for three whole days."

We said good night and Zeb opened the door for me. "Just think, tomorrow night I won't have to say good night to you on the porch."

Zeb went off to his bachelor party, and I walked into my empty house for the last time.

26

Christmas Eve arrived in not so much the same way as in years past. When Agnes and I still lived together, I always had something planned for the day—usually some last-minute shopping, cookie delivery, and gift-wrapping. Agnes liked to have folks come by so she could hand out gifts and catch up on what she called her end-of-the-year prayers.

Some folks obliged with a list of wants and desires and left behind packages for Agnes to open later. Sometimes the packages held foods and candies but often the gifts were a little more sensible, at least for Agnes, and consisted of pretty sachets for her drawers, picture frames with images of the town in them, or even a book.

But this Christmas Eve arrived quietly. I sat in the kitchen sipping coffee and looking over the list I had made for the wedding. It seemed everything had been taken care of and now it was just a matter of getting through the day. It seemed impossible to wait five hours.

My stomach was queasy but I figured that was nerves. I wasn't hungry at all but knew if I didn't eat and my blood sugar dropped I would be a mess. So I decided to scramble a couple of eggs and butter a slice of toast. The eggs went down like I was eating wood chips, and the toast never made it off the plate.

Suddenly, the house seemed emptier than it ever had. Even Arthur was subdued and hung around by my feet, purring and pawing like he knew something was up. He didn't ask for anything, just an occasional scratch behind the ears. I went from room to room, thinking and praying, thinking and praying, and saying good-bye to one life while waiting for another to begin.

I had done this three other times in my life. Once a few weeks after our parents died. I was only nine years old. I remember I walked from one room to another, lingered a moment in each, and tried to believe that nothing had changed. As long as the rooms stayed the same, then so did my life. The second time was when Agnes decided she wasn't ever leaving the house again and I was forced to turn the viewing room into her bedroom and moved most all of her belongings there. It became the room where we spent all our time even though the house had ten other rooms.

I went from room to room in the big Victorian and tried to remember what they were like when our parents were still alive, when I was young and Agnes was young and we still played with friends. When she slept in a room at the front of the house overlooking Filbert Street. You could see the mountains from her room and I had always been envious. My room was in the back. It had a nice view of the pond, but to me, back then, it was boring. Agnes's room looked out on adventure.

I did it a third time when Agnes checked herself into the nursing home. That time I went from room to room feeling as though I was lost and searching for a friend. And now this time, I would be saying good-bye, preparing for a change that would make the house no longer my own, a place where two would become one in that mysterious way God had designed, where I would not be alone, yet I worried if the only home I ever knew would not feel like home once Zeb made it his.

Would we sleep in my parents' bedroom? It made sense as it was the largest room on the second floor. But it seemed an intrusion. And so I went into each room, each bathroom, the kitchen and den, imagining how it would be with Zeb.

Later I distracted myself with dishes and laundry trying to make the place clean and inviting for Zeb, even though I knew it wouldn't have mattered that much to him. I rearranged ornaments on the Christmas tree and hung some garland on the fireplace mantel. At nine o'clock the doorbell rang. I was never so glad to hear that doorbell ring. I thought it was Ruth come to help me get ready.

It was Cliff.

I stood in the doorway staring at him trying to decide if I was glad to see him or upset that he intruded on this day.

"Cliff. What are you doing here?"

"Hi, Griselda, now don't get upset. I just . . . just wanted to ask you something."

"Do you want to come in?"

"Would it be OK?"

I stepped aside and let Cliff into the house.

"I wanted to ask you if you were sure," he said. "One hundred percent sure that Zeb is the one."

It was like my heart had stopped beating for a second. Stopped like the clock that hung on the hallway wall for years and never ticked for reasons I never knew.

"Cliff, I told you I'm marrying Zeb. I told you I wasn't in love with you."

"I know. You were in love with my plane. But I . . . I don't want you to make a mistake. Griselda, you love to fly. You love the adventure. Can Zeb give you that? Can he take you into the clouds?"

My eyebrows arched. "OK, Cliff. Maybe it would be best if you left. I love Zeb. I don't need to soar through the clouds to be happy."

He stared into my eyes for a long second. "Are you sure?"

My heart pounded now. "I'm sure."

"OK. I'll leave." He reached into the inside pocket of his jacket and pulled out a small package wrapped in Christmas paper. "Merry Christmas. Just don't open it until later."

"Oh, Cliff, this isn't necessary." I wanted him to take it back.

"No. Take it. It's not much. A token, really."

"Thank you."

I turned the doorknob and pushed open the door. A rush of cold air hit me.

"Zeb's a lucky man," Cliff said. He hiked his collar around his neck and stepped through the threshold.

I watched Cliff until I couldn't see him anymore and had the strange feeling I would never see him again. It was only slightly difficult to resist the urge to open the gift. But I set it on the mantel for later.

At 9:45, I took my wedding dress from the closet, packed shoes and a few other things I would need into a suitcase and said good-bye to Arthur. I had planned to drive into Shoops and get my hair and makeup done. But on Christmas Eve? I didn't want to bother the beauty shop people. Zeb would have to take me pretty much as I was.

I picked up Ruth who was ready with her dress and stuff. She smelled faintly of lilacs.

"Are you nervous?" she asked as she climbed into the truck.

"No, I don't think so. I think I just want to get it over with."

"Now you sound like a bride. OK, let's go get you married."

We drove down Filbert Street past The Full Moon Café. I thought I might see Zeb. If I knew him well, and I think I did, he'd be inside cooking breakfast. He worked when he felt nervous. At least, I figured he was nervous. But I didn't see him, and the café appeared closed. And that was when I saw a sign on the door.

"Look, Ruth. It says, 'Closed—Getting Married.'"

"Ah," she said. "He is one happy fella."

"Yeah, I guess he is."

The town hall, adorned in its Christmas best, looked stunning against the steel-gray sky. The large evergreen wreath that hung over the doors was gorgeous as in years past. Carols still drifted from the loudspeaker and would for two more days. It was good to know nothing else had changed.

I didn't tell Ruth about Cliff's visit. There wasn't any need. I was over any infatuation I might have had, and for some reason, I wanted to keep the visit my own. Cliff represented a part of me and my life that I would cherish forever whether I got my wings or not. Cliff helped me cross the mountains I saw every day—the mountains I had longed to cross since I was a child. But that was my business.

The nursing home came into view and my heart started to pound.

"Oh, dear, Ruth," I said. "Why am I suddenly so nervous?"

"It's marriage, dear. Forever, or until death."

"Is that it? Or is it something else?"

I parked the car near the front looking for Studebaker's blue Cadillac. It was early and I hadn't really expected Zeb to arrive more than a minute or two before necessary.

"Come on," Ruth said. "We have to get you dressed and ready."

"In a minute. I want to go out to the gazebo first."

"Sure."

We walked the long path around the building, and what I saw pretty much knocked the wind out of my lungs.

The gazebo was wonderful. It had been transformed into a princess palace with twinkling lights all over it, nearly every inch. The lights shone bright against the dark, overcast day as even more bottom-heavy snow clouds rolled overhead. Greens had been hung in swags around the railing. The crooked roof had even been strung with lights, large red and green bulbs and a large sprig of mistletoe hung down from the center of the roof on a braided gold cord.

A white carpet had been laid on the path leading from a side exit of Agnes's building. Wooden folding chairs were set out in neat rows. Each chair with a small red bow, save the aisle chairs that had large white bows and sprigs of holly attached.

"Oh, my," I said catching my breath. "Who did this?"

Ruth appeared stunned. "I don't know. But it's absolutely wonderful."

Avoiding the white carpet I made my way around the gazebo. The backside was as pretty as the front. Not a space was left undecorated. There was nothing else I could do but stand there looking, admiring, and feeling absolutely mystified over who would have—who could have—turned a crooked gazebo into a wonderland.

All of a sudden I heard a noise, a rustling in the woods behind me. It was too loud for a possum or even a deer. I turned in time to see a red and white flash disappear into the trees.

"Ruth," I called. "Did you see that?"

"What?"

"In the woods."

"I didn't see anything."

"Ah, I guess it was nothing. But I could swear I just saw—"

"We need to get you and Agnes and me dressed," Ruth said.

"OK." My nerves and spirit were at peace.

———∞———

Agnes·was, as usual, sitting in her wheelchair. She was wearing her usual housedress, but I saw her maid-of-honor skirt and blouse laid out on the bed with her lovely hat.

"I've been sitting here all day waiting," she said as we stepped foot into her room. "The aides never came to get me dressed."

"Oh, that's OK, I guess. Ruth and I will get you dressed for the ceremony," I said.

"Sure," Ruth said. "No problem."

I placed my own dress next to hers on the bed. "We have about an hour and a half before guests begin arriving. I don't know how she did it, but Ivy Slocum managed to get invitations to just about everyone in town."

"Ivy's a good egg," Agnes said.

"She is," I said. "People didn't have time to RSVP, but at least everyone in town knows when and where."

"Christmas Eve," Agnes said. "I hope that doesn't upset people too much. And what about the Christmas Eve service at church?"

"There will be plenty of time. Zeb and I will be married by one o'clock and then we're just having a small reception. People will be back to town by three or four."

Agnes looked out the window. "Those flurries are getting heavier. And it sure looks cold outside. Whoever you had dress up the gazebo did a spectacular job. I didn't know they made light bulbs so tiny, so to make them look like stars."

I moved toward the window and looked out.

"That's just it," Ruth said. "Griselda doesn't know who decorated the gazebo."

"Did you see anyone out there?" I asked Agnes.

Agnes shook her head and slapped her knee. "No. I woke up. They got me dressed, to the bathroom, and into my chair. Fed me my breakfast and that was when I saw it. All lit up like some kind of enchanted castle."

"So you didn't see anyone?" I said. "Not a single person out there all morning."

"Nope. It's like magic."

Ruth laughed. "She thinks it was Santa Claus."

"Oh, I do not . . . not really."

"Well, speaking of Santa Claus, did Mildred ever catch Leon Fontaine? I sure wish she would, people around here are turning back to their old ways, walking all hunched over, crabby at each other. Mr. Spearmint lost his teeth and got into a quarrel with one of the nurses. He said she tossed them in with the laundry on account of they came out when she pulled his shirt over his head."

"I got to admit," I said, "that the feeling around here is not very bright, even for Christmas Eve."

"Well, some folks have been picked up by family. And the rest of us are just waiting around."

I swallowed as irritation built in my throat. "Agnes, you're waiting for my wedding. That should make you happy."

"Oh, it is. But you know how much I love Christmas and not to be able to be home, with the tree and opening presents. It's weird."

"Next year," I said. "You'll come home next year."

"And I got to say," Ruth said. "Your room is decorated so nice. You got that little tree and all them cards strung up on the walls and a nice nativity scene on the windowsill. I'd say you're doing the best you can."

"I suppose. I suppose," Agnes said. "And speaking of gifts. Have you gotten any wedding gifts yet?"

"A few. But I reckon most people will bring a gift today."

"And what about the cake or pie?" Agnes asked. "Is that already here?"

"I don't know," I said. "Thought I'd go on down to the Sunshine Room and check on things. I imagine Charlotte has it under control."

"Oh, OK," Agnes said.

I patted Ruth's shoulder. "Can you help Agnes into her dress while I dash down the hall and check on things?"

"Oh, sure, Griselda, you go ahead."

"Thanks."

I did exactly as I said. I dashed out the door and down the hallway. I arrived at the Sunshine Room in time to see Charlotte and Rose Tattoo setting up the Christmas Wedding Cake Pie.

"OK," Charlotte said, "hand me the last lemon meringue."

I watched as Rose gave her the pie. Charlotte carefully deposited it on a deep platelike thing that jutted out from a center pole. I counted eighteen plates and eighteen pies arranged in a tree shape.

"It's . . . amazing," I said. "I didn't expect it to be so special. You did a great job, Charlotte."

"Oh, I had help." She nodded at Rose.

"Thank you, too, Rose. It's incredible."

Rose who wasn't wearing her trademark brown sweater but a long-sleeve turtleneck that still covered her arm tattoos, smiled. "I think it's the best Christmas Wedding Cake Pie in the world."

Charlotte laughed as she backed away from creation. "I think it's the first Christmas Wedding Cake Pie ever."

I looked around the room. Tables had been covered with white tablecloths. A holly centerpiece adorned each one. There was one table that I supposed was for Zeb and me. It was up front and a sprig of mistletoe hung from the ceiling over our two chairs.

"Shouldn't you be getting ready?" Rose asked. "It's nearly eleven o'clock."

"I suppose . . . but, say, have either of you seen Leon Fontaine?"

"Leon," Charlotte said. "Not in a few days. I know that policewoman was looking for him, but I haven't seen him."

"Yeah," Rose said. "Asa said his trailer is locked up tight and there's been no sign of the man. Course Asa shut the fountain down for winter—"

"Oh, that could explain it," I said. "No water."

"That's right," Charlotte said. "So Leon didn't have any more water to fill his bottles to give to the people to make them act young so he just left."

"Well, not without visiting Haddie Grace—"

"Who?" Charlotte asked.

"The old woman who rode around the nursing home on her tricycle."

"Oh, yeah. What about her?"

"She had that accident and was unconscious until—and this is according to the nurses—she was visited by a strange little man."

Rose smiled. Charlotte flat out laughed. "I wouldn't doubt it. I don't know why everyone is so suspicious of him." She replaced a holly sprig that had fallen from the stand. "It's not like he really has powers or that the fountain water had powers. He was just so positive and charming, people listened. Maybe these people just needed someone to listen and be nice to them and stop shoving pills down their throats and telling them when and where to eat or pee or sleep."

"Maybe," I said. "But I was thinking he might have been responsible for something else."

"What's that?" Charlotte asked.

I took a breath as I admired the Christmas Wedding Cake Pie. "Nothing. It's not important. I better go get ready. I'm getting married in less than an hour."

"Yes, yes," Rose said. "Go now. We'll be two of the brave souls that will be sitting outside in the shivering cold."

"I appreciate it. And so will Agnes."

On the way back to Agnes's room I saw Eula Spitwell. I had met her on a number of occasions. I believe she was well into her seventies and usually moved quite slow. That day I saw her leaning against a wall as though waiting for a bus. I had never spoken much to her, but today I couldn't help it.

"Can I help you?" I said as I noticed a distinctively rotten smell about her.

"I . . . I came for water."

"Water? Are you thirsty?"

"No. The water. The Christmas water."

"Christmas water? I'm sorry I don't know what that is."

Just then Leon Fontaine popped out of small alcove. "Shhh. Don't tell."

I nodded. "OK. But—"

Leon reached into his pocket and pulled out a small bottle of water. He helped the old woman drink it. "Go on, Maggie," he said. "You drink half now and half in a month or so. It'll help make you young again."

She smiled and I stood amazed as I watched her straighten her back against the wall as though her spine had not been a straight line in ears. She hunched her shoulders and then straightened them. She wiggled one arm and then the other.

"I feel like I could dance the Hokey Pokey," she said.

"You can do what you tell yourself you can do," Leon said.

"Where have you been?" I asked him.

He smiled. His rosy cheeks brightened. His eyes twinkled but he said nothing and slipped out through a side exit. I thought about running after him, about sounding some kind of alarm, but I also knew in my heart that Leon Fontaine would never be caught—and he shouldn't be.

⸎

When I arrived back at Agnes's room, Ruth was busily trying to get Agnes into her blouse. Agnes was already wearing the skirt, still not straight but at least it was on her body.

"Come on," Ruth said but not in a sour tone, "try to lift your arms a little higher."

"Can I help?" I asked picking up my pace toward them.

"Oh," Ruth said, "I knew I shoulda redone that sleeve. It's tight. Maybe if I snip the seam no one will notice."

"Maybe you should," Agnes said. "My joints are awful angry this morning. Some mornings are like that. Must be the snow that's heading our way."

I instinctively looked out the window. The sky had darkened a little bit more, but that only made the gazebo shine brighter.

"Yes, snip the seam," I said. "We don't have time."

That was when Nurse Sally knocked on the door. "Thought you'd want to know that your guests are arriving."

I turned toward her. "Oh, boy, thanks." A shudder of unexpected nerves wriggled through my body.

"Where do you want them?" Sally asked.

"Can they wait in the lobby for a few minutes and then show them to the path to the gazebo at about twenty of?"

330

"I can," Sally said. "But you got to know, some of them, especially that one tall woman—"

"Edie Tompkins," I said.

"Is complaining about the cold and says she'll watch from the window."

"That's fine. I suppose the heartier of the bunch can sit outside, the rest can wait in the Sunshine Room—but don't feed them until we're all there."

"Right," Sally said.

Ruth retrieved her snipping scissors from the little sewing basket she brought. She sat on the edge of the bed and set to work on the sleeve. I wrapped a blanket around Agnes.

"You'll never believe who I saw in the hallway?"

"Santa Claus?" Agnes said.

I looked at her and wrinkled my brow not sure if she was joking or not. "Not exactly. Leon Fontaine."

"I was right," Agnes said. "You did see Santa."

"Really?" Ruth said. "Did you talk to him? Should you call Mildred or the State Police?"

"No, I decided not to call anyone. It's my wedding day. It's Christmas Eve and besides no one will catch him."

I saw Agnes lift her hand slightly as in a wave toward the window.

"He gave a very elderly woman some water. It was amazing. She straightened right up and smiled wider than all outdoors."

I moved toward the window. "Agnes, did you just wave to someone?"

She shook her head. "Course not. No one is out there."

"Do you think he gave water to everyone?" Ruth said.

"Not sure," I said, still looking out the window.

But our question was answered just a few seconds later when I heard Christmas Carols blare through the PA system and residents scurrying around outside.

Eula Spitwell poked her head in the room, "Is this where the wedding is to be?"

"No," I said. "At the gazebo."

"Hot-diggity," Eula said. "I'm goin' to a weddin'. Will Mickey Mantle be there? I'd like to pet the doggie again."

"Sorry," I said. "But I don't think so."

Eula bolted down the hallway, while I closed Agnes's door. "I think we should keep people out of here and let Sally and the other nurses handle the guests.

27

All done," Ruth said. She shook out the blouse and picked a couple of stray threads off of it. "Let's get this on you now."

"OK," Agnes said. "I'm sorry to be a bother."

"You're not a bother," I said as I pulled off the blanket and tossed it on the bed.

Ruth and I pulled the blouse over her head. Then we pushed her thick arms through the sleeves.

"Much better," Ruth said. "Except now, Agnes, I need you to stand up so I can clasp and tie and get you looking right."

"Oh, all right," Agnes said. Her voiced had reverted to her little girl voice. It made me close my eyes for a second.

"OK," I said grabbing her walker. I placed it in front of her. "Do you think you can do it, or should I get an aide?"

"I can do it."

"OK." I slipped my arms under Agnes's armpits. "Ruth, you get behind her and push a little. When she's up, come around front and help keep her steady until she gets her footing."

"One, two, three." I pulled, Ruth pushed and Agnes lifted herself up. She wobbled a second or two and then grabbed her walker.

"Get steady," I said.

"I . . . I am, Griselda. I think I'm steady now."

"OK." I let go.

Ruth set to work, and in a few minutes, there my sister stood in her red maid-of-honor outfit, hat and all. I pinned a corsage of red poinsettias on her tremendous chest. Then I adjusted the sprigs of holly with red berries on her hat.

"You look so pretty," I said. I wiped tears from the corner of my eyes.

"Can I sit now?" Agnes asked.

"Do you still want to walk down the aisle?" I asked.

"Sure do, Griselda. This is your wedding day. Jesus will be walking right beside me, holding me as I go. Don't you worry."

And that was when I saw my own image of Jesus, walking beside me down the aisle. I had been sad about not having my father to do that honor. But I had my heavenly father. He said he'd be a father to the fatherless. I smiled at the image and decided to keep it with me—in private.

"The Holly and the Ivy" drifted through the loud speaker. Another knock on the door. It was Sally again.

"Thought you'd want to know that Zeb just arrived. He looks so . . . well, handsome, Griselda. I didn't know you could get a green tux with a red shirt. And he's wearing the sweetest green velvet bow tie."

I swallowed and surprised myself by laughing. Agnes, though, must have thought the image was hysterical and busted into a belly laugh. She slapped her knee.

"And oh," Sally said. "You look pretty, Agnes."

I looked at the clock. "Eleven-thirty. We better hurry."

"Won't take me but a minute," Ruth said. "She unveiled her dress. It matched Agnes's except it was one piece. She slipped it on easily. I zipped it up the back and helped pin her poinsettia corsage.

Then they both looked at me like I was about to go in for brain surgery.

"Now it's your turn," Ruth said. She unwrapped my dress and held it up. "This is so pretty, Griselda. Just perfect for a Christmas wedding."

"It is sweet," Agnes said. She started to blubber.

"Don't, don't cry now," Ruth said. "You'll get all red-faced and puffy."

Ruth and I looked at each other and then Agnes burst out laughing. "Yeah? So? How could anyone tell?"

The levity helped and I slipped my dress over my head.

"I still don't know why you didn't get your hair done this morning." Ruth said as she zipped me up. "But I'll do something with it. You have pretty hair, getting a little gray here and there, but that's to be expected."

"I thought I'd pull a comb through it and maybe you could put it up, you know, like in a bun or—"

"Beehive?" Ruth said. "I don't believe we have the time and I didn't bring any hair spray."

"I'm certain someone around here has a can," Agnes said.

"Whatever you can do, Ruth," I said.

"OK, OK." Ruth opened her purse and pulled out a brush. "Let me see." She started pulling and twisting and teasing while my stomach started churning, flopping, and making embarrassing sounds.

"I'm sorry," I said.

"Don't have time to worry about body noises," Ruth said. "Agnes, call for the spray net."

Agnes wheeled toward her bed and squeezed a small rubber bulb on the end of a wire. A few seconds later Sally opened the door. It was almost like she was waiting for the call.

"Can I help you?" she asked.

"You surely can," Ruth said, not looking at her. "I need a can of hair spray and twenty-seven bobby pins and a rat-tail comb, stat!"

"Right away," Sally said, and off she went.

Ruth pulled and tugged on my hair. "Ow. Ow," I said. "That hurts a little."

"No time to mollycoddle. You're getting hitched, and I got to get all this hair piled up on top of your head and then make it stay there for the duration."

"Of my marriage?"

"No, the wedding."

Agnes laughed. "Griselda, I can't remember a time when you allowed anyone to do your hair. Except the one time when Mama put a million curls into it. You looked like Little Orphan Annie. You remember that?"

"I do." I winced from the pain in my scalp. "I was so embarrassed I refused to go to school."

Sally returned. "Here you go. Aqua Net, bobby pins, and one rat-tail comb."

"Put them on the tray table please," Ruth said.

Sally stood near.

"Comb," Ruth said with hand out.

Sally placed the comb in Ruth's palm.

She fussed a little. I couldn't see what in the world she was doing. And frankly, I didn't want to. But I could feel my hair getting bigger and taller by the second.

"Bobby pin," Ruth said.

Sally obliged.

"Again," Ruth said.

This went on for a few minutes until Ruth asked for the spray net. She sprayed all around my head and a small cloud enveloped me. It smelled a bit like alcohol and lilacs.

"That should hold," Ruth said. "What do you think, nurse?"

Sally touched my hair. "I agree."

I touched my hair. It felt like it had been shellacked. I found the top and it seemed to be about nine maybe ten inches high.

"Go on," Ruth said. "Take a gander at yourself." But then she pressed on my shoulders before I could stand. She dug deep into her handbag, which was the size of a bed pillow. "This won't do."

She fussed in my hair a few more seconds and said, "Now take a look."

I stood and peered at myself in Agnes's mirror. My hair had been wrapped in a tight beehive. Ruth pinned a large red bow on the front.

"I look . . . ridiculous. I look like a Christmas tree."

"No, you don't," Agnes said. "You look very pretty. Wait until Zeb gets a look at you."

I took a deep breath and blew it out. "There's not time for anything different now. It's five after twelve."

The view from the window was astounding. Nearly every chair was taken by someone from Bright's Pond or Paradise. I saw Boris and Asa, Charlotte, Rose, Ginger Rodgers, and Harriet Nurse. Ivy even wore a dress. She sat on the end with Mickey Mantle by her side.

"I can't believe she brought that dog," Ruth said.

"It's OK," I said. "I think it's funny . . . and sweet."

Sally moved toward the door. "I guess I better get going."

"Are you coming?" I asked.

"Are you inviting me?"

"Sure. Can you get away for a few minutes?"

"I sure can."

Agnes grabbed my hand. "Griselda, I . . . just want to say before we go out there, that I love you. I'm very proud of you and . . . and thank you."

"Thank you?"

"For taking care of me. Even when I didn't really deserve it sometimes."

"You're my sister," I said. "I will always take care of you. I love you."

I kissed her cheek. She pulled me close.

"Come on," Ruth said. "The guests are turning into popsicles out there." She gave me my bouquet of poinsettias.

Ruth pushed Agnes. I followed behind. When we got outside the room, residents were lined up along the walls. Clyde, the orderly was there also. I called him over.

"You look so pretty," he said.

"Would you go and tell them we're ready?"

"Sure."

I took another breath.

"Good luck," shouted Eula Spitwell.

"God bless," said Clive Dickens who was standing with his bride. She blew me a kiss.

My heart pounded, but that was OK.

"Here we go," I said. "Here we go."

I expected to hear the traditional wedding march when Clyde opened the doors. But instead I heard "Pomp and Circumstance" blaring over the PA system.

"I'm sorry, Griselda," Clyde said. "We couldn't find the right record. This was the closest we could get."

"It's OK," I said. "It's fine."

Ruth pushed Agnes to the start of the white carpet and stopped. "Now wait until we get all the way down there before you start down. And remember walk slowly."

"Right. Got it."

Clyde helped Agnes out of the chair.

"You sure?" I asked. "It's not that far but—"

"I can do it," Agnes said. "And no walker."

I think I might have gasped, but I could see it in her eyes. "Agnes will walk down the aisle on her own steam."

Clyde followed behind with the chair just in case she had to sit down.

Ruth followed Clyde. She looked so nice in her red dress with the white poinsettia corsage. She walked slowly. But I knew the scene only made her miss her Hubby Bubby.

I looked down the aisle and saw Zeb standing with Studebaker. Zeb was looking right at me. He smiled so wide I thought his face might break.

I waited until Ruth was all the way down. Agnes had sat down in the chair.

Just as I took my first step the music changed to Bing Crosby crooning "White Christmas" and the flurries started falling again. I felt tears well in my eyes and I sailed a prayer amid the snowflakes thanking God for Zeb and friends who would sit outside on folding chairs at a nursing home on Christmas Eve.

28

I took the first step down the aisle, and at first, I was caught off guard by the noise of seats moving as all our guests stood. Then I needed to swipe at tears when I realized they were standing for me. I was amazed and humbled all at the same time even if it was tradition. It still felt like it was the absolute first time any group had stood for a bride. I walked slowly like Ruth told me to. I looked from side to side nodding at people, making eye contact, and trying to remember to smile. Edie and Bill looked happy and smiled. Janeen and Frank Sturgis seemed proud to know me. Frank held his Super 8 movie camera cradled in the crook of his arm as though filming the bride making her entrance was somehow off limits.

Cliff was not there, and it made me feel sad for just a second or two. Like Leon Fontaine, Cliff had disappeared. About two-thirds of the way down I looked at Zeb and never took my eyes off of him.

When I reached the last row of chairs, I saw Pastor Speedwell nod to Zeb. He joined me. I slipped my arm in his, and we took the last few steps together. I smiled at Agnes and Ruth and Studebaker. Pastor raised his arms and then lowered them— a signal for the congregation to sit.

"Join your right hands," Pastor said.

And suddenly the cold went away and all I could feel was the warmth of Zeb's hand holding mine. Although to be honest, it was difficult not to whisper to him about his choice of tux.

Pastor Speedwell looked out over the crowd. "Dearly Beloved, we are gathered here in this—" he looked around at the twinkling lights and the mistletoe. "Beautiful place to join Zeb and Griselda in holy matrimony."

Zeb's palm went sweaty but I only held tighter. We looked into each other's eyes.

"If there is anyone here who knows any reason why this union should not take place let him speak now or forever hold his tongue."

A distinct hush fell over the crowd. I could feel the people looking around, waiting for someone—Eugene Shrapnel, who I saw sitting in the back, or even Agnes—to speak. But all was still.

Pastor spoke a few more words on the sanctity and mystery of marriage, about two people becoming one, and about miracles in general. We exchanged vows as the snow began to fall harder.

"The ring, please," Pastor said.

Studebaker handed him the gold bands we picked out. Pastor gave the ring to Zeb.

"With this ring," Zeb said as he slipped it onto my finger, "I thee wed."

Next Pastor Speedwell took the ring from Agnes. She smiled at me. And I at her.

"With this ring," I said. "I thee wed."

Pastor Speedwell smiled. "And now I pronounce you husband and wife." He looked up at the sprig of mistletoe and then back at us. "Go on, kiss your bride."

Zeb and I kissed. But it was more like a peck. A quick acknowledgment. And that was OK.

Then we turned, and I looked out over the guests. They applauded as we walked down the aisle holding hands, married, husband and wife.

The walk back to the Sunshine Room was the happiest walk of my life. Residents still lined the halls, a few holding IV carts, most in pajamas or robes, yet all with smiles as Zeb and I made our way to the reception. There had been talk of a receiving line but both Zeb and I felt that would be a little too much.

"Nah," Zeb said. "Let's just mill around, you know mingle and greet people like that."

"That sounds good," I said. "I don't think I'd like to stand and shake hands and hug like I was the Queen of England or something."

The day was still overcast and gray so the lights were on in the room giving the place a kind of odd yellow glow. But the Greenbrier kitchen lady, Babs, set about lighting the candles in the center of all the tables while Zeb and I waited for our guests to arrive. The plan was to hold them back until we were settled. Then Agnes arrived and took her place next to me, Ruth popped her head into the room. "Woo hoo," she said. "Congratulations."

Studebaker, who pushed Agnes into the room, sat next to Zeb. He slapped Zeb's back making him lurch forward and nearly knock over a water glass. "You did it, Old Man," Stu said. "Congratulations."

Zeb smiled. "Thank you."

By then, all the candles had been lit and Babs turned the glaring overhead lights off. Between the glow that leaked in from the kitchen and the candlelight, the reception area now had a romantic ambience.

"This is so nice," Agnes said. "I don't think I've ever been in this room."

"It is pretty," I said. "Whoever set this all up did a wonderful job."

"It was mostly Charlotte and Rose and that midget—"

"Little person, Ginger Rodgers," I said.

"Right, didn't mean no disrespect. They decorated the place."

Long ribbons of red and green crepe paper were strung from corner to corner across the ceiling. Wreaths made from pinecones and holly were hung from the windows, and a fully decorated Christmas tree stood in the center where what I assumed were our wedding gifts sat underneath.

The Christmas Wedding Pie Cake was sitting proudly on a table off in a corner but still attracted attention. I heard someone say, "That is the oddest wedding cake I ever did see. Who has pie at a wedding?"

Charlotte, who sat with the Angels at the table closest to the cake, simply smiled.

It took a few minutes but all the guests were seated for the meal when it occurred to me that these people were expecting some kind of luncheon. I whispered to Agnes, "Zeb and I didn't really plan on food. We thought we'd just have pie, coffee, and soda. Nothing fancy."

She patted my hand. "Edie, Janeen, and the Society Ladies took care of it. They wanted to surprise you."

"Oh, that's so sweet."

"It's pretty much a pot luck," Agnes said. "Church food."

Studebaker tapped his water glass with his knife and stood.

"Ladies and gentlemen," he said. "Lunch will be served in just a few moments. It's pot luck, so we have all kinds of choices over there."

I looked in the direction he had nodded and saw a table crowded with pretty casseroles, pots filled with baked beans, dishes of already sliced beef and pork, salads, macaroni and cheese, and Jell-O Surprise.

"But first, I just want to welcome you all and to congratulate Zeb and Griselda."

Applause echoed through the room.

Zeb pointed at the mistletoe. We kissed as the applause grew louder. It had started to become a bit embarrassing. But that was OK.

Also at our table were Milton and Darcy Speedwell. What they did with the boys I didn't know and didn't ask. We moved to the buffet table first and piled our plates with macaroni and cheese, roast beef, tomato casserole, biscuits, chicken legs, some kind of Jell-O Surprise, meat loaf, and meatballs. Well, Zeb did. I wasn't all that hungry and ate only some macaroni and cheese lovingly prepared by Harriet Nurse. It was her specialty.

It didn't take long for everyone else to line up and get their food. Christmas carols played in the background although broken up every so often by the sound of a resident's call button ringing for a nurse—most of the nurses were at the reception.

I spotted Nurse Sally with Doctor Silver. They seemed more like a couple than colleagues.

"I just want you to know," Janeen said as she hugged me, "you are the prettiest bride ever. Ever, Griselda. I am so happy for you."

"She's right," Edie said. "I didn't think you two would ever tie the knot but this day couldn't be more perfect. And that gazebo, what a fabulous place."

And so it went for a few minutes. Friends came one by one, two by two to congratulate us. I watched some of the men slip envelopes to Zeb that he discreetly shoved in his pockets.

It was as though the world had stopped spinning when I looked up from my macaroni and saw Mercy Lincoln standing in the doorway. Tears streamed down her cheeks. She wore nothing but a slight, thin dress, no shoes. She shivered and cried.

"Oh, no." I pushed my seat from the table and ran toward her.

"Grizzy," Zeb called, "where are you going?"

I moved quickly toward her. "Mercy, what's the matter?"

She flung her arms around me. "Miz Griselda. It's something awful. I need to find that little man. Where is he?"

"I . . . I don't know," I said.

"O, Miz Griselda, I am terrible sorry to interrupt your weddin' and all, but I need to find him."

"Why?"

By then Zeb had joined me. "What's the problem?"

"I'm not sure, yet."

I took Mercy's hand and led her to the hallway. "Now tell me why you need Leon Fontaine."

"He's the only one what can help. It's Mama, again."

"Is she sick?" Zeb asked.

Mercy sobbed and nodded. "Where is he?"

I looked at Zeb. "What should we do?"

"Get Doc Flaherty. I saw him sitting with Dot Handy."

"Listen, Mercy," Zeb said. "You stay right here. We'll get help."

"Leon Fontaine," she said.

"Stay," I said.

I found Doc. He had just put a large fork full of beef in his mouth.

"Doc, can you come with me?"

"Is it Agnes?" he said looking in her direction.

"No. It's someone else."

The others at the table asked questions, but I ignored them.

Doc knelt down next to Mercy. "What's wrong? Are you sick?"

Mercy shook her head. "It's Mama. I need Mr. Leon."

"Leon?" Doc said looking at me. "What can he do?"

"He can help Mama," Mercy said.

"I knew something like this was going to happen," Doc said. "That man has no right to—"

"Shhh, Doc. Let's help Mercy."

"Come on, Mercy," Doc said. "Take me to your Mama."

"We'll be right behind," I said.

Zeb grabbed my hand. "Griselda, it's our wedding day. Let Doc handle this."

"But Mercy. I can't just ignore her. I need to help."

"Later, let's enjoy our day."

"I can't," I said. "I can't go in there and . . . and have a party."

"Shhh," Zeb put his finger to his mouth. "OK, we'll catch up with Doc in a little while."

"Think we should send Mildred out there?"

Zeb looked around the room. "She didn't even come."

"I know. She's been looking for Leon."

It took a few minutes with people both congratulating and asking questions, but we finally got back to the table.

"What's going on?" Agnes asked.

"I'm not sure," I said. "Doc went with Mercy. Something about her mother."

"Is she sick?" Ruth asked.

I don't know yet. We'll figure it out later. But she wants Leon Fontaine."

"Leon," Zeb said. "I knew he'd be trouble."

Studebaker stood and proposed a toast. I guess he hoped it would settle the chatter down and get people thinking about other things.

"I'm not very good at explaining my thoughts," Stu said. "So this will be short and, I hope, sweet." He looked at us.

Zeb draped his arm around me.

"There are some who said that Griselda and Zeb would never make it official. But I always knew that when the time was right these two lovebirds would get hitched."

Applause and tapping of water glasses. We kissed—again.

"Anyway, I just want to say that there isn't a couple around who belong together more than these two. But, Griselda, we already know who wears the apron in your family. And from what I hear about your cooking, that's a good thing."

Laughter filtered around the room. The sad thing is, he was right.

"But Zeb, my friend, Griselda is the one with the pilot's license. You might want to keep that in mind when she says she needs to go out for some milk. Oh, and don't forget you'll be living in a funeral home now." Stu swallowed and then smiled with a twisted grin. "So, congratulations and here's to a long and happy marriage."

We all sipped from our glasses.

"Thank you, Stu," Zeb said.

Babs approached me. "Should we cut the . . . cake, pie thing now?"

"Yes," I said. "Let's do that."

Babs signaled for two men to wheel the Christmas Wedding Pie Cake to the center of the room. Zeb took my hand and we made our way there. A pie slicer sat on the table with red and green bows tied to the handle.

Zeb picked it up and made the first slice into one of the lower cherry pies. Then he handed me the utensil. I made a second slice and gently lifted it out of the pan. A cherry glopped onto the floor. I knew there was a silly tradition of smashing the cake into the groom's face, but I couldn't see myself doing that. So, I lifted the pie to his mouth and he bit and chewed and smiled.

"The best pie ever."

More applause, and Zeb and I returned to our seats while the pies were sliced and distributed to the guests. Yet my mind was still on Mercy. I worried that her mother had taken ill—or worse. And when Mildred Blessing arrived and stood in the doorway my heart sank into my shoes.

29

"Zeb," I said. "I better go see what she wants."

"OK, but come right back. I don't want you going to the woods."

"I won't."

Agnes stopped me. "You can't take care of the whole world," she whispered. "Your life isn't your own anymore."

"It never really was." I regretted the words the instant they left my mouth.

Ruth snagged my hand as I tried to slip past her. "You follow your heart."

I could tell from the chatter and laughter in the room that most have forgotten about Mercy, and they hadn't even noticed Mildred standing there in her police uniform.

"What happened?" I said.

"Nothing. Yet. But we need to find Leon. Have you seen him?"

I shook my head and walked into the hallway. Mildred followed.

"Tell me the truth, Griselda," Mildred said. "Now I hate to interrupt your wedding day but if you know anything you got to tell me."

"All right, all right. I saw him earlier today."

"Where?"

"Here."

"Here?" Mildred said. "At Greenbrier?"

"Yes. He was helping Eula Spitwell."

Mildred twisted her mouth and then said, "Why would he help a woman spit well?"

"No, no, that's her name, Eula Spitwell, one word."

"That's unfortunate. But when, how long ago?"

"A couple of hours ago, maybe three."

"Why didn't you call me? You knew I was looking for him. I had an APB out on him."

I swallowed and glanced into the room. I wasn't even missed yet. I saw Zeb talking with Stu. He looked happy enough.

"Because I didn't want him to get into trouble. He's a good man—"

Mildred wrinkled her brow.

"OK, maybe he's a little crazy. But he means well, and no one has really been hurt."

"Oh, no? Tell that to Charlamaine Lincoln."

My stomach churned. "What happened?"

"I was just at the shack. Apparently Leon had given Charla—"

But before she could finish, Zeb appeared behind us. "Can this wait, Mildred? Is Griselda in any trouble?"

"No, Zeb," Mildred said. "I just need some information."

"Then get it later." He took my hand. "Come on, Griselda. Let's get back to our wedding reception." There was a tad of anger in his voice. "I told you we'd figure this out later."

When we got back to the table I leaned toward Agnes and Ruth. "Something happened to Mercy's mama. I don't know what. Leon might have done something."

"Oh, dear," Ruth said. "Really? But that fella doesn't hurt people."

"I know. But now I'm sorry I didn't say anything when I saw him earlier."

Harriet Nurse stopped by the table. "I just want to say you look lovely, Griselda. And best wishes."

"Thank you, Harriet."

I watched her return to her table. She was sitting with Jasper York and some other residents.

"Now look," Agnes said, "you did what you saw best to do. Like I keep telling you, the weight of the world is not yours to carry."

"I know, but now I'm not so sure."

"Why?" Ruth asked.

"I was just talking to Mildred. She said something has happened to Charlamaine Lincoln. She thinks Leon might have something to do with it. But Charlamaine's just so mean-spirited, I wouldn't put it past her to try and make him take the blame for whatever it is."

"Of course not," Agnes said. "He's like Santa Claus or a leprechaun. He'd never deliberately hurt anyone."

I saw Mildred strutting toward our table. "Shh. Here comes Dick Tracy."

"Just tell me where he went," Mildred said.

"I don't know. He slipped out the side door."

Mildred took a breath and waited until a nosy resident passed by. "Charlamaine Lincoln needs him."

"Are you gonna tell me what in the heck is going on?

"Mercy said he promised he'd help when the time came. And Charlamaine is crying out for him."

Now I was even more confused.

"Just go back to your party. But, Griselda, if you see him again tonight, please tell me."

I didn't say anything. Going back to the party was a little harder. I really wanted to go the woods, to Mercy's home, and see what was happening. But I knew Zeb wouldn't allow it. Married less than three hours and already I was wishing I wasn't.

Zeb turned to me. "We'll leave in a few minutes. Everyone will think we're on our way to Jack Frost, but we'll stop by Mercy's first."

I threw my arms around his neck. "Thank you, Zeb. I have to know what happened. Mercy could be in trouble."

"I know."

I waited anxiously until Zeb signaled that we could leave. He stood and tapped his glass.

"I just want to say thank you to everyone for coming out on Christmas Eve to be part of this incredible day. Thank you for the food, the gifts, the fellowship, and—" he patted his thigh— "the cash. But Griselda and I have a reservation to keep up on Jack Frost, soooooo . . ."

"Have fun," someone hollered.

More applause and cheers as Zeb and I made our way out of the Sunshine Room and back to Agnes's room. I stopped at the door. "Should I get changed?"

"I think so, if we're going to Mercy's. I don't think you'd want to get your dress messed up back in those woods."

He followed me into the room and my nerves got the best of me. "Zeb, I . . . I need to change."

"I know. I had Studebaker bring me my blue jeans and a flannel. I'll change also."

"But . . . but, I'm nervous."

Zeb smiled and looked into my eyes. "You can change in the bathroom."

I snagged my clothes from Agnes's bed. "Good idea."

A few minutes later, we ran to the truck followed by friends tossing handfuls of rice and, I think, Rice Krispies. I figured the nursing home residents had an easier time finding cereal.

"Oh, good Lord," I said. "Will you look at that?" A large "JUST MARRIED" sign hung from the back and long ropes with tin cans and a pair of work boots hung from the bumper.

"You want me to take them off?"

"No. They'll get insulted."

"Let's go."

Zeb opened the driver's side door, and I climbed in thinking for a second that I would drive but he climbed in next to me and I moved over. He turned the ignition and Old Bessie started right up, almost like she knew there was an emergency.

"You sure you know where she lives?" Zeb asked.

"I do. But go to the library. It's easier to park there and then walk the rest of the way."

Snow must have been falling harder during the wedding as it had accumulated about an inch on the grass. The roads were still pretty clear, so Zeb drove fast into town, which was deserted on account of the wedding. Still, the carols blared from the speakers atop the town hall and the lights on the town Christmas tree shone bright. The huge star on the top seemed to light a small path toward the library. It was almost eerie to see the place with no people—kind of like a scary movie.

He stopped the truck at the library. "Let's go."

We hurried through the snowy woods as quickly as possible, twigs snapping and leaves crunching underfoot. We startled a deer who took off like a shot.

"Watch out for the traps," I said.

"I know, come on."

I saw Mercy's house. "There it is. Over there."

"That place?" Zeb said. "It doesn't look fit for mice or possums let along human beings."

"I know, but still, it's their home."

I didn't bother to knock and pulled open the door. I saw Doc crouching near Charlamaine who was lying on the bed. She was moaning and groaning. Mercy spotted us.

"Miz Griselda! You find him?"

"No, Mercy, I didn't. What's wrong with your mama?"

"I don't know if she'll make it," Doc said. "I should get her to the hospital, but the baby is coming."

"Baby?" I looked at Mercy. "I didn't even know your Mama was—"

"She's so thin," Doc said. "She didn't look it. The baby is early. Very early."

"Oh, dear."

Zeb took Mercy's hand. "Where's your daddy?"

"Don't know. He comes by now and again but then he leaves. Says he'll be back, but I never know."

Charlamaine cried out. I shuddered. "Dear Lord," I prayed. "Take care of this."

Zeb kept Mercy as far away from her mother as he could. But she kept breaking away. "Don't cry, Mama. The baby is coming."

I pretty much held my breath waiting to hear the baby cry. A few moments later Doc said, "It's a boy."

Zeb took his shirt off and handed it to Doc.

"He's not crying," I said.

Doc handed the tiny bundle to me. "Massage him, gently. Gently."

I sat on the floor and lightly touched the infant's chest not wanting to look at Doc who was busy with Charlamaine. I blew into his tiny face.

I saw so much blood out of the corner of my eye, my stomach ached. Zeb continued to shield Mercy until he couldn't anymore.

She cried, "Mama!"

Doc shook his head. Zeb carried Mercy outside.

The baby cried, just low, a whimper. "We got to get him to the hospital."

"What about . . ."

Doc shook his head. "She's gone. Too much blood."

I held the baby close while Doc looked at him. "Good. His color is good. Little, but—"

"What should I do?"

"I'll take care of things here. You and Zeb get the baby to the hospital."

"OK. But why did Mercy want Leon?"

Doc wiped the back of his neck. "It's weird. All I could ascertain from Charlamaine was that Leon said he would help when the time came. She had no one else. The midwife in these parts hasn't even been here. She didn't know Charlamaine was pregnant. Charlamaine only figured it out a few weeks ago."

I tried not to look at Charlamaine. But I couldn't help it. There was no peace on her face.

Zeb and Mercy waited on the porch. Mercy looked up at me. I leaned down and showed her the baby. "This is your brother."

Mercy smiled and touched his cheek. "Mama?"

I looked at Zeb and shook my head.

"Doc said we should take the baby to the hospital to get a checkup," I said.

"Mama?" Mercy said.

I held the baby as close as I could to my chest. Zeb took Mercy's hand. "Doc is taking care of her, Mercy. You come with us."

When we left the woods and arrived at the truck. Zeb ripped the tin cans from the fender and tossed the JUST MARRIED sign into the back. "Come on. We should hurry."

Snow fell harder as the winds whipped up. Zeb had the wipers going full speed and the heat going full blast. Mercy snuggled as near to me as she could. "Miz Griselda," she said. "What's gonna happen now?"

I leaned my head on hers. "It's going to be OK, Mercy. Zeb and I will take care of you and your brother."

Zeb put his arm around me. His fingers touched Mercy's shoulder. "That's right, honey. We're here."

———⚬⚬⚬———

Mercy and I sat in the waiting room while the doctor tended to the baby. Zeb went off with a nurse to explain what happened. He wasn't gone long before he came and got me.

"You need to sit here, Mercy," Zeb said. "Griselda and I have to talk to the nurse a minute."

"I can't leave her," I said.

"You have to. We'll be back." He smiled at Mercy and reached into his pocket. "I got you a candy bar from the vending machine." She eagerly took it.

"What's wrong?" I said when we were out of earshot.

"They're giving me trouble. They say with the mother dead and the father nowhere to be found, the children will be turned over to the state."

"What? No. We'll take them home with us."

"It's not that easy Griselda. We can't just take children."

"But . . . but they have no one else."

"There's a state home. Not far from here."

"No." Tears flowed down my cheeks. "I won't let them take her."

The nurse approached us. "I just got off the phone. They can take the girl tonight."

I noticed a small Christmas tree in the corner. "But . . . but it's Christmas Eve. Can't we just take her home with us? It's Christmas. Her mother just died. The baby." I sniffed.

The nurse shook her head. "I can't do anything. It's not up to me."

"But—" I fell into Zeb's arms.

"They'll send a social worker out tonight to get her. We'll keep her here."

"Well, I'm not leaving until—"

The nurse handed me some tissues. "I'm sorry. I'm so sorry."

Zeb and I walked back to the waiting room. "Let's just take her," I said.

"We can't do that."

"How's the baby?"

"Don't know. The doctor and nurse took him away. I haven't heard a thing."

I sat next to Mercy and pulled her close. "Mercy, I need to tell you something."

"I know, Miz Griselda. Mama's dead."

"That's right, honey, but there's something else."

She looked at me. I wiped chocolate from her mouth with my thumb. "You can't go back to your house tonight."

"Am I going to your house?"

I shook my head.

"The library. I can stay there. With all them books."

"No, Mercy. In a little while someone is going to come get you from—"

"From a special place for children," Zeb said.

"That's right, they need to find your daddy."

Mercy looked away. "They won't find him."

"But they have to look."

She grabbed onto my arm.

"We won't leave until they come and get you."

We waited nearly two hours until a stern-looking woman arrived. She barely looked at us and marched straight to the nurses' desk and signed papers.

"She looks mean," I said.

The woman in a long, black wool coat approached us. "I'm sorry it took so long for me to get here. The weather. My name is Mrs. Strickland, Hildegard Strickland."

Zeb stood and let her take the seat next to Mercy. "You'll like Framingham," she said. "There's lots of girls there."

I fought back sobs.

"I don't want to go," Mercy said. "I got to stay for my brother. He'll need me. I bet he's crying just this minute for me."

The woman looked at me. "You'll see your brother. But for now, you need a place to stay."

"I can stay with Miz Griselda and Mr. Zeb. They said so."

"That's right," I said. "She can stay with us. I . . . we have a big house in Bright's Pond."

The woman shook her head. "I'm sorry, we can't just give children to people, and in this situation, it's . . . different."

"Different?" I said. "She needs us. That's what matters."

The woman paused and then said, "She's a Negro girl. She'll need to go with her own kind. Besides, we can't just give children away without going through the proper channels."

"Own kind? She's a human being. That's all that counts. And I love her. Please don't take her."

"Please," Mercy said. "Let me go home with Miz Griselda."

The woman shook her head. "I'm sorry. We have certain policies. And even if that wasn't an issue, I couldn't simply hand her over to you without the proper procedural tasks being attended to, now could I?"

I instantly hated her condescending tone. "Zeb, do something."

"There's nothing we can do tonight," he said.

"But it's Christmas," I said choking back tears as I held on tight to Mercy's hand.

Zeb uncurled my fingers from around Mercy's hand. "Come on, honey, you have to go. But we'll do something."

"You promise," Mercy said. "Right now, promise you'll do something to get me."

"I promise," I said. And then I hugged her. "What about the baby?" I asked looking at Mrs. Strickland.

"The hospital will keep him until he can be transferred to the orphanage."

Orphanage. I hated that word. Mrs. Strickland gave Mercy's arm a slight tug. "Come, child."

"But it's Christmas," I cried.

Mrs. Strickland turned back and looked at me. "I'm aware of the day."

Zeb shook his head. "No one can be that hard-hearted, Grizzy, can they?"

The nurse came by. "Hers is a thankless, hard job. If she wasn't mean, she'd probably slit her wrists."

"Come on, Griselda. Let's go home."

We got into the truck and Zeb turned the ignition. This time Old Bessie complained. "Come on, start," Zeb said. He pumped the gas.

"I don't blame her. I don't want to go home either."

The engine finally turned over. The snow still fell and I could hear the wind whipping around outside. The trees shook, the traffic lights dangling from wires over the middle of the roads shook in the wind and the cold. The Christmas lights on the houses we passed and stores closed for the holiday still bright with Christmas cheer did little to warm me.

"Let's not go to Jack Frost tonight," Zeb said. "I'm not in the mood."

"Me either."

Christmas morning arrived. Zeb and I had not been to sleep. Instead we spent the night talking about Mercy and her tiny baby brother. We opened wedding gifts that had been dropped off the night before and marveled at the love and generosity of our friends and community. But the joy of the Christmas Eve was overshadowed by the intense sadness that had fallen on Mercy.

Zeb did everything he could to cheer me that day. He even gave me a gift.

"I wanted to show you that I really do listen when you tell me stuff."

I ripped the wrapping off the rectangular gift, an old version of Emily Dickinson poems, the one with the flowers on the cover.

"This is lovely," I said. "She would understand what Mercy is feeling, I think. What I am feeling. There must be something we can do."

The doorbell rang. It was a sound I didn't hear too often since Agnes moved to the nursing home.

"Who would come calling on Christmas?" Zeb said. "And besides, everyone thinks we're on our honeymoon."

"Don't know." I set the book on a table and waited for Zeb to return.

I heard voices.

"Griselda," Zeb called, "come here."

I went to the entryway and saw Mrs. Strickland standing there.

"Merry Christmas," I said.

She nodded.

"Mrs. Strickland has something to tell you. To tell us. Go on, Mrs. Strickland, say it again—for Griselda."

"I'm not certain exactly how the events transpired but the child's father and a weird little man came to the orphanage last night."

I looked at Zeb. "Leon?"

"Had to be."

The woman clicked her tongue. "The father signed custody of the minor children over to you and your husband if that's what you want. Course it's only temporary until a suitable home can be found, but—"

"Of course, where is she?" I looked around Mrs. Strickland's wide hips.

"She's in the car with my driver."

"Can I go get her?"

"You may."

But I didn't wait for her answer. I was halfway to the curb before I heard it. I pulled open the door and Mercy leaped into my arms.

"Miz Griselda," she said. "They said I can come stay with you!"

"That's right, Mercy."

We walked to the house.

"Thank you," I said to Mrs. Strickland.

"The agency will be in touch with you soon," she said.

"Fine," Zeb said. "Now if you'll excuse us, it's Christmas."

Zeb, Mercy, and I went to the living room.

"What's that?" Zeb said, pointing to the Christmas tree.

"What?" I said.

"It looks like a gift. I didn't put it there."

"Me neither," I said.

"Open it, Miz Griselda," Mercy said.

It was another rectangular gift with my name scrawled across the odd brown wrapping. I ripped the paper off.

"I don't believe it," I said. "It's . . . it's a first edition of *Don Quixote*."

"Leon," Zeb said.

I ran to the back of the house and flung open the back door. But I didn't see anything, just crooked little footprints, making a crooked little path in the snow, but a straight line to my heart.

Discussion Questions

1. Strange things are happening at Greenbrier. The residents seem younger, spunkier—apparently thanks to Leon Fontaine's water. Why do people want to remain young? If there really were a fountain of youth, would you drink from it?

2. What, if anything, is wrong about the people believing in the water? Isn't the result more important?

3. Who was Leon Fontaine, really? Who did he remind you of?

4. Discuss Griselda's decision to marry Zeb. Do you think she really loves him? Is something else going on? Did she make the right decision?

5. And what about Zeb? Just cold feet, or does he really love Griselda? And what effect will Mercy have on them?

6. Mercy becomes very important to Griselda, but there was objection to Mercy living with white folks. Discuss this.

7. What were your feelings about Mercy playing the part of Mary in the pageant? What about Griselda's deception in getting Mercy's mother to allow it? Does the end justify the means?

8. Once again, pie is everywhere in Bright's Pond. Discuss pie. What does it make you think about? What memories arise? What is it about pie that is so inviting?

Want to learn more about author
Joyce Magnin and check out other great fiction
from Abingdon Press?

Sign up for our fiction newsletter at
www.AbingdonPress.com/fiction
to read interviews with your favorite authors, find tips
for starting a reading group, and stay posted on what
new titles are on the horizon. It's a place to connect
with other fiction readers or post a
comment about this book.

Be sure to visit Joyce online!

www.joycemagnin.com

Welcome to Bright's Pond

More Books from Joyce Magnin

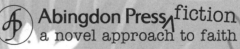